I've travelled the world twice over,
Met the famous: saints and sinners,
Poets and artists, kings and queens,
Old stars and hopeful beginners,
I've been where no-one's been before,
Learned secrets from writers and cooks
All with one library ticket
To the wonderful world of books.

THE LAYING OF THE NOONE WALKER

When brash American architect Charles Gelhorn buys and starts to smarten up the dilapidated rectory at Noone Ampney, things start to go wrong: tiles are smashed, wallpaper slashed. Kate, Charles' wife, begins to wonder if there is any truth in the old ghost story of the "Noone Walker". As the mystery deepens and events take a violent turn, Kate's passion for Noone Rectory and her increasing obsession with its "Walker" lead her to the edge of madness but also to the possibility of the love she had never expected.

ROSALIND ASHE

THE LAYING OF THE NOONE WALKER

Complete and Unabridged

ULVERSCROFT
Leicester

First published in Great Britain in 1987 by
Bantam Press,
London

First Large Print Edition
published August 1988
by arrangement with
Bantam Press,
London

British Library CIP Data

Ashe, Rosalind
The laying of the Noone Walker.—
Large print ed.—
Ulverscroft large print series: romance, suspense
I. Title
823′.914[F]

ISBN 0-7089-1844-1

Published by
F. A. Thorpe (Publishing) Ltd.
Anstey, Leicestershire
Set by Rowland Phototypesetting Ltd.
Bury St. Edmunds, Suffolk
Printed and bound in Great Britain by
T. J. Press (Padstow) Ltd., Padstow, Cornwall

For Josephine

1

LAURENCE had never seen it.

Through all those golden summers, with their broad black frames of boarding school, he believed in it unquestioningly, as he did in the verger's gospel truth and the gardener's laconic accounts of the facts; but he never actually saw the Noone Walker.

Back at school, of course, he claimed he had.

"Ghosts? Oh, yes: I've seen one. We have a ghost: old houses just do—everyone knows *that*—and ours is this pale cleric" —the verger's phrase felt stiff but impressive—"with a white face and a black hat—all black and white—"

"Oh, not Gill's precious ghost again! And it walks in broad daylight—doesn't it, Gill? *Your* ghost *would* have to be different of course. I mean, all the others merely come out at midnight and whizz back to their graves at cockcrow, but yours—"

"And it's not even his: he only stays there with his uncle, don't you, Gill? Don't you, Fishface . . ."

"Fishbreath! Fishbreath!"

"Oh, shut up and let's hear about it—you can't rag in here anyway. Your people are abroad, aren't they, Gill?"

"Yes. My father: he works in the Far East; but Noone Rectory is a sort of Family Seat—"

"The Family Bum! The Fishy-bum—!"

"—If fishes have bums—Let's see!"

"Off with his flannels . . . !"

Chaos and ragging. He was a natural victim in those days: small and new, an odd man out, having been so much alone.

"They're called Dodsworth, actually," said Laurence, rather loudly, when order, and his grey flannel shorts, had been restored; "my uncle and his forebears, right back to this ghost. My mother was his sister—"

"The ghost's sister! Did you hear that? The ghoul's sister is Gill's—"

"Shut up, Maudesley. His mum's—"

"What? Oh—sorry, Gill . . ."

"OK, Gill: tell us about this family

2

ghost. I mean, does its blood, so to speak, really run in your veins?"

And that was why he could feel it, perhaps, even if he wasn't psychic enough to see it: his silent companion along the poplar alley, in the woods, or down by the lake where his Riding Tree reached out over the reedy water. He believed it was there, and he was not afraid of it.

Now Laurence Gill was going back to Noone; still some distance from it, but facing the right way: towards the Colombo airport. Going Home.

That word was strange on his tongue, with the flavour and texture of a long-forgotten nursery treat, like chocolate flake, or the fingers of Madeira cake soaked in Cognac that his uncle used to toast over the library fire. It was a word he had not allowed himself to use for so long: shying away from it; stepping round it in conversation, and wishing for some acceptable euphemism—"Blighty", or "the Old Country"—when fellow expatriates in Penang, in Singapore, in Colombo, used it casually. Then, three evenings ago, over a Tiger beer at the Polonnaruwa

Resthouse, he had heard himself use it, dropping it into the travellers' chat like a beloved name; awkward as a bridegroom saying "my wife"; relishing its secret significance.

Of course he must have used it before, on his rounds of farewell; too busy, too concerned with other matters, to notice. Now he was on leave, breaking his journey in Sri Lanka, there was suddenly time to take it in; and that evening at the Resthouse looking out over the pink satin water of the vast man-made lake and thinking: Only three more days and I'll be beside the lake at Noone—there had come to pass one of those rare moments of unreasonable exhaltation: a frisson, as physical as the trickle of his cold lager, that went right through him, pricking his eyes and standing his hair on end.

The three American ladies sharing his table on the crowded veranda—all so well turned out and uncreased in their safari suits—were armed with a stack of postcards and Polaroids to illustrate their travelogue. They drew breath while he ordered their next round of Pepsis, then demanded

4

to know how many of the ancient cities *he* had clocked up so far.

"Ah, there you've beaten me," he said. "I'm not going to manage Anuradhapura. Dambulla and Sigiriya yesterday, here today, Kandy and the tea country next. But then," he said, "I'm going home . . ."

Talk flowed on round him of the wonders he had missed, of this lovely guide, that faulty air-conditioning. Soon he drained his Tiger and excused himself, "to catch the last light, you know". As he walked along the shore, passing a group of small boys swimming and two skinny Tamils washing a white donkey, he still felt light-headed from that visionary moment. He tried to think back to a point when Noone Rectory had been, unquestionably, "home". Prep school? probably later, at the age when his contemporaries started to talk about a future beyond the next holidays, the skiing, the boat in the Med: talk of jobs in the City, or doing Agriculture at Cirencester, or going into publishing, and ". . . So Gresham says but, then, he won't have to work: he's inheriting . . ." "Well, I'll have our place one day of course—if the death duties aren't terminal haha . . ." It was only the plumage display of a tiny minority; and Laurence knew that, for most of them, "home" was something you grew out of and left. Perhaps it was just that, for him, Noone was all he had ever really known; without a proper family, he had invested all his feeling in those nine acres. But by the time he went up to Cambridge he had learnt to protect himself; and when he left to work in the Far East, he closed all those doors, and thought no more in terms of "home". Only a few months earlier, reading *Earthly Powers* by a mothy lamp on his veranda in Singapore, he had almost resented the writer's selecting that magic word as possibly the most emotive in the language: he felt as though Burgess had betrayed and exposed him.

Now at last he could say it, make it his; and deliberately he used it again, to the talkative little Tamil driver of his hired car.

"Tell you something, George," he said, leaning forward to light their cigarettes. "Tomorrow I'll be at home."

"Really, sir, Mr. Gill? Is that so? The wondering of this modern travel, eh, sir?

Is your home in London then, Mr. Gill? —Ah, in the countryside. And as beautiful and highly productive as this we are enjoying here in the hills, sir?"

"It is beautiful to me, George; and it's as green in spring. But there is nothing to compare with these terraces and mountain peaks, of course."

"Indeed, this is the finest in Sri Lanka, Mr. Gill: you are surveying the cream of our cream, up here in the tea country. And up here it is being peaceful and prosperous even as the Garden of Eden itself. It is in the hot plains that you are meeting with poverty and troubles. We are very trusting that the new irrigation schemes, which I will show you if you are not too pressing with time, may ease our rumblings . . . On the way to Negombo you will see . . . Ah, but please let me halt for you to observe the last view of Adams Peak before we depart the uplands. Is it not blessèd and fulfilling with ecstasy?"

There are no ecstatic mountain tops in Suffolk; if painters love East Anglia, it is for the light, nine parts sky to one part land.

There is a wrinkle in that land just north of the River Stour; from upper windows in Noone Ampney you may look across the fields to Brookall and the railway line and Brookall Newtown and out to the estuary beyond—a distant gleaming of seagull sands or choppy buttermilk, depending on tide and weather. Part of this small eminence, and reaching down to the railway embankment half a mile away, were the nine remaining acres of Noone Ampney Hall, now Noone Rectory; the garden itself had been landscaped long ago into lawns, terraces, a hollow with a lake, and woods threaded through with paths. The curtain wall of the kitchen garden— the tallest part, up which the fig trees were trained—was visible from a distance above the sloping trees; coming home at the end of term, Laurence used to watch for it from the train window, and still have time to gather up his bags and comics in time for Brookall station.

The house itself was large, old and dilapidated. The elegant baroque façade with its great porch was covered in ivy, and the long-disused fountain—a tangle of nymph, triton, dolphin—was streaked turquoise with age. A pair of ancient ever-green magnolias leaned out unpruned from the walls, creating a lush, damp shrubbery and towering up almost as high as the galleried crest, a parapet that masked the attic windows. In Eastern gardens or citrus groves, Laurence often remembered the heady-sweet scent of those leathery lotus flowers when you leaned out of a bedroom window on an August evening at Noone.

Walking round to the back of the house, however, you found another world: "stepping back a century", as his mother used to say: she had lived there as a child; and, like her, he loved the homely space created by the embracing wings—rough plaster washed a serviceable brick red. This was a place of washing-lines and scratching hens; there was a big cast-iron pump, the haphazard wheelbarrows, woodpiles, brick-piles, a rusty, elegant pram planted with hyacinth bulbs, and usually, with luck, a trug of earthy vegetables by the kitchen door: carrots to wash under the pump, and as sweet as any Bangkok mango. Such was the back yard; and the kitchen wing trailed off into dairies, larders, storerooms, sheds, and, further down the hill, stables and barns, the dove-cote, and a ruined summerhouse on the edge of the wood.

It was up the rough road between the farm buildings to the back gate, rather than along the formal lime avenue to the front door, that the village taxi used to bring him. He would dump his bags in a corner of the great kitchen, tawny and echoing, and make his way along the passage to his uncle's library off the main hall.

This hall was the largest room by far, more than twice the size of any other, stretching as it did from the front to the corridor at the back of the central block, and rising almost half a storey higher as well: a vast double cube, with seven doors and the grand staircase leading out of it. It was draughty and magnificent; its ornate plaster ceiling, now patchy and crumbling, could only be guessed at, for the six great chandeliers were always bagged, brooding overhead in the gloom like anchored airships; and the light from the tall casement windows was obscured by greenery. A grand piano, an oak refectory table, and half a dozen faded brocade sofas sparsely furnished what was more an indoor court than a chamber. At Christmas or for special company a fire was lit, and logs like whole tree-trunks burned in a hearth the size of a small room—or so it had seemed to the young Laurence.

The dining room, with its broad, circular table, stiff chairs, and red silk walls, was never used; he and his uncle lunched in the kitchen and supped by the library fire—and these two rooms were the only ones that were always warm. Upstairs, the nursery fire was lit on cold, rainy days; and once, when Laurence was ill, the gardener brought kindling and a bucket of coal up to his bedroom. He remembered all too well the terrible urgency to make him stop, and how he managed to croak out: "No, Abbott—you mustn't! There's a starling's nest . . ." So they carried Laurence and his bed through to the nursery; he fell asleep watching the pink firelight as it wavered across an upside-down fantasy landscape of peeling paper; and he peopled it with aborigines and kangaroos.

He loved this nursery, a corner room looking over the avenue and east to the distant estuary. There was a painted dresser full of funny old books, like *Princess Alexandra's Birthday Album, The Pink Knight, The Cruise of the Cachalot*; and a deep window seat with flowered cretonne squabs. There was a doll's-house, a model farm, a rickety Meccano set, and a big wooden trunk of old-fashioned toys and fancy-dress.

In the doorway, up the frame, and still legible on the yellowed paint, were ruled lines recording children's growth over the years, starting near the floor with "Elsie" —Laurence's own mother—"aged 3, 1925" and moving up through "Laurie aged 5, 1916", a mark a year for each child, interspersed with a sprinkling of second-cousins. This old record in various pens and styles made his dead mother's childhood, with her studious, and much older, brother—the godfather for whom he was named—suddenly very real to Laurence; even more than playing with their toys through the winter evenings: toys that were too young for him of course. But no one was there to see and make fun of him—nor to watch him crawling on all fours to read the kids' stuff in the Scrapbook Corridor.

The nursery wing over the kitchen was always less cold than the others, and this corridor ran the length of it, with windows looking down on to the back yard and across to the shuttered western wing; and it was marvellously decorated. The walls were covered with the collage of a century's ephemera: cards, slogans, children's drawings, pictures from magazines and seed catalogues, Sunday School prayers, valentines, pressed flowers and even the jokes from crackers—all varnished and revarnished to a deep amber over the years, and arranged with thought for the viewer's stature. It petered out towards the far end, and Laurence had been allowed to extend it, collecting postcards and pictures and favourite comic strips all term to paste up in the holidays; but years earlier, even before he stopped using that word, he had lost heart. It was not his; not really . . . He continued to enjoy the illustrated walls: it was an unfailing indoor diversion; and, though most of the daylight hours he ranged free in the grounds, his long winter evenings, when his uncle was working, were spent here in the nursery or in exploring the house.

Thirteen of the bedrooms were shuttered and muffled in dust-covers. These, and the attics above them, so hot in summer, so cold in winter, were never entered except by him. Once, however, he had taken the gardener's son indoors to play—and only then did Laurence realise it might be a frightening house. The boy had not stayed long enough even to appreciate the potential of the shrouded four-posters for sailing round the Horn, much less the endless scope for hide-and-seek or lurky. Perhaps Laurence had spoilt it with too many tales of the Noone Walker; as it was, young Bill Abbott backed away from the threshold of the first bedroom and swore he could hear the rain was easing off . . .

The handful of rooms kept in order by a housekeeper who came up from the village were comfortable enough for the bachelor needs of the scholar-parson and his nephew, and Abbott saw to it that they had firewood and vegetables in abundance. There were always eggs; sometimes a rabbit, or a present of pigeons for a pie, a hand of pork, or a brace of pheasant in season; and young Bill taught Laurence to catch perch from the little lake. In those days it seemed that money was only there for railway fares, charity and the odd treat: coins or rumpled notes dug out of a wash-leather bag in the bureau drawer; house-keeping from the biscuit tin on the kitchen mantel. "I swear I'd call Parson a miser if he didn't keep chuckin' his money away," Mrs. Hatton used to say. "Always plenty for some old lag but never for a new kettle —much less a curtain! And I've long given over patchin' them stair-runners."

"Mean as mouse-shit" was Abbott's judgement. "Only fancy bit of comfort in his life is the liquor—and even that's what his forebears laid down. 'Put the old hip-bath under where that rain's coming in, Abbott,' says he, 'and bring me up a bottle of the '96 . . .'"

The fact that the great house and estate were gradually falling apart did not concern Laurence as a child; he loved wandering through the neglected rooms, or scrambling along fallen trees. The long wistaria shoots snaking in through the cracks round his bedroom window frame were marvellous in the morning sun; and he used to lie on his back on the nursery hearth-rug and make pictures out of the damp patches on the ceilings and faded wallpaper. As in time they changed and spread—especially when he had been away at school—he would alter his scenario: he became Caesar dividing Gaul, or Hannibal slowly conquering the known world. After the Great Thaw, he came down and told his uncle he had overrun India, south-east Asia and the China Seas in a single afternoon; and Abbott was sent up a ladder to fix the cracked lead valley with mastic. He came down shaking his head, and sucking his teeth audibly.

Ever since the first visit to Noone when he was nearly six, on home-leave with his mother, Laurence had been happy to play alone in his private domain. He started going there for his school holidays when he was seven; and there he was sent a week before the end of term on the news of his mother's death only a year later. Time, Noone and Uncle Laurie comforted him.

He never really felt lonely until much

later, at his public school, when he went to stay with friends. After seeing their houses, he suddenly realised that he could not ask them back to this crumbling pile, with its mouldy stair-carpet, primitive kitchen, and the curtains you had to pull with caution, if at all. He saw "his" house was different, and did not want to be ragged at school.

After a day alone in his favourite haunts, however, he decided he was glad to have it all to himself. "No one's the best company, when all's said and done," the verger said. And only then, drawing it in the mud with a stick down by the lake, did he see that Noone and no one were the same. School was the place for people; and he did have one or two good friends. Home was his: the last Mohican tracking silently through the woods, exploring the old cellars and passages, the scary game-larder, the pretty, skeletal summerhouse, and the roofless barn. Sometimes Bill Abbott—two years his senior and already a working man—would come over on a summer evening to teach him how to snare rabbits or tickle a trout, adding to his skills and country lore; but Laurence never showed him the most secret hide-outs—and knew well enough how to frighten him off if he turned inquisitive. "The Noone Walker wouldn't like it," he would say darkly. "You see, his territory is sacrosanct."

The Reverend Laurence Dodsworth, though vague and other-worldly, buried in his books or correspondence with Cambridge theologians, was always access-ible, even companionable. He was, more-over, a fund of exotic, impractical knowledge; how adders fly, what Rosicru-cians did, who killed Baldur the Beautiful —and how he once saw a rat lying on its back with a large egg in its paws while the others pulled it along like a trolley . . . His godson never tired of these stories. "Tell me about Sarajevo," he would say, setting up the new logs to dry by the study fire, and lighting his uncle's pipe for him with a sliver of kindling. "Tell about Atlantis —or the Hunting of the Snark . . ."

They were both loners, and respected the rules of privacy; but they had always enjoyed each other's company: treating as equals—authority apart—and sharing an intimate appreciation of the many veils of fact and fiction. "Humans—and dolphins too, I think, and snakes, possibly: creatures that bask or play—need stories as they need food," the old man used to say. Laurence could talk to his uncle about his anxieties—over his father in far Penang, or coping with bullies at school—and be advised, as though for a third party; or relate his "Noone Walker and Tonto" stories without fear of ridicule. "That's a wise old young man," Uncle Laurie used to say: "I doubt he'll lead Tonto into any trouble . . ." Later, it was some comfort to remember this.

Only twice after his mother's death did Laurence see his father in England. James Gill had little else to bring him home, and Laurence did not go out to Malaysia; he was not sent for. To begin with the explanation was his delicate constitution: he was small, skinny, and prone to asthma. Not until he was much older did he realise the real reason had been his father's preoccupation with a half-Malay mistress, whom he married when the second child was on the way. Moreover he had let his business run down, largely through neglect; selling out to Government interests when the chance came, staying on for two years as manager, and building himself a bungalow in the Malay Cameron Highlands.

Here Laurence visited him and the new family in his year off between school and Cambridge. He discovered little in common with them. The children were friendly enough, but strangely incurious; and his young step-mother had quite rejected her background, westernised in a superficial, suburban way; pretty and plaintive—sour that the occidental star she had hitched her waggon to had fizzled out. Laurence stayed only a few days; then he travelled on round the Far East of which he could remember so little. He fell in love with it. The ambition was born to work there after his geology degree; and none of the foreign lands he travelled in his vacations ensnared him as the East had done. His impossible dream was to live in Noone Rectory and explore the world at his leisure, an eccentric country squire; but since he had no home and no real family, he would espouse the Orient.

Halfway through his time at Cambridge, his father died, and he lost touch with his step-mother and half-sisters when she sold up and moved to Australia. He realised then, and even before, that his uncle/godfather was more than both of these titles to him. But now he too was dead.

The foothills about them were unrolling into hot, bare plains. It had been dawn when they left Nuwara-Eliya: still hours to noon, but already the road ahead shimmered like a mirage.

Half-listening to the Tamil's untiring monologue, Laurence felt the lack of sleep. There would be time enough for sleep later. He thought of the old parson nodding over his darning by the library fire, and felt hollow with loss. Friends he had; but now there was no one he was close to.

No doubt he would see Sarah in London. An ambitious lawyer—yet she had proposed marriage when he told her of the job in the East. She still wrote to him regularly, and had been dissuaded with difficulty from meeting his plane. A closer call had been his visiting the family of the Swedish student he met in Cambridge: they assumed quite simply that he and Karen were engaged. And there was the beguiling Californian he encountered in Bali, who had followed him back to Singapore: his most exciting affair. But he was twenty-six, making his way in the world, and marriage was irrelevant; he would see her again, he felt sure ... Perhaps he had always shied away from commitment; certainly he had a poor opinion of the married state. And no lover had ever been so dear to him as that crusty bachelor who raised him.

It was after two years' metal broking in the City—"good experience", as it had proved—and the offer of the post as adviser to a mining firm in Singapore, that he had to take his leave of Noone, his old uncle—very frail by then—and his past life: a conscious act of uprooting. Uncle Laurie told him then it was a simple fact that they were unlikely to see each other again.

"So you may as well know you will be my sole heir," he said. "Noone itself, naturally, will revert to the Church Commissioners—as you've always been aware, dear boy, since with me the direct line ceases; but everything else will be yours."

Seemingly untroubled by its true state, the old man had by that time withdrawn to the only sound corner of the vast rectory— even slept, as often as not, on the library sofa, wrapped in the duvet his godson had given him. Aside from the gifts of his loving parishioners, he lived a monkish existence, happy with his books and his dwindling stock of fine clarets. He had, nevertheless, found money to buy the godson a car to use at Cambridge, and had recently financed a private printing of his theological essays: his head, and his priorities, were very clear.

Faithful Mrs. Hatton, though beset by grandchildren, still came up from the village each day to bring the milk and the paper, tidy round as best she could, and see to it that he sat down to a hot meal.

"But he won't let me leave him vittles for the evening, Master Laurence. Oh no! 'I'm enjoying a new-found skill, Hatton,' he says—making soup, if you please! And I know just what his game is: when I've sat him down to his dinner and gone off home, he'll only eat the half of it, so's he can cook it up with a bit of water—and a dollop of sherry no doubt—in the evening! Two good saucepans I've had to throw away: charred solid they were—but I recognised the spinach from last Monday . . ."

This had been on an earlier visit—Laurence came down most weekends from London—and he drove into Brookall and purchased a toasted-sandwich machine, pocketing the receipt in case the rector of Noone rejected such a gadget out of hand; but, in one of those evolutionary leaps with which Uncle Laurie was still capable of surprising him, the new machine was seized on like a toy, and the accompanying booklet read from cover to cover. Both Mrs. Hatton and Abbott were treated to Surprise Toasties with their morning coffee; "surprise"—as the old man explained—simply meant one could not, in the heat of spontaneous improvisation, be expected to recall the precise composition of each filling.

Mrs. Hatton approved. "Oh, it's lovely, Master Laurence! Mind you, he'll still be saving his good stew from his dinner to toast up of an evening—but all that bread and butter'll do him no end of good, skin and bone as he is."

It was over an evening dish of "toasties" and some noble, illegible wine that the Reverend Laurence Dodsworth told his godson of his inheritance.

"I had always intended it; but when your father was blessed with further dependants, and especially with a new young wife, I summoned my solicitor and formalised those intentions. As I say, so far as the house and grounds are concerned, the direct line ceases with me; adoption will not do, apparently, and quoting them Shaw buttered no parsnips: a pity—I rather fancied myself as an Undershaft. . . . No: you would have to be my son, and in holy orders, to inherit Noone. But you will have what is mine to give. And you may find a solution, dear boy," he added gnomically. "This way at least gives you freedom of choice, eh? Come now—don't be so chop-fallen, Laurence, my dear: I say nothing new, really; it is just the fact that I say it which is new . . . I fear I have not chosen the best moment; why not take a turn in the poplar walk whilst I cletter the dishes?"

Only in the past few days, since breaking the news of his removal to Sarah, his first "serious" girlfriend, had Laurence encountered female tears; and he had almost envied the ease with which she wept, and the release she clearly found. He could recall only two crying fits in his own life: the first night at prep school, and on the news of his mother's death. Pacing the willow alley in the late twilight had only increased the dry ache, a sense of impending loss that could not be wept away. In all his scrupulous avoidance of "home" and the whole concept of Belonging, he had not faced up to the reality of losing Noone and his uncle at a single stroke; the prospect of inheriting such books, pictures, and mementoes as might come his way was bitterly irrelevant. He remained outside only long enough to give them both the needed space alone: it was the balmy close of a false spring day, April pretending to be June, and the warmth of the fading pink light on the old walls gently and firmly twisted the knife.

He had only visited Noone twice after that, and only to see his uncle; the house itself, the wild gardens, even the view of the distant estuary, were too much part of him. He must lose them, shut them away, suppress that part of himself; must even try—God forbid—to forget. It will never be home, he told himself sternly, looking neither to right nor to left; it never was. But if ghosts are true, he thought, then this is where I'll be.

That was in the previous spring. He had planned to return on leave at the end of a year; but the news came of his uncle's death early in January. The family solicitor told him the Reverend Dodsworth had specifically requested that his godson should not rush back for the funeral: "I hope he may return later on a happier mission."

Then Laurence discovered what he had meant by this. The old man had died rich: "sufficiently so, dear boy, to ransom Noone from the Church Commissioners— or 'Mammon, Lord & Co.', as I prefer to call them—if you so wish; and even, I believe, to restore it; for, as you are aware, it has been sadly neglected. Deliberately so, I now admit: I was determined not to keep it up for *them*; but preferred to leave the money and the choice to you. I trust you approve, my dear Laurence."

In the midst of sorrow, the truth dawned slowly: that paradise regained was now within his grasp. Even when it reached him, his dazzled senses still cast about for some comparable glory, trying to find its measure: some light meter that would accommodate it. But neither first love, nor sex, nor hearing of his Cambridge scholarship, nor his brief exploration of hallucinogens, came near this. It was partly the circumstances, he told himself: losing the only person in the world he really loved, and then learning what that person had done for him, was too complete a reversal of fortune. His next telephone conversation with the solicitor made it more real in practical terms, and sobered him a little. "We can fairly confidently assume the Church Commissioners will sell," he was told, "but their deliberations may take time; moreover, though I shall approach them on your behalf—since that is your wish— they may well decide not to sell it privately, but put it up for auction."

By the end of February, Laurence knew

that Noone was to be auctioned, that it was being advertised in national as well as local papers, and that April the fifth was to be the date. Home leave was now due; but he told the head of the firm his plan to live in Suffolk and find a post in Cambridge or London.

"Just take home leave, my friend," said his Chinese boss. "And this is an auction situation? Then you must not tempt Providence, or whatever you believe in, by giving up your job with us. I like your telling me; and I will know and understand if you succeed in the purchase—but I do advise you to leave it open, if only to flatter the gods of chance and mischance."

Laurence bowed to this wisdom and took his holiday; but he knew himself well enough not to allow too much time in England before the auction: he did not want to see Noone until—and unless—he had bought it. He needed no survey, no preliminary searches. So he took three weeks and spent it travelling in Thailand, followed by a few days in Sri Lanka; pleasantly killing time.

Now it was the third of April; three

o'clock in the afternoon and the hottest time of the equatorial day as they set out again across the western plain, heading for Negombo. They had seen over the batik factory, the waterworks, and the spice plantation where they had picnicked and rested in the shade by a small brown stream.

George the driver had explained at length that his decision to take the long way round, and find a nice hotel in the seaside resort where Laurence could await his evening plane, was justified by the news from Colombo, where he had planned to spend his last afternoon.

"Rumblings, sir, Mr. Gill—and my misgivings are truly confirmed by my little chat with the irrigation official. It is not just the wall writing that is crying 'Tamils Go Home', sir"—a nervous laugh with gold teeth, a mopping of the dark brow. "It is the burning and the looting of Tamil shops on the Colombo outskirts. We will take avoiding action, sir: discreetness, as they are saying, is the best valour."

"It's good of you to take me so far, George. If you want to change your mind, perhaps I could find a driver—"

"No, no, sir, Mr. Gill: I am willing, I am wanting, to meet my obligations, as contracted so generously—and I will charge you no more for the longer route: it is, after all, I who am putting *you* at risk—potentially, sir, only potentially. This trouble is rare, and may with God's good grace be all mere imaginings . . . Not far now, Mr. Gill: take heart! The hotel will be cool, and the sea bathing . . ."

And then the plane, Heathrow, London, Ipswich, the sale and, finally, Noone. The poplar alley will be cool; snowdrops over, but narcissi pushing up through the young nettles—or will they have tidied it up for the sale? The lawns, maybe—but not the alley or the walled garden or the paths through the wood . . .

Laurence leaned back against the hot plastic kept on to preserve the upholstery, and gazed across the blanched rice-fields. Here the harvest was over. On the horizon, smoke rose from burning trash. The only other sign of life was by the muddy waterhole where a path led down the steep banks from a little cluster of houses. There under the harsh sunlight a girl stood thigh-deep in a brown pool, washing clothes; a water buffalo tethered nearby shook its great horned head at the flies. The girl wore only a thin shift; and Laurence watched the coffee-coloured shape gleaming wet like a fresh clay vase on a potter's wheel as she turned slowly and shaded her eyes to stare at the passing car.

A better figure than Cissie's—his Californian, his mixed-up golden girl. And Cissie would be too hyperactive and impatient to move with the languor of that waterhole goddess. Sarah, of Kensington W8, was thin and red-headed, with a white skin and a promising career; the muddy dryad would be wringing out clothes for the rest of her life: only the water would change, plentiful and clear or sparse and brown according to the changing seasons . . .

At first he thought it must be a carnival, a celebration of some sort: all the crowds and noise.

But the bangs were not fireworks, and the faces that flashed by were shouting, not chanting. There was a bristle of sticks, a flash of knives, acrid clouds of smoke. The driver shouted something, twisting

32

round in his seat and rolling his eyes, and Laurence was hurled across the car as, with a scream of brakes and the thunder of staves on the car roof, they swung abruptly into a narrow side street and picked up speed.

"Shut up your window, sir! Shut it! I will try this way—"

Two youths were still clinging to the car, crouching on the boot and beating at the back window with their fists. One fell off as they swerved again and bumped over a stony track between shanties. Gesticulating figures fled out of their path. A stall of brightly coloured drinks crashed across the front wing, and, further on, the windscreen was blindfolded by a falling line of washing.

All this seemed to happen in slow motion. Then suddenly they were out on a main street, almost empty of people, and George pulled the car hard round away from the town centre, crouching over the wheel and exhorting God to grant him acceleration: a hundred yards ahead was a level crossing. But the loud bell was jangling, and now the gate was swinging out across their path.

For a moment it seemed that the law-abiding George da Pinta, good Catholic and loyal patriot, the proud owner of a leatherette file bulging with the postcards, snapshots and commendatory letters of past clients, would storm the barrier ahead; but the car halted a hand's breadth from it. Wild-eyed, the little Tamil stared back down the road where the rabble with flaring torches and a thicket of staves was surging towards them. He wrenched open the door and started to get out, shouting at Laurence to run. Then there was breaking glass and smoke—no air—only faces and fire, and the thunder and scream of the train above the roar and battering of many voices, many hands.

People in the passing train said they saw the axes and staves, and the fire. Not even the looters could save the Englishman's luggage—much less the Englishman.

2

THE Ship is a handsomely refurbished hostelry on the edge of Ipswich's new waterside development, with a large upper room for private parties, Rotary Club meetings and auctions of importance. The sale of the Rectory, Noone Ampney, by instruction of the Church Commissioners, was set for eleven o'clock on Thursday the fifth of April; and in anticipation of worthy contenders, a good fight, a rich purchaser or, at the very least, a relieved vendor, two qualities of champagne were already chilling. But at ten-forty, behind the closed curtains of the snug, Knott-Brown Senior had been joined by Knott-Brown Junior and Mr. McKay, their esteemed valuations man, for a strengthening Gaelic Coffee before the fray: a pardonable bending of the licensing laws in deference to Knott-Brown Junior's cold feet. This was to be his first property auction.

"Never fear, laddie," said Mr. McKay:

"it may be a wreck, but the position is fine—just fine. And the building materials alone must be worth a bob or two."

"So long as there's a couple of serious bidders, Mr. McKay. I saw the press going in, but—"

"Ay—and the gossips; maybe a local or two with their wee fears—or maybe hopes?—of a new housing estate. Don't knock 'em, Kevin lad: it's bodies you need for the acoustics. And a crowd makes a good impression on the private punters: only the property development johnnies will appreciate how many are come for the show. Never you fear."

Knott-Brown Senior rejoined them from a hushed consultation at the door.

"Four fancy foreign motors in the car park, according to mine host," he said, rubbing his hands. "Two calls asking for directions. Wates Homes like to walk in on the dot, from past performance—strong contenders, don't you think?—and the Nip investors were already there when *I* arrived, bowing and hissing in the front pew . . . Better than I'd hoped."

"Oh, it's a highly desirable area, as I've always held," intoned Mr. McKay:

"increasingly so—never mind it's the thick end of two hours from the City, and more in the rush-hour. It's still select, you see: that's the draw. It's posh. It's classy" —the Edinburgh refinement bleaching out the words—"and just look, will you, at the quality resident it's attracting these days . . ."

"I'll concede you a minor Eastern potentate"—Old Knott-Brown pursed up his lips—"and a so-called 'foodie'."

"Irene saw him on the TV, you know." The junior partner brightened a little. "Talking about pancakes, she said . . . And what about that Mr. Hogan and the oyster-beds?"

"True—why, he's spent a fortune, I kid you not, on his marketing network alone. And the pop-star turned City whiz-kid? I ask you now: 'retiring', at thirty-nine . . . Oh, granted they're bringing money to the area."

"That's the positive side of it," said Knott-Brown heavily. "When all's said and done, simply purchasing these barns and workmen's cottages at—admit it, McKay—silly prices, then employing local builders to pretty them up: it's all healthy circulation of wealth—"

"That's right!" Young Kevin's eyes shone. "And I like to think of us as instrumental—"

But his father had not finished. "So the small farmers and labourers move into the new towns, the new Volvos; and commute, in their turn, to their tractor sheds. *And* holiday in Ibiza."

"So, everybody's happy," said Mr. McKay. "Time to move, think you?"

Between London and Aldeburgh there had long been a shifting stratum of painters and music-makers, shoring up their arts and crafts by opening small tea-houses, galleries, whole-food stores, and holding folk concerts in barns. A more stable layer was provided by those enlightened, well-heeled professionals, the doctors, bankers and lawyers who were willing to train or drive to London daily in order that their leisure hours and their children might benefit from a home-grown-vegetable environment.

"Benefit" is probably the word they would use. Their softer brethren in Bucks or Sussex might substitute "enjoy"; but the men and women who choose Suffolk's cool clay in which to sink their roots tend to be tougher; somewhat austere, even, and with clearer whites to their eyes, than the easy-option, short-spin-away Home Counties folk—rather as Cambridge Man is distinct from Oxford Man.

Lately their territory was being invaded by a different sort of wealth: you could still find the better country house for less in East Anglia, or the under-developed site not far from the sea, with room to accommodate the mini golf-course or the airstrip without much levelling. In the last year, the Middle East, the multi-media, and one dubiously crowned head had settled in the region—as much as these nomads ever settle—taking over the family seats of various hard-up aristocrats. And these now had to live on their Highland estates all year round; coming south only for a vital vote in the House of Lords or the purchase of a gun, and making shift with Aunt Hermione's sofa-bed in some darkling Knightsbridge drawing room. Knott-Brown père called it the circulation of wealth; but it was more what the recipes refer to as a "slow rolling boil" in the social system, with the New Money bubbles winking at the brim, a bland middle of well-emulsified two-car families, and the old landlords sinking down, with something of an air of specific gravity, into a thick, sluggish and surprisingly rich goulash.

Movement—any movement—is good for the estate agents.

"Time? Pop upstairs, Kevin, there's a good lad, and see how they look. Oh, Kevin: ask—discreetly, now!—if a Mr. Charles Gelhorn has shown up. There's no telling by the cars they drive: he wouldn't necessarily be sporting a Rolls, but that's his league. All right . . . ? I feel this could be our purchaser, now that the most interested party, the young relative of the deceased, has dropped out."

"Ay: I got your phone message. Dropped dead, not to put too fine a point on it. Nasty business."

"Yes, indeed," said Knott-Brown. "The family solicitor has been in touch: one of those Far Eastern incidents, I gather; some racial confrontation or other—well, it was in the papers, wasn't it? Muddled reports, of course, but descriptions seem to fit . . . Which really leaves four possibles, and then this dark horse. Coming up on the inside."

"That you're backing?"

"I'm inclined to, Mac—though he only went over the house last week."

"Yankee architect."

"That's right. With an English wife. He looks, and talks, like a big spender."

"They'll rattle about a bit."

"Oh, I don't suppose it'd be for his own use. I know these successful architects . . ." Old Knott-Brown tapped his nose. "More likely a spec: calculated tax-loss on capital gains. Could even be for an American client—a rich one: let's face it, my friend, even at top whack it'll need the same spending on it, the state it's in."

Mr. McKay's red moustache stretched in a foxy smile. "And of course the Very Reverend Church Commissioners would be relieved just to get it off their hands, I'll wager; at any price—to duck out of this 'shared responsibility' lark."

"What a mess, eh? Some ill-defined

agreement made between gentlemen centuries ago—"

"That didn't hold water—or, rather, let it in!"

"Oh, terrible shame," said Knott-Brown. "And the family tend to be the losers . . . I knew old Dodsworth a little. Sad, really: the last of the idealists, eh?"

"Shouldn't dabble in property—leave that to the Church Commissioners! Ah—Kevin laddie: is there a quorum?"

Knott-Brown Junior was pink with excitement. "Wates Homes have just gone up. And the American, Mr. Gelhorn, approached me and made himself known —*and* introduced me to Mrs. Gelhorn! Ever so stylish: she had a raincoat with a fur lining—dark, you know, like mink maybe."

"This lad will go far. That was a nice wee bit of observation, Kevin: it's just what we like to hear. I do believe we have lift-off," said Mr. McKay.

3

CHARLES took me to see Noone Rectory later that morning.

He was still high. Charles was always ebullient, hyperactive, a fast talker; but, coming out of the auction, he was so high he was out of sight. Hardly uttered; a sort of tense ecstasy: all alone on his mountain peak—a state I'd seen him in maybe a couple of times in five years. Me, I was a bit winded by the speed of it all: he'd only seen this place a few days before. And maybe I'm still not used to that sort of money, but I was alarmed at the price he was paying for it: well above the figure he'd talked about on the way from London.

He hadn't said much else, actually; driving fast with the radio on rather loud —LBC, then Jimmy Young. But he'd wanted me to come with him. Maybe he needed a woman's eye; maybe just someone to witness his victory or flatter away his disappointment. He doesn't often ask me "along for the ride", so I guessed it might be something special for him. Now I knew it.

But I couldn't reach him; not yet. As he stepped out of that pub in Ipswich, he literally leapt into the air, brandishing his fists like a footballer who's scored the winning goal in injury time. He threw his head back and roared: "*Gotcha!*" What they thought back in the pub . . .

I caught up with him at the car. He was grinning to himself as he leaned over to unlock my door, and I could see he was in his own little world of deals and double-deals, plans and super-plans: Charlie Gelhorn had done it again. He'd pulled it off. He'd beaten the buggers. He'd got his baby. Now his brain was racing ahead on to the next stage—and I didn't actually know if this Noone Rectory was going to be razed and developed, or restored and resold within the year for a million, or had been snapped up for some special client. Or if we were to live there.

Charles hadn't said. On the way up I weakened at one point and asked him; he seemed not to hear. In all the banter after the auction, he gave nothing away. Not that he would. And confiding plans—to me, at any rate—was not his style: that was "counting chicks". I only ever heard when my husband had clinched a deal: "that way no one gets dropped in it". "No expect, no regret", a Gelhorn dictum, a bit of his father's ghetto wisdom, no doubt. So: now the deal was done, and if I wanted to hear how it affected me—and he was barely aware I was there—then I must talk him down.

"You're pleased," I said—but it sounded too cool. "That was terribly exciting. And all so fast I could hardly—"

"It was just—*fine* . . ." He exhaled, and leaned back against the seat. He slowed down to the speed limit. I knew that Lee Marvin gravel-voice: Charles was Kid Shelleen, and he'd just shot the man with the silver nose. "Oh, but it was just f-i-n-e . . ." And he turned his grin briefly at me. "Did you see me? Did you *see* all that, honey . . . ? Boy! I played only to win: no fancy steps, none of those—those clever, inscrutable silences—nah! No plays at all, folks! No aces in my turnups! Nosir: our Chuck was in there, beginning, middle and end, popping the bids in—fast—between those mumbling mothers—and topping them by five Gs every doggone throw! Were they *sick* . . . ? Know what? If those assholes had gotten the word they'd be up against some wild Yankee they wouldn't have wasted their time. Oh, it was just fine . . ."

"It was, absolutely, Charles: congratulations, darling," I said. "And the bubbly was a graceful touch, I thought."

"Sure. The good stuff. I checked that out."

"And they couldn't resist staying on for it: that was nice . . ." He was nearly down. "I mean, there they were, the losers, and you made them shake hands with you all round—and Charles, I overheard a couple of them muttering away, 'He's got some cheek, that one: boasting—boasting, mark you—that he'd never even had the place surveyed!'"

Charles slapped the wheel and bellowed with laughter. "I *like* it! Keep that in . . . ! Oh, Katy, it's great you were there to see it all—Jesus! *I* didn't need a survey: all I needed was those guys, the development boys—a nice little cluster of them—so neat: I knew I only had to top the speculators, and I was in business—with a *bargain*!"

I felt like saying, "Aren't you paying a lot more than you meant to?" but Charles had never, so far as I knew, laid out good money on anything that wasn't a good investment—as he liked to tell the assembled company, pointing to me as a prime example. And now "speculators" was my cue to ask the big question.

"Charles, what will you do with this old rectory?"

"Why, Lor' bless you, Miz Katy: just live in it, that's all! Just, this is *it*—this is the Big One, honey; the one I've been looking for. Oh yes indeedy: this is where Chuck Gelhorn turns country squire—with his son and heir—and his gorgeous missis . . . Didn't I say? Hell, why d'you figure I was so uptight? Sure: this is It . . . You'll like that, won't you, Kate?" He turned and laid a large, furry hand on my lap. "It's your scene, isn't it? Back in the jolly old County set-up again: it's what I want for you, honey . . . It's what I want for my boy."

So my line has always been to keep well

clear of these things; I learnt that at the start, and it was almost part of the deal.

Charles was constantly falling for one desirable property or another, some of them in fishnet tights—he was a legs man —and then forgetting them a week later. Occasonally they stuck; like our house in St. John's Wood, or the pink-haired singer on her Chelsea barge. My yoga (especially the breathing exercises, I'm convinced) helped me to let it all flow past: I'd got what I wanted. And I knew I wouldn't lose it. I was sure of that. My insurance policy was four and a half years old. He answered to the name of Henry; and he was Charles Gelhorn's pride and joy. He'd got his heir. Pink-haired crooners would come and go; but this marriage would stick. I believed that, and was content.

The rain had gone away. Driving along narrow lanes between big, dun fields, with the April sunshine stretching out the land and the vast East Anglia sky, Charles was trying to reassure me now.

"Sure it's all a bit sudden. But you like surprises, don't you? Just keep an open mind. And don't think it's all flat as this, Kate: the village, Noone Ampney, is on a rise—almost a hill for these parts—and the grounds of the house itself are very much up and down; landscaped, way back, I guess . . . Then, like I said, I'll put the London house on the market with a real late completion date, OK? So's this place is all ready for us, with the least hassle for you and Nanny—and Henry will just love it, no problem. Matter of fact, old Henry would have gotten a great kick out of all the mess and building works, wouldn't he . . . ? Honey, this is for keeps —honest. It's fantastic: this is the place I've been waiting for. And I've got such *plans*: oh, brother! The Old Rec.—wreck: geddit?—just won't know what hit it . . . And then, like I say, there's your barn: your baby, right? All yours, designwise: as a painting studio—lots bigger than your studio in St John's Wood. Or a rumpus room—a guest annexe, maybe. What- ever."

At first glimpse, coming down the avenue, I was shocked by the sheer size of it. More a landfall: a massive shape that gradually solidified through the veil of spring leaves; that loomed over us as we parked by the fountain. It was like a cliff, part-hidden in dark vegetation; a cave of a doorway at its foot and, high above, delicate pinnacles of a broken balustrade. "Fantastic" was right; but somehow I hadn't been prepared for the size.

"You think this is big? This is just a third of it, kiddo! OK: the biggest third; but you haven't seen the wings—and there's out-buildings and—Kate honey: just you wait till I've fixed it all. You'll be its *queen*! You will love it! You will: *believe* me."

He led me round the outside to see the back.

"Virtually untouched . . . As it was built. Kinda grim, eh? Sort of dried-blood colour—a bit Chas Addams, with the parapets, and all those shuttered windows."

"Oh, I don't know—it strikes me as rather mellow." I realised that a certain jockeying for attitudes was going on: by decrying the place, he'd nudged me into the position of defending it; but I carried on. "Almost homely—homey, that is—as I see it. Really, Charles. That's how *I*—"

I needn't have bothered. He squeezed

my shoulders, but he wasn't actually listening.

"End of line: all change," he said; and he spread out his arms, taking in the weeds, the rusty pump, piles of rubble, an ancient pram, and sweeping them all away. "A great courtyard between the two wings —York stone—maybe marble . . . and a fountain. Floodlighting—or even flambeaux, for parties: great for folks to, like, spill out into, as a basic space—right? But all lit up: every casement—With a fantastic new picture-window the full width of the upper storey; very clean and spare . . ."

"Sounds terribly expensive, darling."

"Sure. All the best things are. Come on inside . . . The old kitchen: quite something else, eh? But a great shape. High-tech boiler room, could be. That's how I see it; and all the pipes and junctions lacquered scarlet: a raw statement of energy. Then there are all these pokey passages: they'll go. Clean sweep . . . OK, cue for roll of drums: the great hall! Should've come in through the front doors, but—hell, there it is! How about that."

51

Whatever I said—"Wow," I think—bounced back at me and I shut up. That elegant, echoing cavern soared up, stretched out, on all sides. There were portraits, and large, formal urns between the casements; and I could make out shapes of curvy Regency sofas in the gloaming. One had collapsed into a grotesque kneeling position under a load of fallen plaster; and, walking over to the fireplace, we crunched through more of it. We craned up at the carved stone chimney-piece; its pale fluting and embossed coats of arms ran the full height of the room above the black yawn of the hearth.

From there I looked round me. "The staircase is later, isn't it?" I said.

"Victorian. And it must absolutely go . . . Then: morning room and library and —through here, the dining room. Must have been quite a colour when it was first put up. Yes, that's silk."

I asked what was happening to all the furniture, the paintings.

"There was an auction a couple days ago. Some of the stuff has gone, but the Church Commissioners stipulated the bulk of it had to stay till the house auction:

reckoned it'd be more appealing—easier to visualise, I guess—before it was totally stripped out. And the proceeds simply go with the rest of the old boy's estate—the cash holdings: a tidy sum, so rumour has it. Oh, to another branch of the family, Australia or somewhere, since the heir is no more . . . Sure it's sad, Katy: but it's an ill wind, and it's blown good our way. He could've been prepared to pay a silly price for it, you know. A strong contender." He looked at his watch. "Hey, I'm working up quite a thirst. The table's booked for one . . ."

He'd fixed that, days ago, in confident anticipation of his victory: even when his chief rival was still around. The old estate agent had told me how the lost heir used to visit Noone when he was a boy, and I found myself wondering what *he* would have done, if he had won, to crown his triumph. Me, I would have brought a picnic and spread it out, champagne and smoked-salmon sandwiches, in the dusty morning room where the sun came in . . .

Charles was saying, "We'll have to drop by at the local pub first: no way can we miss out on that. So, a lightning tour of the bedrooms and nursery wing, OK? Then see if there's time for the attics. Maybe a peek round the garden. And your barn, right . . . But it's quite something, eh?"

After five bedrooms, only two of which seemed to have been actually used, Charles went on up to the attics. I lingered in a corridor where the walls were covered with a collage of old pictures and mementoes. It was like that lovely, roomy downstairs loo at home, papered in postcards: a favourite bolt-hole, with heaps of books and magazines. *Ages* ago: before the dry rot. Before Father died; I think he put them up: memories of travels long before that, in the good old days. Later they were papered over to cover the mildew—when Mother put the place on the market . . .

Charles was shouting down the stairs. "Hey, step on it, Katy! There's another whole floor to see."

"You carry on," I called; "I'll look at the attics next time." And I went back to my varnished cards and valentines. There were elaborate ones with paper-doily edges; and pretty bookmarks, mostly religious, all gilt angels and lilies and improving texts—prizes at Sunday School? Drawings, too, and little watercolours; and poems, or nursery rhymes, some written out in copperplate, so far as I could see. But the electricity was off—it probably needed complete rewiring. I tried to pull the curtains open a bit more; they stuck, then gave way and collapsed at my feet in an explosion of dust. Looking out, I got my bearings: down below was the back yard, surrounded by those red walls; opposite me, the shuttered casements of the other wing, the one we hadn't explored. And the strong sun only increased the feeling of desolation, somehow; cruelly bright, striking across the jungle of weeds, the looped-up washing-line, the high, rusty pram—so eccentrically planted with spring bulbs by someone—and the background of peeling red paint picked out by that harsh, raking light.

I felt stifled suddenly, as if . . . as if the dust and the memories, and those centuries of accumulated lives I couldn't ever find out about—but which I was about to join, to become part of, in the history of the house—were all compressed into that view from an upper window, and crowding round me in that dim, golden, illustrated corridor. All at once I needed to get out.

I heard Charles go down into the great hall, and was glad he did not see my panicky retreat along the passage. It *was* a sort of panic; but he would without doubt have seen it as "fanciful", or "hypersensitive". I was "flaky", according to him: rather more than just "highly strung". At least I'd managed to be supremely cool over the whole auction business. I'd done well—though actually he might have rather enjoyed me being jumpy and asking a lot of questions: the Little Woman. And he'd have turned protective and masterful. It might have helped his own nerves; and the perfect wife would probably have played along . . . But I'm best separate: I'd rather have my own "fanciful" thoughts, good or bad, and keep them to myself to sort out, than have them shot down. I think I was learning, slowly.

He didn't call me, so I went back into the day-nursery. This must be over the morning room, I thought, kneeling on the wide window seat and looking out. Part of the ceiling had fallen and been swept into a pile in the corner. There was a trunk of old toys; and I wondered about the children that had played in there, the boy who used to come and stay. I thought of Henry. Henry playing with them would "earth" them, somehow, just as I could make these rooms mine. I enjoy continuity, really; I wasn't rejecting the past: I just wanted to *contain* it. It felt as though it were lying around loose, sizzling quietly every so often; and I was getting the odd, small shock from it . . . I wished now we could have been at the auction of the contents: I would have bid for those toys. And for a couple of the portraits.

On the way downstairs (I liked the great staircase: a pity it had to go), I stopped and had a look at one of the small paintings that had caught my eye: a pale young person, eighteenth century probably, or late seventeenth, in a narrow black coat and broad hat; rather stern-faced and stark against a stormy landscape dotted with sheep. It wasn't a great—or even a very good—work of art: the pose was stiff, and it was flatly painted, in the manner of a colonial primitive; but the effect was arresting. I would have liked to clean it up; and to keep it right there.

I moved on quickly. I realised that it would have been less disturbing if the contents of Noone had been removed after all. Outside, the light had lent a kind of false liveliness to the rusty pump, the washing-line; in here, it was the presence of pictured faces, and the open book on the library table, the worn wing chair by the hearth, or the pathetic little sandwich-toaster I had noticed on the kitchen dresser . . . The garden would be better, with this year's new, clean growth hiding even last summer's tracks, and all those gone before.

Charles was leaning against the refectory table, scribbling in his sketch pad. "Ah, hi there . . . ," he said. "Look, honey, I've just gotten me a hunch about the layout of this room. Then I'll be done . . . Fine: meet you by the car. It's all these doors, you see . . ."

Back in the sunshine, I realised just how cold I'd been. The barn must be down the slope behind the house; first I wanted to make a detour through the walled garden. I tucked my hands in my mackintosh pockets, made my way through an untidy arch in the yew hedge, and struck out briskly across the west lawn.

I left the house determinedly; but, by the time I had passed the formal rose beds round the sundial, and taken the brick path leading to the kitchen garden, I'd forgotten my "fancies" and the need to escape. (Looking back on it later, I'm quite clear about this; and it is important.) I was simply enjoying the warmth and the springy, mossy turf under my feet. There were marvellous trees: I recognised arbutus, white-beams, ilex, wych-elm, a huge weeping willow, an ancient tulip tree, and another willow, rather exotic—*Salix tortulans*?—with fine, kinky branches like a newly washed perm, and a shock of lime-green leaves that seemed to trap the sun in their twists.

Someone had been looking after the garden. According to Charles, the place had stood empty since the new year; yet the roses were pruned not long ago, judging by the young shoots. A certain amount must have been done with the sale in mind: mowing and edging and weeding, just in front of the house and on this west side, as I noticed from the windows. In the walled garden, however, nothing had been touched for months. The neat rows of cauliflower and broccoli had bolted, a forest of yellow flowers; weeds had spread over the darker plots of winter digging, and in the handsome, long bed of perennial herbs. Maybe he'll come and work for me, I thought: it only needs hoeing and planting; some repairs to the greenhouses and frames . . . And I found myself smiling, realising it was mine. Ours, of course; but Charles would not have time to tear the gardens apart this year. I picked a posy, a *bouquet garni*, tucked it in my pocket, and went across the garden to the door on the other side.

Here a path and a row of poplars ran along the length of the brick wall: aspen poplars, quite young, with tender pinkish leaves shivering even in the still air. Between them, beyond the sloping wood and the further fields, I could see a railway line on its steep green embankment, the arch beneath where the small road ran through to another village and the flatter land, fields, a distant spire, and the huge sky. From here, the estuary of the nursery view was only a bright streak glimpsed through trees at the far end of Noone's high ground; and the village itself was hidden. Nearer, where the slope was gentler, I could see the roofs of the outbuildings; my barn would have lots of north light—but there wasn't really time to inspect it properly now. Charles would not feel I was ungrateful: he was happily absorbed in bigger things; and he would shout when he didn't find me waiting by the car. For what time I had, I wanted to linger here, to follow the path; and somewhere, I knew, there was a ruined summerhouse.

This alley had not been cut for over a year; last summer's long, grey grass lay tangled among old brambles and new snaking shoots. But someone had walked through before me, and I followed the weaving track, skirting a fig tree that had fallen away from the wall, and rambler roses, run largely to briars now, arching sprays that reached right across my path. I lifted these carefully out of the way: they would be lovely in June; they could be pruned after that. Glad of my boots, I stopped to press back the nettles round a clump of white narcissi, and felt down their cold stems to pick them; taking my time. Bulbs were so much later here than in London, and spring there such a public event, held in the parks; Keep Off The Grass. Here no one would miss them: no one even knew about them ... I straightened up, and that's when I saw him.

Charles called from far away by the front door. I came through the yew arch into the forecourt.

"Hey—you're there! You didn't answer—"

"I was on my way. Look: our own narcissi, all amongst the nettles."

"Fine. They're great. Let's go."

And I didn't tell him about the encounter in the long alley; not then, nor afterwards, when I should have done. I never even told the police. Then, Charles would have rolled up his eyes and said something like: "See what I mean, folks? *My* wife's got little men in black at the bottom of *her* garden. Tell you, it's all go ..." But it wasn't that. For some reason I just wanted to keep it to myself.

So I said nothing. He was talking enough for both of us, about planning permissions, I think; while I wound back the scene and ran it through my head again, checking my frame of mind, noting the sharp details. I couldn't have made it up. Everyone, of course, has imagined the Intruder; but this had not frightened me. Disturbed me, yes: my adrenalin was still pumping and my hands were like ice. I still clutched the narcissi, as though they were some sort of proof: it was when I straightened up from picking them that I saw him.

About forty feet away from me, by a clump of rusty brambles, was the black-and-white figure of a man: a flat black hat and narrow dark clothes framing a white face; and white at his throat. It was only for a moment; then he turned and walked away from me. I had already lifted my hand to wave; opened my mouth to call "Good morning". But instead, suddenly curious—about his coolness, his identity, his odd clothes, his right to be there at all —I walked quickly forward, to follow him, to get closer before I hailed him. A branch of briar caught hard in my skirt; I stopped to disentangle myself. And when I looked up he had gone—either through another doorway in the brick wall, or among the trees where the wood crowded close onto the pathway. Then Charles called, and I turned back.

Sitting in the car, with him still talking, I could recall that intruding figure quite precisely, stark as an engraving against the bright green wilderness of the sunlit alley. I was sure I had seen him, and that he had seen me. I remembered his eyes.

"Just gone twelve: opening time—" said Chuck Gelhorn, the new squire of Noone.

4

NEARLY a fortnight went by before I saw Noone again.

Charles had to fly off to Milan soon after the auction to oversee a leisure complex where progress was falling behind schedule, and awkward clients were demanding to see the top man; then he was due to give a talk at some business seminar in Houston. I could have gone too, but I'm not too good at those lush, tax-loss beanos; and I knew he enjoyed them a lot more, all that boozing with the boys, the obligatory sucking-pig barbecues by the pool, and the lovelies—in stetsons and not much else—for afters, without Third Wife watching him across her Perrier water.

Meanwhile there was nothing I could actually do for our newly acquired house, he insisted, until plans had been drawn up and passed: "And there'll be a deal of hassle and horse-trading right there," he said, "never mind the building work itself." I needed simply to see it again, especially on my own; to examine the barn and start thinking what I would do with it; to decide how much repairing was urgent, how much could wait.

But before the house came so suddenly into our lives, I had arranged to spend a week with cousins in Anglesey, taking Nanny and Henry with me: rather straight relations who had only re-established contact once I was properly married—and never refer to the events of my "black sheep" period. They were Family, however—I don't have many—with a house by the sea, and two girls just old enough to spoil Henry rotten. Nanny, accustomed to large, aristocratic broods, and always hinting darkly about the complications of having an Only, was looking forward to three under her wing; and I was made to feel that, if I renegued on account of Noone and my barn, I would be sacrificing an innocent on the altar of a mere "hobby" —her view of my painting career. I could have taken them down to Noone for a picnic; but, before he left, Charles had insisted he should be present for Henry's introduction to his new home.

I might have driven over alone one afternoon: I did want to, as I say. Yet I found myself oddly grateful for excuses: seemingly divided between curiosity and some half-admitted dread that was just a little stronger. Trying to explain this away to myself, I decided it was not the presence —nor even the sudden, mysterious absence—of the Intruder; nor the inevitable sadness of the vast, neglected manse; nor the mammoth task ahead of reclaiming it, since I would have no hand in this: Noone was strictly Charles's baby, his new toy. That was clear and ought to have been a relief; I didn't have to bother my pretty little head about it, as I'd been told more than once.

So why *was* I reluctant to go back there alone? I had, after all, rather fallen for the place; parts of it, the morning room, the library, and especially the nursery wing with its illustrated corridor, appealed to me so much, it was almost as if I recognised them—though I wouldn't say that to Charles, of course. And there was the garden . . .

Then I knew, all at once, it was the combination of these discarded reasons—it was what they added up to—that disturbed me: my dread was not *of* Noone, but *for* Noone. Because I knew, and it didn't, just what was about to hit it: the terrible reforming energy of Charles Gelhorn. Which was really just comic, in a grotesque sort of way—unless you knew the place; and I had let myself identify with it, which was worse: unwittingly I had allowed its past to get to me. That was abundantly clear; and the encounter in the long green alley only clinched it. If I was genuinely psychic (unlikely, whatever Charles might say), then I had seen the ghost of a former incumbent; if not, my unconscious mind had seized on that portrait as a symbol, a summary, of the haunting past, and projected it on to the wilderness.

Small comfort, however, to rationalise my misgivings so tidily; and I didn't go back to Noone alone. I think it was sensible not to; knowing me, it would have been unsettling, either way—whether the place turned out to be more spooky or more desirable the second time around.

Over the passing days, and staying with the cousins, hearing myself describe it, or in bed at night, remembering it in the light of that brief visit, I felt that I might get too involved in it, wandering round alone; have my own ideas about it—especially as I knew that, with Charles's kind of money, it might be properly and marvellously restored.

He could not touch the front. But he would rip out the Gothic staircase and the impractical stone monument of a fireplace and sell them to a Beverly Hills builder who had a market for such outsize antiques. He was going to convert the fifteen bedrooms into five suites with dressing-rooms and bathrooms; and that "pokey" corridor upstairs in the nursery wing would be widened and illuminated with one continuous window: already he referred to it as "my gallery", and looked forward to "getting the artwork together" for it; the Gelhorn Collection. As for the hall itself, the great double cube, I couldn't even imagine what its final form might be; but when he phoned his buddy in New York the evening of the auction, I heard him saying, "That *space*, eh, Mikey boy? Christ, it really starts my motors; like, there's room for—right! That's *right* —and know what? That's what flashed on soon as I saw it. I thought, straight off: Wow, there's the space for the double helix . . . Certainly for the mezzanine concept . . . *Sure* you could conceal them, but why not flying cantilevers? Like, make them a Feature . . . ? Fancy ceiling? No problem. Plaster all shot to hell . . . No, no way—unless you're an Oxford college or something and just a matter of selling off a chunk of Cheshire or an apartment block in Mayfair to foot the bill . . ."

Charles's American-Jewish energy was what he was all about; the first thing you noticed, because it came out and hit you. His enemies/rivals called it brash, bull-dozing, pushy; and they were right of course. But it's also what attracted me in the first instance.

So different from me; my energy is the "nervous" variety. He used to say it was "cold, blue-spark stuff"—like a miniaturised circuit, I suppose, beside his blast furnace: twenty-four hours a day; you can't just turn these things on and off. A one-man, three-shift power-source. Charles was a workaholic who played squash after a seven-to-seven day, then took his buddies out to dinner and a night-club, slaved over hot plans in the small hours, and was up again at six to go jogging.

As I say, I'm different. And he liked it that way; wouldn't have wanted me to compete. His second wife, the Texan bombshell, tried to keep up. "Chuck and me, we do everything together." But she didn't produce a child for him, and was junked. An heir was what he wanted from marriage. Third time lucky; and, old-fashioned though he was, he lived in sin with me (careful, too, hiding me away in one of his country cottages—a speculation buy like me, I think—and saying, only half-jokingly, that he wanted to make good and sure the kid was his), just until the pregnancy test came up positive. Then it was the big "engagement" party and the registry office; and, soon after that, the mansion in St. John's Wood—bought like Noone, before I'd seen it.

When my sister in Canada used to hear

about my life with Charles, she'd say "But what about what *you* want, Kate? wouldn't stand for it!" She's younger than me, and still full of moral fervour and idealism, in spite of ten years wedded to an earnest, struggling farmer, four children and no money for frills. They work shoulder to shoulder, digging the tractor out of the snow, rebuilding fences or whatever—when she isn't driving an old pickup full of kids twenty miles to the Good School. "We make decisions *together*, Kate . . ."

I can't say: "Yes—but what happened to the degree in music you didn't finish? How often do you sit down at the piano these days?" (And they've got a piano now; when he first took us over, to meet his family and for him to meet mine, Charles gave them the spare one from his Manhattan apartment—a white baby grand that looks somewhat out of place in the rumpus room with the sled and the patched dinghy.)

Maybe I didn't make the decisions. Still, I did what I wanted: I was that rich, that free. "But you don't really love him, do you, Kate?" she'd say. There's no answer to that.

You can't expect more than one great love in your life, I believe. It was so simple for Louisa: she was always going to marry the boy next door—or half a mile down the lake, which was the Northumberland equivalent. They worked and saved even in their teens, and finally emigrated, with the help of the money Mother left us. Louisa was still only twenty-one; but they'd been married for three years, and she wanted a farm and kids so much more than the conservatoire and the grind of part-time jobs; she simply got pregnant and left, heading West with her man, her one and only.

I was out of art school then, living in London digs and beginning to sell my prints, mostly to interior designers or shops like Harrods and Casa Pupo. Seeing my lump of capital disappearing in rent and small plain rare beef-burgers, a business-school boyfriend persuaded me to invest in a studio flat in Camden. He nearly talked me into a larger one and a mortgage; but, without the security of a steady income, I was not that confident. As I couldn't afford to rent a proper studio, the flat was always a tip, crowded out with my screenprinting table and paraphernalia, the press (attached to a large second-hand vacuum cleaner to create the necessary suction), and all the clutter of easel, oils, canvases and the withered still-life arrangements required for the originals long before any printing got under way. Friends who dropped in soon learnt to roll up my futon if they wanted somewhere to sit. But it was my own place; I could manage the low service charge and still afford a paraffin heater, and a lager or two in the small, juddering fridge. I worked hard; I got some prints into a Francis Kyle summer show. And that was where I met Leo.

He looked out of place, a bull in a china shop, among the sensitive watercolours and sub-Hockney studies of deck-chairs on balconies. He had been brought along by a reviewer friend *en route* to something else; and he stood in a corner, glowering; a gorgeous, black-haired, outsize genius, silent amidst the high-pitched gossip. Until he suddenly demanded beer instead of wine.

The scatty deb in charge of refreshments was quite thrown by this. I said I'd get some from the nearby pub. "*Could* you? Fantastic . . . Oh, but you can't! You're one of the *artists*, aren't you? I mean— you've got to *be* here to sort of explain your stuff to—"

And at this point Leo Constantine moved between us, his broad back filling her view. He said, "You go to the pub, young woman. That's where I'm going . . ." Then we were outside in the sticky summer evening together; and we did not go back.

We weren't long in the pub either. He had a motor-bike, and a warehouse near Tilbury docks. I stayed with him that night, and moved in my things next day, the canvases by taxi and the rest on the Tube. He didn't offer to help, nor did I expect it; he wanted me there, and that was enough. Because Leo was painting. I had, he said, released his block. I was good for him.

For me, it was the apocalypse. It was Death and Transfiguration; like being killed in a violent accident—too fast for fear, or caution, or even pain—and becoming on the instant a flaming angel in bliss: a state the Bible doesn't describe; unrecognised, perhaps, by our brand of religion. I discovered that the seat of the Soul was (as so long suspected by the sages) absolutely central to the body: between the legs. And I had no doubt that it was my soul: this was an emotion too mighty to be contained in five senses; an elation too fine to be ruled by mere nerves and synapses. I understood about Faith too, when I stopped to think amid my carrier bags on the Underground; for by no exercise of reason could I show that Leo Constantine would be a good thing for *me*.

He hardly noticed my arrival; just told me which corner I could stack my things in, and warned me about a rotten board. But I had brought a carrier of food and drink, and he broke off to make love and to eat. While he ate he pulled out my canvases one after another, and went through my portfolio. He didn't say a lot, maybe because his mouth was full. In bed that night, replete with passion and the fish-and-chips I'd provided, he said, almost asleep: "Your early stuff is fine. Get away from all this decorative shit, woman, and try to say something real. Something hard . . ."

I was twenty-three, and wildly in love for the first, the only, time. It lasted three and a half years, during which I tried not to wonder how or when it might end. Sufficient unto the day.

Friends, the ones that asked "How are you doing?" "What are your plans, then?" —they worried about me for a while, then lost touch. Leo had no time for their sort; and, seeing them alone, I was unsettled both by the straight warnings and the tactful, bright evasions. Even at their parties, all my contemporaries seemed obsessed with "commitment" and "caring"— it was that era, and they were career-persons beginning to think hard about pairing, bonding, reproducing. I pretty well stopped seeing them. Social life was provided by private views, and by Leo's few artist friends, including a silent sculptor—highly successful—who roamed the junk-yards for exciting scrap-metal;

and there was a titled philosopher-turned-Buddhist who lived in a real caravan and slept on our floor when the nights got too cold. I never saw him remove his wilting tweed hat.

Sometimes a persistent dealer, or rich, avant-garde, private collector, would take us out; and Leo, who was sublimely unconcerned with approval, ate well and drank deep at their expense, revelling in his role of elusive genius. He'd drain the bottle of Château d'Yquem into his glass and look around vaguely for more; then admit, on being pressed, that his latest study of Wapping Reach was OK. "No: not 'good'," he'd say, suddenly aggressive after a run of bored monosyllables. "Spare me the hogwash, man. 'Great', maybe. Certainly the new one—same series. It's getting somewhere. Or it was . . . What? Oh, I reckoned it had the bones of something even greater: it's white emulsion now—lovely surface. Like a stubble field under snow . . . No sweat. Plenty more where that came from. I believe . . . Want to know what I believe? I believe 'pleased' equals 'smug' equals 'static' (where the fuck *is* that waiter?) . . . Oh, sure I like some things. And keep them. Those I wouldn't sell out. Hell, you know me, Max: if I paint to sell, it's to pay rent or the trip to Paris. Like that little thing you've got: a quick squit, straight down the middle—eh?"

During the first few weeks I went often to my Camden pad to print: the Kyle Gallery had brought me two commissions and, despite Leo's scorn, I delivered the goods. I could see we needed the money. But I never slept there, and felt only half-alive away from him. What was more, I soon realised I wasn't the only woman in his life. But I was the resident one: I was determined to swallow my pride and envy, to be there when he broke off from work, and looked round him for flesh and drink. Whatever he did on the days, and sometimes the nights, when he simply disappeared, it was just something I learnt to live with. During those first months, wherever I was—printing or delivering or going to a party on my own or visiting my great-aunt in Sussex—I always trekked back to Tilbury. I was determined to become indispensable; and, by the time my friends, family and patrons had faded away, and Leo was, by my choice, the only thing in my life, I believe I had. Aldred, the Buddhist peer, drifting into Tilbury one frosty morning after a long mild season, was surprised enough at finding us still together to tell me, in confidence, that Leo had never been with any woman so long. "Likes being looked after, I suppose," he said broodingly, warming his hands round his mug of coffee: "must be feeling his age."

I did look after my awkward genius; but it wasn't all one way. Leo was making me paint: at first in an attempt to please or impress him, following the leads of the few unfinished experiments he had noticed with approval, and later becoming absorbed in the process of learning, relearning, about paint. While I was still at art school I had produced and sold several attractive little portraits mainly done from photographs. Now I started to draw the "moving head"—the only true model, according to Leo. Leo painting; Leo reading the *Standard*; Aldred asleep; Aldred mending a haversack; Mrs. Patel, of the corner shop, at her till; Miss Patel selling stamps; Leo and his cat; Leo asleep.

He did not involve himself, but he did not dismiss these efforts as he had my prints, with all the labour that went into them; and often he would sift through my newest sketches and ponder over a couple: "You might do something with those," he'd say. By this measure of encouragement, by allowing me, however grudgingly, to watch him at work, but most of all by being there and being who he was —a clever, difficult and entirely dedicated painter, and my lover—Leo changed me. It was a close encounter with integrity writ large—though he'd have dismissed the word as "artsy-fartsy". He may be a millionaire by now for all I know; but I honestly believe he still won't know the meaning of "feedback": he never felt the desire for it, either in terms of appreciation or of sales. "You have to be mad," he said in one of his rare moments of generalisation: "madder than the poets or philosophers or whatever, to paint properly. They need people—poor buggers. Got to communicate—or they feel it hasn't 'happened'. Can't come on their own, poor

bloody wankers. Me, I only need my ey
and the paint. And if some lucky sod like
what I do, then he's a bit mad too."

Maybe I fooled myself that he neede
me. Being told I had "released the block"
in one of Britain's most controversial
promising and difficult painters was th
headiest declaration I had ever—have eve
—known; and though, with the anguish o
trying to become a better artist, and th
greater anguish of Leo's absences, the
were hardly three years of happiness, the
were blissful in parts; and nothing since
no succession of rich, admiring husband
or warm, lavishly equipped studios, o
soft-footed minions carrying up ligh
luncheons under silver domes, could make
me forget Tilbury.

Half in Tilbury, half in the Black Moun
tains of Wales; but afterwards I tended to
suppress that bit, when the outlay in
anguish tipped the balance till it hi
bottom with a resounding thud.

It was when he got the money from his
first US sale. He wanted to clear out of
London, away from critics and media folk.
His painting was changing, and it was the

onjunction of an adverse critic regretting
iis new, "muddier" palette and the first
lays of spring that pricked him into
precipitate action, the only sort where Leo
was concerned. A Sunday morning, and he
went out to the phone; we didn't have one.
Four hours later he was back: he had seen
in advert in the *Sunday Times*, got some
change from Mrs. Patel, phoned Wales
from the call-box; then bought an
Exchange & Mart, and swapped his bike
for an aged pickup truck in Hendon.
"Talked long enough about needing
isolation," he said, and started carrying
down his canvases. There was a moment
then—there had been many before—when
I thought he meant isolation from me as
well. Going down with the next load he
said, over his shoulder, "Could be, with
all the mountains and air and things, you'd
find your own style . . ." So I started
packing too. He'd need someone to cook
for him; and maybe, there, I'd have him
to myself.

The simple life takes time, I discovered:
most of every day, in fact; something that
the noble savage, if his woman is worth
her salt, should not have to worry about.

Winters were bitter. You had to carry
stores uphill a couple of hundred yard
when the pickup was working. When that
was out of action it was a mile to the bu
stop and five to the nearest village. There
were moments in spring, and in summer
when life seemed idyllic; when we ate the
vegetables I had grown, or drank the batch
of home-brewed beer that hadn't spoilt
and watched the sun go down. But much
of the time I found myself on my own
and never knowing when Leo would be
back. Without him there, there was less to
be done: I still had to keep things going
make it nice, ready for his return. After
that, I painted: first for his eyes only, ou
of habit; then to kill the time, to dull the
ache. In the end it took over, as painting
does. I stopped looking for my "own
style", and I found that living with Leo
had not quite silenced me; for though—in
terms of paint—I was still listening rather
than talking, the observation was beginning to tell.

In these terms, Leo was shouting. His
"muddy palette" had built up a heavy
impasto, almost like a bas-relief, with deep
lines incised in it that gave a hard-edge

ook. This "Rouault effect", as he called t, was finding approval, and a market; he now had an agent and much more exposure: a one-man show in the Barbican and television interviews.

Leo was the producers' classic nightmare: either monosyllabic or breaking into an unstoppable diatribe on "mushy art", otherwise termed "the soft squits" or "squit by the yard". At first they took care to record and edit, pruning the longer of the glowering silences, the worst scatologisms; then they looked at the ratings and took the public's temperature, and found that even viewers who didn't go for arty programmes turned on for Leo Constantine. It really happened when a late-night, outspoken, young, leftish chat-show caught him in town; and it went out live and unexpurgated, making headlines next day. The viewers had got wind of it and stayed up. "This artist guy is quite something: switch over or you'll miss out." He became the flavour of the month, the latest *enfant terrible*. At thirty-five.

I couldn't have got that one on Welsh television anyway; but I read about it when he brought the papers back a couple

of days later. He was in a good mood
expansive and highly amused by it all
"Bloody media, eh? One good Anglo
Saxon word and it's orgasms all round.'
He was into wine these days; and we go
very drunk that night. In the morning he
told me he had a larger studio now; and
that he had to be on call while the exhi-
bition was running; interviews all over the
shop, radio, glossies, more television:
"'Just be yourself, dear boy'—and now I
don't need the free publicity, Old Agent
sees I get paid for it! What a lark . . ."

Not that, I hoped. He dubbed her
"Old Agent" because her black hair was
dramatically streaked with white. She was
thirty-three.

I did not see him for two months: too
proud to follow him to London and join
in; constricted, not so much by his express
desire I should keep the home fires
burning, as by the state of my hands, my
clothes; by childish fear: I'd make a fool
of myself, so out of the swim, so "country
cousin". Most of all by the dread of
finding myself superseded in Leo's life.
Then he came home for a weekend. He
was tired; seemed glad to be back. He

consumed the hastily fatted calf, drank a great deal and fell asleep. We didn't make love till the morning, after which he left. I gathered his agent was fixing a show in New York. I said, "Maybe we'd be better off in London now." He said something about the isolation bit certainly having paid off; and that he'd be in touch. We still had no phone.

The London *Standard* is not a paper one often sees in the Black Mountains; but an acquaintance who had once had an affair with Leo posted me a copy, a scrawled line —her only comment—across the wrapper: "Thought page 15 might interest you. Roz." A photograph of Leo coming out of a registry office with his agent on his arm.

I suppose he thought I wouldn't see it. Actually I don't suppose he thought at all: he'd simply moved on to the next stage. Like he had when we met; and I wondered —as I'd so often tried not to—who had been left waiting, vacant, when he walked me away from the Kyle Gallery to look for beer that hot summer evening. I stood outside the village post office and cried for

her, and for me. It was raining, so no on
saw.

Leo's last "weekend" had been s
abrupt, I had forgotten to ask him fo
money. The rent would soon be due. Th
pickup, stone-dead halfway up the moun
tain, was not much of a liquid asset;
might even be fined for dumping, com
the spring. The last of my savings, m'
"running-away money", had gone int
rates and service charges on my unuse(
studio flat; Leo had paid the last groun(
rent and water rates, on condition I sold i
before the next were due. Now I couldn'
raise the fare to London: I had two pound:
in my purse, and the other half of my bu:
ticket. I'd been left high and dry. "Wh}
be high and dry, folks, when you can b(
low and wet?" I said out loud to the
weeping heavens, and caught mysel:
giggling foolishly; so I took refuge in the
ladies' behind the bus station and go'
myself together for the journey home.

I went back up the mountain to think
I knew I must think. But the only rea.
thing was that I loved Leo and he had lef
me. He was my world, my life, and he hac
taken both away. If I felt I could have hur

him through suicide I would have done so; perhaps if there had been gas, or pills—anything easier than the old knife I used for scraping carrots—I might have tried it anyway. As it was, all I did was burn the three or four paintings of mine that, in his cups, he had openly acclaimed, and the three-legged stool he had made for me during one of the idylls. I crouched down by the blaze and drank the half-bottle of whisky I kept for emergencies, and the remains of some sticky Spanish liqueur he'd brought back from a weekend not long ago in Barcelona—"Where the jolly old Rouault Effect is all the rage," I observed owlishly—a trip organised and, as I suddenly saw, accompanied by the agent in question . . . And I hurled the fancy bottle on to the stone hearth we had so idyllically built together; and passed out soon after that.

Two days later I assembled myself and wrote what can only be called a begging letter to an old art-school friend in Oxford who probably didn't know about me and Leo: we'd been out of touch that long. She was the sort of person you could appeal to; the sort of person I hadn't bothered about for three years. But when I went down to post it, I found a letter for me from an art-dealer friend of Leo's, breaking the news of the sudden marriage and the removal of the happy pair to Los Angeles and enclosing fifty pounds. I put together what I could carry, locked up the cottage and left the keys at the post office, as specifically requested by my benefactor. An odd letter: so anxious and caring from someone I barely knew. "I can imagine how you must be feeling on hearing this but I most earnestly beg you not to do anything foolish and sudden: that would be selfish, would it not?" I was touched and read on: "For, though what remains in the country studio may only be sketches, unfinished paintings and early experiments, all are important in the corpus of his work, indeed valuable, and worthy of care. I hope we may trust you, therefore, not to harm them; and I shall be sending an expert packing firm within the week . . . ," etc., etc.

But the fifty quid was real enough. I hitched to Hereford, and caught the bus to London.

It was a pity I hadn't kept up with people; possession by a demon lover is so time-consuming. Now that I needed them, I was totally out of touch; my friends could be dead, or married, or in Australia: I'd feel a fool ringing them up to ask which. And they had all disapproved of my living with Leo; those who cared were certainly hurt by my leaving London without a word. It would have been hard to explain then—and impossible now—that this was the love of my life, the bonfire on to which I threw everything; an act of commitment, while they just talked about it; proof of how much I loved him. (And Leo, need-less to say, hadn't even noticed. I lay in his arms and said, "You know my friends think I'm crazy." "Of course you're crazy," he said, "or I wouldn't fancy you." And shut me up.)

If there had been prospects for me in London I would have stayed on in the flat: my printing table, my oddly dated posters and knick-knacks, were as comforting to my broken heart as childhood toys. But it transpired that "dated" also applied to my pretty still-lifes; "marketable" now meant either the minutely realistic paintings of fey subjects, in the wake of Kit Williams, or the Video Look, a sort of day-glo Dada. I had neither, and learning how would take time.

A beady-eyed sale-or-return gallery in Camden Passage took on most of my remaining prints. I got a part-time job behind a fast-food counter for want of something better (who advertises for artists anyway?) while I sorted out my belongings and put the essentials, with the printing gear, into store. The flat was already on the market and had to look spacious and desirable; so, when I wasn't boxing fried chicken, I painted ceilings and stitched curtains.

I answered hopeful adverts, and even went in for a pub-sign competition, the latest publicity campaign of a big brewery chain in the Midlands: a matter of producing a detailed painting for one of three common pub names. I chose "The King's Head". Once my evening stint at the take-away was over, I would hurry back to the quiet of my gleaming white flat (sad that things only look their best when you're selling them); and it was pure, mindless therapy, working away on my kitchen table which, with a chair and my futon, were the only remaining furniture. I got very fond of my king's head, too: without referring to my old sketches, I had still given him the demon lover's fiery glance. But I delivered it to the brewers' head office in the City, then managed to forget about it. Till I found I had won.

The prize was a commission to paint signs for six newly refurbished pubs in Warwickshire. There was an offer on the flat, which I accepted on the promise of an early completion: I needed money to live on. I might even need a car to get me and my painting things from village to village. Meanwhile, I sold a family miniature for thirty-five pounds, packed, and took a train to Leamington to meet my patrons and see the pubs. That was all part of the programme: even a couple of cub reporters tagged along, and photographed me graciously accepting a surprise advance of one hundred pounds from the jolly brewing brothers—but I don't suppose they see the *Warwickshire Gazette* in LA . . .

It seemed a good idea to stay up there and start work, so I booked into a bed-and-breakfast outside Henley-in-Arden. Early summer, alternately drizzling and bright: buttercups and chestnut blossom, and the odd field of oilseed rape like a patch of condensed sunshine on the hills. No one knew me; I was alone, but not really lonely, what with the builders adopting me as part of the workforce, and the hearty, rich, Brummy brewers drawing me into their families, feeding me Pimms by their heated swimming pools, and buying up my passée prints.

I wasn't lonely: just hollowed out and empty, with memories echoing inside. He was inescapable, unforgettable. Sometimes I wondered if I had died, a ghost living among ghosts, so unreal was life after Leo. I dreamt of him; he walked straight through me.

The nights were bad; but by day I worked hard, and made it an exercise to count my blessings. Twenty-seven, employed, and getting brown in the June sun. My heart had been cut out and eaten; but, to outsiders, there was only a hairline scar, tanning nicely. When I'd done the Pig and Whistle, the Bird in Hand and the Wheatsheaf, I bought a second-hand Mini to commute to the outskirts of Stratford for the Lamb and Flag.

This hostelry, over which my brewers waxed lyrical, consisted of a large Tudor shell entirely gutted and replanned. The architect in charge of updating the whole chain had just returned from foreign commitments; and the historic pub, the greatest challenge in his current brief, was not only highly prestigious but reputedly his favourite—though only peanuts, of course, beside his glass tower of offices in St. Albans, or the "village" marina in Dockland. He was American, and his name was Charles Gelhorn.

A strange courtship. He took a shine to me, and asked me out to dinner: drove me all the way to Thornberry Castle near Bath for an *haute couture* meal. I hadn't eaten that sort of serious food since being courted by Leo's patrons; and I had never eaten so well. He was the famous architect, I was just a sign-painter; but he seemed to be as attracted and impressed by the *artiste assoiffée*—a real live Bohemian, he said— as by my old family, nearly extinct.

"Is that right? Your father was a

baronet? But doesn't that make you an 'Hon.'?"

"Yes—but one that's slipped through the Society mesh. Which means it doesn't really count for much, actually. I don't use it. And I didn't come out or anything: Come Out, you know, with a ball and so on. Not like homosexuals."

"Oh, I get that: I worked for a lord, and his daughters were about to—to do that Coming Out scene. They have something like it in New Orleans, I guess."

He talked; so different from Leo. He said things like: "You are quite something else. Know what? I really like you. We get on, don't we?—So, how's about a liqueur? OK: I guess I just like watching your lips when you sip—and look over at me out of those two great big eyes . . ."

"Well, that's the way to do it," I said: "better with two."

He flattered me, fed me royally; I was too busy eating to say much, but he laughed a lot and told me I was fanciful and witty. A marvellous banquet; I went to bed with him almost as much to say thank you as because he was warm and

96

forceful. Someone to hold me tight and blot out Leo for a while.

Like Leo, Charles was dark; but shorter, and chunky; solid muscle—"Feel that"—overlaid by the peach-fed American glow that proclaims a well-ordered childhood, lacking nothing. Professionally, he was pushy and sharp; dead-pan, if necessary, over a tricky deal. Socially, he was "outgoing", no smoothie: all heart; still pushy. Tan and teeth and thick, beautifully cut, wavy hair receding a little: he was thirty-eight and had done well. But in two marriages he hadn't fathered a child. And he talked about this as easily as he talked about everything. "So I'm good and ready and looking for Number Three, shweetheart—could this be It?"

I liked his Jewish vitality, his enthusiasm. I think what drew me most, physically, were his power and his money. Sex—though it reminded me too sharply of Leo—was very comforting; and he made me feel safe—as I had not done since the time before my father died. Charles made me seem more solid: no ghost, to him. He was a rest cure after the last three years, and especially those months on my own.

I knew we were very different. When he talked, it wasn't my language: I was the silent one now—the "elusive genius", to him. He was attracted and intrigued. I knew, moreover, I was not the least in love with him, nor he with me; alike at least in this, that we were neither of us looking for a grand passion. He was sharp and busy and knew what he wanted. I was disillusioned and didn't much care. Three weeks after I turned up in my Mini at the Lamb and Flag he said, "So how's about me and you, Kate? See it this way: up front, I'm not your usual kind of lover; more the reverse. Like, when you get pregnant, I'll marry you. In that order. How's about it?"

I said nothing. Enigmatic. But one day he packed me and my belongings into his Bentley and took me off to the cottage in Oxfordshire. There was only the White Hart left to do; I was given space to work, a motherly comer-in to cosset me; and my protector returned each night and made love to me.

Two months later I was pregnant. I kept

im dangling for a day after the test was
positive: not really to consider what I was
doing—I knew that—but just to assert my
independence. Then I said "Yes."

5

THERE is a certain bright young
National Theatre director who, al
unknowing, has a lot to answer for
When St. Peter confronts him at Heaven':
Gate, the new soul will glance down
the list of black marks and say, "What':
this about 'justification of architectura
vandalism'? . . . And who on earth is
Charles Gelhorn?"

"Well, not on earth, actually," Pete
will say; "but he met you at a dinne
party, apparently, and he quotes you a:
directly responsible for one of his mos
heinous sins of commission. Not that thi:
one was, in fact, commissioned . . ."

Listening to Charles showing his friend:
round Noone Rectory—and inevitably
heard the spiel many times, with sligh
variations for his changing audience—
found myself embroidering this fantasy ir
my head as I handed round the champagne, or wine, or cans of beer.

The director in question, boyish with a

100

wispy beard, had seemed to me more like an undergraduate than the onlie be-getter of a recent smash-hit production of *Edward II* at the Olivier Theatre. He'd brought it into the present and set it mainly in the Oval Office of the White House, with Gaveston, the top man's favourite, all in black leather, like an Orton anti-hero. At this dinner, I could see Charles hanging on every word; Jaco-bean theatre was not exactly his "bag", so I started to listen.

"My philosophy, as you may know," lisped the infant prodigy, "is quite simply that the best of the old can be used afresh in each generation, like a fine old violin —no more—on which we play our new tunes."

I said I'd always been told it was the other way round: actors being merely the instruments—

"Old hat. You have clearly been brain-washed by genteel O-level teaching." My demurs were brushed aside. "No; that sort of blind reverence only fossilises the past. Not reverence, but Relevance! We take the quality that has withstood the test—the wind-tunnel, as it were, for innovators like myself—and adapt it to our needs. Make it relevant."

Charles could not have put it better; hadn't, until then, put it at all, preferring to ignore anything that made him uncomfortable. Now the Anti-fossilisation Theory was continually on his lips: it perfectly justified his dragging old buildings into the twentieth century by the scruff of the neck. He'd frequently had problems with conservationists in the past: he grumbled about the "arties", the "nostalgia buffs"—sometimes "your typical Islington dropout". But nowadays that unshakeable confidence had a lecturing tone as he squared up with his back to the great stone fireplace and snapped open his lager.

"Oh, sure: reverence is just fine in its place, like in a church—period! But what about *relevance*? I mean, this has got to be a nineteen-eighties family home, right? Now, we can see, we can *feel*, the quality that's stood the test of time: it's 'fine', like a thoroughbred racehorse. But it's tough, too: it can take it! Just look at Shakespeare —and, incidentally, that's near as dammit when this was built, you know: the vintage is right . . ."

To the rest, and especially his tough, successful friends, he could simply demonstrate that Noone was in such poor shape it was more cost-effective, labour-saving and practical, in the long run, to change it than to restore it. As for the appalled County set, a tiny minority, they stayed away. They remained polite—but only because they had known my glamorous aunts in the twenties, or because they were aware that the shooting in Noone woods was first rate, the best in the district.

Charles was amazingly wounded by their cool non-acceptance: the formal, dutiful invitation to the At Home, and then no more; the notes, painful as rejection slips, "So sorry we cannot come to drinks on Sunday . . . So kind of you . . . So tiresome . . ."

"They'll eat their hearts out, when my epic housewarming comes around! . . . Or maybe don't ask them: just let them hear about it, right?"

And he turned for local company to the new aristocracy of seafood barons, television producers, the youngish old-roses or old-wine gurus; while they in turn picked his brains about their home extension, or an exciting *trompe l'œil* painter to transform that dark farmhouse dining room.

I say Charles was "amazingly" wounded by the attitude of the County set; but, looking back, I realise it's really a judgement of myself.

I shouldn't have been amazed. A more attentive wife, especially one who'd come from that sort of background—however long ago—would have seen it a mile off and protected her man; prepared him, at least, for disappointment. In fact, if I'd done my stuff, wooed them a little, patted their horses' noses, gossiped a bit about theirs and my papa's eccentric friends when they were all up at the House, and the famous occasion when they dunked a Buller in the Tom Quad fountain . . . Maybe if I had worked at it, they'd have come over to Noone on my account—to see "that fine filly of old Guy Berry's: spitting image of her mother—now *there* was a poppet and no mistake . . ." And they would have accepted Charles as part of the package: "What with old Guy's death-duties and all that caper—never had much of a head for money, did old Guy—generous to a fault—must've left 'em poor as church mice—makes sense, you know, these sweet penniless gels marrying money—absolutely . . ."

But I stood back as usual, leaving the social contact to my outgoing Yankee architect, content to be private, and lazy: what Charles's designer friend called "your lady wife's quality of intense stillness"—while other buddies, in my hearing usually, judged me "very fine", "ever so unique", and "odd, like quirky, you know". Small wonder I kept quiet. At those posh occasions—the cocktails in the stately homes—I should have been on the alert. But still I stood back—talking to the wrong people, Charles said, over the "drinks after church" at the moated grange, or the "little garden party" at that marvellous pile of Portland stone with a hundred chimneys and a Norman chapel. I remember a pale dowager with a nice, waspish tongue, and a tall, chinless, teenage son who told me he'd got into Pop this half, and offered me a mount next hunting season. Charles was nearby, addressing our host; and I only dimly heard, only half-registered, how squarely Our Chuck was putting his foot in it.

"Nice place you've got here; had it quite a while, I guess! Reminds me of one in Bucks that my buddy Bob Nassau (maybe you know him: very big in the Square Mile) just bought: beat the Arabs to it—by a nose! Doing great things to it—with the help of yours truly, need I add . . . And if you ever want ideas about that old stable block of yours, don't hang back, will you? What are neighbours for? But you must come across and see Noone Ampney Hall, like Before and After, right . . . ? That's its old name, by the by . . . And maybe you'll loan me your gardener some time to give me the low-down on the whole topiary scene: we have these fantastic yew hedges that need a firm hand—and your chap is clearly a real pro—or is it 'chaps', with a show-place like this?"

Only dimly overheard, as I say; and that's an extrapolation—but not wildly exaggerated.

As a rule he was so good with people: he had an awful, wonderful way of bulldozing his way to their hearts. He could outrage, flatter, contradict, cajole: demanding a reaction, then building on it, drawing them out—brickies, bankers, pensioners, the lone boozer, or a whole pool of typists. I used to amuse myself just watching him rope and break them, relentlessly charming till they were eating out of that broad palm; and then, for employees or anyone potentially useful, there was always the spur as well, applied with instinctive timing. I once said to him: "It *is* like horses: they know if you're nervous. And you smell so bloody confident."

That was it, of course: he wasn't, with the County lot. He talked hard to cover up, but he minded too much and it came out all wrong. You could almost see his nervous sweat. And the thoroughbred nostrils dilating.

Rich, sharp, charismatic, accepted in the City, the Bow Group, the solid end of the jet set and the fringe of the art world (Leo would have liked him), Charles had also, assiduously, done time on the fund-raising committees of some of the smartest charities. He was a star in his own architectural field, especially on the Continent and in the States: he spent a week of May in New York for an in-depth television programme on his newest acquisition— *Gelhorn's Noone*—and was a guest on the Johnny Carson Show.

Oh, Charles had arrived all right. Sociable, successful, thick-skinned: a winner. But his weakness—the only spot where his soft centre lay dangerously close to the surface—was this passionate desire for acceptance into the Establishment, and especially that conventional, traditional, British, upper-crust scene. It had certainly attracted him to *me*, even when I insisted I was no longer a part of it. He did his homework so well on most subjects: maybe this is something you have to grow up with—just as I could never learn to be Jewish. He must have thought that by acquiring a County wife, however lapsed, and a real country house, he would qualify. He'd always wanted the ancestral home and an heir for it, or vice versa. So: he'd made it, on both counts. So? Now he wanted recognition from his peers— his neighbours—folk with classy wives-stroke-houses like his; and proper respect from the rest, maybe even a bit of the feudal deference (but still good pals, right?); a sense of being established. Instant roots for the wandering Jew.

It never occurred to me to explain how the system worked; or that being a "winner" and buying a Hall did not automatically make you clubbable. Only after I'd seen him with the first of the rejection slips did the significance, and the irony of it, get through to me: that he wanted the one thing he couldn't have. Because Charles's great strength, and charm, and even genius, lay in the supple, restless, Jewish drive to acquire and exploit, to *change*; while his sentimental dream was to Conform; to fit into the only group who had not the faintest interest in his sort of success (Johnny Carson cut no ice there), and found his energy repellent.

Christ!—he said—he'd *show them*. If only for Henry's sake.

Then, far too late, I said: "But, darling, why should they matter so?"

"*Matter?* Sweet Jesus! Only the Lord Lieutenant of the County over thataway, and, just down the road, a guy whose great-great-great fought at Agincourt . . ."

In June the builders were due; meanwhile, plans were with the Suffolk authorities—and so, much of the time, was Charles: busy-busy, bullying, charming, getting his way. He had hived off most of his work on to a colleague, and found a three-star hotel by the sea where he could jog along the sands.

He would not consider staying at the house, nor even camping in the grounds as I suggested. Much to Henry's disgust: Noone had swiftly become his happy hunting ground, and there were always tantrums when we had to go home. We usually took friends down for picnics at the weekends. Charles showed them round, Henry explored—within strictly defined limits—while I catered, and planned my barn.

This was the largest chunk of the stable block, with a pretty dovecote perched on top: precariously, for most of the roof was gone. I contacted the old gardener, Mr. Abbott, who had been looking after the place while the Reverend Dodsworth was alive. He had taken on other jobs since then: "Come winter I could be back," he said: "maybe see to the digging and that."

But he found me a local builder to fix the barn roof immediately, and willing to tackle the rest as soon as I'd worked out what I wanted inside. It was just a big, plain, open space with a wide door and a few narrow windows; the beams, joists and lintels were sound. My wiry little builder made it sound so simple and straightforward: barns were everyday country matters. "Get her covered: that's what she wants. Let her dry out a bit; then we can bring down the electric and see what she's been up to."

I liked the feel of the place. I would need larger windows, heating, and a floor; probably a damp-course. But, apart from repointing the brick walls and painting them white to brighten it, little need be done to the inside. I would keep it open for now: I could always divide it later if I needed to.

Henry liked it too, romping in the mouldy straw and swinging on the gate. I must admit I enjoyed having him around. He was less demanding and querulous away from Nanny, the television, and his clever Schwartz toys. He didn't seem to mind being ignored: happy mucking about, chatting to his second-best bear or his imaginary friends. Maybe he was getting more interesting and independent; maybe just that I was seeing more of him, or that Noone was what he needed, not the other siblings Nanny kept on about.

I still felt he was hers and Charles's rather than mine. Nanny, now in her sixties, was extraordinarily possessive about him; clearly she had despaired of me, and saw him as her final baby before retirement. She adored him, and was—I considered—wildly indulgent: almost as bad as Charles, for whom Henry could do no wrong; while I tended to be strict in a vain attempt to redress the balance.

Henry knew this, and learnt very early to leave me to my painting and put on the pressure elsewhere. I would work in my studio at the top of the London house most of the day, or go round galleries. I always played with him and read to him each evening; but I wasn't violently maternal. I'd had him to order, as it were; then rather sat back, grateful at that stage to hand him over. Charles—naturally enough, I suppose—wanted several more just like him: in this, at least, he and

Nanny were as one. But I'd fulfilled my part of the bargain, and told him so. I had, after all, been treated like a brood mare: on appro until he checked I was productive. *And* I had presented him with a son. That was it, as far as I was concerned. I put up with him moaning about me, waxing maudlin over the patter of little feet to his multi-offspringed buddies; but I balked at breeding repeatedly with a man I did not love, and who did not pretend to love me.

Not that I put it like that, of course. "It's my life too," I said; "and, anyway, one Henry is enough—surely." He was: both in terms of that fierce, all-demanding energy—his father's—and his undeniable charm; and it amused me to see the skill with which he played Nanny and Charles off against one another, as they vied in their different ways for his favours. I didn't worry: such devotion could do him no lasting damage; and next year he would have a real school and his peers to contend with.

Meanwhile, I enjoyed leaning on the gate talking to my builder, and watching Henry bob about as he served up "tea" on the mounting-block; chiding his bear "Now now! No more bickies for you—and this time I *really* mean it . . ."

The following week, Philip the builder started on the barn roof. When we came down Saturday, he had stripped off the remaining slates, mended and secured the dovecote, and treated the timbers with preservative—"safest with any old place if you're thinking of heating: don't want the dry rot after all this time, do we? Not that there's much danger with you keeping it open, and all the air circulating." He'd bought in enough good second-hand slates to cover it, with a few spare in case I decided on a dormer, he said; he'd start felting and slating on Monday. I paid him for materials, and showed him my sketches for the new windows.

"Custom-built is pricey," he told me. "And slow." He fetched a catalogue from his van and found me some ready-made ones the right size. "Not all the makes are reliable, mark you," he said; "but these are good: they're seasoned; and I'll give them a proper priming. Set nicely between the buttresses, they will: nice and simple."

114

It may have been in reaction to Charles's plans for the house, but I felt the need to keep whatever changes I made to my barn as plain as I could. I reminded myself that the two structures were hardly comparable, except in their urgent need of repair; and, while part of me still yearned for the chance to restore the Rectory using Charles's astronomical budget, I could see that, in terms of running it realistically, restoration was not enough. It needed updating; and the cool-headed survivor in me was relieved not to have that responsibility. Even for the power-plant I called husband, it was quite a challenge.

Noone had been built for the sort of grandeur that might only be sustained, even now, by sacrificing all ideas of privacy. It was designed nearly four hundred years ago for the comparative comfort of the few served by the many: the few who moved from one well-stoked fire to another, passing up and down the great staircase and along wide, handsome corridors, while the many bore wood, buckets of coal, bed linen or flagons of hot water up back stairs and through small winding passages.

To Charles—despite his sentimenta[l]
yearning for an ancestral home—both o[f]
these occupations were anachronistic; s[o]
were the too-high rooms, the vast
ivy-darkened entrance hall, and tha[t]
echoing vault of a kitchen, designed t[o]
house spits, ranges, boilers, bread-ovens[,]
sinks like baths, plate-racks like five-ba[r]
gates, and space for an army of cooks[,]
undercooks, scullions, pot-boys an[d]
hangers-on. "This whole place: it's jus[t]
one great big beautiful nonsense in thi[s]
day and age," he used to say, leading hi[s]
tour down the great staircase and over t[o]
refreshments on the refectory table (it had
not sold at auction, so it remained).
"Noone is a mega-folly—OK! And I love
it. But I want to Use it—you get me[?]
Make it work, in *my* terms"—thumb
thrust to mighty heart—"and that mean[s]
nineteen eighties, *plus*!"

For a potted history of Noone, h[e]
referred to the late incumbent. A tall[,]
old-fashioned accounts book in marbled
covers had been sent us by the deale[r]
who had bought the Reverend Laurence
Dodsworth's library desk; he found it in a
drawer and deemed its rightful place to be

116

with the new owners. Parish accounts may once have been kept in it: some pages had been neatly cut out. Most of the remainder was filled with notes on the life and teachings of St. Augustine of Hippo, and two short, witty sermons which, as Charles observed, must have been Greek to the solid farmers of the parish—all in a graceful italic hand that rode confidently across the double-entry columns. At the back we found the parson's summary of the Rectory's past, and a sparse family tree, full of gaps, queries and even a couple of exclamation marks.

"*Noone Ampney Hall*," he wrote: 'built, substantially in present form, as manor house and working farm c.1590 on older farmhouse site with distant prospect of sea; by seafaring Dodsworth retiring to Suffolk to establish new dynasty, but originally of West Country family (NB. Born and lived in Glos. till ran away to sea; hence explanation of Glos. name *Ampney* added by him to local *Noone*: nostalgia of black sheep?). This founder reputedly a ruthless privateer grown rich on Spanish gold; sufficiently wealthy, grateful, and (they say) penitent, to erect small church

by front gates about same time (more
prob.—says sceptic in me—to house fine
family monument, see left of altar; and, on
practical level, to provide self and descend
ants w. snug resting place!). Married
eldest daughter of Essex baronet (plain—
see portrait on stairs); multiplied
flourished. Family kept 'low profile' in
Civil War, but harboured Royalists, for
which given more lands, some in Herts.
by Chas II. Flourished even more; putting
on new façade. A Dodsworth fought under
Marlborough and knighted by Q. Anne
built new house in Classic style in Herts
left Noone. Younger son, Laurence (also
on stairs), parson with seven children
inherited N. A. Hall; too poor to keep up
alone, made agreement with bishop
(friend, and godfather to eldest), viz:—
that Church should have one half of his
harvest in return for one half of running
costs 'until such time as no proper heir
wore the Cloth' (i.e. ecclesiastical male in
direct line)—at which point Church would
inherit house and land. Renamed *Noone
Rectory*. Since when, in each generation, a
son, frequently the eldest (departure from

norm!), only too willing to take orders and inherit This Blessed Plot.

"Over years, land gradually sold by mutual agreement; both Church and incumbent pleading poverty, and sharing proceeds: classic 'Catch Twenty-Two' in modern parlance, as less and less 'yearly harvest' for upkeep, with generations of jolly hunting parsons, lulled by shared responsibility, preferring to lay down good wine or commission portraits of favourite retrievers than embellish Rectory. (NB. Myself equally culpable.) Exception proving rule: early 1800s windfall from West Indian property produced Neo-Gothick main staircase and stained glass; but slaves emancipated before more practical improvements could be carried out (see plans for conservatory and servants' quarters). Last serious attempt to update was installation in 1890s of water-closets and 'modern' cooking ranges: the Church Commissioners' *quid pro quo* on starting a small orphan school in the unused wing; but this was closed within a few years as 'unhealthy, dispiriting and inappropriate for those of tender years'. Probably true, for, though my father, then a small boy,

survived to become the penultimate recto
of Noone (and, indeed, to modernise th
bathroom in the '20s as I remember), thre
of his siblings have small graves in th
churchyard.

"Of the final generation, I am the sol
survivor, and have produced no heir. M
dear sister Elsie predeceased me; her onl
child, Laurence, my godson, canno
inherit. Noone will go to the Churc
Commissioners. RIP."

There was usually a small silence a
Charles closed the marbled ledger. The
someone would say: "You know, that'
really sad . . ." "End of an era . . ." "Bu
now for the new Gelhorn Dynasty—eh
Charlie?" Or: "Amazing—like a sort o
time-capsule . . ."

"That's right! Sealed up in one hous
and virtually unchanged," says Charles
"Pretty unique—and I could see tha
straight off; so I got the whole plac
professionally photographed before the
moved the furniture out—didn't I, Katy
(She's a sentimental old thing: wouldn'
touch a hair of its head. Let it fall dow
around you—wouldn't you shweetheart?
So I've made up an album of these ol

photos—you can see them—the 'Before' situation, right?—Oh, sure: sepia would have been great; but I didn't want to miss out on some of these colours: in here, the greenery over those windows—'verdurous gloom', somebody called it—and the old, yellowish look of that corridor I showed you—right: with the collages. And what about that bedroom, and the creeper sneaking in through the cracks in the window frame? I mean: *taking over*! Fantastic—we've just *got* to have a record of that, I said—and there it is: captured for posterity, before I fix it all. Hey, and I told you about the TV feature—? Right: they're putting in some old stills. Terrific. OK: so you want to see the plans . . . ?"

The baroque front, mentioned in Pevsner's *Suffolk*, was protected, as everyone kept telling us. "That's what I call Style," said Charles; "this old Dodsworth had it, in spades: get knighted, and go home and stick on a really grand façade—OK, OK, Katy, for Chrissake: so I've mixed up the generations—so what? It's the Grand Gesture—I like that." He was quite contented not to change it; just restore the balustrade, repoint, and add maybe an urn or two, maybe statues over the porch—in keeping, of course.

And he would not touch the barrel-vaulted cellars running under most of the house; apparently they were sound as a bell, and served their purpose, keeping the ground floor above them dry and well-aired: all that damp had come in through leaking roofs, cracked balustrades, over-grown walls. No, he wasn't even going to put his great multi-fuel boiler down in the cellars: a waste of good heat. And ruinous for wine: that's what he'd use them for when he got around to it. "That's a must: masses of room for the everyday bottle as well as the good stuff—and a pipe of something really fancy for Henry's twenty-first. So—pencil that in, folks!" Anyway, those vaults down there, what he'd seen of them, simply wouldn't house this *particular* boiler, plus no existing opening big enough to take it . . .

"Hey there, let's cut the boring, nut-and-bolt stuff: that's shop-talk! I mean OK: it's a sort of passion with builder-architects like little ole me, but I wouldn't lay it on my best buddies . . . Sure? Well, now: like, ducted air? Secondary solar panels? Heat-exchange pumps on the refrigerator principle, *and* runs on any fuel—you name it—with automatic changeover, automatic de-coke, self-servicing . . . ? Don't worry: she'll work, believe you me. A real lulu: going to house her in that old kitchen, paint her red maybe—a statement of raw energy—and boxed in with plate glass to keep her pristine: on show. The 'Pompidou effect', right? No, but this hall is the big thing. Like: Watch This Space!"

Here, the remaining two-thirds of the elaborate, moulded, and mouldering plaster ceiling would come out: too costly and labour-intensive to replace—"Unless, of course, you're an Oxbridge college, or happen to have an apartment block in Mayfair to sell off . . ." (or "a chunk of Gloucestershire" or "a mile of fishing on the Test"). "No problem: the visual interest will be provided instead by this 'Minstrels' Gallery', right along here; very light and high-tech, cantilevered, to house all the sound-systems for parties, dances and so forth, and maybe some really neat abstract sculptures—very clean. Banish the gloom! Oh, sure: that chimneypiece comes out: I mean, full-height carved stone, *now*? Crowthers would buy it; more likely it'll be shipped off to this guy in Beverly Hills—sheer size is in great demand. And I might still have a real fire, I guess, in a simpler, a more human-size, space."

Of course the Victorian staircase had got to go. "OK, *OK*: 'late Georgian Neo-Gothic', honey—but a dam' close call —and the Victorians went a bundle on it, that grim religious-type stuff, all that fretwork and pointed arches; all right in a cathedral, or the Houses of Parliament— just. It'll go like a bomb for some Dracula set. I see something very spare and light and open-plan: a double helix, with some slender neon handrails to light your way —make all these fussy wall-brackets and chandeliers totally *de trop*, and still show off the height . . . But in all the other ground-floor rooms, including the so-called library, the ceilings'll be lowered so as to accommodate—not just the indirect lighting for those rooms—oh, no: sunken baths—sure thing!—on the first floor, where—like I showed you—those fifteen bedrooms are going to be five suites with

124

double-bed, bath and dressing room. OK? Are you with me? Now then, the bedrooms will remain 'antique': a concession to the tastes of my dear, old-fashioned little cabbage-patch lady here. Like, the chimneypieces will be left in, with gas-log fires. They do some very good ones nowadays; and I'm installing a big gas-tank outside for the cooking as well, so that's cool. The wallpaper? My decorator agrees that some of those tacky old patterns up there—the striped floral, the Chinoiserie stuff ('Chinese junk', huh?)—can't have been changed since Christ knows when—1900? He's coming through with an appropriate *motif* for each suite, picking it up with these hand-painted tiles in the bathrooms, and the basins and so forth all tying in.

"And—wait for it!—not only sunken *baths*, folks: the old nursery on the corner is going to be the games room, with a billiards table that disappears into the floor on hydraulic stilts! This golfing buddy of mine down in Surrey has one, and it's real neat. And there will be not only your real Beverly-Hills-type video room (that's it: and this section here covered by a mural

125

that slides back to reveal, da-dah! a whole wall of screen), but your audio room as well—the ultimate music experience: carpeted on floor, walls and ceiling— Right! 'Audio womb'—I like it! All in the morning room as was . . . Then sauna and jacuzzi of course, in the old dairy—end of this west wing. Plans for a workout complex in the stables; there's even room for a squash court—but hold it: not the whole lot at once!—though I promise I'll get moving on the swimming pool right after the main work is complete. Well, I guess that'll do for starters, with the repairs . . ."

In London, the sale of the house went off quite painlessly: the first couple who looked round made us an offer in excess of the asking price to take it off the market, and agreed to wait till mid-September for completion. This gave Charles a good three months for building —so long as he could get the plans passed quickly.

The most time-consuming element of the negotiations was to explain, and get agreement on, his building methods and materials.

"You will appreciate, Mr. Gelhorn, we have to satisfy ourselves that your proposed alterations meet with the requirements laid down in Section—"

"Sure," said Charles: "I appreciate all right. Meantime, you have my specifications now and you're very welcome on site without notice, before, during, and after alteration."

In the end, so long as the work inside was sound and the changes did not cut across any of the health or safety regulations, he knew they could object to nothing within the body of the house. The stained glass, however, in the casements of the great hall: this was borderline. Charles held it was only properly viewed from inside, and saw no tenable objection to his replacing the panes. The strict conservationists on the planning committee disagreed. "Surely," they wrote, "these constitute one of the features of the façade when observed from the exterior, lit up at night; and we deem this dual nature to be the special glory of stained glass."

I thought it was rather well put, if a

little pompous. I liked the windows. But
Charles crowed with delight when he read
me the letter.

"Too much! This is just what I was
waiting for. 'Now then,' I say: 'A and one,
I trust not too many sightseers will be
sloping around outside in my yard at
night; and B and two, that glass is totally
out of sync, periodwise, with your
precious façade . . .'—and I whip the late
lamented Rev. Dodsworth out of my hat
and prove those 'special glories' were
installed in the nineteenth century with the
West Indian windfall. Now, ain't that
sweet?"

The planners decided to consider the
problem a little longer. Charles meanwhile
filled his spare moments by taking an
active interest in the proposal for a
Newtown sports complex; helping to
create interest and support by organising a
competition, and promising to serve on the
panel of judges. The removal of the
stained glass was approved. There was a
note—not quite a proviso—to the effect
that it would be public-spirited if he
gave his contract to a Suffolk building
company. Charles had foreseen this too

and—though he would vastly have preferred to ship in a big London firm—had already sorted out the local talent; now he confirmed a June start with the builders of his choice. "Craftsmen", of course, were a different matter: Spaniards for the tiled kitchen and sauna, Italians for three marble bathrooms—but no need—eh, folks?—to declare imports when you're halfway through the green sector.

Mid-June; and the builders moved in. And so, within a fortnight, did the Jinx, as they called it. Just a joke to begin with: playful—even witty—in its manifestations. It took a little while to show its claws.

6

NONE of the workmen on the site was able to pinpoint the very first incident, or even agree roughly where and when they noticed anything wrong. In fact their disagreement was the first sign, as far as we were concerned: raised voices when we got out of the car one sunny morning (I had come up with Charles to see my plumber), then sudden silence once we'd slammed the doors, and a certain *froideur* in the mumbled replies to his bright "good morning's".

He had looked round and was having a cup of tea with the foreman when I came back from the barn. "What's up, then?" he was saying. "Someone not had his Wheaties this morning?"

"Beg pardon, sir?"

"They just seem a tad out of sorts, that's all. So it's Monday—but it isn't exactly raining; and this lot are usually pretty chipper as a rule."

"Oh, that's just young Terry, sir:

grumbling about someone pinching his trowel—and it's not even as if he'll be using it today; I told him—like you said, sir—all that plaster rubble's got to be loaded into the skip before they can start anything like plastering—right, Terry lad?"

Terry shambled closer and said: "There's someone nickin' things, that's all." Sullen; eyes down. Stirring his tea with a small screwdriver.

"Sure you didn't leave it up on the tower? Or knocked it over the edge: that's what. It's most likely in among the rubble, Mr. Gelhorn. Don't you concern yourself with—"

"There's someone *nickin*' things," said Terry fiercely. "It's not just the trowel neither. And I weren't using it up the scaffold Friday."

"You mean other people have missed things?" Charles asked.

"That's what I said."

"Mind your manners, Terry!" growled the foreman. "Lot of fuss over nothing, Mr. Gelhorn . . . About the roof, sir, now that the sheeting's here—"

"So I see; and they're getting on pretty

quickly with the scaffolding round the back."

"Ay: made a good start. Weather's set fair by all accounts and could be a chance to strip off the worst and make an inspection before the covers go on, if they get the platforms up there sharpish . . . Oh, indeed yes, sir: we'll have the back pitch well covered before we knock off this evening . . ."

I saw my plumber, who turned out to be Philip-the-Builder's brother-in-law. He could only work evenings as he was employed full time by a central heating firm in Ipswich; but he had taken an hour off, before doing a nearby boiler-servicing job, to discuss where to run the pipes in my barn. When he had gone there was still some time before Charles was ready to leave for his lunchtime meeting back in London; so I visited the scrapbook corridor.

The power was on now, and the few sound runs of wiring in use. I was able to read the copperplate verses and explore the far end where the collage petered out in postcards of Malayan butterflies, neatly labelled, chunks of *Beano*, and a photo of

Buster Keaton. I had brought a tube of glue with me, and I fixed back the odd ear and dog-ear that had come adrift; determinedly closing my mind's eye to the new plans for the nursery wing that Charles had been elaborating over the weekend. This outsize, walk-in picture book was mine for now, and I would cherish it.

Going back towards the staircase, I could feel through my sneakers where, a couple of feet below me, the last edges of the plaster ceiling were being hacked away; and I heard young Terry's voice: "Needs his head examining, silly bugger. It weren't Thursday: it were *Wednesday* he found 'em gone—and I weren't even around Tuesday!"

"Leave it alone, Tel, eh? Give it a flaming rest."

"But like I'm saying: it's my day-release Tuesday, isn't it?"

"If you say so . . ."

"And it's Wednesday first thing that he was missing his flipping hacksaw blades and stuff!"

"What about old Angus, then, and his soldering irons?"

"How'd *I* know? Could a' been nicked from the flippin' van! Why *me* for God's sake, when I'm in the same—?"

I was halfway down the stairs before they saw me and shut up.

A few days later, Mr. Fawcett the foreman telephoned Charles in London over breakfast and talked loudly and at length. "Trooble at t'mill . . . ," Charles mouthed at me. "Sawn through, Mr. Fawcett . . . ? I see, leaving an edge—the front edge . . ." He raised his brows at me and shot his brains out with his forefinger; but he wasn't smiling. I leaned over and listened.

". . . in a hurry to get the last of that plaster rubble into the skip, and what with the pickup waiting like I said. Else they might have noticed—And straight off: one shovel handle then t'other. Snapped like twigs, sir: barely a splinter! Just short of the reinforcing flange running up from the blade . . . That's it, sir: soon as they took the weight on 'em. So I went and picked up the third and—well, you could *see* it, Mr. Gelhorn, knowing where to look: a pretty piece of work; and—would you

134

credit it?—the cut smeared over with like a crust of plaster, so's you couldn't tell, if you weren't rightly looking . . . No, sir: that's the trouble. We went for that couple of all-metal ones we'd been using outside and you could see the mess on the handles —like cement, it were—see it a mile off: not the way my lads are in the habit of leaving their tools; I mean, they take a pride . . . That's just it, Mr. Gelhorn: I was getting to . . . Yes, sir, cut through with a hacksaw right to the front edge. Both of them. But there's something funny going on, Mr. Gelhorn. And the men don't like it . . . Of course you don't, sir: that's why I got on to you right away . . . Won't slow down the work, sir, no: I'll see to that. But, as I say, my lads are quite upset."

"So that's where the hacksaw blades went," said Charles thoughtfully as he pushed the phone away.

"Where?"

"Who knows? They're calling it 'the Jinx'. The others seemed to think it was young Terry at first—well, you heard all that the other day. He's the one who's always skint: gets through his wages on a

Friday night, they say. But quite a few
things have gone missing, it seems, over
the last couple of weeks. The final outrage
—before this lot—was a fruit cake Terry's
mum had baked for him. Quite a flare-up
I gather; at least our Terry was absolved.
A sassy Jinx: left just one slice in the tin
—for Mr. Manners as Nanny would say—
and took the rest . . . And now this.
Which isn't funny."

"Is vandalism covered by the insurance?" I asked.

"Oh, sure: no problem. Just the guys
getting hot and bothered."

"Bad for morale?"

"Argh—just a pain in the ass, basically.
And it means putting in a night-
watchman."

Routine security was tightened. Bolts were
fitted on the ground-floor windows, all
tools locked in the dairy after work. The
electricity, usually turned off at the main
switch as a potential fire-hazard, now had
to be left on for new outside lights, and
for the watchman: Vince Edwards, an
ex-boxer, installed in the library (my
beloved library) with Camping Gaz and a

bed. Charles added a refrigerator on expenses: cost-effective, moralewise.

But morale remained low. "It's not a happy ship that suspects one of the crew is stealing from his mates—plus maybe the odd thing from his own locker to cover himself. And now this nutty vandalism: patently a skilled job, as they keep saying; and I don't want to lose my master-carpenters right now . . ."

A niggling distrust; and disputes kept interfering with the calm progression of Charles's carefully planned schedule. Then, indisputably, the spray paint.

It was the third night of high security; and, despite the locks, the bulkhead lights outside, front and back, and Vince the Watch—so he swore—doing his regular rounds, the Jinx got into the hall. Next morning, not twenty feet away from the library door, the building plans on the refectory table were found defaced with a liberal coating of black aerosol paint.

Charles was furious. He drove straight over from the hotel without stopping for breakfast and blasted everyone in sight. These were the master plans and builders' specifications, covered with notes, alterations, detailed measurements, lists of stores, time schedules, vital phone numbers. The spray job had been thorough; each page of blueprint and worksheet had been treated generously and now lay there in a glued mass: one vast, black *mille-feuille*, still soggy in the middle, crisping at the edges.

The refectory table, however, was quite unblemished. With the same obsessive precision applied to those neatly sawn through shafts, the Jinx had covered the oak top with discarded copies of the *Sun*, laid the plans back on top, then meticulously defaced them one by one. The final touch was to lay another layer of newspaper on the top plan, and replace the outside "title page"—white and clean except for *Noone Ampney Hall*, and a list of contents—over the lot; which was why Vince on his rounds noticed nothing. It wasn't until the foreman needed to refer to the plans next morning that the outrage was discovered.

The police could not find a single black fingerprint.

"Nor even spray on the floor, as we have checked, sir," said the detective inspector 'or we might have hoped for a fresh foot-print at the very least." He had come in on the case over-hastily—that was my own impression—because it was a break-in at a country house: he was on the track of a team who specialised in big, well-planned hauls of jewellery and antiques, and seemed a bit down in the mouth to find mere building-site vandalism, however quirky. He closed his notes, asked the routine questions for most "invasions of privacy", from obscene phone calls upwards: "Can you think of anyone who might not wish you well, Mr. Gelhorn? Made any—well, enemies, recently?"

"Not recently, no, Officer; not since the auction, I guess." He laughed harshly. "Can't rightly picture Link Homes, or Wates, in this sort of vendetta, can you? Involved in some crummy *crime passionel*?"

The DI didn't crack a smile. "Ah! But that's precisely what it is *not*, sir—is it?" The thinking man's LeStrade. "If I might explain. This was carefully planned and executed; and I gather that some shovels—"

"Yes, Inspector: too obviously the same sort of—"

"'Trademark', we call it, sir." Six foo four of slow, solemn bear undeflected by angry bull. "They can't hide it; maybe don't want to: there is an element, as i were, of pride in a trademark, you see And in this case, Mr. Gelhorn, it would seem to be the only real clue we have to date: this tendency to what one migh term conspicuous—ah, perfectionism; thi attention to—"

"Right. And what d'you propose to do Officer?"

"If you will report any irregularity however small. And you will continue witl your security person, will you, sir? Wise I think. Well, we can only hope that nex time our villain will—"

"Give himself away? Fine: just so long as he doesn't get jumpy—set fire to the place maybe? And destroy any clues we could have added to our rather brief list And meanwhile—"

"Meanwhile, Charles," I said quickly "we'll take every precaution to see thi vandalism doesn't happen again."

I walked with the DI to his car. "

may have missed it, arriving late from London," I said, "but did you mention how you thought the vandal had broken in?"

"That's a tricky one, Mrs. Gelhorn," he said, and the young constable with him nodded knowingly. "Didn't really want to talk about it too much in there; and I hardly felt your good husband was in the most receptive frame of—with respect, madam; quite understandably upset . . . Now, Constable Moon here was first on the scene and checked security. The kitchen door, into the back patio area, has a Yale lock; but the catch was not down: that right, Moon?"

"Yes, sir; and the night-watchman swears he 'snibbed' it."

"So that must be how the villain made his exit. How he got in boils down to whether or not we believe in the night-watchman, Mrs. Gelhorn: not so much in his good faith, mark you—no discernible motive; and clearly shaken by what had occurred so close without his knowing."

"Could have dropped off, sir," said Moon: "not the type that likes to admit that sort of lapse, by my reckoning."

"Just so, Constable: might well lie about the small things; though he could simply have been mistaken over the catch on the Yale."

"Or someone could have hidden in the house before the workforce left," I said. "I don't suppose the watchman looks in every cupboard."

"My thoughts run along those lines, Mrs. Gelhorn; but, as I say, I did not want to expand on it in there: after all, it could be one of the builders."

"Some of them have their own cars or bikes, you see, madam," said Moon. "They wouldn't all be leaving the site together."

"Point taken, Moon. But, considering that the damage is comparatively super-ficial to date—more in the vein of a prac-tical joker—it would do no serious harm to wait and catch him in the act. And we are only a phone call away."

I didn't think Charles would agree on the subject of superficiality: those plans were virtually irreplaceable in his eyes. But when I joined him inside he was already working on the duplicate set from his briefcase in an attempt to bring them roughly up to date; he had both Mr. Fawcett and Mr. Bunter, the senior partner of the building firm, checking their specifications and running round with tape measures. The plasterers and brickies were hard at their tasks, and unnaturally quiet. I escaped to my barn. At midday I got Charles to knock off and come out for a pub lunch.

We took it into the beer garden at the back so we could talk. I told him what the DI had said to me.

"An inside job? Could be; except there's no motive that makes any sense. Plus none of that lot's bright enough to carry it through—or kinky enough, I figure."

"That's the bit that bothers me," I said. "The shovel incident, the stolen cake and so on, were almost farcical. But this is—"

"More like a black comedy, eh? I ask you, will I ever get this stinking paint off my hands?"

He had cheered up a bit with his gin and tonic and his ploughman's lunch, so I didn't go on. I'd been going to say "sinister". And driving back to London alone (Charles had left his car in Suffolk at the weekend, and anyway was staying on to sort things out), I wondered who could want to hinder the work on Noone: some nutty conservationist? Some sort of Antiquities Libber? But one who would risk his neck in order to destroy the infidel's blueprints (and our Vince was of the tribe that smite first and question after); who chose to spend precious minutes arranging the pages of last week's *Sun* to save a table top: rustle-rustle, replace plans, start spraying, sheet by sheet, right to the edge . . . Obsession scares me, I suppose.

Nanny was waiting anxiously when I got back, with Henry straining at the leash, togged up for the Punch and Judy show in Regent's Park.

"Mr. Gelhorn's been on twice and wants you to phone your new house immediately," she said. She never referred to it by name: a mute protest. She was anti-Noone as a dirty and disruptive element in the life of her lamb. "It sounded very urgent, Mrs. Gelhorn: you won't forget, will you?"

I waved them goodbye, poured myself some juice and phoned Noone.

"You took your time," said Charles; the calming effects of lunch had been short-ived. "Look, Kate, we got round to checking out the stores, since I lost my lists along with the plans; and all that stuff in the dairy . . . Yes, yes: padlock on the door—intact . . . Well, he's gotten in here too and defaced all the cartons. You know: all that door furniture, the gold bath-fitments, six different lots of tiles, not to mention the boxes of bolts and screws and angle-joints and brackets and suchlike . . . Sure, mostly from the same firm, in virtually identical packs . . . No, nothing's been damaged: that's not the point. They've all got to be sorted through and re-labelled, maybe re-boxed: must be two or three grands' worth of stuff in there to be gone through. OK, so it's not, quote, Serious, but this guy just seems like he can get anywhere he damn well pleases and it's really *bugging* me . . . Yeah—groan—the Law is back and taking notes. Look, they want to know if your barn's been broken into as well, and any damage done there: you got the keys—you and your builders, right? So we can't check it out . . . But you didn't notice anything this morning?

145

No: think hard now, please, Kate, wil
you?"

I told him I was sure: I'd been meas
uring and inspecting the new load o
copper piping for the radiators. Yes, or
my own, now that my plumber only came
on weekday evenings—"A chance'd be a
fine thing!" said Charles tartly—and]
wouldn't be seeing him and the builder til
Saturday.

"And they've only got keys for there:
No others? Right. If you're sure of tha
. . . Well, you're sometimes a bit woolly
about these little things . . . No, nc
further developments—hell, isn't tha
enough? Oh, Vince, the night-watchman
says now that he heard a noise when the
wind got up last night and went to investi
gate; found a window banging way up ir
the attic. Wasn't gone that long, he
swears."

"Why didn't he tell the police this
morning?"

"Says it was 'too routine to mention'
and the Law didn't press him."

"D'you suspect Vince?"

"What *motive*, honey? Stealing, maybe
but this *mindless* . . . Anyway, no rea

grounds to fire him. Fact is, I was suggesting to the Law I give him the heave-ho when he walks in and demands either there should be two of them or I double his pay—or he'd go. Spiked my guns . . . Right: couldn't leave the place empty, and no way am *I* . . . So, since I can't find a pal for him at such short notice, I'm paying double till I do—and looking for double productivity, I can tell you: like maybe he'll swat this creep twice as hard for me . . ."

There was an uneasy lull; just how uneasy, I only heard when I went down with Henry on Saturday. Work had progressed, but slowly. It seemed that the builders were "jumpy as a bunch of old maids: they'll be seeing things next". (They had, of course, as we found out later; but at this stage they were far too sheepish to let on.) Things had slowed down because, as the foreman explained to Charles, they'd had a "bad go": and so he had arranged for them to work in pairs on the more isolated corners of the site; many of the jobs involved at least two, anyway. 'Makes sense really, Mr. Gelhorn sir; and

147

they seem happier. It'll be wasting no time in the long run."

Once I had double-checked no vanda had visited my barn, I decided not to say anything about it to my gang: freelance self-employed or moonlighting, their odd working hours meant they seldom coincided with Charles's builders. But gossip obeys no such divisions, I found maybe the night-watchman had been visiting the stable block for the loan of a cup of sugar—though he wasn't meant to leave the house. Anyway, Philip broached the subject almost before he was out of his van.

"Well, seems like they got a spook up the Rectory, miss: count ourselves lucky down here, eh? Sounds like they got the Walker on their tails."

"Who's the 'Walker', then?"

"Haven't heard of our Noone Walker Mrs. G? Ah—but I wouldn't want to spoil your beauty sleep, my dear . . . No, no good asking me . . ." He winked, nodding his head sideways towards Henry, who was busy cleaning his bear's knee with spit. "Small pitchers. Any rate, I don't hold with all that nonsense; and we've work to

148

do—haven't we, Henry me old son, me old beauty? Unloading tools first, eh?"

The lull lasted perhaps ten sunny days, during which time Terry, Desmond, old Angus and the rest recovered their former high spirits sufficiently to whistle on the job and tan their torsos in the lunch breaks: they had found two old mattresses on a shelf of the dairy, and took them out on to the west terrace.

Charles was happier too. Since his visit to the States in May, he had a special project on the boil: the Audio Womb. He had described it in the American television programme on Noone. "But that sounds sensational, Chuck—like, literally! I'd sure like to see how that shapes up." "Why not?" said Charles, never a man to be cramped by mere cue-cards. "Come on over and I'll show you, personally."

Afterwards they agreed it would have been better to wait for the follow-up programme they'd planned, but viewers, including a number of the home-handyman brigade, rang in wanting to know more; and the television producer decided to go with it: a mini-article on the

Audio Womb—if Charles could get his act together in July at the latest, while interest was still "on simmer". "No problem," said Charles: "that room, the morning room as was, won't need much basic work once the ceiling's lowered. July it is."

There were times when the disruptions altered schedules and Charles regretted his hasty promise; but now "Nationwide" wanted to be in on it too, and he was determined to meet the deadline. He got in a London firm of shopfitters accustomed to fast, neat work, then the hi-fi technicians and, finally, the carpet-layers with their very special brief: "Operation Spiderman", as Charles called it.

I could not bear to watch what they were doing to that lovely morning room; when Charles reported it was going just fine, looked fantastic, and would be ready in time, I heard myself saying, "Great— well done . . . But terribly vulnerable to sabotage, I suppose?"

"Right across from Vince's library? They wouldn't have a prayer."

And—not for the first time—I

discovered in myself an uncomfortable ambivalence towards our vandal.

So I felt like a traitor when the lull came to an abrupt end, and the sabotage moved into its second, more violent, phase.

It was on his final round one early morning that the night-watchman opened up the dairy storeroom and found a great pile of pottery shards: virtually all that remained of Charles's highly coloured Spanish tiles and the first consignment of the wildly expensive hand-painted ones as well. Box after box—now so helpfully re-labelled—had been ripped open. That was not all: two of the decorated Bonsack hand-basins had been smashed in half. The vandal seemed to have known about and used the tools to hand; in fact—for me—the eeriest part of it was the absence of any impromptu element in that scene of methodical annihilation.

He had unrolled the lunch-break mattresses on the floor, and laid out the tiles on them. The sledgehammer, kept in a corner with the other tools, had been muffled in two layers of carpeting underlay —offcuts from the audio room—strapped on with insulating tape: all to hand; and as though to demonstrate his method, the final batch of tiles lay in rows of exploding squares on one mattress, while a great tip of fragments overflowed the other.

"Still must have been quite a noisy business," observed Constable Moon. "But, as Mr. Edwards here has pointed out, it's right the other end of the house from his base."

"Must have taken one hell of a time to get through all these, though," said Charles, crouching amid the wreckage, picking out the few tiles still intact.

Vince was immediately on the defensive. "Now look here, Mr. Gelhorn: I gave up the routine rounds like you said, and I'm doing the random checks as per orders— but with a place this size it's hard to remember sometimes just where you've *been*, isn't it? Especially now I'm taking in the out-buildings and all . . ."

"That settles it," said Charles. He was sallow and peaky under his tan, and oddly quiet for him; Vince looked alarmed. "I'm getting in a security man from London. Today. Two, if you want out."

"I'll stay, sir. Will the money—?"

"Same double pay, for both guards. And I want a police presence outdoors as well: time the Law took this thing seriously—right, Moon?"

"Very good, sir; I'll report to the DI."

I happened to be at Noone for the next—and in a way more disturbing—discovery later that same day; and only because, while Charles drove to London to bring back his extra security, I had decided to stay and work on the garden.

It was about four, I think, and I was clearing the nettles in the stable yard outside my barn, when Mr. Fawcett and old Angus came down to find me. Angus was wheeling a barrow. They wanted to borrow two bags of cement: I'd had a delivery at the weekend as my screed flooring would soon be under way.

"Certainly," I said, "so long as you replace them. When? Tomorrow, fine. What's happened to yours then—all that lot in the shed?"

They shuffled their feet a bit: been used up faster than they thought, hadn't it? Angus suggested. Then the foreman told me. Three sacks out of four were found spoiled: slit open (neatly, of course; with the good bag laid on the top: I knew before I was told) and watered. The outside tap and hose were only a few yards away.

"Does my husband know?"

"Only just found out, Mrs. Gelhorn."

I let them have two bags from the barn and went back with them to view the damage. "Here," I said: "these are still damp!"

"That's right, madam: nearly going off."

"But when d'you think it was done then? I mean, it could have been this morning, couldn't it?"

"Oh, must've been, yes, Mrs. Gelhorn. Difficult to put an exact time on it . . ."

"But you've all been around all day—so have we. You mean, someone must have—?"

"That's right, madam: doesn't bear thinking of."

Angus ventured, "Maybe when we was all in there, in the dairy, like, looking over the damage—the other lot of damage. Same feller of course. Or maybe there's more'n one of—"

"And no one *saw* anything?" Even with he sun on my back, I felt cold.

"Haven't had the time to ask around et, madam. But most likely they'd say omething soon enough if they had."

"Not that Terry and the others up in he top of the hall would have seen much —nor them on the roof, come to that," aid Angus: "behind them great parapets."

Charles delivered his uniformed security nan and received the news of the watered ement with stony calm. He decided to tay at his hotel and cancel his London lates; he drove me to the station with no pare words. I got home just in time to out Henry to bed. It felt like a long day.

He asked me why Daddy wasn't coming fter all, and I told him about the bags of ement. Not the tiles and the basins: there vas an element of violence there, what vith the mattresses and the muffled ledgehammer, that might be the stuff of nightmares—though, for me, the daytime visitation was far more disturbing.

I was right in guessing that the mud-pie spect of hosing the cement would divert nim; and felt only a little guilty over such subliminal advocacy. But when he had done laughing and wishing he'd been there to make "*very* hard sandcastles" out of i —"And they would be, wouldn't they Mum?" "Super-hard, absolutely"—he frowned and sucked his thumb.

"But that was naughty of Doddy," he said sleepily.

"Not 'Daddy', darling: a naughty vandal. He'll be caught, I expect."

"Maybe he thought they was Gro bags . . ."

7

NEXT morning early Charles phoned me to say, despite two heavies inside and a police car in the grounds, the saboteur had struck again. In the old kitchen, this time: the five spanking new "antique" gas-log fires for the bedrooms had been stacked up and soldered messily together into a grotesque abstract sculpture.

I couldn't tell at first whether Charles was giggling or crying.

"Darling? Are you all right? Shall I drive over?"

"Oh—no point, Kate." He sounded suddenly flat and tired.

"But what about the guards? They must have been a bit dozy—"

"Dozy! Christ—they were flat out! It was the police that rang me. They were just going off duty and they couldn't raise Vince and Sterndale—the new guy—so they phoned me; and by the time I got out there they'd broken a window in the library and found the two of them snoring peacefully. I told them they were fired. And they claimed they'd been doped . . . Right: just his style. *Sure* he could— simply tamper with their snacks in the refrigerator. Like I said, this mother can get anyplace—no problem . . . What'll I do? Oh, business as usual: you know me, honey. Maybe the discreet type-face notice like 'We regret any inconvenience to our employees as a result of', etc., etc. And of course some clearing up here: a skipful of rubble and junk going out—junked grates —tiles—basins—*Christ!*—But we're going to burn all the old laths and timbers on site. And then, being Friday, next week's schedule to check out; then home, I reckon. And I'm not coming up here over the weekend: with the Law and the heavies it's no fun—and good to have a couple of days away from this circus." Already he was bouncing back: he always did. "Tell old Hen I'll be home before bedtime. Don't worry: things are under control." So confident. Not even "touch wood".

It was a rubbish tip, mainly consisting of

rotten roof-beams dumped in the nettle patch at the far edge of the back yard: the open ground before it sloped down to the stables. Eventually this area would be cleared, extended, paved and adorned with balustrades and steps, for the grand terrace Charles had planned out on our first visit. Now it could be treated rough, and cleared just enough for deliveries of the heavy stuff—breeze blocks, drain-pipes, concrete-mixer. I had saved the old pram and the cast-iron pump, given them sanctuary in my stable yard, before they could be overlaid by the growing pile of reject timbers.

Best to burn such rubbish in case of any dry rot, the foreman said. Friday lunch-break on a still, muggy, overcast day, and they all took their sandwiches and bevvies round to watch. Terry did his stuff with the paraffin can and tossed a match into the pile. The old timbers had dried out well, exposed to more than a week of sun; they caught quickly and it was a fine blaze. Then there was a deafening bang, amplified and thrown back by three courtyard walls.

"Hey! Did one of you jokers chuck a

pressure can—?" drowned out by a fusillade of explosions that sent burning fragments flying in all directions. "It was like a B movie with the ammo dump going up," said Desmond, the West-Indian master-plasterer and hero of the day. Most of them hopped about swearing and shouting orders, or took cover as the detonations persisted—random fireworks, with smouldering chunks of blackened timber landing yards away, and the fire itself fierce and spitting: far too hot to get near and pull it apart. Desmond edged round the wall to the standpipe, fixed on the hose and gradually got the blaze under control—the middle kept igniting—until together they doused and dismantled the blackened monster, still steaming, and raked out the heart of it.

Charles, lunching at the pub with a gossip-column writer, had been annoyed to miss the planned bonfire. No way round it: this was a future neighbour "dropping in", curious about work-in-progress, and even more about rumours of the Jinx; and he was only diverted by Charles's promise of a decent hock, scampi-in-the-basket, plus a personally conducted tour of Noone ust as soon as the messy structural stuff was out of the way: "Like it's always worse before it's better—right?"

Right. Charles returned to find a flooded and smoke-blackened courtyard. There was a collection of aerosol-can shrapnel, a little pile of burnt-out bangers—your basic twenty-pence squib—and the police poring over them. The local press and Radio Colchester were in attendance. Noone's "happenings" had provided good silly-season copy recently, and promised even better; news of this lot had travelled fast, as more than one startled cottager at Noone Ampney rang through with reports of gunfire.

The spray-cans and squibs were quite enough to proclaim the mark of the Jinx; but Exhibit A was found at the bottom of the pile, wedged in under a large joist and still reeking of the packets of firelighters that had been strapped to it: the file of plans. They had been kept in the late Reverend Dodsworth's safe—set into the thick wall of the old kitchen—ever since the black paint episode; nor had they been brought out that morning, what with all the alarums and diversions. Later they would have been, of course, for the routine Friday-afternoon update/projec tion meeting between the architect, the foreman and the heads of each section There wasn't much sense to be made o them now, after the fire and the water and the raking out. Not quite so neat as the black paint; but very pretty timing. The police statement phrased it differently while Desmond gave exclusive interview to all comers.

Charles left them to it, not even looking back over his shoulder when Fawcett pursued him.

"Could have been real dangerous, Mr Gelhorn—and the men wanted me to tel you they're very unhappy about all this very dissatisfied with the whole—"

"We'll talk Monday," said Charles already behind the steering wheel. "I don' feel too happy neither, chummy." And he was gone, in a spurt of gravel.

Now it was up to the police, and the bouncers on double pay. "I'll have to ge some fresh plans together, I guess,' Charles said, home and pouring himself double whisky. "And if our joker decide o pay a call over the weekend, he'll find hem dug in and waiting. This is War."

They waited a week. The war spirit that had made Britain great—crouching behind the sandbags, coiled to go over the top, greyhounds in the slips: all that—cooled a little. Unfair to them? Perhaps; still, there was a certain macho relish about the big battalions lying in wait for one small, slender vandal who slipped like a black cat from doorway to doorway . . . (But could it be only one man . . . ? Why did I think he was small and slender? And the "black cat" bit . . . I realised I was romanticising, casting him as the sympathetic anti-hero. I was being disloyal again; and, though one half of me feared him, the other half of me was intrigued, and hoped he would get away.)

We went down with Henry the following weekend. Charles, of course, had been in and out during the week, and reported that things had perked up a lot, the mess cleared away, and nothing left to upset his lad. The hall ceiling was finished, major work on the double staircase going ahead as per schedule; the steel cantilevers for the mezzanine, custom-built, had been delivered, and looked good. "And—know something, sonny boy? You can be the first to try out the audio room! Not really Mom's bag, eh? Just too technical, I guess man-talk, right? But then she's got her barn, hasn't she?"

The waiting policeman switched off the music on his car radio and told Charles there was nothing to report. "We'll be here in shifts over the weekend, sir, but then we're being taken off: my superiors believe this villain's moved to pastures new, so to speak. One theory is that he was after some imaginary haul in that old safe of yours; that he broke the combination, and when he found the cupboard was bare—excepting your file or course, sir—he went and burnt that: sort of a rude gesture, if you get my meaning; then cleared out . . . You'll be keeping on the night guards, won't you, Mr. Gelhorn? And we'll still be doing spot checks every now and again, just to make quite sure. But it seems to have paid off, doubling your security system, sir. Money well spent. As our crime prevention officer put it—and I'm sure you'll agree—there's only one thing that's better than a good arrest, and that's a good deterrent."

I left Charles and Henry to roll about in their deep-pile audio room with all eight speakers going, and went down to my barn. The screed floor was done, marvellously level under its rough combing (the sort of surface, I thought, that Leo would have found irresistible), with bright little periscopes of copper pipes surfacing at intervals round the walls where the radiators would be. None of the gang was there today: an important cricket match; so I laid out my tile samples in separate corners and left them there to see how they'd strike me on Wednesday, when Philip had arranged to come over in his lunch hour.

Getting the picnic basket out of the car, I was reluctantly impressed—as I frequently was—by my husband's ingenuity: what with double glazing and the heavily insulated walls, hardly a murmur came from the morning room on the corner; and indoors I could only sense the beat of the music. Henry came out through what he called the "air-lock" and

I caught a brief, muffled blast of Gerry Mulligan.

"Know what? There's even *blinds* made of carpet over the windows! Push-button carpet blinds, Mum! And I *worked* them! And *great* for birthday parties, you see: you can just shove our food and stuff in the air-lock and forget all about us—and we can shout and jump about and behave like cannibals and not even Nanny will give a tinker's fuss—"

"Cuss."

"Cuss. So Dad says."

Vince and Sterndale came on duty before we left. Now Vince too was sporting a dark shirt and sunglasses; the hip West End Security look with its paramilitary undertones had rubbed off on him. The situation was cool.

So, it seemed, was the trail; and the two security men were quite clearly a little disappointed by the lack of action. Even the press coverage had ceased. We left them comforting themselves with Budweisers, deep-pan pizzas from a take-away in swinging Ipswich (they trusted no local vittles since the drugging episode), and the colour television that was part of the deal. They had already done their first rounds of the house and stables. Seven o'clock of a fine night, and all was well.

By Monday evening, the builders had finished one flight of the double staircase, and half the treads of the second, working overtime: the television session was due at the end of the week, and Charles wanted to have his neon corkscrew, as well as his Audio Womb, on show.

In the small hours of Monday night, about one-fifteen, they reckoned, Vince and Sterndale heard a thud from the direction of the audio room. The door from the hall was always kept bolted despite the extra locks on the windows; they opened it and charged in.

No one was there: easy enough to see in a room furnished with nothing more than carpeting on ceiling, walls, and floors, and built-in hi-fi. Then the door shut behind them. Both doors; distantly, bolts and wards could be heard chunking home; then that perfect silence. Audio tomb.

The window keys, still linked to their duplicates, had been removed. There was no stick of furniture, no ornament, to break the glass; nor did they carry weapons: by agreement, but more a matter of pride. They were both ex-boxers, and Sterndale had done judo; individually formidable, together invincible. Fists and feet, however, do not break wired glass; nor do even the fanciest sneakers, *de rigueur* on duty for speed and silence. In desperation they tried to dismantle part of the hi-fi: a stereo-receiver might make a dent; but on consideration—by the time Vince had had a go and broken the blade of his Swiss knife for want of a Philips screwdriver—it seemed preferable to preserve their employer's favourite, and most costly, installation, and lie low. Then the lights went out, turned off at the mains.

They started shouting and banging again: they admitted as much. "But that place sort of sops it up . . . So in the end —well, sir, we decided to sit tight." Muffled in deep pile and darkness, like an up-market exercise in sensory deprivation . . .

"Anyway, so far as we can see," said the constable, "it was just another practical joke. The foreman here, Mr. Fawcett, reports nothing untoward with the building works, the stores and so on; is that right, sir?"

"Looks like it," said Charles. "Business as usual."

The builders dispersed to their different tasks. The carpenters in charge of the staircase were diverted to help replace a cracked lintel in the attic. Moon was left ushering out reporters, and Charles went off to supervise old Angus in clearing up the audio room: mostly a matter of hoovering and airing—though a bucket and detergent were involved. After all, two grown men primed with Budweiser cannot be expected to spend five and a half hours in a locked room, however comfortable, without accidental spillage. They had smoked too—their only solace—but managed to douse and store their stubs in the cigarette packet. The windows were opened to air the room: their keys had been left on the refectory table. No prints, of course.

Work on the helical staircase did not resume till later in the morning. I spent some time weeding my tiny rows of lettuces, carrots and beetroots, then

carrying water from the standpipe by th
greenhouses.

Even at that distance, I heard it: th
clanging and commotion from the hall
Someone shouted from an upstairs windov
as I ran back to the house.

In the great room, part of the scal
folding had fallen to the floor. The nex
section leant drunkenly against the wall
Fawcett was sitting on a box, sipping fror
Charles's hip flask; Terry was on th
phone. Most of the others were ther
swarming around with ladders, peering a
the stairs or studying the splayed scal
folding from a safe distance; and every
body talked at once.

The carpenters, I gathered, had climbe
up their half-flight of newly fixed treads t
get on with the next, and the two top one
had given way with them: sawn through
just as the shovel handles had been—bu
on a rather different scale of risk. One ma
clung to the stringer, the other ducke
back, missed his footing and slithere
down a few steps before he got a hold
Two of their mates nearby came runnin
to help; and Mr. Fawcett, whose firs
thought was for his showpiece, swarme

up the scaffolding beside it to check the damage.

It seems the saboteur had not wasted those undisturbed small hours after all. He had not only sawn through the three-inch planks of red sapele, but loosened the coupling brackets on the scaffolding as well: it only took one man in a hurry to climb up ten foot or so above floor level for the Meccano structure to slip apart like a drunken giraffe.

"No joke this," pronounced Constable Moon, swiftly on the scene. "This was dangerous: potentially lethal."

So was the fire in the audio room.

It happened very quickly: all our saboteur's aces coming out in a rush. They were still milling around in the hall, examining the power-saws and the stairs—two more had been sawn on the finished flight —to decide how he had done the job. It was Constable Moon, probably the only non-smoker present, who said he smelt burning. The airlock was shut, and there was nothing to be seen, nothing to be heard—until Charles ran across and pulled open the first door.

Then we saw smoke in the air-lock;

and we heard a sound like heavy, splat-tering rain; and I shouted "*Don't* Charles . . . !" But already he was running for safety from the inferno, as five hundred square yards of deep-pile Wilton caught the cross-draught and went up like a torch.

8

AFTER the roaring, the shouting and the coughing, the hoses and the fire-engines, the endless questioning, more shouting, and the fuss, the revving and backing when the builders left, it was suddenly very quiet. All doors and windows were open to let out that terrible smell. We sat at one end of the refectory table in the huge, smoke-stained, half-finished hall with a bottle of whisky between us; and the only sound was the ceaseless dripping.

Charles poured us both another—we didn't have far to go, staying at the hotel. Then he got up suddenly, went over and slammed the morning-room door.

"Chinese water-torture," he said. "That bloody ceiling—they sure drowned it."

"And it's raining now," I said. "Outside, I mean."

"Jehovah right on form," said Charles, sitting staring into his glass. "Too little and too late . . ."

"Even a noon-day cloudburst wouldn't have helped. Darling, it's pretty grim here with no electricity. Let's go soon. I need a bath; we both do—and these clothes stink . . . Is there any point in hanging about for our vandal?"

"I guess not. I guess he's shot his bolt. Sure: we'll lock up and go."

"Pity we can't leave some lights on."

"Only attract sightseers. Police reckon Nosy Parkers and kids'll try and take a look—since it made the evening papers already; but they'll patrol a bit and move folks on . . . So"—he stood up and screwed the top on the whisky— "tomorrow's another day. Busy one, too: that's for sure. New builders, new scaffolding, new schedule. Whole new time-scheme, Katy. Could be. Depending on how soon the next bunch can get their act together." He went round closing windows, checking, bolting doors, as he talked. "Busy time, high summer: all the outside jobs. And half the blue-collar boys off to Marbella—Palm Beach . . . Or is it the Seychelles this . . . ? *Christ*, if this mother hasn't warped on me . . . !" He kicked the inner door of the air-lock and I heard it splinter.

"Leave it," I said: "let's go. At least the fire was contained. Come on. It'll all seem better in the morning, when we can see." But my heart sank at the thought.

I was padlocking the front door, Charles was already in the car—passenger seat and whisky bottle—when headlights emerged from the dark avenue. It was Philip's van.

"Heard about your trouble, Mrs. G. Just wondered if I could be of help." He got out and stood in the drizzle staring up at the blackened brickwork over the windows. "That old Walker of yours really had a field day, I see. Structure looks OK, though. Want some help clearing up and that?"

"Oh, Philip . . . ," I said, suddenly near to tears.

"You'll be all right, love." He held my arm and peered at me in the gloom. It was the old raining-and-crying thing again, the story of my life; and laughing weakly.

"Don't mind me," I said: "I've had a couple."

"Best medicine, Mrs. G. . ."

I could hear Charles champing.

"Philip: I must go. I can't see tomorrow, somehow, but I think: Yes, please—and I'll try and give you a ring early. Bless you for coming up . . ."

"Sightseeing?" Charles snapped as I got in. "Wot, no camera?"

"My builder," I said. "Offering to clear up the mess."

"Huh! Plus an estimate for completion of building work? He's a fast one and that's for sure. A suspect and a motive I must confess I hadn't gotten around to. I guess the Law might be interested in—"

"Charles, there's no question of . . . ! Come on—he's a 'little man'—a freelance builder with the odd friend or relation he gets in for the other jobs. *He* couldn't take on your contract: he wouldn't want to! This is a Little Man, Charles: a mini-operator, who works—"

"Who works after hours? Like our freelance saboteur? And a skilled worker as well—right? Rather convenient, just popping up from the village . . ."

I shut up and drove. Getting out at the hotel I said, "Look, I'm ringing him tomorrow early—about helping to clear

176

p. You speak to him. Offer him the ontract: see what he says."

But that night I lay awake thinking bout it.

I was sure I was right about Philip: a gentle man, a preserver not a destroyer, with rock-solid alibis—if it came down to hat. What bothered me was the sabotage tself (the sound of that fire still roaring in my ears), and all this talk of the "spook".

Amidst the noise and bustle, the accusations and counter-accusations, claims and counter-claims, there had been this continuous low grumbling about "being spooked": always quashed by Fawcett, gnored by Mr. Bunter, the head of the building firm, or angrily brushed aside by Charles; the only patch of no man's land n their battlefield. "That'll be enough, Terry," said Mr. Fawcett. "I'm not telling you again . . ."

"It simply isn't an issue, Mr. Gelhorn," said Mr. Bunter. "Symptom maybe—what with these repeated disruptions making them so jumpy . . . No, Mr. Gelhorn: they did not 'go to pieces', not at any point; and 'seeing things' is only a manner of speaking. The point is that there was a

contract, and my firm agreed to carry ot
the work . . . Now wait a moment, sir: th
money in question—agreed it was a grea
deal of money, as you say; and it was a
great deal of work—you accepted the est
mate—but that is not the *issue*. Surely th
issue is: we have a contract that we . .
Let me finish, please. We have a contrac
we cannot fulfil . . . No, we are not 'givin
up on the job': the working conditions ar
simply *impossible* . . . Again and again m
men see the work they've done messe
up, destroyed . . . And then there will b
the other question, of compensation."

"Compensation? Right, chummy: an
it's *me* that'll be wanting the comper
sation, so get a load of *this* . . . !"

And it went on and on, the endles
high-pitched wrangling—over severa
hours, it seemed—and still ran throug
my head; but always, underneath, th
drone-note of Terry, of old Angus and th
rest as they listened in. Or later, whe
Fawcett sent them off to pack up thei
gear (they would come back for the heav
stuff, the concrete-mixer, the scaffolding
in the morning), I could hear them talkin
of it among themselves. Like the firs

178

me, when Angus had been carrying the
op end of the ladder up the back stairs,
nd . . .

"No, stupid: that must've been later:
ig staircase was still viable like—"

"He's right, though: designer bloke and
hat lot was all over them big stairs, and
Mr. Fawcett sent us round t'other way—
nd old Angus here shouts from halfway
p, 'Hey, Tel, I just seen a funny feller
own that corridor . . .'"

"Very nippy he must have been: not a
ausage when I got up round the corner."

Angus: "You took your time—and me
oing all the manoeuvring."

"Stuck, wasn't you, Tel?"

"Right, I was stuck—went and dropped
is flamin' end, didn't he?"

"Small wonder: poor old sod, he looked
hite as a sheet when he come down.
haking, wasn't you, Angus old son? Had
o settle down and take a nip."

"Had too many nips, Mr. Fawcett says
hen I tells him. 'Have a heart, Mr. F,' I
ays: 'it's only just turned noon! Bevvies
n't till dinner break, you know me . . . ,'
says. 'Just felt it my duty to report a
intruder, Mr. Fawcett sir . . .' And I'd

like to know what you lot are so bus[y]
laughing at: what about Desmond for [a]
start? Nips out the yard for a jimmy an[d]
sees a geyser standing there among the[m]
nettles—"

"Ouch, man—!"

"You wasn't laughing then, mate[:]
blimey, you'd a' been white if you hadn['t]
been black . . ."

I was keeping out of the way, sitting i[n]
one of the window embrasures of the ha[ll]
with a colour sup. left over from som[e]
Sunday picnic. They went to load th[e]
truck, and Terry was saying, ". . . A[ll]
coming out now, i'n't it—eh? All a bi[g]
joke—tell the lads at the pub—now we'r[e]
shot of it, right? No calling it a joke
though, that time we was all together—n[o]
you wasn't, Angus; just the muscle-men—
when Des here found the Newcast[le]
Brown, remember? Getting that load [of]
stuff into the old kitchen . . ."

"But it's ever so creepy—that ol[d]
kitchen is. Like it sort of echoes . . ."

"It's *cold* in there . . ."

"That's spooks for you, man: chill you[r]
very bones . . ."

"But you saw him too, Desmond[?]

through the door into the passage. 'That's him!' you said. Same like you saw in the yard, you said."

"And you saw him, OK? Not just me . . ."

"That's right. We saw him clear as clear that time . . ."

One of the Irish brickies leaned out of the cab and said: "So there he was, then: three-D and all, no doubt, in glorious Technicolor: your friendly neighbourhood vandal just passing through, like—just casing the joint—"

"Not Technicolor, matey: black and white . . ."

"Always black and white . . ."

Mr. Bunter and Fawcett had gone; Charles was outside hunting for more cigarettes in the car, and the last van-load of builders was revving impatiently, when Angus scuttled back into the hall for his lunchbox. I caught him.

"Angus," I said, "what's this about a spook?"

"Nothing, miss, really. They're waiting for me, see? Nothing but talk, miss."

"When was it last seen? When did *you* see it last?"

"I never! Why"—he dropped his voice to a whisper, and glanced over his shoulder—"this morning as ever is, that's when. I ask you, miss: any wonder we're—?"

"Tell me."

"Oh, just afore noon it were, ma'am, after the accidents, and everyone running down to see what the commotion was about and left me up them attics stuck atop a wobbly ladder and me shouting for help out the window best I could, for someone to hear maybe—when I sees him: standing by that big hedge, miss, nearby the drive and that. And I saw you and all, running over from the garden: reckon you passed right close . . . Had to wait, I did, till one of 'em come back up and helped me off it: stuck up there and no one . . . They're honking for me, miss."

"What do you call him, Angus? Tell me, does he have a—a name? Did you never try to speak to him?"

"Wouldn't rightly *speak* to him, miss . . . But could be the village people got some name for him—ever such bad luck

182

to say it out loud, though. That's what Desmond says, and he should know: Phisic, Desmond is." And he was gone.

Philip, who "didn't hold with such nonsense", had dared to put a name to the spook. A punning spook? It was around midday when the morning room was set on fire; midday when Angus first saw him on the back stairs; and again this morning —yesterday morning now, I thought; and wished I could turn on the light. There were no streetlights, down here by the sea.

And it had been noon on the day of the auction when I saw him in the poplar alley . . . I lay thinking, unable to sleep. It was a still night; but not even the gentle sound of the surf lulled me: I seemed always to be listening, anticipating the seventh wave. Waiting for something.

It was four by Charles's luminous digital alarm-watch when I sat up, had a drink of water, and told myself I was being silly. I realised that I had got to the point when I hoped it *was* my village builder sabotaging the works to land himself a fat contract. Anything was better—and less crazy— than a ghost who defended its haunts: a long-dead vicar apparently prepared to maim and to kill.

Our ex-builders were there when we got to Noone next morning. This was the "brute force", as Charles called it, rather than the workforce as we knew it: the belted weightlifters, first and last on any given site.

One weight, however, they could not lift: the pile of concrete blocks behind the dairy, bought in cheap by Bunters for probable use in the stables. Clearly they had not been checked for a while; and, to be fair, they were stacked up so high, well above eye level, that nothing seemed amiss until you tried to shift them.

They had been cemented together from above by pouring a liquid mix into the neatly stacked, well-aligned holes. "Could have been done days—maybe weeks—ago," said Charles: "at least he didn't use reinforcing rods, or it would have been hell breaking it up. As it stands, one good man-day with a pneumatic drill should get it into manageable chunks, I reckon."

Not even the chorus of grunts from the brute force signalling all too eloquently "rather you than me, matey" could dent his positive mood: this morning it was the old powerhouse at full blast. Up early (not long, it felt, after I finally got to sleep) for his jog along the foreshore; a hearty working breakfast, telephoning London builders for immediate appointments—if not sooner—to inspect and submit estimates. "Up front," he told me, with his hand across the mouthpiece, "it's not about money: it's who can get in there soonest. But you got to keep 'em guessing, of course, and use the cash as an incentive bonus: lots of juicy overtime, and we could still move in by completion date on St. John's Wood."

He also had an assessor from the insurance company coming down from London; and I arranged for Philip and friends to start clearing the mess in their lunch hour. Till then, I went round with Charles taking notes for him, while the builders dismantled and loaded their scaffolding with a great deal of language and clangour. It was reassuring to have Desmond in charge; and the only real flare-up was when the concrete blocks were found—particularly as they had been

referred to by Mr. Bunter the previous da
as "materials not disbursed to date"
Normally such deliveries would stay o
site for the next builders; but at tha
moment Charles had been in no mood t
reach for his cheque book: they coul
"clear the lot, and welcome", wit
colourful suggestions as to where the
should store them.

Now, viewing the immovable tower, h
clapped Desmond on the shoulder an
said, "Looks like I'm stuck with 'em, eh
You just tell old sourpuss Fawcett to ma
me the bill, OK?"

When they were going, Desmond cam
down to find me in the barn.

"Just to say 'so long', ma'am, an
thanks for the coffee and all. And tell yo
that old spook's gone, Mrs. Gelhorn
cleared off—OK? Our Angus was goin
on about it last evening, that you was
little bothered—So I thought I'd just . .
Oh, and he says he picked up this old coi
in the drive when we was leaving. Flori
or something."

"Well, how kind . . . ! But *he* mu
keep that . . . You can tell it's gone, ca
you, Desmond?"

"Yes'm: I can tell. Man or spook, he's gone."

"I don't see how a man could have done it," I said: "how he got around like that, through all the security. Only a ghost could walk through guards—and walls, and locked doors. But I don't really believe in ghosts: not ones that can uncouple scaffolding . . ."

"Maybe some feller with paranormal powers . . . Gotta go, ma'am. So, thanks again, and see you around . . . You certainly done this place nice," he said, stopping in the doorway. "Whatever It is, seems like you got Its blessing down here all right."

The main job for Philip and his moonlighters was clearing out the morning room. Charles had planned simply to include this in the new builders' brief; but he agreed that the house would continue to smell of roast and parboiled Wilton— probably with a light dressing of mould in a day or two—until it was stripped and removed. He suggested a price for the job; cash, of course. Philip agreed, they brought the ladders in and started on the ceiling. Charles's attitude to Philip amused me: polite, circumspect, almost formal—not at all his usual manner with employees; more like the way he treated old boyfriends of mine when he met them at parties. And—also unusual for him—he left me to cope with them and arrange when they should come back. He busied himself with the man from the insurance.

I don't remember much more about that day—probably because I prefer not to. There was a great deal of sweeping and mopping; and the house wore the general air of a deserted billet that even an orderly exit of workmen leaves behind it; simply because they are men, I suppose. The library was the saddest of all: Vince and Sterndale had decamped at speed and without a backward glance, leaving grey bedding, beer cans full of cigarette stubs ends of take-away meals, well-thumbed girlie magazines, two odd socks and a persistent locker-room smell that even wide-open windows and spring-fresh aerosol from the village shop could not quite disperse. And I found that my feelings for the sad old library—an odd, very female mixture of protectiveness and embarrassment—prevented me from letting Philip and Co. in there; so I tackled it.

"Don't overdo the spit and polish, Katy," said Charles, bringing me lunch from the pub (I was "in no shape to go public", as he put it). "Remember this is to be my study, and I guess it'll be just about gutted and sterilised by the time I even get around to wall coverings—and Donny sees it done out in gold hessian: I think he may be on to something . . . Like: restrained, but rich—"

The only other thing I remember clearly from Black Wednesday was an overheard exchange between Philip and his brother-in-law. It was just after the insurance expert had looked in, prodded the soggy, charred walls rather gingerly, and moved on.

"Reckon it makes sense these days, that insuring against vandalism," said Paul the plumber.

"Oh, it does and no mistake," said Philip. "Mind you—from what folks say, with the clergy involved and all—reckon this lot'd come under 'Acts of God', like as not . . ."

The television session, of course, was cancelled; "postponed", said Charles. At least he had lots to do. Representatives of two London builders, and of a well-known Essex firm based in Bishop's Stortford, had all been round Noone with Charles by Friday. I was back in St. John's Wood, and he joined us on Saturday for a quiet weekend: a fund-raising squash match, two parties that evening, and most of Sunday in Surrey visiting his hydraulic-billiards-table friend, Sam. They also had a swimming pool, and Henry was learning to dive.

It was quite a gathering, and the menfolk spent a happy day watching the billiards table go up and down (Charles explaining the improvements he would introduce for his games room at Noone); or recording, then observing, their golf swings on video. This was Sam's newest toy, hot from Japan—though the system of retrieving golf-balls hooked or sliced over some two acres of rough meadow was still medieval: every time the balls were used up, a small man would emerge from behind a stout tree in the middle distance, carrying a large basket.

"He's meant to use a motor-bike to speed up delivery," said Sam: "then it's a pretty slick operation. But seems like his kids borrowed it . . . As you say, Chuck: the human factor. So what? Means we have us a pleasant break for refreshing our glasses."

Charles took notes on the swimming pool, its filtration plant, its auxiliary solar panels; and sketched out his plans for the one at Noone. It's always entertaining to watch an architect drawing out his pet projects; and Sam did not seem the least bothered by this comparative one-up-manship. Like Charles, he was a gadgets man, eager to learn the latest refinements. His wife Zee moaned a little.

"Hey, Charlie, cut it out, will you? We just get it working right, then you come along and he starts all over, ripping out the works—like the stereo, last time you visited . . ." She gave up and joined the girls. "Why do I bother?" she said. "Know what? Sam never listens to all those new records we ordered: he's far too busy messing with his newest graphic equalisers."

"Keeps them happy," I said. "And it's

good to see my old man so bouncy, after this last week."

"Poor Chuck—and having to cancel the TV session!" said Zee, busy arranging her chin-reflector. "Poor sweetie! Sounds like it's been real rough on the both of you. Sam swears he should have stuck with the big boys all along instead of tangling with those hick-town builders. I just hope and pray for your sakes, honey, they'll fix it up real fast. I mean it's such a fantastic place, your old parsonage—have you folks been there? Oh, you just have to: we adored every minute of our visit . . . But even so, no fun living with the builders— Right: even dishy ones! And if I know Chuck (and I do, girls: we introduced him to wife number two—*and* he's forgiven us!), I know that no way will that guy stand for a home in shit order. And neither will Nanny, from what I know of nannies —nor even your darling cook, Katy, come to think: not living with that plaster-dust —nohow! You'll be just fine, of course: you classy Britishers are brought up tough —and Henry will have a ball . . . Hey, you want to come see how we've fixed the guest annexe? Sure, honey: you rest. Hey, how's about you, Charlie?"

"Yes: do take Charles."

One of the many delights of buying a country house, they say, is the sudden relevance of other people's—even if, as with Sam and Zee's little palace, it helps define what you would not do. For me, however, this delight was two-edged: I knew I had no power, either way, over Noone's refurbishing; and, whilst I was certain to admire the comfort and the practical good sense of much I saw, I did not want to hear Zee, Charles, Ada *et al.* discussing Good Taste, or Donny's new way with drapes. There was, of course, no absolute—no Golden Mean—in taste, I reminded myself: like a sense of humour, it was personal. But this was definitely not my bag; so I lay in the sun with my eyes closed, except when I was called upon to witness Henry's froglike plunges; and I thought about my barn, the first dwelling I had ever owned outright. I thought about the shallow old stoneware sink I'd discovered among the nettles in the yard when the builders removed their gear: just the thing for washing out paint pots, or

keeping flowers fresh overnight. It woul
fit in; it would be right. And it would no
be broken in half like the Bonsack basins
it would have *his* blessing, I thought.

Driving down with Charles that Sunday,
talked to him about our ghost. Henry ha
been tearing round since early morning
and was fast asleep on the back seat.
simply passed on what Desmond and th
others had said, and Philip's version—
which I finally got out of him on Blac
Wednesday—of what amounted to a loca
legend. Brazenly flouting the dire warning
of old Angus, I made myself name it: th
Noone Walker. I said nothing about th
poplar alley.

It started as an attempt to amus
Charles, and divert him from his Builder
Blues. The two London firms were t
produce estimates within the week, but fo
him it felt like standing still; and any in
activity made him wildly restless. He wa
put out, moreover, at being turned dow
by the fine old Bishop's Stortford builders
he had taken to them, their style and thei
ideas, after the rather cool, unresponsiv
inspection tours of the others. "Not rightl

urned me down': just phoned—wasn't
ven either of the guys I saw—and said
ney couldn't take it on. And when I
ressed for an explanation, they gave too
nany reasons—know what I mean? Like,
ne truth is always simple—so my daddy
ays . . . Yet I got the feeling from going
ound with them that they were real keen;
ood as said right out they'd the time, and
he men, to take it on."

"Maybe they heard it was spooked," I
aid.

"That load of baloney? Got it from
¡unters, you mean?"

"Or local chitchat."

"That the London firms wouldn't get to
ear?—or be fussed if they did . . . But
vho'd turn down a contract like that for
ome old wives' tale?"

"Quite," I said. "Still—vandals, or
engeful spirits—they mightn't want to
isk it."

"Your 'little man' doesn't seem too
othered, and he's local."

"Philip has no time for all that
onsense, he says, since he simply doesn't
ee ghosts, whatever other people do.
nyway, he told me the story . . . It's

meant to be the first Parson Dodsworth
looking after his old rectory."

"Pity he couldn't stop it falling apart
then: fat lot of looking after he's done, him
and his descendants . . . But your guy say
folk actually see it?"

"Apparently: a black-and-white figure
not very tall. With a parson's black clothes
and white bands—you know, neck bands.
White face . . . So they say, anyway. At
noon—midday, I mean—"

"A *punning* ghost! Oh, wow—
punning ghost is too *much*!"

"And there's a little rhyme, too: your
genuine 'folkloric' verse! Here, I wrote it
on the back of my cheque book . . ."
Hunting in my bag, I felt hot with
disloyalty. "As relayed by a sceptic, and
rather garbled no doubt: 'First time 'e sees
un—'"

"Aarh, moi deario . . . !" Charles
always liked my Loamshire act.

"'First time 'e sees un, 'e sees un a
noon;

Next time 'e sees un, he'll bring 'e
boon.

Third time, if it be by the light of the
moon,

Then there'll be a death at the rectory of Noone.'"

Charles loved it.

"Too *much*! Our very own ghost—*and* a warning—in *rhyme*! Oh, brother, what a turn-up for the books: all that lovely bricks-and-mortar and a spook thrown in for free? But a real classy spook, with a rock-solid pedigree! Sheer bloody bonus . . . Hey, all we need is a portrait—was there a portrait?"

"Hush," I said, "or you'll wake the holy terror . . . Here, watch the road, Charles! What's *wrong* . . . ? I said, Don't wake our sleeping cargo, darling: that's all— OK? Yes, I think there was a portrait maybe, on the stairs—D'you remember it?"

"Not so's I'd be able to—Hey-hey-*hey*! Can't *wait* to tell Sam—and, oh boy, will he be sick as a parrot . . ."

I had certainly diverted Charles from his builders. When he stopped slapping the steering wheel and wondering at his luck, I said: "So d'you think the builders really saw anything?"

"Three times? By the light of the moon—? Oh, it's rich, Katy . . . No, honey: they'd simply heard the old tale and used it for an excuse—like, scapegoat —for the whole screw-up. Maybe not deliberate; I mean, Noone must seem a touch weird when you're used to working on office blocks and housing estates. Could be it made them a little jumpy—then something goes missing, goes wrong, and the local guy delivering cement says 'Aarh! Must be that old Noone Walker, moi dearios . . .' and they start seeing things."

"But, Charles, how did the vandal *do* all that? Get past the guards and so on? Do you still think it was an inside job?"

"Sure it was. Which is why I was quite glad to see the back of them. Motive? Oh, money, I guess—what else? And, come to that, there are some really screwball conservation characters around with money to burn . . . I don't know, honey: does it matter? They've cleared off; and looks like the vandal has too. Which proves my point."

"Yes . . . Desmond, the plasterer, said it had gone."

"And—don't tell me—Desmond's meant to be psychic, right? Sure: that figures. Like, he's one of my chief suspects. Can't prove a doggone thing, though . . . Oh boy, is poor old Sammy going to be sick about my spook!"

Actually, Sam came up with a bright idea. We were talking over lunch about the problem of finding a caretaker for Noone until the builders could move in: a fortnight at least. Philip was working on the barn at weekends, and the police had promised to keep an eye on the place at night; but Charles really wanted proper surveillance.

"And I don't figure, after our little fiasco, security men are such good news: I've had the professional heavies right up to here . . . No, Zee honey: no students —no school-leavers—they'd just get their pals in and start up their own hippie squat . . ."

"Hey, how's about spook-hunters?" said Sam. "All those psychic researchers on TV? *Ghostwatch*: that's the one. So you got this fancy ghost, right? I say: cash in on it, feller! And these characters'll sit up all night waiting, you know: can't miss much with their infra-red cameras and tripwires and all getout . . . Oh, sure: load of baloney; but these are the guys to install, see? Like they'll do it for free— and they just might trap the odd vandal as he flits through—"

"I married a genius, that's all," said Zee.

Never one to stand and stare, she had fetched the Yellow Pages and was already riffling through them. (Zee had clawed her way up Sam's firm—her words—to become his Girl Friday, before she'd got him away from his wife. Henry, who was mesmerised on meeting her, asked me afterwards if you could wipe your bottom with nails like that.)

"But it's Sunday, Zee . . ."

"Go on, Zee baby: no ghost-buster worth his salt observes the sabbath trading laws . . ."

"Skeleton staff—right! Oh yes, I like it . . ."

The whole buffet gathering was involved now.

But I was thinking of my sober cleric, monochrome in that green alley; and I sat back hoping that Desmond the plasterer was right; and fearing, too, lest psychic research might somehow sterilise a haunt.

Hopeful, and a little fearful, that one day I would see the Noone Walker again . . .

And Charles observed my detachment. He leaned across and grabbed my arm.

"You didn't tell them the *rhyme*, honey! Come on now: your party-piece! Hey, folks, this is the best bit . . . Hey, Zee, wait up: you simply gotta hear *this*."

9

THE psychic researchers were quick
to accept. High summer was not
really the open season for hauntings, and they tried to fill the gap taking
sightseers round the most notable
"atmospheric" sites, where visitations had
been observed. But for the committed
ghost-spotter, many of them students on
vacation, this offered little satisfaction.
Noone was a windfall.

They arrived later that week, eight or
nine of them in a camper and a van, and
immediately started unloading their equip-
ment. Charles showed them round; then
happy in the knowledge that Noone was
under the closest twenty-four-hour surveillance, and that Jaggi Brothers, "of
Hampstead and Mayfair", could start
work at the end of August, he took Henry
and Nanny off to his holiday house in
Nantucket; happy, too, that I should elect
to sit tight and paint in London, and so

be available for the psychic investigators' daily reports.

I was as much concerned for my corner of walled garden in the long dry spell, for my ripening rows of peas and runner beans, as for my Art. Very soon I realised that the ghost-busters, too, were whiling away the summer pleasantly with little to show for it. A hard core of four, with a fluctuating group of students and hangers-on, they camped in tents and the caravan, using the great hall as base for their gear, the whole house for their experiments. Meanwhile they grew brown with sunbathing, and the dark rings under their eyes from night-watching faded away: there were more than enough in the team for a generous roster. Those off duty went sightseeing to Orford, Ely and Dunwich. Some took to helping me, when I turned up to work on the garden; two students cleared the path through to the lake, and a lecturer in Comparative Religions started mending the summer-house—but to this Professor Leonard, the head man, called a halt: it would tamper with the "paranormal ecology". He didn't really like even the fallen branches being cleared from the wood—and agreed so long as no chainsaws or "similar disruptive appliances" be used.

Three weeks of sunshine; the scented magnolia in glory; and if I could have been alone at Noone, I believe I might have moved in. Or so I told myself. Alone there, I could have painted. At St. John's Wood, I'd started sorting and making lists for the move in September. So the cause of Art had been neglected; but now that the psychic investigators had taken over watering the vegetables (there were enough there for them and for my freezer: a bumper crop), I went off to Paris. I knew, and they knew, nothing was stirring at the Rectory. Professor Leonard waffled on at length about the reasons for this. "As soon as I walked in, dear lady, I felt the site had been raped—it is not too strong a word— and, believe me, intends no disrespect to your lord and master, that very gifted architect. What *drew* me, however, and what keeps us here, and continuously observant, is the fact—I think I may say 'fact' after such numerous and independent sightings, so many occurrences, some of a most violent nature—the fact that the disruptive elements were triggered (oh, quite clearly so) by that very rape. And 'rape' is the only word for it—with all the outraged innocence that rape implies . . ."

I did not like his relish, nor the fine spray that accompanied it, but I was glad he seemed content: they were excellent guardians for Noone, however odd. To keep them there, for Charles's sake alone, I had been as helpful as I could. I showed them the late Laurence Dodsworth's short historical account; I tracked down two of our ex-builders for them. But I did not tell them about my encounter in the green alley.

Professor Leonard phoned me in Paris one evening. Regretfully, he admitted, they had drawn a blank; even the well-known medium they invited to Noone agreed their efforts would remain fruitless. She held a seance in the great hall and another in the nursery, choosing those rooms as the most and the least "tampered with", and her findings only supported the opinion she had expressed on arrival: "Something was here, and it may come back one day. It is not here now." In her trance, he said, she mentioned "traces—

so many traces—but I am receiving only the wordless echoes of old happenings". And I thought of my first visit to the illustrated corridor. I knew just what she meant.

Completion day came, as even the furthest and most isolated dates in a diary's crisp back pages have a way of doing. By then those pages were filled up with names, numbers and times, of packers, of movers, of carpet cleaners—and one, in red, for a "last-call" van, specially ordered by Charles, who had moved house many times. When the final pantechnicon had slammed its gates and headed for Suffolk, this carried what remained: our immediate life-support system of kettle, groceries and liquor, a step-ladder, two lamps, Henry's toy-box, the portable television, work-in-progress from my studio, and an urn, overlooked in the garden shrubbery. Then the carpet steamers moved in, and we left.

But between the time when the new London building firm took over Noone and our going to live there, there came a moment when I deliberately challenged its huge past—or tried to. I suppose I wanted to make it accept the new era: my dominion, at least, as Charles, his men and machinery had dominated the house itself. Me, I had to go back to the willow alley alone.

It was six months. I'd been several times with Henry, and once with Charles, who wanted to replace the aspen poplars with formal cypresses and create a paved vista; I'd been there with the psychic research students to show them the other way to the lake, the steep way: quite precipitous in parts—and this had always been an excuse for keeping Henry away from it. Three days before the move, the packers were already busy in St John's Wood; so, to escape them, I drove down to Suffolk with Charles. Next time, we'd be sleeping there: a silly moment to choose, maybe, for what had accumulated into an "ordeal"; the sun was coming out, and that would help. On the way, I chattered a lot about practical things, but I knew this was only to divert myself; underneath I had decided to do it.

Charles needed an hour or so to check the rooms that were being rewired as our makeshift living quarters, and show his new "co-ordinator" the plans on site; I did not need to rush at it. I went off to the greenhouse to pot the winter bulbs I had brought with me. During the summer I had discovered a stack of good old bowls stored away under the staging there, and so disguised by grime and cobwebs as to have escaped the auctioneers' eye. As I worked, washing them off under the standpipe, lining them with pottery shards and filling them with peat from my bright new sack, I decided I no longer felt I was cheating the heirs of their rights in accepting this treasure trove.

But the dead nephew himself, the "strong contender", lingered in my thoughts. This Blue Doulton I was planting with two layers of crocuses: might it have been a favourite of his, always there on the hall table when he came home for the holidays . . . ? Then I saw he had mingled in my vague imaginings with Henry a few years hence; and told myself sharply that the "patina of devotion" was nonsense as far as pottery was concerned: far more likely that I was freeing the rich lustre from a generation or more of disuse; that the dead schoolboy had never set eyes on it. Anyway it was mine now: *I* was the heir.

Only one creature from Noone's past had challenged my heritage and, in the past weeks, encroached more and more upon my thoughts. Both waking and sleeping; twice now I had dreamed of him. The first time, simply a figure, a guest among others, in the great hall after one of Charles's conducted tours; and when I asked Charles who he was, he replied, "Some old retainer I guess: just crawled out of the woodwork." Nanny (who had never been to Noone, but was busy setting out paper cups—which we never use) said: "No manners, keeping his hat on at a burial service!" And I realised everyone was in black, and there was solemn music. Charles was saying, "Why not?—poor bugger: it's his funeral"—and laughed loudly, and I woke up.

The second time was only two nights ago, and prompted, no doubt, by my determination to revisit the scene of my encounter. This time, I saw Henry beside the ruined summerhouse, talking to someone hidden by the wistaria. Then suddenly I *was* Henry, and looking up at him: pale grey eyes under the dark hat, very close to me. I was afraid, and trying to be brave; and then he smiled and held out his black-gloved hand to me—and I woke up, shivering.

I knew he had not spoken; but also knew that I, Kate, was "his": he had told me so. What he meant by "his" I did not know; and I hastily dismissed it as a schoolgirlish whimsy: the sort of romantic escapism, Love Tinged With Fear, in the tradition of all those heroines "claimed" by dashing villains—whether they were brigand chiefs or pitiless sheikhs or lithe cat-burglars.

It amused me that I was—subconsciously—so oddly fixated on this ghost-vandal; and I realised that I thought of him far more often nowadays than of Leo Constantine . . . Deliberately I pressed down the last layer of damp fibre, brushed off my hands, and set out for the poplar alley.

On the other side of the stiff, peeling door, the low sun was suddenly blinding: almost due west as it neared the equinox, splintering through giant cow-parsley directly into my eyes along the pathway. I

shaded them and stared ahead. There was
no one in sight. The alley was just a green
tunnel now, after a summer of hot sun,
and heavy rains at the end of August; the
arching briars were brilliant with rose
hips, and the brambles bore the largest
blackberries I had ever seen. A magpie
took flight from the top of the high wall,
'one for sorrow"; but of my black-and-
white ghost there was no sign. I waited a
little, standing very still, feeling foolish
after psyching myself up for a confrontation; then I picked some blackberries
into a big dockleaf and turned back. At
least I had done it. "Tell them I came, and
nobody answered . . ."

There was a sort of revelation, however.
Standing there alone, it was the first time
the truth of living there, of *being* there,
permanently and continuously, had hit me:
a moment comparable with the realisation
that "all this is mine", in that same alley
way back in April when I picked the damp
young narcissi, *my* narcissi—but comparable only so far as (for example) knowing
that you are hooked on someone compares
with the awful certainty that you will be

spending your one life with them. It was solemn; frightening, even . . .

Come on, I said to myself: it's only a house. But I knew it wasn't.

Zee had been spot-on in her dire predictions about living with builders. Cook gave notice after three days; Nanny went into a depression, knitting fiercely and watching endless television—previously so despised —in her room, between bursts of fighting back the plaster-dust; and Charles could not take it at all. Soon he was spending more nights in his Barbican flat than at Noone. I could see this made sense: the "co-ordinator" he had taken on, one Brian Bostock, was highly trained, highly paid, and far more powerful than any site foreman; no part of Jaggi's, the building firm, but accepted by them as Mr. Gelhorn's right hand, looking after his interests and taking the pressure off him.

"And there's one helluva backlog of work I've got to deal with, Katy: I've been messing around with Noone long enough. Brian's just the ticket—worth every penny: you'll see. He knows my ways, and he won't bother you folk one bit:

answerable only to me. He knows the plans backwards: he's even rejigged the whole schedule for the weather situation, and . . . Hell, why keep a dog and bark? There's nothing here for me, honey—except Henry of course—and the pleasure of your company . . . But life must go on, and other projects are priority now."

I could see it made sense, but I did not much like it. OK, so I was a "classy Britisher"—as Zee had pointed out—and had coped with more exacting briefs than keeping Henry from danger, Nanny from leaving, and some sort of order in the midst of the desolate building-site that was Noone. I could not paint yet, but I had the satisfaction of overseeing my barn's slow, steady progress. In the house, it was almost impossible to escape from noise and dirt and the all-pervading grit; but our rooms in the nursery wing were cleaned by our Mrs. Furze, and she cooked us a sustaining lunch every day. Having lived through Asian flu, and an abortion, virtually alone in the Black Mountains, I knew about survival; yet I was unhappy, hard-done-by—and jealous.

This is what it felt like, anyway. Not

only had my husband left me holding the "baby"—his, all messy and disfigured—but he had effectively isolated me from London and jollity and such friends as I had. He knew very well that Nanny would not stand for nights alone at Noone: however he chose to ignore what had happened in the summer, local gossip—via Mrs. Furze—kept it alive; and I had heard Nanny lock her and Henry's door each night.

It may not have been a deliberate move on Charles's part to rusticate me. But I was aware that he had embarked on a new affair; and I suspected it was something big: he had been less interested in sex recently. However routine it had become after six years, I missed it; and such abstinence in Charles meant someone new; it always had. Before, I'd managed to convince myself I did not mind: I had other things in life—and, at best, it was a poor shadow of Leo's brand. Nor did I have the right to be jealous: this was a marriage of convenience . . . Now, suddenly, I felt it threatened. And I wondered if the "Principessa" had come back into his life.

I believe he met her in Milan the previous spring—more likely than Houston—but it was Bob Nassau, I knew, who had given him her address: I had heard them joking about it at Sam and Zee's party in the summer. "Don't fret, Katy dearest: you'll meet up with her soon enough," said Zee; "she always likes to come over to London for the Fall."

Maybe I felt it was unfair that I should be shut away in the country, in my dirty tracksuit, keeping the family spirits up, instead of—as in the course of previous affairs—meeting, mingling with, and sometimes very satisfactorily outfacing, the opposition; confident in my budding career, my couture clothes, my mini-title, and universal acceptance that I had produced an enchanting son for Charles. Or was it that I suspected the mysterious Principessa, with a trump over each of my aces (including, Zee told me with relish, an elegant little daughter of seven), might be playing for higher stakes than I was used to? Might clean me out of all I owned, and take my place?—though Noone Ampney Hall would be complete,

clean, magnificent and comfortable before
that, I'd wager . . .

But I must keep smiling through
"We'll be fine," I said. "And you can see
Henry's loving every minute, now that I've
persuaded Nanny not to try so hard to
keep him clean. Oh, don't worry: *she*
won't leave—far too firmly hooked on her
little prince—and quite convinced I'd
neglect him, let him catch cold. I'll find
her little jobs to do that aren't too menial.
As for Cook—I think this woman from the
village may be better under present
conditions; we don't need *haute cuisine*
just big, hot meals."

"She sure is one plain cook, I'll give you
that," said Charles. "And you'll cater
weekends, will you?"

"It makes sense, surely? If you can take
it. That little stove and the gas ring
couldn't cope with large numbers, of
course; but I don't suppose you'll be
bringing too many people down just
now, will you? I mean, you'll have to get
proper caterers, darling, if you're going
to throw your 'Pull-Up-A-Packing-case
party."

"Forget that one," he said, zipping up

his bag. He checked his watch and patted me on the shoulder. "You're doing a great job here, honey—but no way am I going to bring my buddies down to this tip at this moment in time. Life-enhancing it is surely not—Jesus, just look at it!"— gazing round as we crunched our way across the cavernous hall. "Come Christmas—or spring, maybe . . . Sure you'll be OK? Barn making progress? Must see it some time . . . Well, gotta get rollin'! This breakfast meeting's a tall order, but what the heck? I gave it—so. At least the roads'll be clear. Be back— oh, Friday? With luck. Talk to you before then."

It was six-thirty; and dark and cold, standing at the front door, watching him drive off. I made tea on the gas ring in the pantry, took it up to the old nursery we used as a living room, and watched the sun come up over the estuary. Soon the builders would arrive. Nanny and Henry were still asleep. So Noone was mine. Cluttered, dirty and cold; but beautiful in its way, and all mine. That was something —though maybe not for long.

Meanwhile, apart from the runs of new

wiring, and the replacement of musty old
curtains with makeshift calico, the rooms
we used were untouched; and so it would
remain until the final phase. Being so
much later in the year than originally
planned, Brian Bostock was concentrating
his workforce on roofs, guttering and
damp-proofing; aiming to make the place
watertight before the weather turned
nasty. Inside, the plumbers were running
pipes through corridors and up to the
other floors behind the wooden shutter
cases of the windows. We were fairly
untroubled in the nursery wing, apart
from a day of laying copper pipes under
the floorboards of the passage. All the rest
could wait until the main bedroom suites
were complete: heated, carpeted, decor
ated and furnished. Then we would
decamp; and our old rooms, together with
the nursery itself and the scrapbook
corridor, must be torn apart.

I tried to see this stay of execution, and
the Indian summer of those first weeks at
Noone, as a golden time, to be treasured.
I had no real duties as such, except to keep
up morale. Such little cleaning as was
possible was cornered by Mrs. Furze from

the village, our plain cook and maid-of-all-work: she even took the washing home with her—except for Henry's clothes, kept back as therapy for Nanny. I was free to oversee the decoration of my barn; and the official switching on of its own small heating unit so inspired Nanny with a vision of progress and order that she took on the stitching of the curtains for my new windows. When the weather broke in October, it was a haven for us: warm and clean, and ready for furnishing.

"Gives you hope, madam. When you look round and think: In time the Big House will be all like this."

"Well, yes, Nanny. Not quite, of course: much grander, I mean. This is very plain, you see."

"But it will come to pass, madam—and the grander the better for my little princeling . . ."

While I thought: When they start on the nursery wing, maybe I'll sleep down here —if Charles is still away so much . . . But probably Nanny wouldn't like being on her own up there with Henry; I had heard Mrs. Furze asking her if the building works were going ahead all right now after "all that trouble in the summer".

"That bit of hassle in the summer", as the cause of delay and the present necessity for speed, was, in fact, the only reference to our intruder Charles made. So I did not say anything to him when I first began to suspect the hauntings were not entirely over. Charles would have seen it as "nutty": I did not want that. It was only by being there all the time, and being very alert, alone at night, to noises, draughts, doors left open where no one had been that evening, that I became aware of it. One night I was woken by the distant jangle of a bell, and I thought sleepily: I'm not answering that; it's far too late. Then I thought: But we haven't got a bell . . . It didn't ring again, and I fell asleep. Not until the workmen were going next day did this come back to me; I said to one of them in passing: "So we have a bell now."

I don't think he heard me properly. He said, "Bell, Mrs. Gelhorn? Oh, that won't be for a while yet: the electricians are starting at the back, you know, for the boiler room, new kitchen and so on. This here hall area won't be on the ring-main till later. But they could maybe fix you up something temporary, with a battery, like."

"Oh, no," I said: "the knocker's fine . . . But those bells in the—the boiler room—"

"Them old-fashioned ones? All ripped out. Getting 'em gilded, Mr. Bostock says. Very ornamental. Could hang 'em up on the Christmas tree, eh?"

So there had not been a bell. I must have dreamt it. But what about the light in the far wing? That was the week before. It certainly hadn't been on when I looked across from my bedroom, pulling back the curtains before going to sleep; yet I woke in the night, saw it—and didn't have the nerve to investigate. Then there was the packet of nightlights missing from the pantry . . . Little things, and all were either fanciful, or explicable with workmen around: not worth mentioning. There was no vandalism. The work on the roof, the heating and wiring were going ahead according to plan. I caught myself thinking: Clearly he approves of all that; how sensible. But what about when they start on the nursery wing?

At the speed they were going, all the various carefully orchestrated groups, it would not be long now. Already the decorators had arrived. The dining room—furthest ahead, for it would be our next living room—was to be papered with a sort of tapestry in shades of a colour that Don, the designer, called "Regency Cyclamen"; and the lobby leading to it was painted the same, but skilfully graded from a pale pinky-mauve up to deepest purple, above which the cornices were picked out in gilt; "Airbrush technique," said Don unveiling it. "Pity the boss won't see it till he gets back; but I think he'll be pleased."

I couldn't quite believe my eyes; and I did not go back to make sure—until Henry burst into my room early on Saturday morning. "Did Daddy come back late? Oh . . . Then who painted the funny black mountains on that fadey wall?"

By the light of the builders' powerful lamp, they were clearly scorches: a wavering line of sooty candle-smoke—quite deliberate, with the flame held close enough to the fresh satin-finish to bubble it in places. I was trying to scrub the marks off when Charles walked in.

He was angry, and it broke over me. He knocked the bowl of water out of my hand. "For Christ's sake, woman! You're only making it worse—I'll do it . . ."

He spent most of Saturday laboriously re-spraying it.

"Aren't you going to tell the police?" I asked, watching him mixing up shades of purple while lunch got cold; Henry and Nanny were into their pudding.

"No," he said. "Let's keep this one strictly between ourselves, OK? And above all I don't want the painters and decorators to know. It's an isolated incident. Not worth rocking the boat." He did not look round. "And if you think the vandal is back wandering about at night and it makes you nervous, just lock your door . . . OK: I'm sorry if I shouted at you. But *you* knew I'd designed a landscape here . . . ? Come *on*, you must have heard me talking about it. Yes, a range of mountains—what else?" He stirred silently, preoccupied. Then: "I'll fix this —don't worry. It's really pretty harmless stuff, and I don't reckon it'll happen again

—do you, Kate? Look: if you're really nervous here without me, I'll get Brian, or the foreman, to sleep on site."

"No need," I said. "Don't do that: it might start people talking about jinxes again."

"Are you sure, honey?" He stopped mixing and looked round at me. Perhaps I had been too emphatic—I should at least have been seen to consider it. "Is this some twisted, British, determined-to-stand-alone-type stuff? Come on: *I* might be a bit jumpy if *you* weren't here."

I thought: *You* come on, Charlie boy; if I weren't here some new girlfriend would be—and smuggled out in the morning back to her hotel before Nanny started bumbling about . . . But I said, "Nothing twisted. I just don't find this place scary at all. And maybe our being around is deterrent enough: as you say, this is kids' stuff beside the earlier sabotage . . . Anyway, they wouldn't harm *us*."

He was still watching me. He smiled. "I guess not. OK: please yourself."

I was emphatic because, of course, I had considered it. There'd been lots of time to,

224

during the last two weeks, with Charles in London, and Nanny and Henry sleeping the sleep of the innocent, behind locked doors; time to conclude that I was not the only one awake in Noone Rectory. I wasn't afraid, because I had decided—No: I had realised—the house was haunted. Why should I fear *him*? It was his old home, and he had returned. I admit that discovering the candle scorches came as something of a shock to me; but then, I had not liked the new colour-scheme either. As so often before, he and I were in sympathy. Had he not "blessed" my barn?

It was rather unnerving, however, to think how much he must know about us. If this spirit were not simply some sort of visible echo, bound to certain paths, then my interpretation might not be so far from the mark, attributing him with new thoughts and feelings. How else could he have disrupted our lives so effectively?

I began to accept that he might be observing us constantly, only appearing when he wished to: three or four times to the workmen, and once to me. And we had all seen the same figure: no mere coincidence, surely? Did he watch me watching late-night television alone? Could he walk through Henry's wall and watch him sleeping? Could he harm us? What sort of a man had he been? I wondered. Might it be some guilty deed, some dark unfinished business, that brought him back from the grave?

He knew all too much about us; we knew next to nothing of him.

According to local gossip, filtered through Philip, the spectral walker was the guardian of Noone, a kindly ghost—but I could not forget that he had nearly killed harmless workmen, as well as my not-so-harmless husband, on the morning of the staircase, the scaffolding, the fire. I re-read the brief history provided by the late incumbent (the last vicar, as he had been the first, with the same name: full circle) and how, in his lifetime, our ghost had saved Noone and his seven children from insolvency by co-opting the Mother Church as a business partner. That was the only mention of him.

Then I remembered that a Mr. Glyn-Jones, whom we met at a summer garden party, had told me how the elder brother

Sir Henry Dodsworth, had built an even grander house in Hertfordshire; but that his son had gambled away his inheritance, and *his* sons emigrated to Canada and Australia. That house passed through many hands, he said: in this century it had been a smart prep school, then an officers' billet, and was now divided up into rather expensive retirement flats, with a resident matron. It was still called Dodsworth Hall; and I telephoned impulsively to see if they had any family papers. The caretaker put me on to the matron, and with both I drew a blank.

Next I rang the Ship in Ipswich, hoping they could tell me the name of the auctioneers who had sold the contents of Noone. Mr. Knott-Brown Senior would be my man, I was told, and I ran him to earth that evening, fresh and expansive from a day's golfing. I asked him if he remembered who bought the contents of the Noone library, other than the desk in which our ledger had been found. Several dealers were involved, he said, as the books were sold in separate lots; but a job lot of "damaged" books and mixed papers had, as he knew without reference to his files, been bought up by a local Ipswich junk dealer (his description). He recommended a personal visit: Mr. Flynn was notoriously uncertain about the contents of his shed.

Following directions, and losing my way only once, I found Mr. Flynn in his back-street lockup, among second-hand television sets and sad fur coats, tending three kittens. These, like the rest of his stock, were somewhat past their prime for home-finding: three leggy, obstreperous teen-agers.

"The muvver's gorn," he said mournfully; "and I for one don't blame her . . Papers, you say . . . At some old rectory: Books? I remember'm—and they've gorn too. There's that box, though, miss—that's wot she *had* 'em in: papers—old newspapers and such. Not worth much now . . ."

I recognised the late Reverend Dodsworth's Italianate hand as soon as I got the box into the light; and Mr. Flynn was quick to sniff an interested party.

"Not as I likes parting wiv old papers, miss: never know what's vallibble til they've bin gorn through proper . . . Any road, them kitties'd miss 'em now . . . Oh, no, miss: fresh newspapers'd *smell* all wrong . . . Till I can find homes for the little beggars I can't rightly see my way to—"

"Look, I'll take two of the kittens," I said. "You keep that big one to scare off the mice, OK? And then I can have the box of papers. Ten pounds?"

"For the papers," he said cautiously. "Wot about the kitties then? Half-Persian those are, I'll have you know . . ."

"Which half?" said Charles with distaste when he got home next day. "How much did he pay you to take them off his hands?"

"I paid him; twenty pounds, actually. He had some old stuff from the Reverend Dodsworth's library that looked interesting; and these little angels were using it as a bed."

"Just keep them out of my sight, OK. . . ? You're *mad*, Katy! Way out of sight—You knew I wanted to get some real classy cats once we'd settled in—something with a pedigree, for Chrissake—but you go off on a wild-goose chase into the skid row of Ipswich and bring back some smelly old papers covered in cat-shit—"

"Just hair, as a matter of fact. And a lot of tooth-marks of course—"

"—And two mangy, bat-eared delinquents—though with this goddam house in shit order anyway, I guess they'll be right at home eh? But listen, and listen good: when I get Donny laying the new carpets and putting up those brocade curtains in here and all around, no way will your stinking moggs—"

"Hush, Charles: Henry. And he thinks they're great. I'm only sorry you don't—"

"Hey, Hen—what's cookin'? Did you know you had a real flaky lady for a mom, Hen me lad? That's right: a regular nutflake. Lucky you take after your good old pop, eh? That's my boy . . . And, Kate, mind you burn those junk papers: Christ knows what diseases they could be spreading around."

"It's all right: I'll keep them in my barn until I've sorted out what I want to save."

"Just keep Henry out of it—and if you get sick, don't come crying to me, OK? What you do down in your goddam barn is your business—maybe your precious Philip's business as well, for all I know—"

"Or care—"

But he was steamrollering on: "And as for that—my buddies have gotten quite a kick out of your little 'restoration' project, and all these 'little men' and plumbers and so forth that can only come on weekday evenings . . . ! That just slays 'em!" He laughed weakly at the memory and wiped his eyes. "Jeez—I guess flaky little ladies are good for a whole load of laughs, eh, Hen . . . ? No, honey: you're doing a great job . . . and if twenty quid on two stinking lousy cats and a box of rubbish keeps you happy, it's a bargain at the price. Now if all the ladies were that easy to please . . ."

It was Sunday morning a week later. I woke to a shout from Charles in his make-shift dressing room down the corridor: "Kate! What the hell is going *on*?"

On the chest of drawers lay his own private "artist's impressions" of the Gelhorn Gallery in the nursery wing, which he'd been working on the evening before. Across the drawings from corner to corner, cancelling them out, a thick red X had been scrawled.

Charles was trying to wipe it off; but it was obviously lipstick—a dark, greasy blood-red—and only smeared across the paper. He dropped the drawings and rounded on me—then snatched my hands and turned them palms up.

"Had a good wash then, dear? Little walkabout in the wee small hours, was it?"

It took me a moment before I caught up with him. And then I saw that the candle scorches in his precious lobby had been part of it.

"You think I've been sleepwalking?" I said slowly.

"You never sleepwalked in your *life* . . . ," he hissed, throwing my hands down like a gauntlet. "You're a pretty flaky little lady, Kate, but this is the limit. You don't like what I'm doing here—do you? Never have: admit it. And now you're busy taking up where our absent vandal left off, right? *Right?*" he pushed his bristly face up to mine, livid and shouting.

Anger—any loss of control—is so repellent to me that it makes me quite cold:

ust a reaction, like an unfortunate allergy. Even the alien lipstick did not move me. I wished I could shout back, let rip, see red—instead of that cool, clear appraisal of his gold back fillings and quivering uvula. I could see just as clearly that if I convinced him it wasn't my doing, the armed guards would be back, the hunt would be on. Charles would not understand about the Noone Walker: that we had to find a way of sharing Noone with it.

I said, "But, darling, it's not even my lipstick."

"What? That's totally irrelevant, for Chrissake! Who else could have—?"

"Well, it's highly relevant to me. Does your new girlfriend use that shade? Or was it left in your briefcase by the one before last?"

"That is not the . . . Ha! So how come *you knew* it was in the briefcase, unless . . . ?"

Only an assumption; and I said so: there were the drawings, here was the open briefcase. Going over to it, I could see the small gold missile glinting among the papers. So what was new? Charles was a

tidy man and tended to pick up these
things left lying around in the Barbican
flat . . .

"—Which only makes it *doubly*
malicious of you, Kate: admit it—
psychotic, even."

I said, "Look, if you suspect me, it
would be better if I moved down to the
barn." It wasn't the answer; but I needed
time: time to think, and to let him calm
down. "It might be a good idea anyway
the way things are."

I went and got dressed. I could see
Henry playing in the back yard and Nanny
standing over him: they hadn't heard any
of it. I gathered up some clothes and a
duvet, and carried them down the hill
then came back for a single mattress
proper furniture could wait: I'd need help
with that.

The shock of that accusation still stung
like a slap on the face. It came as a
surprise that, in Charles's book, I was
vicious, or mad, or both. "Flaky" I was
used to: this was different. It occurred to
me this might be the thin end of the wedge
if he considered junking me for a new
model; and my mind raced ahead: does the

divorced wife automatically keep the house? Not if she's certifiable . . .

Trudging and breathing in the cold morning air, my head cleared a little. I decided I didn't care: he could prove nothing, yet. Maybe it was better this way, if somewhat bizarre—to act as a scapegoat for my eighteenth-century parson.

And it could only have been deliberate, using that lipstick to deface Charles's precious drawings and discomfit him thoroughly. Nice one, I thought; and found myself smiling.

10

CHARLES was busy cooking breakfast for himself and Henry when I came in.

"But why's Mummy moving her bedclothes?"

"She wants to camp in the barn and see what it's like."

"I want to camp in the barn *too*!"

"No, Hen old son: I need you here."

"But you're always *away*—"

"*Especially* when I'm away: you and Nanny and Brian—you know Brian—you're going to be my official nightwatchmen, OK?"

"With brassières and hot chestnuts and all that?"

"That's one great idea: we'll have chestnuts on the open fire this very evening."

Next morning early I heard Charles driving off. I'd slept well in my barn. I went up to the house, drank my tea by the glare of a red sunrise, and contemplated the emptiness of my gesture. Charles had clearly written it off as a "married tiff". I could tell the lipstick episode had put his nose out of joint when, after supper, he turned magnanimous and forgiving to his "nut-flake baby"; but I put on my boots, got my torch and strode off into the night. He shouted, "*Be* like that! Huh! I should worry . . . !" It all felt rather petty.

What had I achieved, if Bostock or someone was being detailed to guard the house? I found Charles's note to him and pocketed it; then rang the London office later and said I would move back, and I really didn't think there'd be more trouble. Charles was preoccupied. "Up to you, honestly, honey—looks like I may not be able to get back at all next weekend . . ." Bugger him, I thought as I rang off. Weekday affairs were one thing —but this was getting too heavy for comfort. I nearly rang up Zee to find out if the famous Principessa were still in London, but decided it was unwise: the grapevine would go into overdrive. I would wait: there was a party at the Nassaus' London house in ten days. Even if I did not meet her, I would learn more by listening than by asking: in their cups, Charles's buddies could be very confiding; and their wives would give me several good reasons why he had to be in town, and point out how tired he was looking . . .

As it turned out, Charles came back with a rush on Thursday, thanks to the wallpaper crisis.

Work had progressed rapidly; already two of the main bedroom suites were altered, plastered, equipped with gas-log fires, marble-lined bathrooms, and dressing rooms with walk-in cupboards. The lovely, faded Chinese paper in the master bedroom would be supplanted: something "very Jacobean", Bostock told me, had arrived from Coles and was waiting—still shrouded in a bulky parcel —to be put up. But when the packaging was opened, early on Thursday morning, and the new rolls of paper stripped of their polythene wraps and spread out, they sprung apart into a useless multitude of short pieces, and lay, like so many unstrung corn-stooks, all over the bedroom floor. Every single roll had been sliced through with a sharp blade, right to the centre of the tight coil, then carefully replaced in its polythene sheath; and I could see, with hindsight, that the two layers of wrapping had been opened and resealed with fresh, slightly narrower, tape. I did not point this out.

Two of the dismembered rolls were laid out on the refectory table when Charles arrived. He greeted no one; examined the paper silently.

"Can you beat that?" he said. "Sabotaged at the factory! Just my luck . . . ," and telephoned Coles. Brian Bostock was trying to tell him he'd phoned already, that they said something about the replacement being already on the way: "Didn't quite seem to take in that this lot was ruined—or maybe there'd been a rush of complaints . . ." But Charles was shouting down the phone.

"No: I want the manager himself!—No: this *is* Mr. Gelhorn!—Christ . . ."

I went off and busied myself with Mrs. Furze in creating a lunch out of assorted scraps and tins: I was far too intrigued by this destructive master-stroke to miss the outcome by going to the shops.

Charles marched in. "They keep saying

the new paper we ordered by letter will arrive today or tomorrow—and something screwy about feeling certain that, as I said in the note via my secretary, the 'hand-blocked Chinese design will be far more fitting for the room as described'; and that fortunately they 'always keep a small supply for special customers'. Kate, if this is your idea of a—"

"Thank you, Mrs. Furze," I said: "I think that will be all for now . . . Charles, do be reasonable: it's really—no—no, I'm *not* laughing—but it's all so—so way out . . . ! Charles, I *wouldn't*. And I couldn't, in my sleep, could I? Cut those rolls like that?"

"I reckon you're schizo, Kate: mad folks have access to unusual strength, you know."

"But the ingenuity . . . ! I wouldn't even *begin*—"

"Look: just don't keep on about it, OK? And I'll try to stay calm, and cope. I'm sticking to the story that this was done at the factory, for Bostock and the men. Coles say they've had no other complaints, but who needs to know? I mean, I've got to cover for you somehow. And I will—for all our sakes. But I'm getting them to send back my—quote—secretary's note. Then we'll talk, Kate. Things have gotten out of hand ... Reckon you're ripe for the funny farm: flaky ladies with sharp knives can't just run loose, you know. Not with kids around."

The comparative quietness of this accusation chilled me; and, for a moment, I actually wondered if I might have done it —and the smoky mountains—and the lipstick cross through his precious sketches. I could see motive, ample opportunity, a lack of convincing alibis—and also a peculiarly well-informed malice— behind each act of destruction.

Only for a moment. Then I remembered I simply was not like that. I might not approve of what Charles was doing to Noone; but I was still a good, responsible and grateful wife to him, and wanted him to be happy. From the start, I had accepted that the nursery wing must go, just as the hall had done: I had never objected. The same with the master bedroom: I could survive the lumpen Jacobean-style wallpaper—I was a tough

Brit, wasn't I . . . ? But Charles couldn't see this: he did not really know me, after all. Now, living in London, he could have no idea just what I was putting up with—though he'd decided very rapidly it was not for him. He was more out of touch than ever.

Later that day I tried to explain this. I heard the workmen leave, and came up from my barn. Henry would be watching television; and I had been sufficiently shaken by my momentary self-doubts to want to sort things out.

I actually needed reassurance. Sitting sewing at my cushion covers, and trying to anticipate his case against me, the phrase "attention-seeking device" kept nagging at me—even though I knew he would not have the gall to use it. If I was the neglected wife unconsciously creating situations that would bring my straying husband home to me, he would not be the one to suggest such a motive. And I knew, deep down, I did not really want his attention as such; Noone was easier without him, on the whole; allowing me, moreover, the time and privacy to piece together what little I could of my earlier, and far more appealing, Master of Noone ... But I wanted a reason—even more than a reward—for keeping these home fires burning: my sojourn in the Welsh hills had taught me that much. I needed some assurance of security. I was even prepared to tell him of my conviction that the Noone Walker had returned, and all the odd things that proved it ... But not until I could see Charles was taking me seriously. Otherwise it would be "Well of course that's your story, honey, and I guess you're sticking to it ..." As things turned out, we did not get that far. Charles was already preparing to go out.

"Looking in at Adrian Pearce's to talk about his loft—and dine, I guess: he's got some buddies up from London."

"Was I invited?" I asked.

"I told him you were too tired," he said, sorting through the papers in his briefcase.

"It's not fair to punish me for something I didn't do. You should know me well enough to see this vandalism just isn't my style, Charles—but I feel we've got out of touch, don't you ... ? Charles?"

"So who says I want to be in touch with someone so sick and kinky-minded?"

"Now, see here—"

"See where? No, thanks: we'll talk when I've had a good look at this famous note that Coles are on about. Right now I'm off to greener pastures: this dump is getting me right down."

"And what d'you imagine it's doing for—?"

But the engine drowned me out; and he had gone.

The mysterious note arrived, with a compliment slip, by post next morning, and later the wallpaper was delivered: a reproduction of the Chinese tree-of-life that had been stripped off. By then we knew it would be: a tattered fragment of the original was pinned to the offending letter.

Below, on stiff, yellowed stationery headed *Noone Ampney Rectory, Suffolk*, was one paragraph of spiky black handwriting. Regrettably—it said—the consignment as delivered had been damaged (deliberately ambiguous?); and in the interim, Mr. Gelhorn had decided to restore the original design. There followed a brief description of the master bedroom:

then: "Mr. Gelhorn believes the fragment enclosed to be one of your old stock, and that you still carry it. He regrets any inconvenience caused, and will be happy to defray the added costs, if necessary, of a small reprinting." He remained, etc., p.p. Charles Gelhorn Esquire. Gazing down at the ghost's angular, sprawling, illegible signature, I think I began to love him then.

Charles had handed it to me silently across the breakfast table. I knew I was under close surveillance, and his suspicion sobered me enough to prevent me smiling as I read. I handed it back.

"Quite a little work of art," he said, still watching.

"'A reg'lar Tin'eretto,'" I answered: "but not mine."

"Where did you find the paper?"

"There was some left in one of the library shelves when we first came, you remember: you pointed it out to me. I don't know where it went. Maybe the workmen took it—but it wasn't there when I cleaned up after the night-watchmen."

"And I wouldn't find any in your barn, I guess."

"Come and search," I said, "if you're prepared to brave the disease-ridden papers I've got laid out down there."

Henry looked up from the free-gift plastic dinosaur wading through his muesli.

"If you got any fleas down there, Mum, I want to try and train them—OK? Julie Andrews and Katisha are quite vacant, you see—all sprayed out."

"Praise be for small mercies!" said Charles, dumping his newspaper and getting up. "I'm going to see the builders. I'll talk to you later, Kate."

"Down at the barn?"

"No way! Gotta be here to see that wallpaper . . . Then I'll be packing up to go back. Give you a shout before I go."

When he called me, he already had his suitcase out by the car.

"I'll be off now, Kate," he said. "Just wanted to tell you I reversed the order with Coles. I'm taking that Chinese stuff back with me now, and I'll make good and certain a new batch of the vandalised paper comes up with Jaggi's men on Monday, so's they can start. It's only delayed us a couple days: no sweat—hardly worth all that goddam 'ingenuity', eh?" He grinned knowingly, and chucked me under the chin.

"Look, Charles—"

"Not now, honey: it's all taken a whole lot longer than I reckoned on. Back to the bread-winning, OK? Another day, another —*No*, Kate—for Chrissake! Just drop it! I know it all. *Sure* I've no proof—you're quite a bright little lady. Nutty, but crafty with it: no flies on you—So let's just give it a rest, right? Right. Now then, honey: I've got to go to Rome—did I tell you? Well, I'm booked already—towards the end of next week; and I might just grab me a break as well while I'm about it. I've had a lot on this past month. And all this muckup here—and the mess, the delays and so forth—naming no names . . . It's really been getting to me. I'm bushed."

"Poor old Charles," I said. He couldn't look me in the eye.

"Now, it'll take them a fortnight to get those three main suites fixed up—and locked up: I'm having no more hassles there. And they can get on with my study.

Then I'll be back to kick the shit out of that old nursery wing." That's when he looked at me. "But you'll be OK, won't you? Won't go doing anything silly . . . ? Because, vandal or no vandal, this house is going to be just like I want it come Christmas. You be good, play your cards right, and everything'll be just fine." He patted my bottom and got into the car. "Be back Wednesday I guess: not to stop; just to pick up some travelling gear—see the lad . . . And who knows? I could bring home some real lulus from Italy—fancy busts and urns and so forth. You'll like that."

I said: "Wait: what about the party? Next Thursday, isn't it?"

"I've gotten out of that, for the both of us, Kate: I'll be in Rome—and you wouldn't want to travel up and down just to drink with the old Nassaus and Zee and Co. now, would you?"

He came back, as promised, to pack; and I could tell, by the time he spent on it, and all the Jermyn Street carrier bags that the thrifty-minded Mrs. Furze rescued from the dustbin, that he had virtually refurbished his wardrobe, and was going all out to impress. One might almost jump to the conclusion that some female was involved—and more than a mere secretary, it would seem . . .

Alone once more, I ordered myself to forget it. He was with this Principessa creature, and I might as well face that fact, then put it out of my mind.

It would soon be dark, but I went over to the greenhouse to get some eating apples, and sort through the boxes we had just picked. Henry came to help, and wandered off; and I caught myself nibbling a hangnail off my grubby thumb and thinking: God! I'm a mess; how can I hope to compete with that sort of opposition? Self-pity came flooding in as I imagined a holiday in the sun: heat, and the clean, whitewashed hotel by the sea, and breakfast on the terrace in an elegant, short dressing-gown; browning my legs, and eating papaya; pouring Charles coffee, seducing him back to bed . . .

How *pathetic*! shouted the Free Woman in me, drowning out the sound of the surf and scaring off the flock of rainbow parakeets: So it all comes down to knowing

which side your bread is buttered! Do you
have to seduce your own husband in order
to keep yourself in the manner to which
you've grown accustomed? Women died to
get you the vote, and you—

But I'm only trying to keep my family
together! I shouted back.

"What's up, Mum?" Henry was in the
doorway. "What you staring at so
funnily?"

"Nothing, Our Hen; just thinking about
holidays and sun—silly old me . . ."

"Watch *Blue Peter* on telly with me? It's
making Advent calendars today, they said
—and you can draw better'n me, you see."

I'm Henry's mother, so I can't be
replaced, I thought, as we watched the
cheery, well-scrubbed girl cutting little
windows for the pictures to show through.
I thought of the sliced wallpaper. If, on
the other hand, Charles really believes I'm
ready for the funny farm, I could be
replaced overnight.

When Nanny announced bath-and-
bedtime, I went to work on my
"Dodsworth papers" in the barn: the
surest way I knew of diverting my circular
anxieties; for I had decided that I must

very deliberately, cope with this affair of Charles's like any other—as a passing fad. The stalled engine, the nosedive into depression, might be spectacular, might bring him hurrying home; but it would not help my cause. Instead, I must count and consolidate my blessings—and I was determined to clean myself up, get my hair done, dress to kill, and go to that party. Fly the flag—and not even a touch of ladylike white at the throat . . .

Many was the time, however, during the next three weeks (as it turned out to be) that I felt jealous and bitter. The foul weather closed down on us; the clocks were changed, bringing darkness at teatime. Henry grizzled that he could not play outside. Nanny retired to bed with a heavy cold and the portable television: there was no question of my going to London. And even among Jaggi's workforce of automata, morale seemed low.

They hadn't much liked the wallpaper incident, Brian Bostock told me, and were beginning to imagine things. I felt I had heard it all before.

"What sort of things?" I asked.

"Oh, little things, Mrs. Gelhorn. I believe they've been stopping in at the local public house after work these dark evenings and hearing silly gossip . . . But I talked with Mr. Gelhorn in Italy yesterday, and we're putting the incentive-bonus scheme into effect as from this week."

"Fine," I said. "Maybe they're just missing the bright lights. It must seem such a gloomy old house to them— especially in this miserable weather. But whatever the gossips may say, I'm certain they have nothing to fear."

I meant it, too; the Jinx was working in a new way: no longer the frontal attack endangering life and limb, but a silent almost secret, guerrilla warfare directed at Charles himself. The scorched mountains of his projected landscape, the invasion of his dressing room, and the use of his girl-friend's lipstick to deface his sketches; the sly destruction of his chosen wallpaper and then that letter, so swiftly effecting the delivery of the original design: so cunningly making a fool of him, knowing his weak spots, slipping in the blade where it hurt most; and even the manager of

252

Coles, with his warm approval of the saboteur's choice, rubbing salt into the wound . . . No, the workmen were not at risk.

Before I discovered his suspicions, I used to imagine what it must be like for Charles to have something still working against him, prowling round his house; I decided it was hardly surprising—even without the lady-friends in town—that he stayed away, waiting only for the workmen to finish and go, when proper security would be possible: the electronic eyes, the Dobermann pinschers. But I had to remind myself how very differently we saw things; and that the element I would find most upsetting in this skilful persecution might not have occurred to him: that the Jinx seemed to know him so well. Now, of course, I could see it was both more convenient and less disturbing for Charles to believe the Jinx was me.

For, once he accused me of "taking up where it had left off", it was clear that his case—when he put it—would be based on this apparently "special" information: the most inside of inside jobs. But the very fact that he had avoided any straight-talking, together with the dark view I now took of my future, convinced me that his "suspicions" were just a neat way of easing me out of his life: the thin end of a powerful wedge. In fact, I had no means of telling what Charles really believed. Meanwhile, however resentful I felt, I could see he was involved in a more dangerous game than he guessed; and it troubled me that, of his true adversary, my husband knew nothing—not even what I might have told him.

He wasn't interested: to Charles, conquering the house was paramount; the ghostly saboteur was just a good joke. And an alibi for his nutty wife. So there was no hope of compromise, of treating with the first Reverend Dodsworth, of halting the systematic destruction of Noone—or the Walker's vendetta.

Once I accepted this, I tried to see it quite simply as a contest (it amused me to do so, and I needed amusing): the drama of two magnificent obsessions locked together in combat; I, the impartial observer.

It seems so cold-hearted now.

There were no disruptions while Charles was away; not to the building work.

It was two days to his return, between four and five on a wet afternoon, that I went upstairs to summon Henry for tea. As a rule, we simply called from the bottom of the stairs; but he had been set the task of gathering up his playthings and sorting them into boxes, ready to be moved. I went to inspect.

From the head of the stairs I heard his chatter: one of his imaginary friends must be "helping"—they often did, and took the blame for slowing him down. I looked into the nursery to close the curtains, saw that Nanny had done them, and turned along the illustrated corridor, calling him. But the Noone Walker was there.

I stopped dead. The afterglow from a tawny sunset lay across the wide lobby; beyond, a rectangle of light through Henry's bedroom door. On the far side, some twenty feet from me in the gloom, stood the figure I had seen once, and imagined so often since. The white of its face, high stock and ecclesiastical bands stood out in the darkness like a skull and crossbones—or I might not have seen it at all. Then I thought: *Christ!* It's been at Henry . . .

There was only a sort of keening from his room.

"Henry? Henry . . . !" I cried, and ran a mile of corridor to his door. "Henry— are you—?"

He was flat on the floor, crooning to the trains from his worm's-eye view as he shunted them into their box. I stepped back into the passage, but of course there was no one there. I stared for a full minute into the darkness and saw nothing; walked forward a few paces to reach the light switch. No one.

"Did you hear, Mum? *And* the inky-pens *and* the crayons . . . ," Henry's sing-song ran on. "*And* the biros, *with* their tops on like Nanny said. So . . . so can I watch *Captain Caveman?* Mum?"

I did not want to go to the end and hunt round the rooms for it. I was cold with fright. I did not want to see it again.

Back in Henry's room I grabbed him up and hugged him.

"Hey, Mum, you knocked over the cattle-truck!"

"Are you all right?" I said. "Did anything—?"

"Not finished the trains quite," he said, slithering out of my arms; "but see: there's the crayons and there's the inky-pens and—"

"T'riffic!" I said: "haven't you done well? It's—it's teatime, darling: come quickly—now, with me."

Switching out the table lamp with a shaky hand, I saw the sprig of tiny white flowers lying by it. I didn't know we had an autumn prunus. I picked it up and took it with me.

"Where did you find this, Henry?"

"Um. Doddy was here. He picked it. He knows his way around, Doddy does . . ." He was busy not stepping on the cracks along the landing.

I steadied my voice carefully. "Come, on, Our Hen: where did you find it? I don't mind you picking it, darling. I'd like to get some more."

"Oh, somewhere in the wood, I'spect. *I* don't know, do I? You should've asked *him* . . . Nanny! I've done the biros like you said, *with* the tops on, *and* the inky pens *and* the crayons—so I *can* watch

257

Captain Caveman, dearest Nan? . . . You
know you love it—Oh yuk, Mum! . .
Nanny, why is Mummy putting Dad'
brandy in her cup of tea?"

I had been completely thrown by it. And
yet, until now, I was continually won
dering if I would see him again; hoping
might. Remembering him.

Among the old newspapers I found i
my kitten box—and the notes for sermons
estimates for repairs, plans for th
grounds, lists of plants, copies of ol
parish records (all dating from differen
periods), there was one special prize:
faded black-and-white photograph, four b
six, of the portrait I saw on the stairs tha
first day at Noone. It was little more tha
a patchy chiaroscuro, and looked a
though it had been taken years ago with
long exposure and a hand-held Bo
Brownie; but it was still my greatest find
and I put it between tissue paper and lai
it away. That very morning I had starte
a watercolour sketch from it—squaring u
to twice its size, and filling in the back
ground colour as I remembered it.

Now, even in a state of shock, it di

not take me long to work out that the last time I had encountered the ghost was immediately after seeing the original painting; and here was I in possession of the photograph, seeing him again. A simple case of projection, I told myself firmly as I patrolled the house, locking up.

It was no good. I knew I had not imagined it: this time I had proof—but I shied away from that. I would face that later . . . Meanwhile I just tried to think as clearly as possible about the encounter. I had wanted to see him again for so very long, it seemed, filling my imagination, and even the hollow that Leo had left. And suddenly he was there—only twenty feet away—in the illustrated corridor: black and white, stern and slender; the eyes intensely alive in the shadows, holding me breathless. My beloved ghost.

Why, then, was I so shaken? What is so peculiarly alarming about a second sighting? That awfulness of certainty? Was I happier with speculations? I think I'd built up the noonday visitation into a pretty fantasy, invented round the portrait. When the workmen talked of the black-and-white ghost, surely the image only took its shape from village gossip from a legend? Even when I decided I was "not the only one awake at Noone", it had been with a sort of adolescent frisson; did I really *believe* it? So many levels of belief . . . I think I had romanticised him into the Spirit of Noone.

Trying to be dispassionate about it that evening, alone, with a cup of coffee, and the television programme of my choice passing before my eyes, I could see myself as a lonely, jealous, and—OK—dissatisfied lady of nearly thirty-three, building a fantasy; founding it on my growing involvement with the house, and around the man who had loved it most. Loved it so much that he virtually handed his birthright to the Church in order to remain there. So much that he was back two centuries later to defend it from Charles Gelhorn. Naturally, I told myself, you would try to suppress a nonsense that played havoc with your loyalties—and especially if you were already regarded as more than a touch insane . . .

And so I spent the evening, twisting and turning to explain away what I had seen, preferring any alternative, even the convic tion that Charles was right after all: that I *was* mad. If I could have taken refuge in sleep . . . I envied them: Nanny and her cold had gone up when Henry did; both were quite untroubled.

But Henry was not mad.

That was the point. I watched the television screen fade to a spot, got up and switched it off. "You have to face it," I said out loud in the midnight silence: "You know he saw it too. It's his friend 'Doddy'."

That was the horror. The creature had approached him, and won his trust. I'd even heard Henry including him in his prayers, along with "Booterful" and "John Lewis" and the rest of the imaginary friends. And I thought of the things our monochrome visitor had done, with saws, with knives, with fire; thought what he might do. And forced myself to see it: wooing Henry was the real master-stroke, the crowning coup of this guerrilla war.

What a truly fearsome way to get at Charles.

Next day, "just for fun", we all three moved down to the barn.

Charles phoned from Paris to tell us he was returning by boat, and a day later than planned. "Don't come down: I've got a van meeting me. Must keep an eye on these things . . . Ah! You'll just have to wait and see, won't you?" He sounded ebullient. "Should be back with you mid-afternoon—and I'll need some of Jaggi's men to help."

"Can I tell him about sleeping in the barn?" said Henry, hammering at my arm.

I shook my head. "OK, Charles," I said; "and I'll hang on to them if you're running late. See you. Henry sends love . . . Sorry, Our Hen, but he was in his usual rush. Tell him when he gets back." I knew Charles would be put out to hear the house was empty at night. I'll cross that bridge when I come to it, I thought. Anyway, Charles sounded so high on his truckload of Italian booty—the Merchant Adventurer's Return—that I would have a breathing space.

We moved our things back from the barn on Friday morning, and Charles rolled up before sunset.

"No, honey: no tea now. Got to get these things unloaded. 'Ey there, 'Arry

262

boy! How's tricks? Come on and see what Daddy's been buying—"

"I've done my toys, Daddy: all of them —even the biros! And we slept in the barn and it was really neat—"

"Great, great—now take a look at *these*, son. Katy, come and see. Two urns—I got those first: don't know just where they'll go . . . Fine, Brian: a couple of trolleys, I guess, and four strong men, OK? But get a load o' these little beauties! Meet— da-*dah*! The Four Seasons!"

Four brand-new statues, six foot tall, Spring, Summer, Autumn and Winter: semi-clad nymphs in dark red composite marble. "For the top of the porch," he said, stroking them. "Copies, I'm told— but lush, right? Pricey little ladies, I can tell you."

To me, they looked like ornaments for a Mafia gambling den, crudely carved and garish. "Amazing, darling—" I said. "And they'll mellow very elegantly and fit in . . . But d'you really think over the porch, Charles?"

"Sure. Over the porch, honey. Hell, that's what I got them for—"

"Hey, Dad! Dad! There's a yellow crane coming up the drive!"

"Correct, son: gonna get them up there right now."

At six they were still working with the floodlights.

"Charles, why not finish the job tomorrow—or even Monday? What's the rush?"

"The rush, honeychile, is I want to see them up, OK? *In situ*—get it? *I* want to. And furthermore I phoned old Adrian, Adrian Pearce; phoned him from Paris— and that other guy—Hogan, that's right: the oyster guy—to drop round and see. Hogan, he's got a house party—but I said, 'Bring 'em all!'—OK? Surprise party? You used to like surprises—"

"And feed them, Charles?"

"Sure! I bought the food already: ordered and waiting at Harrods—picked it up on our way through. It's cool, honey: you haven't got to do a thing—maybe a bit of tidying around, tarting up the hall— and yourself while you're at it . . . Right, coming, Brian . . . See? They're good as up now: only one to go. We're just setting them there, OK? Nice and steady—and

264

we won't mess with concrete and such till Monday. But I've sweated over these dames, and I'm gonna get them up there —should be a full moon if it clears—and drink to the mothers, if it's the last thing I do."

Which it was.

We drank to them by the floodlights, ten of us, and went in to a magnificent picnic in the hastily swept hall. With the candles lit, you hardly saw the dust. It was all a bit unreal for me. Charles had drunk a great deal even before the guests arrived. He came into the pantry when I was getting some more ice and said, "Hey, Katy—how does the idea of divorce grab you? Reckon old Hen boy could handle two mothers? Think about it—OK?"

About ten o'clock, Charles announced the moon was up. "Gotta see 'em by moonlight, right? Charged glasses, folks— more brandy needed over here, Katy—and come on out when I call you—OK?"

I could see through the uncurtained windows that he was turning off the flood-lights. He shouted through the open door:

"Come on out, folks, and drink with me to the finest little—"

But it turned into a scream, and a loud crash—then silence.

I was the nearest the door and ran out. One of the statues had fallen, and Charles lay beneath it on the gravelled drive. He died without regaining consciousness before the ambulance arrived.

I think we stayed the night in the oyster man's house; and it must have been there that the police questioned me. They were very patient and kind with me, and kept Henry amused outside. One of them gave him his whistle. I didn't know policemen really carried them. I thought they went out with Dixon of Dock Green.

"You were the first outside, you see, Mrs. Gelhorn. We just wanted to know if you remember anything—anything odd or, well, untoward."

"No. Not really. I'm sorry. Nothing."

"Well, we wouldn't expect you to recall the—situation—in detail, of course, considering the—"

"Oh, I do, Officer: very clearly. It was as I said: moonlight, and him there on the ground . . . And the head of the statue was broken off—And I. . .”

"And you looked up."

"Yes. And saw the porch and the four statues—the three statues, there in the moonlight: very clear—I can see it now, very clearly—I can—”

"Don't distress yourself, Mrs. Gelhorn. No more questions at present. In a day or two, if the doctor sees fit, we may need to follow up a few . . .”

They left, I suppose. Or I fell asleep again. I was terrifically drugged. The oyster man was so kind having us there. I don't remember what happened to his house party; maybe they'd gone. But it was a big house, of course. Very comfortable. I slept a lot.

And it was only when the druggy state cleared, and the police were coming to see me again, that I made myself think back over that bright moonlight scene; made myself count the statues. You see, there *had* been four moonlit figures on the porch, one at each corner.

So I knew then that I had seen the Noone Walker a third time.

11

I DID not intend to kill him.

Back in my lair, I was appalled at what I had done. All at once the game changed; I had overstepped the mark. Killing Charles Gelhorn, I swear, was never part of my plan. To scare him thoroughly, yes: but not to kill him. He lurched forward suddenly, glass in hand, just as I eased the statue past its point of equilibrium. And I was so horrified by the scene below, I simply stood there, paralysed, looking down. She saw me. I know she did: she looked straight at me. She could be blurting it out to her friends, telling the police, giving a statement, a description—at this very moment.

No time to light my little stove, warm up. I was deathly cold; but I had to get out, and rapidly. No time even to change: I gathered up my clothes, my lamp, my tools, and packed them into the haversack. Fortunately I was travelling light—not like the summer months when I had virtually pitched camp: too cold now—and retraced my way along the tunnel as swiftly as I could with my bulky pack; then set out across the wood. I heard the ambulance arrive, but no sounds of tracker dogs, nor heavy feet. Out of the trees, following the protection of the hedgerows, I crossed two fields and the railway line to my car in the lane beyond.

This was a nice quiet layby. I tried to use a different place each time: sometimes even the park behind a village pub. Sometimes I just turned off into the woods; but now the leaves had fallen, there was less cover. Behind high banks, invisible even from the lane itself, this was probably the nearest safe spot to my hideout under the hill. How lucky I chose it tonight, I thought, as I changed out of my clerical clothes: to stray beyond the boundaries of Noone in that startling disguise was strictly against my rules.

I cleaned off the thick pancake makeup in the rear-view mirror; remembering, replanning. The sight of the broken body beneath the broken statue haunted me. I have murdered that wretched architect, I thought, and here is old Scarface, the killer . . . But only one person saw me—not close, and by moonlight; had seen me twice now, fleetingly and ill-lit, reinforcing the spectral image. It would not lead them to me.

Meanwhile, my private crusade was over: I could see that, even in a state of shock. I must leave the area, go back to New York, maybe. First, I must collect my things from the bed-and-breakfast hotel in Orford and pay my bill—without unseemly haste, moreover: any abrupt departure must seem suspicious, once the news of Gelhorn's death was out. It would be almost as foolish as clearing off now and heading for London, for the airport, as my panic instincts urged me to do. No: I must go back to my lodgings; tomorrow morning early I would take the incriminating costume away and dispose of it.

First I had a hot bath; then I sat down with my second whisky and the remains of my lunchtime sandwiches to survey the wreckage of my hopes. And only then did I begin to see that all was not lost. Gelhorn was dead, but I hardly thought his murder would be traced to me. I must go away, certainly; but, now that I was forced to drop my double life, I should return as myself, scarred but socially acceptable, and contact my uncle's friends, justify my absence in terms of amnesia and prolonged convalescence—maybe buy a cottage, settle down. Above all, be there when Noone came back on the market.

With her husband dead, she would certainly sell.

It had not, I confess, occurred to me before: fortunately, perhaps—or I might have arranged his death quite deliberately when I found I could not scare him off. Now, inadvertently, it had come to pass; and my way was clear.

I went to bed. It had been an eventful, but not unsuccessful, day. Disposing of the Walker's trappings was my most urgent task; and I decided to make a parcel of them, with the jemmy and my makeup, and send them poste restante to a fictional name in London: the most effective way of losing them. Her description would be in terms of that black-and-white disguise: that is what the police would look for.

Between waking and sleeping, I kept seeing her, and the horror in her upturned face. Never mind: she would want to escape from such memories. She would sell.

Only two people knew who I was, and only because I told them. The family solicitor rightly refused to accept my story until he saw me; and then, as I had warned him, found little about my face to recognise. As for Charles Gelhorn's second wife, whom I sought out when I was in New York, she did not really care who I was so long as she could help me "fix the crummy bastard". I realised now that even dear Dolores might consider I had gone too far. Hearing of his death, she would be certain it was my doing. But I doubted she would talk: as I pointed out at the start, giving useful information about the enemy to a saboteur would make her an "accessory". "Sure: the best," she said: "in alligator—right? From Bergdorf's . . ." And told all. She was in this, though not so deep as I.

Old Glyn-Jones must be visited and reassured as swiftly as possible. I had been keeping in regular contact with him, and not just for money: he had bent, if not broken, the law on my behalf; and he was clearly concerned about my state of mind. To preserve his innocence, I should tell him as little as I could; but in respect of his trust and his concern, I must tell him I did not murder Charles Gelhorn.

My sudden reappearance had been an embarrassment, at the very least. This conservative country solicitor, nearing retirement, was faced with problems—legal, ethical, emotional—for which nothing in his long life had fitted him. He was a pillar of rectitude; only his loyalty to the family—indeed, since Uncle Laurie died, he considered he *was* my family—and his ill-disguised conviction that I was still a little deranged by my experiences, that I needed humouring, helped him to justify his unprofessional behaviour.

I agree that I was in no fit state to be crossed when I first arrived in England, and summoned him from Ipswich to the private room in the North London clinic where I lay, under an assumed name, in a state of semi-sedated disrepair. He turned his back to me and studied the view while I set about convincing him I was none other than Laurence Gill back from the dead; that amnesia had lost me the best part of two months (my only lie, as required by the man who saved my life) and that for the time being I needed to remain unknown. I had one question that I begged him to answer, whether he believed in me or no: Had Noone been sold?

He stayed silent for a while, then turned round; clearly upset by what he saw and heard, by the demands made upon him. He spoke carefully.

"I do believe you are Laurence. I do not believe in the tale of amnesia: that is to protect someone, possibly myself. I agree to respect your desire to remain incognito, and I propose to advance you money since yours is in probate; and I shall, if you agree, tell the relevant department of Probate that some doubt has arisen about the fact of your death; that you may be alive. And: yes, Laurence, Noone was sold at auction. Now I'm leaving. I shall return in two days to talk at greater length— though I shall not, as you said, 'put the very clock to sleep'"—he smiled, for the first time: "an expression of your late uncle's that reminds me very sharply of the dear man . . ."

It was a relief to me that I had found so staunch an ally; one, moreover, who did not demand the whole truth. That I could not tell him yet. My story of seven weeks' amnesia, however, was far less bizarre than the facts.

The man in the crowd who pulled me from my burning taxi was one of Mahatmaya Docapenee's followers. He rolled me in a flurry that put out the flames, carried me away on his shoulder, and laid me at his master's feet. "Revered Doctor, I have brought you apes, Tamils and trash-heap babies to raise from the dead. Now I am bringing you one burned-up foreigner." So my healer told me later; and he said I had indeed "died a little death".

Docapenee, Professor William Chambenay, born in Manitoba just before the Great War, was the first "alternative" medic to grab the headlines in the flower-power sixties. He had dropped out of surgery; "turned against the knife" (his words in the famous *Time* interview) "in favour of that infinitely more precise

instrument, the laser of Pure Thought".
His detractors said he was simply making
a virtue of necessity: experimental drugs
had given him the shakes. *Time* quoted
an ex-colleague: "'Alternative'? Oh, sure:
there's gotta be *some*! Hell, who wants a
zig-zag appendectomy?"

At that time, *The Mind Force*, his
"simple guide to meditation in healing"
had just hit the international best-seller
lists; but Champenay, never one to stag-
nate, had already moved on into his Green
phase, and was building acres of glass-
houses on his dude ranch to create the
controlled environment for his collection
of "world palliatives".

Most of this, of course, I only
discovered later; but I do recall—it must
have been my last year at Cambridge—
reading a jokey piece in the *Guardian* on
The Alternative Medicine Man who had
gone off to darkest Gabon to learn more
about herbal stews from a witch-doctor,
leaving his followers to cope with some
gothick scandal of body-snatching in the
respectable suburbs of Marin County; and
how their statement to the press, that the
professor would return "almost immedi-

ately" to sue for defamation, was displaced by banner headlines of a far more serious law suit arising from the post-mortem on a dead patient. Lawyers for the bereaved family were using phrases like "grievous assault", "terminal allergy" and "gross negligence". Champenay did not return. He had disappeared.

Years later, and quite by chance, a handful of his flock discovered him. He had quitted Africa to wander round the Far East, a much-wanted man, owing millions in compensation. They found him not only alive and well, but still practising (and what a field-day the prosecution had enjoyed with that simple gerundive!) his Alternative Medicine in a disused Rest-house on the western coast of Sri Lanka; respected by the people as a sort of guru, by the Establishment as an eccentric phil-anthropist. And no questions asked: he was wealthy, he was peaceful, and he seemed to be a good doctor. He cured people.

The high-class Sinhalese came to him very privately between certain hours; I saw them: smart, richly veiled women stepping from Mercedes, or sipping lime juice in the lofty, shuttered salons of the old Rest-house, cooled by old-fashioned ceiling fans, and the breeze from the sea. It was these invalids who subsidised the poor that lined the wide back veranda, waiting from first light and through the hot afternoons for a potion or a salve from Mahatmaya Docapenee. Most of them came by the canal or along smaller, winding waterways, their boats laden with fish, fruit and live chickens as payment: usually enough to feed his staff, the two small wards, the out-patients and the many relatives they brought with them for company.

It was in a small upstairs room of this Resthouse that I was installed; wrapped in cool, sticky gauze—some ointment that smelt of mint juleps and wood-smoke—and laid out in what must have been a large porcelain sink from the old kitchen or laundry. I was hardly present: cocooned in ice, like Frankenstein's creature, and somewhat less human; only dimly aware, at intervals, of those perfumes, and that there was cold, but no pain. When I began to think, I assumed I had died and been consigned to the icy regions of Purgatory. The first time that I became clearly conscious, it was of the moving fan above me; then of a white coat, dark face, dark hands delicately basting my chest with a large watercolour brush; beyond that, at the end of my coffin, several pairs of eyes, startlingly white in the slatted gloom, all bent on me; and a mumbling, humming noise. "Stop them praying," I said. "I'm not dead, you see." "Do not speak, please. Do not move, or smile. But take this tube into your mouth. You must have nourishment." I sipped, and slid back into my cool, numb world.

Days—or weeks—later, awake and freed of my ice-floe, I still spent much of my days like this: a marvellously tended mummy, daily rewrapped, hourly anointed, and topped up with delicately spiced broths and compôtes; and—for part of every day—hummed over. The good doctor, it seemed, still had the old "mind-force" bee in his bonnet, busily cross-fertilising now with African homeopathy and the meditational disciplines of the Far East. When his faithful band were not busy working on the Resthouse vegetable garden and the livestock, or brewing ointments and possets in the small herbal factory, or dosing patients, they sat cross-legged near the hard cases and meditated them back to health. As for me, I cannot say that I saw new skin growing—any more than you can sit and watch a pond freeze over—but I knew, as the slow weeks passed, that my body was mending, and whether this was brought about by the herbal poultices and potions, or such inviolate peacefulness as no Western nursing-home—however costly—could hope to achieve, or by the old man's mumbo-jumbo, I cannot tell. Maybe Champenay was just hedging his bets.

I began to move, to sit up, to walk; I was human again. But I was never shown a mirror; and, growing anxious, was given to understand that my face had proved the most difficult. So Champenay told me.

"By the calendar of Alternative Medicine, Laurence, and in terms of meditational healing, these are early days. You had to travel a long way back to us from your little death, strangled by those fiery fumes. And after that, there was the danger of waking into intolerable pain; but you have responded to the cool resting period, combined with Nature's own medication and the power of thought-healing. Give us, give yourself, one year, maybe two, and you will be entirely renewed: re-created. What is so little time? Life is pleasant enough here; you will become one of us, and make your own progress up the ladder of creation with the assistance of my teachings."

His gentle, singsong mingling of fringe medicine and oriental philosophies, like a thin old temple bell, was curiously seductive . . . But I did not have that sort of time. I was worrying obsessively about Noone. For God's sake, *what had happened to my house?*

When I considered leaving, however, I realised it could only be with Champenay's blessing: I was not simply weak, I was effectively a prisoner. (Were his followers too, I wonder, now I know his history? Once they had discovered the master's refuge, how could they be allowed to go?) This Resthouse he had turned into a nursing-home was much older, more spacious, than the one at Polonnaruwa. With its fretted archways and flaking wooden lattices, its high ceilings and wide, curving staircases, it had a certain genteel shabbiness that was very appealing. But, beneath the decoration, it was solidly built of stone; and, in truth, a very private place, open only to the sea. Its five or six acres were guarded by a fine old wall, and iron gates which were opened and closed for the visiting Mercedes by a large, mild-mannered bouncer; while the River Lodge, half boat-house, half folly in the Moghul style, covered the only entrance from the lagoon. There seemed to be virtually no means of communication with the real world. And what need? The inmates were amply sustained by the gifts of grateful patients, supplemented by the flourishing model farm within those walls; among the faithful, all possessions were shared. Passports? Money? For what? And there was, so far as I could tell, no telephone, no newspaper, no radio.

To be fair, however, there was nothing *else* the least disturbing, in any sense, about Champenay's little kingdom. Never once did I feel menaced by his absolute power, nor uneasy about his methods (sceptical, yes; but I am not a natural Believer); nor did I hear, during those eight weeks, any muttering among the ranks of the faithful.

I did sometimes wonder, as I began to cast about for ways of deserting this happy hive, whether drugs played a part in that unquestioning dedication; and, indeed, whether an outsider showing signs of excessive curiosity might not gently be brought to heel . . . But my fellow prisoners were all too bright, clean, busy, and selfless for addicts; so sweetly (for me, over-sweetly) reasonable in everything— except discussion of the underlying Faith. "What should we 'justify', friend?" they would say, uncoiling gracefully from the lotus position to return to their tasks. "Look at us, and look around you. See that we are happy; that this place is good. Then see that these two things are interdependent, are One; even as we are, with each other, with Creation."

And so they would leave me resting on my pallet in the shade of a fig tree, robed in my cool shirt of gauze—with only the chuckling hens, the munch and breath of a tethered ox, and softly hushing waves on the beach, to answer me.

It was towards the end of May by my

calculations—give or take a week or so of unconsciousness—that I was recovered enough to grow restless. My progress had been miraculous even by their standards. I begged to be released; but the Reverend Doctor prescribed patience, study, rest. I complained I could not sleep for worrying; that when I did, I had terrible dreams. Then I had a recurring nightmare, dredged from deepest childhood fears: of being locked in a mask, unable to breathe; and woke to find I had torn at the new skin of my face.

Suddenly he panicked—or so it seemed. He arranged to fly me to London, to a private clinic. I had never seen him disturbed or distressed: it was oddly unnerving. When he told me, I saw him alone for the first time. He sat by me and held my hand.

"I send you on trust, Laurence, that you will not betray me. I have had many troubles, much persecution, in the world outside. I took you in as dead; but *they* would say I had exploited you: that I should have told the authorities of your Rebirth. *I* knew they would take you from here; that assuredly you would not survive

. . . So I am guilty of concealment, at the very least. My concern, however, is less for legal niceties than for my subject's wellbeing; and, though in the resurrection of your body I am clearly succeeding, in the renewal of your spirit I seem to have failed. Your soul is troubled beyond my reach. I could mend you further; but I feel I must send you back to your 'real' world and let you make shift with plastic surgery. They will patch your face—see, here are the names of the two clinics who knew me and will understand my reports —and it is for you alone, now, to mend your spirit. One day, I trust, you will visit me again.

"But I must ask you to agree to take a new name, at least for a while, so you cannot be traced back to this place—and this may not be so hard for you: some men I have known would be happy for the opportunity to start a new life. Will you accept my terms? That is the only price, the single compensation, I ask."

Any terms, I said; and thanked him. I promised to come back. And so it was that I returned to England in a wheelchair, bandaged, with a new name, and a beautifully forged passport in my gloved hand. I could have been anyone; but the lush clinic he was paying for asked no questions and treated me as discreetly as a film star in for a nose job. The newspapers they brought me, and the view from my window, declared it was June: eight weeks had passed since George drove me down from the tea country. Eight weeks since Noone went up for auction, and I was not there.

On his second visit, Glyn-Jones did his best to reason with me. No use, he said, to dwell on such misfortunes: I must think of other, hopeful things; and it was priority now for me to rest and get strong enough for the plastic surgery. He talked about my inheritance that was waiting only for me to claim it. In desperation, he suggested I divert myself by watching the television, and marked some programmes of interest in the evening paper.

I thanked him for all this. He meant so well. Then I cross-questioned him about the auction.

He left soon afterwards. Understandably, he could tell me little, having been far too concerned at the time over my reported death. But he could see I was obsessed. On his next visit he brought me photocopies of the property columns that had reported the sale in April. He tried to comfort me by telling me that, as soon as my money was released, I would have more than enough to buy some other house: just as fine, and as old, and in better repair. He even produced a copy of *Country Life* as proof. His kindness was touching. But it was cold comfort: I could see no good reason for living; and turned my face to the wall, bitterly regretting my resurrection.

In the days that followed, I lay there with the television set on "mute" and imagined the American architect, Charles Gelhorn, taking over my home. I thought I was hallucinating when one morning, during some vapid breakfast show, the unforgettable silhouette of Noone Rectory appeared; then the handsome front, in sunshine. My tray and flowers went flying as I hunted for the autocue and turned up the sound. By then the house had disappeared; but Gelhorn himself was being interviewed. ". . . A little matter of planning permission?" said the breakfast-show lady.

And the monster spoke: "'Little' being the operative word there, Chris. I'm not laying a finger on the front—like that's, quote, Protected, unquote—but the interior situation will certainly change more than somewhat; and, however they play it, the planning-permission guys carry no clout in that area. And I'm happy to say the alterations to the great hall—I believe you have a visual—Right: that's my baby!—the alterations start next week . . . Sure it'll take time; but we don't intend moving in yet a while."

"Tell me, Mr. Gelhorn, aren't you bothered by legends that Noone is haunted?"

"Hey, Chris, is that so? Well, now, that's kind of a status symbol with these old country properties, right?"

"And"—smiling through a last-question voice—"what would *you* do if you saw a ghost, Mr. Gelhorn?"

"Tell it to get lost, I guess!" He laughed. "Reckon it'd feel pretty damn lost anyway, Chris, by the time I've rearranged the old Rec.—'old wreck', geddit?"

"Thank you Mr. Gelhorn; and good luck."

"Maybe some time you'd like to film the finished article, eh, Chris? Quite some . . ."

But they faded him out.

And whether it was this visionary glimpse of Noone which revived me, or my hatred of Gelhorn and his monstrous smugness, I do not know; but I switched off the set, got up, dressed and sat by the window. With the blind up, morning sun flooded the room; and not fifty miles beyond my garden view lay the grounds of Noone. Already his builders might be there . . .

Buy him off? No. One look at that flashy Yank architect, with his heavy good looks, his big, expressive hands, confirmed what Glyn-Jones had told me: this was not the sort you could buy off—and the articles on the auction, as well as his plans, hinted broadly at limitless wealth. Scare him off? He was not even living there. Delay the building operations? Or scare the workmen? Or both?

And so my role as the Noone Walker emerged, inspired by a breakfast show seeming far-fetched and desperate at first then possible, then feasible, with careful planning.

Much, I could see, depended on what *he* had planned. I might get some idea from his application at the proper department in Ipswich; but how would I justify my queries? And might he not hear of them? No: I really needed to see the working plans. I must go to Noone. The plastic surgery would have to wait. needed to get fit; and I wanted money, a car, a costume and makeup. I rang Glyn-Jones, British Rail Information, Nathan & Berman; I summoned the matron. Suddenly it was all action; and, where before I had dreaded it, I was now looking forward to my release from care: it would be a sort of escape, I thought, unpacking the parcel of clothes from the costumiers next day, simply to hide my scars beneath heavy pancake. The smell of the waxy sticks reminded me sharply of school plays. So: "Fishface" rides again . . . slept well that night.

The old solicitor was harder to convince

han any doctor or nurse; but I persuaded
im not to visit me, since I was leaving by
rain for Scotland, to rest and get fit. He
ad already opened a bank account for my
lias; all I needed to do was to telephone
im at intervals and keep him happy. In
he light suit, sunglasses and hat provided
y Champenay, I took a minicab to the
City, where I bought a few clothes, and
aught the Colchester train from Liverpool
treet. Children tended to stare at me,
while adults, especially businessmen,
ooked away: no fear of being recognised
when, in the dining-car, I passed a metal
roker I used to know. Even behind the
road-sided glasses, enough of the scars on
he burnt upper part of my face were
isible to set me apart. Which suited me
erfectly.

So started my siege of Noone: mingling
with the holiday crowds on the sea-front,
esting my strength, breathing the ozone,
aying my plans.

believed the "sapper" approach was the
nly way. I knew the passages that ran
nder the house; and, when I made my
vay in, and looked at the working blue-

prints, I saw that these lowly and ancien cellars played no part in them. He had no even made a plan of them; just marked th main entrances, with *Wine Store* writter across them. And I made myself a wage there and then, standing alone at night in the desecrated hall, where his filthy blue prints were spread out across my old prep table, that I would drive him out befor he moved in his wine. At the latest— calculated—that would be Christmas.

Now, thanks to the unfortunate acciden with one of his ill-made, ill-chosen statues I had as good as won.

Initially, perhaps, I was foolhardy intoxicated merely by being back a Noone. I came in daylight the first time and as my inscrutable self, to relearn m way; hiding at noises, meeting no one And it was strangely exciting to take it so by stealth: to park my rented car far of and walk through the fields, approachin; the house from behind, from the north through the deep woods; within th grounds, moving from tree to tree, some times losing my path in the dense spin neys, but always knowing my direction; homing pigeon. When I arrived at th lake, and saw the little oriental bridge was still there, with a few more planks missing, I sat down in the friendly curve of my old Riding Tree. It was all a size smaller than I remembered, all so inexpressibly dear to me; and the discovery that nothing had really altered yet made me hopeful I might have the grounds, at least, to myself. I could have lingered there contentedly for hours: every line of rock and shore, of stump and branch, were so perfectly familiar. It was like watching the sleeping face of the beloved—so secretly to enter my own home ground, to sit there so still, and silently move on.

Next I made for my planned base-camp. As a small boy I had named it the Hidden Grotto; later, the Mountain Lair. For myself I named it: no one else knew of its existence. The entrance was low and narrow, concealed, summer and winter, by the tangle of wild rhododendrons clothing the precipitous side of the slope above the lake. It was Uncle Laurie who pointed out to me that, though the Rectory and part of the village were sited on a gentle whale-back of land, this rocky hillside and the little amphitheatre of the lake were clearly man-made: many cartloads of rocks must have been imported to alter the line of the slope in pursuit of the Picturesque, and "filled" with the "cut" from the lake-bed.

But not entirely filled, as I soon discovered in my earliest explorations; and I told no-one—especially not Bill Abbott —about the secret passage that wound along the hill behind the terraced rose-garden and under the back yard, where a stone slab among the nettles marked one exit; and on into the cellars.

Now I used my first visits to establish my hiding place, stocking it for basic needs, making it watertight and clearing some of the small rubble and leafmould that had gathered over the years. It was a time-trip: I had not been there since my last year at school; and I found a dissolving Penguin paperback, *Rogue Male*, that I had read there by candlelight—my survival handbook, on the tactics of whose lone hero I had slavishly modelled mine.

The passage, I discovered, was as sound as ever; and I quickly relearnt its twists and turns, where to bend double under its low lintels, and the various exit points— some of which, I knew, had been boarded over and forgotten long ago. There were places, too, as I found on my daytime incursions, where I could eavesdrop on much that was being said in the hall above me, in the library, the morning room; and I listened to the monster's voice outlining his "audio room", and expanding with relish on the helical neon staircase ("Hey, Chuck, that is so *conceptual* . . . !" I heard one of his groupies squeal, before the feet moved on), his gold hessian study, and the Gelhorn Gallery that would replace my nursery wing.

That was when I began to be destructive.

Before, I had merely pricked them: so easy, the swift night raids to liberate tools, a groundsheet, that excellent cake. Now I cut through the shafts of their shovels. They countered with a night-watchman; so I decorated their plans with aerosol paint.

By then I had become fit, learnt to move fast, and grown into my part; happy to be doing what I could in so great a cause; relishing every tremor of Charles Gelhorn's boat. And there was clear evidence his builders were not happy at their work;

especially since I started the Sightings granting them glimpses of the black-and white ghost in broad daylight, amongst the tall nettles, or at the turn of the stairs . .

It was psychological warfare, as I planned it; with an increasingly menacing physical edge to it, the longer Gelhorn persisted. But my encounter with the small boy, Henry, was quite unplanned. He came down with his parents for picnics at the weekends, when I preferred to stay away; but I had heard there was going to be a delivery of bathroom fittings on Saturday, and needed to know where they were being stored. I was standing in the cover of the old summerhouse behind the thick curtain of wistaria, watching for the lorry to come up the back drive, when he stepped out of the edge of the wood and said: "Boo!"

Then, uneasily, almost apologetically: "I tracked you down. Please, what's your name? Why do you wear those funny clothes?"

He stood at a safe distance, and I saw he was being very brave: I must have looked most odd, with my dead-white face and crumpled black costume. "I am the

Reverend Dodsworth," I said; "and I lived here long ago. I was a parson; these are old-fashioned parson's clothes."

"Can I call you Doddy? Would you like to be one of my friends? You see, this is John Lewis—and here is Booterful . . ." He pointed to the thin air on either side of him. "They helped me track you down."

"Clearly you make an excellent team," I said: "I should be honoured to join, and count myself one of your friends—but on one condition: that I remain a secret. As secret as—as Booterful, or Mr. Lewis here." I did not like resorting to such blackmail: children do not talk to strangers, and especially those who require them "not to tell Mummy". But too much was at stake. Moreover I knew that, as long as I was "haunting" Noone, I could watch over him and see he came to no harm; and, if I avoided encounters with him, he might even forget my existence.

It was oddly upsetting, meeting Henry: as though, on my time trip, I had come across myself. He was only a little younger than I when I first discovered Noone; independent and curious as I had been, I think, and enjoying his private tracking

297

games just as I had: another loner. There
the likeness ended. He was sturdy and
ginger-headed and bold, a modern child
with that American precocity—"outgoing-
ness", they call it: making the first move
in an encounter. I had been a shy and
somewhat sickly child, pale and solemn in
the early photographs with my mother; it
was my many summers of running wild at
Noone that toughened me and taught me
self-reliance—but I would never have said
"Boo" to the Noone Walker . . . I liked
his nerve, and his friendliness, and wished
I could spend time with him. It occurred
to me then that, in my war against his
terrible father, he might be a complication.

(And now? Not merely a complication:
more of an Achilles heel. Yes, he could
shop me—the mysterious black-and-white
"Doddy"—with or without pressure from
his mother; but it was not that. Only for
Henry, I found, did I mourn Charles
Gelhorn. And Henry alone was worthy of
Noone—yet I intended to take that from
him too.)

As for the wife, she seemed a sensible
sort of person, judging by her voice in
the hall above me, her quiet, somewhat

evasive, counters to her husband's blustering. Apparently she had been given the old barn to play with; and during those weeks when I was busy sabotaging the work on the main house, I observed the repointing and the roof repairs with grudging approval; I even liked the plain sash windows she put in. Her casual labourers were a nuisance, as I never knew when they might turn up; so I was glad to observe the bathroom fittings were stored in the old west-wing dairy rather than down in the stables. Night-watchman or no, I could get to them at my leisure. They were hideous, and they were so gloriously vulnerable, with all the stored tools conveniently to hand. Carefully planned violence can be very satisfying.

So can improvisation: not all my outrages were elaborately set up. They were gathered together there in the dairy early that morning—architect-boss, foreman, workforce—surveying the wreckage, when I had the happy thought of watering the cement sacks in the shed close by. My only sadness was that I could never be there to enjoy the outcome, the full flowering, of my labours; never on the spot to witness the discovery of the soldered "Queen Anne" gas fitments, or the lighting of the booby-trapped bonfire —though I could hear the results well enough, even down in the wood.

I suppose I thought that might be enough to put Gelhorn off, to show him I meant business; at least to scare away the builders. I retired from the scene, taking with me my sleeping bag, stores and stolen tools, and covering my tracks. It was sunny; I bought a tent and went camping in Norfolk for a few days, during which I telephoned Glyn-Jones to report that I was fit and relaxed, busy exploring Britain. When I had had enough of this, I told him, I planned to get the plastic surgery over with and to buy a nice house somewhere: I had put Noone behind me. He must have believed me: he said not a word about the disturbances there, though recently the local papers had made a meal of it. I longed to ask him whether the building works had been suspended.

But when I returned to find out for myself, my morning room had been transformed into the dread audio chamber. And there was much talk of it, and of the television crews, both English and American, that were due the following week. Moreover, security had been tightened: on my arrival I saw a police car in the grounds; and in my long hours of eavesdropping, I listened to the locksmiths working on the morning-room door, and to the voices of the same two night-watchmen that had slept so well on my Mogadon.

Perhaps it was the thought of that lovely room now cruelly stripped of its old cornices, its arching alcoves, and choked and blinded with deep pile: I had seen the blueprints . . . Or maybe my desperation stemmed from those endless vigils in darkness beneath the hall floor, biding my time and dreaming of revenge: what I came up with was more a gamble than a plan, encompassing the hall, the guards and the audio room.

Carpet now covered the old trap door I meant to use; the windows double-sealed with wired glass, and locked from inside —or so I must assume. Yet somehow I had to create a disturbance in there that would attract the guards, and then make my escape. I could only get in by easing the trap open and slitting through under-felt and carpet above it; but until I was in, there was no knowing if the rest of the plan would work. If I found that Gelhorn had ripped out the cupboard in the small lobby, I must give up and go back through my trap door—with no way of ensuring a neat alignment of the slit carpet. In my favour was some slender evidence that ten days of tight security, and not one single untoward happening, had lulled them. Police visits were few and brief; the guards in the library above me, when I checked on them that night, were drinking and watching television and laughing too hard to listen. I could have put my knife-blade between the floorboards and tipped over a can of beer—freaked them utterly. But I liked them the way they were.

I crawled through the passage under the hall till I was below the old trap door, eased back the bolt I had oiled the night before and forced up the lid far enough to reach the underfelt with my knife. It took time to slice round three sides of underfelt and carpet; then I was through the hatch and inside the terrible woolly cavern Gelhorn had created. By the light of my torch I saw that even the windows were covered with carpet blinds.

But the cupboard in the tiny lobby was unchanged. I pocketed the window keys, pressed down the flap of carpet neatly, and removed any loose tufts. Now for the disturbance—difficult in a sound-proofed room: a matter of creating vibrations. I got up on the window sill and jumped heavily down to the hollow floor below. In the silence it sounded like thunder, and I ran through and hid in the lobby cupboard. Feet and voices, the door being unlocked close by me. Then they did just as I hoped: they both charged into the morning room, switching on the lights and shouting something that sounded like "Geronimo!"

I slipped out, bolted the inner and the outer doors. The muffled hammering and shouting was sweet music. Next they would try the windows; but I had the keys, and there was nothing they could do to break that glass. My trap door was the only way out. In the long hours ahead, they absolutely must not find it: so I went through to the fuse-box in the back corridor and switched off the mains. This meant that now I must work on the staircase by torchlight—till I saw the powerful battery lamps were right there in the hall; and a cordless chainsaw that would save me precious time.

The helical staircase, intended co-star of the television session, was nearly finished; and I worked happily away at the higher treads for nearly an hour. By then the hammering from the morning room had ceased, and my saw sounded very loud in the stillness. That was when I decided to uncouple some of the scaffolding: using the wrench was quicker, quieter and, in its way, just as devastating. About three o'clock, I tidied up and went back to my lair in the woods to sleep; I did not want to miss the denouement.

It took its time; they must have been working elsewhere. But I stayed above ground, and as near the house as I could, using the sprawling shrubberies and yew hedges for cover: having slept through the release of the imprisoned guards, I was determined not to miss the excitement in my great hall. Indeed, I meant to use it; and could see, from where I stood, that they had found the window keys where I eft them on the hall table, and the audio room was being given a good airing.

When at last it came, the outburst of crashes and cries was profoundly satisfying. I saw the wife running in from he garden; and one of the builders was shouting for help from the top floor. To keep under cover, I had to take a long way round to the side windows of the morning room before I could be near enough to toss in my improvised firebrand. There was a lot of smoke and a low roar; but I wanted to see the flames. Then, as I watched, the windows brightened with a sudden blaze: I knew they had opened the door, and I could hear the shouting. I thought: May he roast—with deep-pile Wilton as his winding sheet . . .

But I don't believe I really meant to kill him, even then. In fact, I remember reading the papers and feeling relief that he had survived. By then I was back in London. I stayed long enough to hear that work on the house had ceased: the building firm had pulled out. It was not a "For Sale" sign, but it was something; it would take him time to get his show back on the road with another company,

particularly after such a bad press; and
decided to use the cease-fire to make my
face more socially acceptable. In order
effectively, to disappear for a while,
chose the clinic in the States. Only Glyn
Jones knew.

And later, Dolores Gelhorn. She was—as
I quickly discovered—almost as good
gossip-column copy as her ex-husband
the "architect-playboy" (sic) "presently
resting up in his Nantucket holiday
home". Nice to hear he needed a rest . .
While I was convalescing in up-state New
York, I contacted her and asked her to
visit me "to discuss Charles". She was
eager to; and it was she who told me some
thing I had carelessly overlooked: that the
one thing that really "rated with Chuck"
as she put it, was his son and heir.

I did not like this—maybe that was why
I had not seen it—and I was both
intrigued and disturbed by the possibilities
it raised for tightening the screws on
Gelhorn. I would use it only if I had to
and I decided that, when I did, I would
let the wife see me first, somewhere near
the boy. I could count on her to raise the

alarm; to turn against Noone and persuade her husband to give it up.

Confronting her in the corridor, therefore—that dark November evening—was a desperate measure. And not quite as I planned. I had not meant to scare myself.

But so much of my return visit was miscalculated. I did not think they would move in; and was shocked to find my nursery wing furnished, inhabited. Dodging a nightwatchman or two had been hard enough; now I had to contend with a watchful housewife, a nanny, an inquisitive small boy, and a daily help, as well as the new builders. Moreover, now I knew him better, I had decided to concentrate my efforts on needling Charles himself—but he was never there. Time was growing short: very soon the nursery, the corridor, my old bedroom (now Henry's), would come under the sledgehammer; and any moment, at Gelhorn's whim, the preparation of my cellars for his wine would put a stop to all the guerrilla war. The Wallpaper Plot delayed them a little; but there was no knowing how soon the straying husband would return, to move his family out of the doomed wing, and create the Gelhorn Gallery.

Meanwhile the wife was in charge: alert rather nervous, by my reading; and arranged to scare her thoroughly . . .

Apparently I succeeded: they moved down into her barn. Most of the next two days I spent trying to discover from scraps of conversation whether she talked to anyone about me. It was cold, thankless work; and all the while I wondered what it was about the brief encounter in the corridor that so unnerved me. A simple communication of terror? Or was it the flash of recognition in her eyes: almost as though she knew me, had encountered me before, face to face; almost as though she were about to speak of it—until a sharper fear, for Henry, had drawn her eyes away.

Had he described me to her, and put her on her guard? No: the recognition that looked out through the terror was her own. And I began to regret the visitation by the Noone Walker I had so carefully arranged. I felt suddenly involved, uncomfortably aware of her as "Kate", mother of Henry, with feelings of her own.

—not just an offshoot of her monster husband.

The husband I killed.

Well, now she *had* seen the Noone Walker again: up there on top of the porch, playing at statues. But not Laurence Gill: he would emerge in time to purchase "this fine old rectory, partially modernised". She need never meet him— probably would not want to. That might be best for me too, burdened with the guilt of Henry's double loss. Meanwhile, there was lots to be done. Once the incriminating evidence was wrapped up and posted into oblivion, I must tell Glyn-Jones my surgery was complete. I was ready to come back from the dead.

12

LADY CHLOË was larger than life, and exactly as I remembered her, in spite of the years between. We decided we had last met at a hunt ball that I was coerced into, one Christmas at Noone, because males were in short supply, and my uncle had had a soft spot for the Chetham girls.

"But we didn't dance together," I said. "Or did we?"

"Oh, false and ungallant!" she cried. "For that you will have to eat up all your bread-and-butter before I let you get at Nanny's fruitcake. Yes, Laurence, we danced the Valita; and you were fearfully aloof because you'd just got into Cambridge or something. *Why* I bothered with a pipsqueak like you eludes me: I was ancient and engaged and merely chaperoning Harriet with her little friends. But I suppose I felt somewhat guilty for dragging you into the party at all—and thought a spin with a glam Older Woman would positively make your evening—"

"You can't be that much older than me: girls just grow up so much sooner."

"Good try but—dammit, Beccy's pushing nine; and I'd been engaged twice before dear old Percival nobbled me . . . So you can tell just how gracious I was being granting you the Valita you've so utterly forgotten . . ."

"Well, I remember you best at a tea party my mother took me to: the first time we met, I suppose. And you were so—tall, and—"

"Large, darling: large—"

"And so self-possessed, that I thought of you as a grown-up, and very grand."

"I jolly nearly was. Grown-up, anyway. And you must have been about seven—though you looked younger . . . And my bloody little sisters were being rowdy and tiresome, I remember . . ."

And Lady Chloë had seemed to be above it all, fifteen and pouring the tea for her mother: tall, broad-shouldered and black-haired, with bright pink cheeks. As she was now. It could even be the same silver teapot.

"Is it the same teapot?"

"Yes. I got it, sucks-yah-boo to them. But they couldn't argue: they found a sticker underneath it when we were going through Mother's things. Just to make doubly sure. I was always rather good at her writing . . . So, young Laurence, and what about you? I declare—after the shock-horror of you not turning up for the auction—Oh, *bitter*, my dear, to let it go out of that family! As Percival said to me at the time, 'Glad yer mother wasn't alive to see the day . . .' But you, you've certainly been in the wars—No, I don't mean the scars, silly! They're rather intriguing, you know: like a sort of half-mask—madly Venetian—what's visible under those dark glasses? Do take them off: I feel you can see me and I can't see you . . . That's better. I say, isn't it nice how after the dread age of, what, twenty-one?—we all even out: we're contemporaries now, I feel—don't you? And, of course, with all you've been through—Tell me, can you remember much of it? I thought you were being wildly tactful just now with Perce: he's so funny about these things. But now you can tell all."

"I don't remember that much, honestly—though I do still dream about fire. Someone saved me—don't remember him: I'll go back and say Thank You one day . . . Then I was at this clinic in the States: must have lost weeks under sedation or whatever; then all the surgery. And now, here I am; as you say, back from the very jaws."

She leaned across and cuffed me lightly. "Glad you got in touch, me dear. I mean, I know we can only have met each other at those church fêtes and things—and, of course, the hunt ball—but you're still part of the old days: young Master Laurence up at the Rectory, you know. And not that many of the old faces are around these days—" I grimaced, and she flashed out angrily, "Oh, *stop* being so mixed up about those bloody scars! Want us to censor the word 'face'? Drape all the looking glasses when you're coming over? I was going to have fun showing you off—No, listen. You just wait: you're going to be a bit of a hero—social asset, all that, you know: you are a highly eligible bachelor, my dear, attractively battle-scarred from your adventures, unattached rich . . . You are, aren't you? So rumour has it."

"Quite rich, yes. Not by your standards."

"Luck of the draw, old thing; and Perce spoils me shamelessly. But you could still buy Noone if she was put up for sale couldn't you?"

"I believe so. Why, is that what you think I should do, Chloë?"

"But of course! That mill cottage of yours is all very sweet—and probably even dries out in the summer—but don't tell me you haven't got your eye on Noone because I simply won't believe you. My dear Laurence, when that poor—dreadful—Mr. Gelhorn died, and then, within the month, your letter was brought in, we both said—didn't we, Percival?—Noone my love, and the architect chappie snuffing it, and then Laurence here—"

"Oh, absolutely!" Sir Percival wandered over to the hearth and knocked out his pipe, then blew on it thoughtfully. "'What timing,' we said. 'Give her a while to get her bearings . . .' The wife, you know nice girl, actually: m'father rather set his cap at her mother back in 0–four . . . But married to a fearful tick—the daughter, I mean—'Give her time,' we said, 'to get over the obligatory nervous breakdown and all that'—(Don't mean to be heartless, Laurence, but the ladies must do what's expected, you know . . .)"

"And then she'll sell!" said Lady C triumphantly. "Percival, do ring for the drinks tray: this tea is water bewitched, as Nanny used to—"

"Oh, she'll sell all right. What would she do rattling round on her own in a big place like Noone?"

"Her, and the boy," I said.

"Aha!" crowed my hostess. "See, Percival? He's been doing his homework! Now then, Mr. Gill, deny it if you dare: you've come back to rescue your beloved Noone, haven't you?—Not that we'd breathe a word—"

"And a fine chance too, I'd say," intoned Sir Percival. "Ah, Barnes. Her Ladyship—I say, Cloclo, what was it I rang for?"

The mill cottage was on a small, winding

tributary of the Stour. I was lucky: it was only the second place I looked at; cheap, too, because the "fairweather sale" as a holiday house had fallen through just after that market dried up in the autumn, and the farmer needed cash. I moved in the week before Christmas.

Once the coroner's verdict on Charles Gelhorn had been published as Accidental Death, I knew that, for some reason— probably a merciful blacking out of the whole occasion—his widow had not reported the intruder on the porch. Might it come back to her? More immediately, did the police know more than they were telling? And how could either of these eventualities lead them to me?

I decided that the safest, least suspicious, course of action was to re-establish myself in my homeland as the mild-mannered, respectable member of that fine old family, and beloved nephew of the late rector.

It had been strange to return to Suffolk as myself—recognisably, this time, thanks to the surgeons—and stay at a good hotel in keeping with my new wealth, while I looked at houses. I made a point of visiting

Noone Ampney and calling on Abbott—"young" Bill was away in the army—on Mrs. Hatton, and on Miss Wilkins, the shopkeeper-postmistress. They all wondered at my resurrection, and gave me their versions of the architect's end; none mentioned foul play—nor did the village bobby, Moon, who stood me a home-coming pint at the pub. It seemed the case was closed. So were the gates of Noone, when I drove slowly by; Mrs. Gelhorn ("Poor lady: she was a good 'un . . . ," said Abbott) was still away; "in the nursing-home, most like". All building work had ceased.

From a small rough lawn beside my mill-pond I could see through bare willows to where, four miles away across fields and water-meadows, Noone's long whaleback broke the level skyline. Even from this distance, the Lebanon cedar on the west lawn was a landmark; and on a clear day I could make out the frail silverpoint of the aspen poplars against a pink smudge of brick walls, rising above the dark tangle of woods and evergreens. Of the house, however, I could only see some upper windows and a slice of the west wing: the

clump of sycamores above the stables—
planted long ago as protection from the
north-east winds, and spreading every year
—hid the rest.

My cottage itself was pretty enough,
especially as reflected in the mill-pond;
inside it was dark, damp and, apart from
a hastily installed bathroom, quite unmod-
ernised. But—as I knew the moment I got
out of the car—it had all I wanted: that
homecoming view of my Blessed Plot;
bleached and shrunken by distance, but
still my train-window view from long ago.
In spring, I realised, it would be lost
behind the nearest willows: maybe I
should pollard them now. By spring,
surely, I would have stepped into that
distant watercolour prospect . . . Surely?
From the big window on the upper
landing I observed it with my binoculars;
I even took to eating and reading up there.
Through the tail end of December and
most of January, I saw no movement at
Noone. Surely, thought I, the signs are
good.

As the social life that Chloë had threatened
gathered momentum, there was less time

for watching; and I soon realised there was more to be learnt from party chat and local gossip than from those closed shutters beyond the swaying rooks' nests.

Back in December, a couple of lines in the *Telegraph* and a paragraph in the Ipswich paper had announced my Lazarus act; and I wrote to the few neighbours I remembered from my uncle's day. All his life he had spent time on his humbler parishioners, the lonely, the sick and the needy; with the others, he tended to trade on his reputation as a recluse. Neither of us had been socially inclined: too content with our nine acres and our own company; but his calling, and his position in the community, involved him in certain formalities which he took pains to observe, especially in the early years. These were mainly church occasions, or the token appearance for a drink on Sunday at one of the great old houses; and then the return visit—once a year, as a rule—when the fire was lit in the hall and Mrs. Hatton brought an economy pack of potato crisps from the village and dressed in her blue wool to carry round the tray.

By the time I was of a proper age to be

involved, Uncle Laurie was withdrawing into almost total seclusion; but I remembered old Admiral Chetham (he had died recently, I heard), and Mordecai Pope, a retired Cambridge don, and one or two others who visited him and talked by the library fire—as well as the rather discouraged roster of "excellent women" who tried to, and were fobbed off with charming aphorisms and, like as not, the pot of jam left by the one before.

But I could not forget the rather startling Chetham girls of those early days; and that the eldest had married into a dull but gently bred neighbouring clan. Two days after my letters were posted in the village, Lady Chloë drove down to the mill in a mud-splashed Packard and blew the horn imperiously. I bundled my binoculars and a half-eaten meal into the cupboard on the landing (bossy ladies who blow horns are liable to demand a guided tour), and met her at the door.

"Found you! Chloë Bender, Chetham as was. You're Laurence. Welcome back to Suffolk—oh, and to the land of the living of course. Am I your first visitor? I do hope so."

She had stared at me quite shamelessly, manoeuvring me into the light from the window. "I think I'd recognise you," she said. "But I know you're not a fake— How? The grapevine, dear boy: one of old Glyn-Jones's grand-daughters is at school with Rebecca—my eldest—and reported you'd been to tea there and that you were battle-scarred but madly dishy and her grandad said you were the genuine article . . . So you see, after the bit in the paper, then hearing that old rascal Molton had sold the mill cottage at last, and to a Mr. Laurence Gill who used to live at Noone Rectory, we were all agog to call on you. I got your card this morning—but I confess I'd have come over pretty sharpish anyway! You mustn't mind us, my dear: not morbid or anything—we just don't have many excitements in our lives. Oh, there was the Gelhorn kerfuffle of course —but he was hardly 'in our lives'. Did you hear about all that—? Of course: old GJ will have filled you in—Oh, lovely: gin and tonic, please . . . By the way, you do remember me, don't you . . . ?"

She hardly drew breath; yet managed to quiz me fairly effectively while she inspected the whole house, g-and-t in hand, opening the landing window to toss out her cigarette stub—"I say, rather a fine 'Diftant Profpect' from here! Might have to pollard your willows, though"— and left after ten minutes, exacting a solemn promise that I would come up to the Grange for a "long slow tea" at the weekend.

I knew I was being "taken over", "taken up"; but it was very useful. And I enjoyed it; liked them both, found her amusing and got on easily with the children. Chloë had already arranged a dinner party when I left the Grange late that Saturday— having stayed on to share their excellent leg of lamb, and a television programme about Royal babies on which Chloë insisted most vehemently. "No, you *cannot* go off and play billiards, Percival! Anyway, you know how you adore Princess Di . . ." Putting me into my car with a portable television set ("You've got to have one, Laurence: just to catch up on things after so long in limbo . . .") she pecked me on the cheek and reminded me to do up my seat-belt.

"Quite enough fascinating scars to be going on with, eh? Now, you will come to my dinner party for you, won't you? Mind you," she added, leaning in through the window, "don't expect to meet La Gelhorn: she doesn't go out at all—won't see a soul."

"But I thought—Isn't she away? I heard—"

"Oh, no: she's there all right. Whether she's still having a nervous breakdown or what, no one knows; but she's there. Must be fairly grim, living with all the ghastly half-done remains of the updating—much as he left it, I gather; can you imagine it!"

I could. I did little else; so near, and yet so far.

Christmas I spent with the Glyn-Joneses; New Year in London. It was late January when Miss Wilkins told me local builders were starting work again up at the Rectory; while the talk at Lady Chloë's was all of the astonishing fortune Kate Gelhorn would have at her command: not just her late husband's personal wealth and his massive life insurance, but the proceeds from the sale of his majority holdings in the Anglo-American firm of Gelhorn Designs.

"Well, lucky old her!" said Lady Chloë; and, as soon as the others had gone: "So she's hardly going to be in need of the ready . . . But—chin up, Laurence: the way I see it, she's not going to stick around at Noone—the house where it all happened, dammit—when the world and its oysters will be up for grabs."

"So will she, poor sweetie," said Percival heavily, coming back from seeing the guests into their coats. "She'll have to be on the watch-out for gold-diggers, mark my words. And it's not as if she's a bad looker . . ."

Rebecca, among the golden retrievers on the hearthrug, sat up with sudden interest. "Then Laurence better marry her quick, bettn't he? He's a geolil—like you said, Laurence—aren't you? Digging for rocks and gold and things?"

"Rebecca! I'm shocked at you."

"Now, Cloclo: she's no worse than you, my dear. You're a fearful old matchmaker, you know."

Emboldened, the precocious Rebecca stood up and smoothed out her rumpled skirt. "Don't blush so, Laurence." She sat on the edge of my chair and put her arm through mine. "I really wanted you to wait for me, you see—but you might as well marry a rich elderly lady while you're hanging about with nothing to do—don't you think?"

"Rebecca! Percival, I'm not like her, am I? *My* mamma was far too strict. Get on with you, hussy: call the others for lunch."

"'Down Rebecca . . . ! Drop him then, there's a good doggie . . .'" Rebecca unwound herself and exited gracefully.

"I'm sorry, Laurence, but children these days! Whether it's the vitamins—"

"Laurence doesn't mind, do you, old man? Rebecca's taken to him—that's all, my dear."

"Oh, she can do no wrong in your eyes, Percival . . . Well then, what about it? Marrying Kate Gelhorn. Are you going to tell me it hadn't crossed your mind?"

"Yes, I am, as a matter of fact. Just that: it hadn't crossed my mind."

"But you do *want* Noone, Laurence? You must have seen it as one of the ways . . . Women do it all the time, for goodness' sake—and often for less. It's called a 'marriage of convenience', my dear."

How could I tell these nice people—for whom even their worldly wisdom was a touch rakish—what I was really like? That I wanted Noone for *myself*? Or just how far I had already gone in my secret campaign to remove the usurpers of my kingdom? Suppose they discovered they had taken up with a murderer?—for, given my motive, and that witness, I would undoubtedly be convicted as such in a court of law . . . Yet I tucked into their Sunday lunch, and it did not stick in my throat: I had everything to gain by this cushy duplicity. I must smile and smile and be a villain. It was for a Cause.

Anyone who has ever become infatuated with a house—unique in its street, perhaps, "across a crowded room"; or alone on its hill, or its clifftop, or nestling in some green valley—anyone who has known the pang of recognition (This is it, the only one I want: that brow, that aspect —profile—texture—), will also know that this is the only truly "hopeless" love we are exposed to: no woman, nowadays, is so unattainable. Romantic tales there are —never first-hand—of knocking at the door, agreeing on a price: idle daydreams. Because houses are Property. Rich women were once, maybe, when you took possession of their dowry; not, in themselves, long-term, to be bequeathed to future generations—and, in terms of simple real-estate, of less account than a sturdy garden bench.

But a lovely house has all these qualities, and more. It has, in abundance, the extra dimension of Time, of Continuity, like a desirable painting; together with the virtues of a good wife, a good mother— and over *centuries*—in that it actually cares for you and yours, protects you, keeps you warm, and pleases you. No wonder their owners prize them; and prize them even more when others come coveting at their door. Yet there is no seducing a house . . . So we learn, if we are wise, not to exchange those long, dangerous looks; not to imagine them ours.

It occurred to me that afternoon, sitting freezing in my coat and gloves by the open landing window, gripping my binoculars and thinking these dark thoughts, that even one's most normal friends can behave quite outrageously over property. Honourable men in the grip of such a fever cease overnight to recognise the "gentleman's agreement". Suddenly no holds are barred —except the handshake. All is deemed fair in real-estate and war.

And mine, I saw, was a case in point; but one so desperate, so entirely exceptional, that it obeyed no rules, fitted into no category—unless perhaps alongside the great, timeless love stories. For my love, believing me dead, had resigned herself to the possession of another. Now I watched her across that wintry East Anglian wasteland, and observed a dreadful activity far worse than the previous neglect: watched them corseting her in scaffolding—and realised I could do nothing, legally, to rescue her. And now, I knew, the aconites were out in the woods; soon the snowdrops would cover the ground beneath the old magnolia . . .

Marry Kate Gelhorn? I hated the woman. She had what was properly mine. She might be as attractive and as rich as she liked, and in other circumstances I might even have found her desirable; but so long as she kept me from Noone, she was the last woman on earth for me. And as for sharing it with her—I had rather turn my back on it and never see the place again.

At Christmas with Glyn-Jones, a pleasantly old-fashioned family affair, with goose and crackers and grandchildren and excellent port—a gift from my uncle the year before —we had time to talk.

He confessed he was relieved to see me so well, so "sane": it meant far more to him than my "excellent face-lift", as he judged it; and, seeing me sane, was prepared to be nudged into talking about Noone itself. I had taken trouble to allay any fears he might have about my motives for settling in Suffolk by outlining my five-year plan for the mill cottage and its few acres; we got round to likely builders —and that was when he started telling me, tentatively at first, about the "mishaps" at Noone.

He had known the house well in the old days, and it was fascinating to hear a third-hand report, however sketchy, of my reign of terror. "Terrible thing," he went on—long before I had had enough of the details—"terrible tragedy about Gelhorn himself: must have been November, when you were still in America—but of course it would be in the papers over there too; he was quite a prophet in his own country, I gather."

"I must have missed it," I said; "maybe while I was staying at this log cabin in the Adirondacks."

"Ah, yes. Anyway you'll have heard all about it since. They say it was just asking for trouble, craning these very heavy statues up on to the old porch and leaving them there without any fixing: not so much as a rope, or a lick of cement, to hold them; the last—and so much the worst—of a whole series of disasters."

"But the earlier happenings sounded like sheer vandalism, surely . . ." I left the half-question in the air for a moment, then went on as smoothly as I knew how, "While this, I gather, was an accident."

"Oh, indeed: of a different order entirely—and magnitude, of course. Just a tragic accident. That poor woman—what she must have gone through . . . I mean them, by the way. Only once, and quite briefly. Early in the summer; Admiral Chetham—only weeks before his coronary —asked them to one of his little garden parties, as newcomers you know—though she's one of the Northumbrian Berrys, of course—" (old GJ was, as Chloë said, snobbier than Crawfie) "an 'Hon.'; and the breeding shows . . . while he—*de mortuis* and all that. 'Nough said."

"And how is she now, d'you know? What on earth will the poor lady do?"

"Recover, I suppose: what else? Time, as they say, the great healer . . ."

I could with decency probe no further; the prospect of a grieving Hon. dictated a short, sympathetic silence. I could not say, But will she sell? I must bide my time. Such a fount of hearsay—and I could not pump him.

I was helpless and thwarted; heartsick with waiting, and burdened night and day with this off-beat passion that dare not speak its name—if it had one. "Lithophilia?" Or did the Greeks have a word for bricks-and-mortar, I wondered, watching the distant parapets through my field-glasses.

331

At least the snow seemed to have halted any outside work; but what fearful plans might be afoot inside, now the wretched woman had all that money to play with? Chloë had decided La Gelhorn must be "tarting it up for the spring market". Whether this was to comfort me or not, I chose to agree: I had to believe in something.

Poor little rich boy. And to my new friends, and those I had rediscovered, I played the part of the wealthy, still vaguely convalescent, bachelor. I had gone up to London to see the New Year in with red-haired Sarah and her fiancé, a pleasantly eccentric accountant who tended to sail across the Atlantic or explore the Amazon basin in between landing better and better jobs. He had taken over Sarah after the news of my "death", helped her to cope with my resurrection, and clearly knew just how to handle her. But it was not just that he relieved my guilt; I would have liked him anyway.

They, and Chloë, and my hosts at dinner parties, all generously provided spare ladies, from debs to divorcees. I had two light-hearted affairs, one with a spiky, bright Italian girl in her last year at Cambridge. Old Mordecai Pope, the retired theology professor, introduced us —"And I feel, dear boy, your uncle Laurie would have approved—despite the Vatican connection." She was hardly a typical convent girl, I found, and certainly not eager to marry and settle down: she wanted to be the first female communist head of Fiat and/or prime minister; yet, with her courtly foreign grace and eaglish good looks, was accepted (and vastly amused) by the Suffolk County folk.

We were no more than a welcome diversion to each other; and welcome to me in another, more selfish way, since Chloë had thrust so many marriageable girls upon me —including one of her younger sisters— without any "follow-through" (as she called it) on my part, that she had once, in her cups, accused me of "not being the marrying kind". There was a brief frost, until Mordecai, a wise old goat who missed nothing, observed that the absence of central heating at the mill cottage did not seem to deter certain hot-blooded young ladies of his acquaintance.

It was really through Flavia that I finally

met the new aristocracy, people like Adrian Pearce, the Hogans and Dickie Bone, pop-star turned impresario. Adrian had produced a short television documentary on Vatican finance, and promised Flavia's uncle, the cardinal, to look out for her in England; he asked her to a party, and she took me along.

I had heard tell that Adrian and the Hogans were among the guests on the night of Charles Gelhorn's death; indeed Chloë herself, stung by his widow's rejection of not one, but two, invitations to the Grange, had said crossly, "Well she must be seeing *someone*: those fearful Hogans, no doubt, who whisked her away from the scene of carnage. Would you believe it? Mitzi Hogan actually put on black—and a hat!—and *gloves*, my dear!—to make a statement to the press . . ."

So of course I was fascinated. I could not actually ask for their impressions of that evening ("And what did you think of the play, Mrs. Lincoln?") when we had all been present, gathered there to see the new statues—albeit from somewhat different angles. Nor could I cross-question them about Mrs. Gelhorn's health, building plans or selling dates. They would certainly talk about Noone if I announced I had lived there, but that profile I kept deliberately low. ("Yes," I would say when I was asked: "I used to stay with my uncle sometimes"; and even the thick-skinned Chloë accepted that I preferred not to be labelled with it in introductions. Percival had taken her to task, insisting that any matter of the Rectory's resale was a no-go area in general conversation. She clearly thought this was "a bit wet"; but I was glad not to have her elaborating loudly on its "returning to the right family", my happy childhood there, or—worse still—how "Laurence here knew every nook and cranny of the old place".)

At Adrian's party the talk was of showbiz and food and cable television; they gossiped, too, but not of the Gelhorns or of Noone. Only when we were leaving did Adrian say to Cliff Hogan, with that drop in pitch that announces the sombre news item: "Oh, have you folks any news of dear Katy? I tried to get her to come today, but she won't, you know—"

"Oh, we know all right. Think we haven't tried—?"

"But it's *not* all right, Clifford, shutting herself away like that," said Mitzi. "She should get about—and especially now, while her little boy is off with his cousins —No: she should see friends, live a little. 'You can't grieve for ever,' I said to her. I said that nobody would think the worse of her if once in a while she had a bit of a fling."

"Quite; and it's not as if—let's face it, lovie—they were that close really—did you think?" said Adrian. "I mean, I even heard tell they were on the point of parting company . . . Just so: the Principessa, no less—and I know you heard it too so I'm not speaking out of wotsits."

"But she's a very attractive lady, is our Kate," Hogan weighed in. "She should marry again—give young Henry some young company to—"

"That's what *I* said!" Mitzi again, fastening her mink. "I told her I had just the chap for her and she just said 'No thanks, Mitzi—I'm far too busy with the builders'!"

"And now it's the landscape gardeners

too!" Adrian cried. "Oh, yes: that was her excuse today. 'On a *Sunday*, love?' I said. 'And in *this* weather?' 'It's the plans,' she said: 'so much research to do . . .' Or something . . ."

I listened, willing them to ask the right questions. Mitzi was clearly the most suggestible.

"So she still isn't thinking of selling?"

"Oh, no, love—I don't think so. Well, she—doesn't really need to, does she? I *mean*—"

"Anyone'll sell if the price is right," said Hogan. "Come along, my dear: can't keep Mario waiting, can we?"

"Oh, Clifford! Mario's our sweet little Corsican chef," she explained to me; "and my husband is terrified of him! But it's only a cold collation, dear—so there's no real . . ." A clunk like a safe closing cut her off as Hogan shut the Bentley door on her.

Flavia commented on my inscrutability that evening.

"Something you imported from the Far East, no?"

I was thinking about Cliff Hogan. He said: "If the price is right . . ."

Next day I wrote to Mrs. Gelhorn, "on behalf of a client who wishes to remain anonymous", making an offer for Noone. I was sorely tempted to use my Noone Walker handwriting and give her a nasty shock; but this was another game, one that called for another heading, that of my London flat, and typing. I signed it John Dekker, the name I had been given by Champenay; and I posted it in London. Then I waited.

I planned to stay there to receive the answer. This flat was now all mine: the banker I lodged with when I worked in the City had been posted abroad a year ago and, when I "came back to life", he first rented it to me, then decided to sell. So I had a place in town; and I was far more comfortable here, particularly in this cold weather, than in the mill. However, even with lots to do and see, I felt—once I knew Kate Gelhorn had got the letter— that I needed to be there, watching Noone through my glasses, as though I might be able to glean some clue to her response from the angle of a ladder, the colour of a

338

van, or the way a pin-figure moved across the snow-patched west lawn. It was a choice between giving in to this strong impulse, but getting her reply at least a day later, forwarded by the porter; and waiting—blind—in London, but getting it sooner. I felt like some feverish lover, hovering between twin hells, twin heavens, unable to choose; and I saw that for my sanity, I must somehow reveal my intentions to Glyn-Jones and get him to act for me in future dealings: my answers would be a mere phone call away . . . I could concentrate on nothing. After three days, I went back.

Chloë heard in the village of my return, drove over and caught me in the act of setting up the telescope I had bought.

"You're pretty serious about wanting Noone, aren't you?" she said. "Either it's that, dear boy, or I'll be forced to assume it's La Gelhorn—this secret passion of yours."

I admitted I felt very sentimental about Noone; as for the lady in question, I had not actually met her. And I apologised for being bad company: I tended to get these depressions, I said, and simply needed to be alone. In truth, I did not want to hear again about the good sense of marrying Kate Gelhorn, and getting a wife, a lot of money, and my house, in a package deal. I wanted no more talk of her: she filled my thoughts quite sufficiently as the recipient of my letter. How many times, like a hopeless suitor, I imagined my offer lying on the mat inside Noone's big front door; saw her cross the hall (and each time the hall was different, more monstrously Gelhornised, in my heated imagination); watched her reactions as she read it; saw her tear it up, or throw it on the fire, or drop it disdainfully in the waste-paper basket, and Henry rescue it to make a paper dart; saw her summon her solicitor, or Cliff Hogan, or the police, or a private eye, or a thuggish bodyguard with steel jaws . . .

Chloë was saying, "Anyway, *I* wouldn't like being without a man in that big gloomy house. And in her dodgy state . . . Fair enough, Laurence, I'll shut up and shoot off. But I don't like leaving a chap with the blue meanies one bit. Promise you'll come to supper tomorrow—?"

I did, and she left. I set up my telescope

to watch Noone—but by then it was too dark.

Early next morning I was back at my post on the draughty landing. Apart from the vast blurred twigs of my own trees, it was an excellent view. I could see a magpie flying into the wood, and make out black footprints across the snow. I could see a white-coated figure, a painter, open a window and shake out a brush: he must be working on the lobby, the one I decorated so artistically in Operation Smoky Mountains. Later, two muffled figures walked out to the old tulip tree and round it, pointing up at it. Christ—they were planning to cut it down! Then they trudged over to the arbutus.

I could not bear to watch. I went down and paced around my own small lawn until I was too cold to stay outside; I came in and wrote another letter, and rewrote it several times.

It was longer than the last, and the offer was higher. I said my "client" fully understood his request to purchase the Rectory was unusual; but not, I assured her, insensitively put forward; and that he was prepared to wait for as long as it suited her: he asked only the assurance of being the agreed purchaser. "Moreover," I added in the final version, "my client will be happy to handle the completion of any necessary building work or modernisation: the state of the house and garden is immaterial." I enclosed a stamped, addressed envelope to Glyn-Jones's Ipswich address: he was familiar with my alias, and would think it simply belonged to my previous, my twilight, existence. I need not reveal my machinations to him yet. I drove into Ipswich to post it, waited impatiently for thirty-six hours, then telephoned GJ on some flimsy pretext.

He said: "You've got a letter here, by the way—under your old name; I was just forwarding it to you—"

"No: I'll come over."

"Good! We'd love to see you. We'll be out all day, so come to supper."

"I can't," I said: "could you leave it in the porch for me?"

"Well, certainly, if you think it's urgent."

"Oh, I don't suppose so—but I'm going to Ipswich anyway and might as well . . . Sorry about this evening, Edward: you must come over here—later in the week maybe. Oh, when are you going out?"

"On our way now, I'm afraid—or I'd wait for you," he said: "I don't really like just leaving it—"

"It'll be fine," I said: "I'll be there quite soon."

It was the longest half-hour's run. There was a car in the drive, and I was afraid they had waited after all: I did not want them to see what a state I was in. But no one appeared; and the letter was there in the porch under a brick: my typing, and the telltale fold. I took it and hurried back to the car. I drove a block, parked, and opened it.

"Dear Mr. Dekker, My client, Mrs. Charles Gelhorn, has asked me to reply to your letters. She states that she does not wish to sell, under any conditions, and requests that you make no further approaches on this or any other point. Please inform your client to this effect. Any further correspondence will be regarded as an invasion of privacy. I would add that Mrs. Gelhorn is in a delicate state of health and must not be disturbed."

Delicate or no, she was going to be

disturbed. "Dodgy," Chloë had called her: alone, without a man, in that house. I turned the car towards the motorway, filled up with petrol at the shopping centre, and headed for London.

I was in time to catch the post restante parcels depot just before it closed for lunch, and collect the package I had sent to my alias three months before.

"Proof of identity, Mr. Dekker?"

"I didn't know I'd have to . . . Oh, I've a letter addressed to me somewhere here—"

"That will do."

In the car I opened the parcel, removed the jemmy, and spread out the crumpled black-and-white clothes, straightened the hat.

Delicately balanced was the way I wanted her now; or maybe her so-caring friends, her pushy solicitor, were exaggerating, and she just wanted to be alone. Either way, the return of the Noone Walker, her husband's killer, would put her over the edge; would drive her out of Noone, or out of her skull, or both. Which would suit me admirably.

13

IT was eleven that night when I set out. I had made myself wait, though I was dressed and ready an hour before. Taking the back roads to avoid the village, I made my way to the old parking place, hidden from the lane. A coat covered my clerical clothes, with my white makeup stick and a small mirror in the pocket. But I need not have been so cautious; Suffolk was asleep under the icy crust of last week's snow, and a sharp east wind had kept even the lovers and the poachers at home.

The hard ground took no footprints; in the woods below Noone, the only sound was when a gust of wind shook slivers of ice from the high branches. My pencil torchlight led me along the familiar paths, and I crept in through the entrance to my lair just after eleven-thirty. Out of respect for phantasmic credibility, I intended to appear to her on the stroke of midnight. I took extra trouble making up my face for

345

a third encounter of the close kind, and
set out through the winding passages to
the cellars.

The easiest point of exit, and the one
most likely to have remained unchanged,
was among the old nettles in the back
yard: but I decided that a lone woman
(Henry and his nanny being too frail a
bodyguard to count as such) might by now
have installed God knows what elaborate
electronic beams or pressure pads to doors
and windows: so I went on to try the latch
in the hall—and found it free.

The porch carriage lamp had been left
on, shedding a little light into the great
room through the casement windows.
Even in the gloom I knew the place was
changed: the gross cantilevered mezzanine
had been removed, and the helical staircase reduced to a single flight, with delicate spindles supporting a wooden
hand-rail. The old refectory table was still
there, covered with bowls of flowering
crocus and narcissi, and a sheaf of plans,
old plans mostly, yellowing and mended
or photocopied from originals: "The
Terraced Garden", "Proposed Lake
Garden", "A Summer House". So—was

she restoring Noone to the way it had been? Damn her: that was what *I* wanted to do. And I didn't even know of these old plans . . . But I was wasting precious time.

Deciding that the fastest way to the master bedroom was by the main stairs, I started up them; using my little torch, and still wary after my night-time surgery on them in the summer. They were no longer open-tread, but filled in and lined in a soft, dark Turkey carpet; and the handrail was silken, polished and pleasingly turned. I had not thought of saving one like this . . . Then, flashing my beam upwards, I saw the ceiling.

I stopped, shining the pencil beam slowly round as much of the huge canopy as it could reach. The gloriously intricate interlocking squares of plasterwork had been completely restored, according to the original pattern—and it was like looking on a dear, dead face, and seeing it smile, and open its eyes. I heard myself gasp, and found I had been holding my breath. It was beautiful, and right, and must have cost a small fortune. So this was what had been going on so secretly over the months

—it would have taken that—since Charles Gelhorn had died . . .

It was still unpainted: I went up a few steps more and examined it where the crisp edge of icing had been shaped round the new stairwell; and looked closely at the tender pinky grey of the moulding, luminous and fresh as young skin. What a magnificent, mad and perfectly judged extravagance, I thought. And suddenly I wanted to leave—as though I needed time to absorb this new and totally unexpected element in the battle for Noone.

But a clock somewhere in the hall below me struck twelve; and the ghost I was moved silently forward on to the landing, obeying the time-honoured summons. All my resolve flowed back with the flood of adrenalin, like saliva to Pavlov's dog; and I stood in the lobby leading to the master bedroom. The cause had not altered, I told myself: I wanted Noone even more now if that were possible.

The door was not completely closed and swung open noiselessly at the pressure of my black glove. A dim light came from somewhere near the window, and seemed to wane and wax with the opening of the door. The fireplace was opposite me, logs burning low and red in the grate; above it was a mirror—for in the gloom I saw the shape of myself. It halted me in momentary surprise, that pale face and bands framed by the dark hat, the dark, narrow coat. Then I took another step; but it did not move. She had brought the portrait back to Noone.

She was sitting in front of the uncurtained window at a dressing table. The candles on either side of the mirror flickered in the dark panes, and Kate Gelhorn watched me from the oval glass.

She did not turn round; and she did not seem afraid. It was as though she were waiting for me: unsurprised, unsmiling, serene; but her eyes, as I came closer, were full of a carefully contained joy, like a well-behaved child in front of a Christmas tree. She was expecting me, and there I was, and she did not want to frighten me away.

Frighten *me* . . . ? And in a sudden rush of anger, of impatience to break the spell of this eerie tryst, I stepped up close behind her and put my hands round her neck.

Her reaction came like an electric shock.

"But I can feel you!" she said quietly; and reached up and held my gloved hands; she laid her head back against me, stroking my forearms. "This time I can feel you!" Her smile was radiant. I had only seen her face properly twice, never close: in the dim corridor, and below me in the drive; scared, both times. I did not know she was beautiful.

I drew away my hands, my eyes, from hers, and stepped back out of the light; then turned and fled. It was a disorderly retreat: in no way the mission I had planned. An unscheduled stop of the heart.

I stumbled along the old passages, and into the refuge of my lair, like a wounded fox gone to earth. There I spent much of the remains of that night, attending to my hurt. Automatically I began removing my make-up; but my face in the mirror slowed me down. It was this face she had been awaiting; the one over her bedroom mantelpiece, the one she watched for in her looking glass. Did she sit there every night? I wondered. So it would seem; and she was clearly mad. She even believed I had come to her before.

So, I thought—and the face of the Noone Walker smiled back at me grimly from my small mirror—so I didn't scare her quite as effectively as I had hoped. All the alarm had been on my side; and it reminded me once more of the unexpected frisson of fear I had suffered on our first meeting, outside Henry's room, when I had planned to get at Charles Gelhorn through her panic: how I felt that she knew me, even then. But at least I had succeeded in scaring her too. Now her attitude seemed to have changed.

And so, as I began to realise, had mine. For—whether it was the physical closeness of our encounter (my gloves still smelt of her hair, her skin); or that passion blazing out at me; or the miracle she had worked in my house, that had struck me to the heart—it seemed to me almost as though Noone and Kate Gelhorn had become inextricably fused into one. What price now, my great cause . . . ? Disgusted by my faithlessness, my sudden preoccupation with my sworn adversary, I finished cleaning that shifty, scarred face—and told myself brutally it would hardly do in the part of a lover. Kate Gelhorn wouldn't look twice at it.

And that was the irony. As I moved through the still woods, making my way home—before the first streaks of day, like the ghost I was—I saw not only that the joke was on me, but was far richer than my clumsy change of heart: it was that, quite clearly, Kate Gelhorn had become exclusively infatuated with a creature of my own making.

That was in early March. And now the spring began in a rush, with a week of warmth and showers, and all the relentless sweetness of bud and birdsong and tender leaves catching the sunlight in a luminous net among my willows. Before the week was out, and the cold winds returned, I could barely see Noone through this golden haze. I packed away my telescope.

Life, and social life, went on. The engagements I had made before crossing that midnight Rubicon came round none the less; and I kept them, and my counsel; behaved obligingly and felt all the while as though my lifeblood were draining into my shoes, and might any moment spill on to their drawing-room carpets. For the wound I had received that night did not heal as I had hoped it would. I had never been in love before, I realised. And I did not like it; all the less that the poisoned shaft had come so carelessly under my guard. The prognosis, moreover, was not good: my only hope was Kate Gelhorn; and I was patently the last man in the wide world to win her heart by telling her the truth.

"Rebecca says you're not yourself," Chloë remarked. "Have you quarrelled with Flavia or something? Can I help?"

"No, Flavia's OK, I think: she's working hard, you know—finals next term and all that. But Flavia and me: it's no big thing, Chloë. No: this is probably just old-fashioned *ennui*. I'm just too idle. Should get a job."

"Are you sure you're really ready for it, Laurence? Not just spring and all that jazz making you restless?"

She seldom mentioned my hopes about Noone these days; the general concensus of opinion, having nothing more solid than hearsay to nourish it, was that the widow was sitting tight, spending money like there was no tomorrow in order to realise her late husband's dreams—and going quietly battier as the weeks went by. Adrian Pearce had tried to get Philip the builder over to his extended farmhouse, ostensibly to mend the roof, but really to find out what he was so busy with at Noone Rectory; and drew a blank on both counts. Nor did he get much ease of mind, it seemed, from Mitzi Hogan's comparative success. I was having a drink with him on my way home from London when she called in especially to announce that the perfect man to take Kate Gelhorn out of herself was coming down for the weekend.

"Ever such a hunk, my dears, and from the loveliest old Cape Town family, with acres of his own veldt to play with—mid-thirties, just looking for a proper English wife . . ." It all came out in a rush. "And dear Katy has said she might be able to dine on Saturday! But we're not asking anyone else, you understand. We want to keep it small for her sake: she's so fragile and nervous still, so shy of company—rather like stalking some rare animal . . .'

"Then the great white hunter should be

just your man," said I, controlling my rising gorge. Two weeks ago I would have been delighted, wished him luck: he would stalk her, trap her and export her; and Noone would be mine. It was still the perfect answer; but now this no longer suited me. I did not know what I wanted now—it seemed to involve Charles Gelhorn's widow as well as Noone in the same fierce possessiveness.

Adrian was saying, "She won't show. Nice try, Mitzi my love, but I'd lay money on it. Give us a tinkle if you find yourself a guest or two short: the dearest little PR person has invited herself down, and you wouldn't want to go wasting good *haute cuisine*, would you?—or Mario will be *wildly* upset."

Chloë too had been busy along parallel lines, I discovered; and it was before lunch at the Grange on Sunday that she drew me aside conspiratorially.

"You won't believe it, but I broke all my rules and had a third try at La Gelhorn: it just seemed so wrong no one seeing her except builders and gardeners —or even being able to check on her real state of health. Dr. Pond of course: but

he's so damned ethical about the Hippo-
cratic thingy. So I sent her a note saying
I would adore some roots from her Iris
Reticulata—by the west terrace, you
remember? And best when they've just
finished flowering, you see—and when
would it be convenient to pop in and get
some—wouldn't disturb her, et cetera.
And back comes a note—quite charming
—apologising for being so unsociable, and
would I come for some tea on Thursday
and she would have the iris roots ready!
Breakthrough! The Mitzi gang will be
sick up to here . . . And, Laurence, now
I've got a way in, why don't you tag
along?"

"Oh, no. I couldn't do that. I mean,
thank you, Chloë, it's such a kind thought
—but she wouldn't want any old bod just
turning up with you when—"

"You're not just any old bod, my dear:
you used to live there, dammit. What
more natural than wanting to see it again?
—if you can stand it, that is: anyone's
guess what ghastly 'improvements' have
been going on up there . . . But it's a way
in, that's the point. Who knows? she may
even relax in the warmth of our combined

charm and talk about her plans, when she means to sell—*Oh*, yes, she will. She'll sell in time. She can't be happy there alone —and if she's a bit batty anyway it'll only make her worse. That is one thing Jamie Pond did let slip; 'no place for a single woman,' he said: she really needed a change of scene, and he had told her so. It was after that he clammed up. I said it must be pretty uncomfortable anyway—or something vague to keep him going; but he said: 'It's perfectly comfortable, Lady Bender; I can assure you of that'!" (I too could have assured her—about as much of it, at any rate, as could be studied by the light of a pencil torch.) "So you will come, won't you, Laurence?" I was saved by the gong. "Never mind now," she said: "lunch. I've got to ring her anyway . . ."

Next morning Chloë telephoned me to say she had "played it by ear"; "wildly sensitive, I was, Laurence (I can be, you know), and she made no objections. Honestly, my dear: she said something about not really being 'up to company', and having had to get out of some fearsome dinner party of Mitzi Hogan's; but that she must start seeing people some time, she supposed—and left it at that. So: Thursday, as ever is! And I promise not to be brash about your happy childhood there. Pick you up at four?"

Turmoil in the breast. I had always thought the expression was a romantic extravagance; now I found no other way to describe it. I was going to Noone as a guest: through the front door. I had not done so since I last visited my uncle, two long years ago. And I would meet Kate Gelhorn formally; be introduced to her, and shake the hand that had gripped mine and stroked me; I must encounter —briefly and decorously—those eyes that gazed with such consuming fire from the oval glass; and must see them go blank, politely dismissing me. "She won't know," I said out loud in the quiet cottage. And it was because she would not know what I knew that we could meet.

An unchivalrous supremacy; but to me, as I inspected myself in the cheval glass that Thursday, dressed to visit Noone, it seemed I needed all the head start I was offered by such doubtful advantages. I was no thing of beauty; confident in this alone:

that she would not recognise me as the ghost she loved.

I had never known Chloë so gentle, so restrained; she had even toned down her flamboyant style of sub-King's-Road dress and put a layer of powder on her scarlet cheeks. The Packard had been washed, and she had painted her "gardening" nails a pale, safe pink. Clearly she was trying.

So was I; and I liked her observing: "You look good." And I said, "That's an irrelevance, surely . . . ," as she would expect me to. She hardly spoke driving towards Noone Ampney, except to remark, as we turned in through the gates, "But you do look good. I didn't want you to look like a 'suitor', you see. Mitzi Hogan tried to slip one in at this Saturday gathering, so I hear—some vast bronzed South African who's come wife-hunting— and Kate got wind of it. Percival is always right about some things . . . Here we are. All very neat, what? She's not too dotty to get those yews in good order."

Spring bulbs—daffodils and narcissi— blowing in the breeze along the lime avenue: those were new; all rough grass in my time. And the neat hedges. And the fountain working. But that house, with a backdrop of slate-blue clouds, and the sun shining . . . It was the first week of April; a year ago I set out from Singapore to buy this place, and failed to turn up at the auction. Now I was here: sick with excitement, with love for the house and for its new owner. We drew up on the gravel and got out.

A Mrs. Hatton figure, but younger and smarter, opened the door to us. While we waited in the morning room (no close carpeting now: polished boards and fine rugs; no wired glass: the open windows framed by pale chintz; the old white marble fireplace and the alcoves were back), Chloë smoothed down the points of my collar and patted my scarface as though I were a son on his first date. That was just how I felt.

"You don't need those dark glasses, you know," she said.

But I knew better than she how much I did: if anything might remind our hostess of the Noone Walker, it would be my eyes. Part of me wanted to remind her; enough, at least, for her to like me a little.

She came in swiftly, out of breath, pulling on her shoes as she stood in the doorway.

"Sorry," she said: "I was gardening. It's impossible to stay indoors and paint in this heavenly—Now, we did meet before of course—briefly—at your father's. I was so sorry to hear . . . Anyway—how do you do. Oh—please excuse my hands: I didn't want to keep you—"

"Good clean dirt," said Chloë. "And this is Laurence Gill."

"How do you do . . . ? Look, come to the library, will you? I usually have tea there. I'll just wash and—yes: across the hall there. We could have it in the hall, I suppose—but the sun is so lovely on that side."

"Lots of choice, anyway," said Chloë laughing.

"Yes," said Kate Gelhorn with a quick smile. "But you knew the house before, didn't you, Lady Bender?"

"'Chloë'—please. Yes, in old Laurence Dodsworth's day. My dear, it's looking simply splendid! I do believe you've saved it—restored it all, you know—haven't you? I must be a little careful how I put

it, Kate; you see, young Laurence here i
the old rector's nephew—so I mustn't b
too rude about the state it was in."

"This is beautiful," I said quickly. "Jus
what it needed. I congratulate you."

"And the ceiling! It's quite lovely! I say
you *have* been busy."

Kate Gelhorn stood silent, glancing
from one to the other of us in our doubl
act. She looked a little dazed, and we wer
covering for her. Then she said: "I'm s
glad you like it . . . Do go through, an
I'll be back in a moment. Hopefully wit
tea: we're still a bit rusty about thes
ceremonies." She smiled at me and m
heart lurched—the romantic script-write
was still hard at it. Then she went ou
towards the kitchen.

Chloë whispered, "That staircase is new
surely: I don't remember that wide spirall
shape."

"Yes, that's new," I said.

"I think I like it," said Chloë: "so muc
lighter . . . Do you?"

"Yes, I think I like it too."

We went into the library. The gol
hessian had gone. Bookcases were back
painted white, and not so many as before

Between them the walls were a deep honey colour; the fugitive western sun flashed from the gilt frames of oil paintings and lay warm on William Morris covers.

"All very acceptable," said Chloë. "I say, d'you suppose these are hers? She painted them, I mean? Look, there's the front of the house; and here's—a bit of the garden? Those aspens are rather good."

"It's the alley by the walled garden," I said. "And here's the lake and the little bridge . . ."

"Funny—d'you see? They've all got one rather sombre little figure in them. To give the scale, I suppose: human interest, like taking holiday snaps. But it's always the same figure, if you go up close—here again, of a summerhouse: almost hidden, you see—but it's there. Black and white . . . I don't think I like it: a touch too sinister for me. I mean, OK in that wintry one—but rather a blot in all this lush greenery . . . Ah, Kate: this is lovely. And we were wondering if these were yours."

"Tea's just coming. Yes, some of them —not the old ones of course!" She laughed nervously and cleared a low table for the tray. "I don't suppose I'll keep them there; but if you feel something's worked, you know, it's fun to frame it and try it out—see how it 'wears'. Thank you, Mrs. Furze: that looks good. Did Nanny and Henry get back from their walk?" (The transatlantic influence, I noted—so much more pronounced in Henry—still lingered in her use of the past perfect, and some emphases.)

"Not yet, Mrs. Gelhorn; but I've got their tea ready for them in the nursery when they do."

Chloë asked, "And how old is your Henry?"

"Five. Five and five-twelfths, he will tell you."

We sipped our tea. She turned towards me and said, "Mr—Gill?"

"Yes, but 'Laurence', please."

"Laurence Gill. I thought right away—when we were introduced—that the name was familiar. I'm sorry if I seemed a bit odd or—surprised. You are the one my husband used to call 'the strong contender' —at the auction, you know. For Noone. And—and I thought you were . . ."

"Dead? So everyone thought—

including myself at times. I was in a fire —a Far Eastern street rumpus—and was given up for dead; but someone saved me, and after a long time in limbo—hospitals and so forth—I got back—oh, just before Christmas."

"I didn't know. I'm sorry: I should have. I feel rather . . ."

"You had troubles enough of your own, my dear," said Chloë. "I do hope life is beginning to seem possible once more."

"I believe it is. The spring helps. And being busy: I have lots to do, you see . . . But—Laurence—it must be very strange to come here now. Is it silly to ask how— how you feel about it?" So straight, under the straight, worried brows. She was older than me by some five years; standing up in her blue espadrilles, her eyes were only a couple of inches below mine. Straight-backed on the sofa, they were level with mine. They were dark blue, and they took me in, as much of me as they could see around and through my dark glasses.

I looked too long: she was waiting for an answer. She said: "Do you mind my asking?"

"No, no: not at all. And I think the

house is fabulous. I think you've done wonderful things with it. Do you like it—Kate?"

"Not absolutely, at first. Then—well, I was alone a lot here, with Charles in London, and I began to get—oh, I don't know—terribly involved with it; terribly protective and silly, I suppose. Then poor Charles was killed—so suddenly—and it was all mine. And I think it saved me, in a way: it was a job to do. I've grown very interested in it . . . Yes, I do rather love it. It's far too big of course, but it's terribly worthwhile—worth saving, you know. Well, naturally you do: you must feel that, what with—Ah! here's Our Hen . . ." She went to the window. "Henry! Nanny, I'd like Henry to come in and say hello: his tea can wait a moment longer." She turned back to us and the sun swung on her bell of conker-coloured hair. "He's not great with 'company', I warn you. Not enough of it, I suppose—and spoilt rotten, what with all his womenfolk bending to his will. Thank God school starts in the autumn . . . Hi, Henry—are your hands OK? Fine. Come and say how do you do, then, to Lady Chloë Bender and Mr. Laurence Gill."

Henry came across, rebellious, head lowered, and shook Chloë's hand jerkily. Then he came to me.

I had hoped he might remain elsewhere, watching children's television perhaps. It was hard to take his hand in mine, and make the right patronising noises: we had been such good companions; but I had murdered his father since I last saw him. On both counts I felt vile and sad. And there was another, more urgent, matter for concern. Henry might recognise me as the Noone Walker.

He looked at me quite hard and said: "What happened to your face?"

"Henry! That's not—"

"It's quite all right," I said. "I was in a fire, Henry. And I had to have it patched up by surgeons so as not to look too much like the creature from the black lagoon, and alarm people. I don't alarm *you*, do I?"

"Not one scrap. Not even a fraction of one scrap," said Henry, and sat down on a stool beside me.

Chloë stepped in and asked him if he would like to finish the icing from her piece of cake, and whether he had any pets.

He accepted the icing and said: "I'll save it, thank you, as I mustn't talk if my mouth is full. I have a cat and a *great* pup called Gnasher. Or Fang, sometimes: White Fang."

"What sort of dog will he be, then?"

"A bastard, I think."

"A mongrel, darling."

"A mongrel. And I have a kind of dull hamster; and some special friends who come and play with me."

"Where do you like playing best?" I asked.

He put his stubby hand on my knee. "Do you know my lake?"

"Mr. Gill used to stay here sometimes when he was a little boy," said Chloë, "so I expect he does."

"Well, I like that lake. Last year I was too young. And I like the summerhouse— and now I'm making a *tree* house! But I need a good guy to help me out . . ."

"OK: teatime, Henry. Then a bit of television maybe." She stood up and held out her hand.

"So what's on the telly today, Henry?"

I asked as he lingered, studying me. It was the sort of question the Noone Walker would have formulated quite differently, once Henry had explained at length the wonders of this newest invention, and acted out some of his favourite programmes. He had enjoyed "teaching" me.

"*Captain Cat*, I guess," he said: "something like that . . . Mum." He turned in the doorway, with the long arm of the nanny already upon him. "Mum, can Mr. Gill come again some time?" She may have frowned: he dropped to an urgent stage-whisper. "You see, he could help me with my tree house. I like him: he's a Doddy sort of person . . ." And the door closed.

Kate Gelhorn, who had been so well balanced, so in command, till now, was apparently thrown into confusion. "Oh—I—I do so apologise—No no"—when Chloë tried to help out—"it's not his father, actually . . . No—this 'Doddy' is one of his secret friends, you see—an imaginary friend . . . A little odd maybe —but you know what small children are —Do you have a boy—Chloë? Oh, three! *And* a girl! Well—this is probably an 'only child' syndrome, this Imaginary Friends nonsense . . . just a phase. As I was saying, roll on the autumn term! Now—what about another cup?"

As soon as we were in the car, with our newspaper bundle of freshly dug irises, and starting down the drive, Chloë said: "*Well*! How very intriguing! I mean, why the confusion and the blushes, I wonder . . . ? But otherwise, I must say, she seemed completely on the ball: quite charming, in fact. I think she's just used her nervous breakdown or whatever as an alibi for getting on with her own life: a bit of a loner, perhaps—and clearly quite clued up enough to know that money in any quantity sets you up as a target—and not just for begging letters and boring social climbers . . . Maybe she just doesn't feel ready for a husband, or anything else, just yet—and so is very sensibly keeping her pretty head down and getting on with the job in hand—don't you think?"

"No: 'pretty' isn't the right word," I said. "But I agree with all the rest. She's got a good life going there."

"Poor Laurence. How was it?"

"Fine. Much easier than I'd expected,

370

actually. Perhaps I'm getting over it—Noone, I mean. I do genuinely think it's lovely—after all the chat about monstrous conversions there's been from Adrian and company . . . No: I think she's done well. Thank you, Chloë my dear, for taking me."

"Don't mensh. And the punchline is: you'll be asked again! You made at least one hit there: 'Our Hen'. Now *he's* your way back, Laurence. And if I were you, I'd play it for all it's worth . . ." When I remained silent, she glanced at me and back at the road; then she added, "But of course men are so much less devious than women, bless them . . ."

14

EMOTIONAL overload can be treated in a variety of ways. My cure, when I resorted to it, fortunately hurt no one, but is hardly recalled with pride.

When I had waited precisely a week to hear from Noone, growing increasingly hopeful and desperate as the hours went by, my spirit broke. My watch announced it was seven days, to the hour, since Chloë had dropped me back by my gate; I got into my car—no time for trivialities like luggage—drove to Cambridge, and snatched Flavia from her revision, for dinner and a room in a lush hotel. I could not contemplate another night at the cottage alone, and sleeping so little. But it would have been less selfish to head for London and the establishment of a good Madame: I was not pleasant company; and, as a lover, merely fierce and sad.

"I judge you are in love," said Flavia. She had propped up the pillows, opened

372

the economics manual she brought with her, and lit a cigarette. "You have met your Waterloo, I think. Can't you woo and win her, like a proper English gentleman? —Or is she belonging perhaps to another?"

"She's belonging to another, actually. And if I managed to get close enough to tell her he's—up to no good . . . well, she'd just hate me."

"And now she just ignores you—right?"

"Right . . ."

So hadn't she liked me at all? What really lay behind her piercing questions about my feelings for Noone? And was I quite wrong—merely day-dreaming—in the belief that our love of the place could be a bond instead of a barrier? Then there was Henry, my "way back". Had he too failed me? Found some other "good guy" to help him with his tree house? His mother clearly knew perfectly well that "Doddy" was his name for the ghost she awaited each night by candlelight; surely Henry's whispered announcement—briefly confounding both her and me—that I was a "Doddy sort of person" should not have put her off me; might even intrigue her a little, incline her in my favour . . .

Unless it had nudged her, forced her, to the conclusion that the Noone Walker was just a man in an eighteenth-century clerical costume; and that the man in question was Laurence Gill, miraculously returned from the dead.

Put like this, it sounded so perfect an equation, the only thing still puzzling me was why she had not guessed long before; then I reminded myself that the final piece of the jigsaw, for her, had only fallen into place a week ago, when Chloë introduced me . . . And I wondered, even while I waited for my invitation from her, whether Kate Gelhorn might not already be starting proceedings against me—on charges so numerous I must surely serve my sentences concurrently to fit them all into one life: trespass, vandalism (on several occasions), endangering life (ditto), harassment (terrorism, maybe, if you dress up for it), impersonation of a dead man, child alienation, murder with malice afore-thought—

I had been through all these stages of argument many times during that week, even before I could with reason have expected to hear from her—and always ended with the same dark conclusion, and my list of crimes. I had written her several thank-you letters and sent none: not one would do. How could I hope to hit the right note, when I veered between a wild faith in our future together, and the leaden certainty that she had uncovered her husband's murderer? What room remained for polite thanks, when I should already be entrenched, either in my willow cabin at her gate, or in some zinc lean-to in Montevideo, waiting for Glyn-Jones to send me money? For there was nothing, logically, between these alternatives. And since I always ended by believing the worst, clearly now—even *now*—was too late to flee the country. And as for money, I could not see old GJ so readily taking on the role of "accessory" this time round.

"I'm meant to be in Montevideo—or Buenos Aires," I said.

Flavia marked her place carefully and looked up. "Why, have you done something very wicked, Laurence?" She was smiling indulgently.

"Why not come with me?" I said.

"Thank you, no. Not even after my finals: too many plans for my life." She lit another cigarette. "And all this is for being ignored? Better you should tell her the truth about this other guy, surely, and make her hate you, *caro*: hate can turn to love—or so we passionate Latins believe. Try it, no? Now I finish my chapter, we make love, we say goodbye, I am in college for breakfast. And you go home—to tell all, like your *Woman's Own*, your *True Confessions*; or, of course, to pack for Brazil—OK?"

"You're a good girl, Flave—know that? You're the—"

"Hush, Laurence. Till the end of the chapter."

There were no police cars waiting by the mill cottage. I opened the door and found two letters on the mat. One was an electricity bill, and the other was from Kate Gelhorn.

"I tried to telephone you today—no answer, so I am getting Philip the Builder to drop this in. Can you come to lunch on Saturday? (This Sat.) Rather short notice, but Chloë Bender has been away and I didn't want to pester Sir Percival for your address. C, now back, says you weren't too mixed-up about Noone, she thought, to want to come again—and Henry is very persistent. So. And if you don't get this till next week or something, give me a ring —if you'd like to—and we'll arrange another time. Yours, Kate."

Elaborate arrangements, dire conclusions—all crumbled away like shed skin: I wondered now how they had ever fitted. I telephoned her, got Mrs. Furze and left a message: that I would be there at one for lunch next day. Kate herself rang briefly that evening to say that, if the weather was still lovely tomorrow, could I come a bit earlier, at quarter past twelve, to help with the tree house: "work up an appetite," she said. I agreed.

Neither her letter, nor her voice on the telephone, I felt, could possibly conceal a trap for a murderer; they were too like her: light, warm and a little scatty. Again that night it was hard to sleep—and not just because my wildest hopes suddenly seemed possible. It became painfully clear to me, in the light of the week's questions and conclusions, that if Kate Gelhorn had *not* rumbled me, then she was too deluded by the Noone Walker, too much infatuated, to see what he was. She was indeed mad. To take it a step further: either she was mad, or . . . Or there really was a ghost at Noone. As I could accept neither of these, I switched on the transistor radio to jam my thoughts, and fell asleep.

That Saturday lunch was the first of many such occasions, and set a pattern. I quickly got the message—and accepted it—that I was there for Henry's sake; she treated us rather as a pair of children—a running joke which delighted Henry ("Hey, Mum, Laurence hasn't eaten up his greens!")—and always thanked me, when I left, for "being so good to him". Once she said "He does so enjoy having a man around, boys together, you know."

Another time she said: "I know he needs a man around." Then, quickly, "School will be the answer, of course . . .'

"Not entirely," I said, chancing my arm a little. She seemed so relaxed with me after the first few visits: still cool; very objective—but easy. (*I* could not relax, of course: I was horribly in love; and it seemed as much a relief as a pain when she would disappear—as she frequently did—leaving us to play together.) We were mixing *kir* for ourselves at the end of a long, pleasant day, while Henry had his bath.

"No, not entirely," she said. "And that's the argument well-meaning friends use when they say I should get about, meet people: 'come out of mourning'. But of course, they're all just busy matchmaking really. You know, they simply can't resist having a go? Producing their eligible stud, or their safe older man—well cut, with the touch of grey—honestly! Mitzi, Adrian Pearce; even old Professor Pope."

"What do you do?" I asked.

"If I suspect a suitable male is involved, I say no—in fact I usually say no anyway, these days; sometimes at the last minute. Largely so I won't have to ask them back here, I think: I do love being alone."

"Ah . . . Shall I go now, Kate? Or may I finish my drink?"

She clapped her hand over her mouth; then threw back her head and laughed—as I had only seen her do when Henry came in wearing the Groucho moustache-and-eyebrow spectacles I brought him that first Saturday. She said, "Oh—I'm sorry! But it's so lovely—laughing . . . ," and wiped her eyes. "Sorry, Laurence—do sit down: I've got so bloody rude and anti-social, I don't even hear myself doing it. Come on, have another and pour me one. You know you're different, for goodness' sake—don't you?" Heart leapt, like a salmon in the aorta. "You're a pal—" Salmon fell back gasping: "No, dammit: not just for Hen; for me too—with so much that you're able to tell me about Noone, and your—your sympathy? With what I've been trying to do . . . Your suggestions—and helping us in the garden: all that. I never had a brother, and neither has Henry of course—nor likely to. But I can see what a boon they must be. And you never had a sister—so: I hope, well—that you're enjoying it too . . ."

"It's time for me to go up and read to him," I said, looking at my watch. "I promised I would before you kiss him goodnight . . . Of course I'm enjoying it, Kate. I wish I could ask you back; but now that the builders—"

"Oh we wouldn't mind *that*. But we're terrible home-birds, I guess."

"Understandably," I said. "I must go up—and then I'll be on my way."

"D'you want some supper?"

It was the first time she had asked me to stay on—but her tone was too flat; and I too proud, and sick at heart. I did not fancy supper with a sister, or a pal. "Some other time maybe," I said. "I'm due at Chloë's."

It wasn't true; but I called in there for scrambled eggs and sympathy. I knew Chloë was on her own, and pining to hear how my siege was progressing. Usually I fobbed her off with vague assurances, but this time I needed hers.

She made me suffer a little at first, to pay my dues.

"'Pals,' you say. Oh, Laurence, that's not so good. And I thought you were practically *living* there ... But—tell me honestly, my dear, are you actually in love with her—honourable intentions and all that? Or have you still got your sights set on Noone? And all that brave talk about 'getting over it' won't wash with me, so don't try it on."

"I won't, Chloë. I'm afraid I am in love, and I do want to marry her. She remains cool and charming and elusive: absent, as it were; I'm just a playmate for her rather lonely little boy. And, at times, a useful man to have around—for carrying a sack of peat from the car or fixing Henry's train set. Or as a safe confidant, like today."

"Oh? Did she open up, then?"

"Certainly she seemed more relaxed. And, yes, she opened up a little . . . She had the gall to talk about the bore of matchmakers; and tell me of all the suitable males she contrives to evade—as though I were some cosy eunuch sitting there—"

"—On a pouff at her feet—oh, poor Laurence!"

"And even worse: she confessed she really said no to invitations because she didn't want to have to ask people back: she loved being alone at Noone! Then of course apologised—so disarmingly—for being so rude."

"My dear, she is shooting a line! Or talking through her hat: by my calculations you've been over there five times in the last fortnight—"

"Ah! But for Henry; kindly remember that. And she does like to be alone, Chloë: leaves us playing for hours. Doesn't go out . . ."

"Paints, I suppose; or wanders round the garden." (Especially the poplar alley, I thought: it seemed she often went looking for him there.) Chloë was asking just how batty she seemed to me: "You know the way she sort of looks through one a lot of the time. And then all this chat about pals and brothers: is it entirely normal? I suppose she could still be mourning the late Charles to the exclusion of all else—though Mordecai's theory is that it was more a *mariage de convenance*. Especially on his side . . . When I dropped in the other day to lend her some gardening books, I did say, woman to woman, that she looked tired and how was she really, and so on. And she said 'Short of sleep, and of course a bit depressive still; but at least I'm off those beastly tran-quillisers.' And she kept looking at her watch, then leapt to her feet—'No, don't go,' she said, 'I'll be back in a tick.' Must have run down the garden: it was during one of those sudden showers, and she got back quite wet and out of breath."

"What sort of time was all this?" I asked.

"Oh, mid-morningish. Well before lunch—because she offered me a drink when she got back and I felt it was a bit early for the hard stuff. Had a lager . . . Why? D'you think maybe she was meeting someone? My dear! D'you think she's got a lover?"

"Well, it's not inconceivable."

"Oh, Laurence! And *that's* why she only wants you as a brother? You men just have to have a nice neat reason, don't you? Her husband's been dead, what—five months?—and she doesn't seem to want you as a lover; ergo, she's got one. My dear beastie! At that time of day, why— she was probably paying old Abbott the gardener."

"I'm sure you're right," I said. (But Kate never allowed me to arrive before twelve-fifteen: it had become a joke now. She claimed she painted till twelve-fifteen; "Precisely?" "Why not? Aren't I? About other times?" "Never, Kate . . ." And Chloë, of course, had "just dropped in".)

"Still, to be fair, Chloë," I said: "it was you who thought she was behaving oddly, on this occasion."

"Well, yes: very jumpy. Don't you find her so?"

"Yes, I do sometimes. But not batty. Charmingly eccentric, in my eyes."

"Poor Laurence!" she said again. "I'll make us some coffee . . . And meanwhile you're getting nowhere. A fine romance, with no kisses. Maybe you should pounce."

"And immediately be relegated to the ranks of predatory fortune-hunters? No, thanks: I'll play it her way. Maybe I'll become indispensable."

"That takes time."

"Softly softly catchee monkee."

"Just so long as she doesn't make one out of you, dear boy. I still don't like this pally stuff. I'd pounce."

Now it was late April; and, instead of looking for a job, I was hunting far-flung nurseries for plants worthy of Noone: species roses, and old-fashioned herbs, and exotic water-liles for the "Proposed Lake

Garden". Usually I took Henry; once Kate came too.

She still contrived never to be alone with me for long; some days I barely saw her. When I did, she seemed to be avoiding my eyes. Often she looked pale and blue-smudged with tiredness; and I thought of her fruitless midnight vigils, and cursed the day I invaded her house—our house —in my black-and-white cleric's clothes. I longed to hold her tight and tell her it was all a foolish trick. That I was the one she really loved.

April sun had browned young Henry; he was growing, getting tougher and more useful, less temperamental, all the time. As for me, I had caught the sun too, and felt confident now that I looked less ghostly than ever before. I had abandoned my dark glasses on my second visit, at Henry's insistence. And as my face—even the scar-tissue, more slowly—grew brown with the hours of gardening, and cricket, and croquet, and exploring, I could see just what a good job Champenay and the surgeons had done: the seams, so to speak, were flat now; the edges smoothed out.

In the days when I used to meet Henry

in my spectral guise, that face had always been clown-white, my hands gloved, the broad hat shading my eyes. My behaviour then was sober and dignified; we had walked and talked, and shown each other special things—a buried nut-hoard, forgotten by the squirrel that made it, a curly ammonite in the landscaped hillside. And he would bring Dinky toys, a battery torch, his Mickey Mouse watch, and explain them to me. Good times. But now, I believed, we had moved on; and I had effectively diverted him from that Imaginary Friend. As myself, I romped with him, swung him by the feet, climbed and bicycled and swam with him—and not all in an attempt to catch his mother's vague glance: I liked Henry; and enjoyed reliving my early years at Noone. For an unsuccessful lover, I was extraordinarily happy.

Only once did Henry disrupt this mood by announcing solemnly one evening, when I was leaving rather earlier than he approved: "OK: then I'll go and play with Doddy—he keeps on about being left on his own too much; poor old Dods . . ."

"I thought you'd grown out of all that kid stuff," I said. Far too sharp.

He frowned blackly at me—reminding me suddenly of his bullish father—and stumped off. I got into the car, rather sick with myself; then decided to go after him. But Kate appeared.

"You're off, are you? What's up with Our Hen?"

"Nothing: he was just being a bit silly, and I snapped at him . . . No—not worth carrying on about."

"Well, maybe I'll have a go: see what he's up to, anyway."

I bet you will, I thought. He probably announced he was off to see Doddy; and she would trail after him. I drove off. Just for the moment I'd had enough of the pair of them. Of all three of them.

May was cold and wet. The plants and seedlings we had established in April did not progress—some were even washed from the ground—and others, annuals we had put out too hastily, were nipped by night frosts. Unable to garden, we tramped across the meadows or along the hedgerows in macs and wellies, taking

White Fang for walks, and washing the mud off him in the back yard when we got back—with the same hose I had used on the cement sacks. Then we would change out of our wet clothes (the first time I had to accept Charles's designer jeans, and a sweatshirt emblazoned *Basil's Bar, Mustique*; after that I brought my own); and have tea by the nursery fire.

Kate seemed to be out a lot more these days. She even asked the Hogans over one Sunday, and invited Chloë.

"Can you come, Laurence?" she said: "you'd be such a help."

"I can't actually," I lied. "But thanks. Cliff Hogan is very handy with a champagne cork." Petty stuff; and she actually looked at me: the first time that day.

"OK. . . See you next week, then."

"When?"

"Oh, just come. Whenever. You know you're always welcome . . ."

"I'll be in London two or three days: jobs I'm following up."

"Really? I didn't realise that you—What sort of jobs?"

"One in Sumatra that sounds interesting; and another that involves moving around: largely advisory stuff—not really me. And then of course my old job in Singapore: they seem to want me back. Which is nice."

"Golly—I didn't know about all this! Well—good luck. You'll be badly missed." (The careful passive. "Henry will miss you"? Too hard: she must know something of what I felt about her by now.)

So I said it for her. "Well, I can't play around with Henry indefinitely, can I? So. And have a good drinks party, Kate. I'll ring when I can get over—OK? And I'll have a look for Hen's rope ladder whilst I'm up in town . . ."

I would hear all about the drinks from Chloë: I knew that the Benders did not really like the Hogan gang—much less the prospect of Charles's old buddies who had threatened to turn up, now that word had gone round of his widow's emergence. Percival would probably slide out of it, but Chloë would go, from sheer female curiosity.

It was a good time to get away: the builders were making me a small gothick conservatory while they waited for the central heating hardware to be delivered. I got back on Thursday, determinedly staying away an extra day. My talk of jobs had been perfectly genuine. During one of those all too frequent moments of black despair, when I acknowledged I was getting no closer to Kate Gelhorn, I started writing off about possible posts abroad; and saw, moreover, that her reaction to the news might be some measure of how much she cared—if she cared at all; then found myself postponing such a moment of truth, the longer to protect my illusory hopes. Only that moment of pique, prompted by the dreary vista of being useful at her drinks parties, wrung my plans out of me.

I returned to the mill cottage with the assurance of two good positions in my second favourite part of the world, and a fierce determination to make up my mind and take one; for—though the income from a well-invested inheritance was more than enough to keep me handsomely—work and travel, combined, might be the only antidote to such a powerful double-dose as Kate and Noone. I tried to see it in terms of mere addiction. This too will pass.

Chloë rang me, to "tell all" about the Sunday drinks.

"I'll come over, if that's OK: Nanny's back from her hols, and the twins are being fearfully tiresome, playing us off— 'Well, *Mummy* let me . . .' and disapproving looks from Nan: you can imagine. So you could give me lunch—if you're not on call *chez* Gelhorn—OK, OK: Sorry, Laurence! No, I'm not really jealous— though I did find you first. I'll bring some Pouilly as penance. I've something quite interesting to tell you. Well, odd, anyway . . ."

When she had sat herself down with a large gin and tonic, she said: "Laurence, you've heard of the 'Noone Walker', haven't—? Goodness, are you all right? Here, let me help you clear up; that's the trouble with these quarry tiles . . . Oh, it's only one glass; sounded like the whole tray—"

"I must put a light in that corner," I said. "I've missed the edge of that damn table before—even on a bright day—need a bigger window, really—and I'm getting these builders to put one in, when they've finished the conservatory . . ." I was talking too much. "Sorry—you were saying: the Noone Walker. Yes, I remember some sort of a legend: probably just young Bill Abbott trying to scare me when I wouldn't lend him my bike . . ." I was still doing it. Nonsense talk, now: *I* had scared *him*. Shut up, I told myself, and listen. "So, what of it, Chloë dear? Planning a fancy-dress ball?"

"Not exactly . . . Actually, I should have put two and two together long ago, when I heard from my little antiques man in Orford that Mr. Hogan had been trying to track down some of the portraits at Noone for the present owner (the paintings that were sold off, you know—so sad), and especially the one of the first Reverend Dodsworth, he said. The poor lady, a widow he thought, particularly wanted to restore it to its proper home. Well, Laurence, this Noone Walker johnnie is meant to be the ghost of the first rector—did you know that? And at the drinks on Sunday, Mr. Hogan was looking at her pictures (he's not bad, is he? A sort of teddy-bear figure —rather a sexy teddy-bear . . .) and he asked her where the 'first rector' was. She said she'd got it upstairs; and I asked

'Where upstairs?'—Nosy Parkering as usual—and she said, 'Well, my bedroom was rather bare, so it's in there.' Later she took them up to see it—the Hogans (*she* was even worse than I remembered—or I'd have gone too). But, while they were gone, my dear, Adrian Pearce (fearful little toad) said he supposed that this must be the creepy black-and-white figure in all her paintings: 'Just too too obvious for *words*, my dears: the lovely Kate is carrying a torch, as they say, for this reverend *revenant*! No, duckie, you can't call it necrophilia, actually—but, dear me, what a fearful *waste*!' And then they came back, or he might have gone on . . . So maybe she does have a bit of a thing about this ghost chappie, Laurence. I know it all sounds somewhat far-fetched—but lonely ladies do develop bees in their bonnets. Why, it's almost as if she was trying to sort of conjure him up—don't you think?'

"Oh, come now, Chloë! Aren't you being a touch fanciful about this? You'll be seeing pentacles on the parquet next, not like you at all, to get so—I mean listening to Adrian Pearce's pet theories about *anything* . . . !"

"Not fair: you're the one who's making too much of it now. No, it's all about strategy, Laurence: you could take an interest, tell what you know of the legend, where he's said to appear and so forth— and isn't there some folksy jingle about him?"

"But if she's really so fascinated by this nonsense, surely one shouldn't encourage it?"

"Oh dear—you men are all so fearfully 'white', aren't you? This is no worse than laying bait. I just thought it might offer you some sort of breakthrough . . . But you're dying to hear about the opposition, I'm sure. Well, the dread Mitzi had brought along not one but *two* eligible men—'just my weekend guests, Katy dear: I knew you wouldn't mind . . .' But that was only for starters: the Yanks arrived!"

And over lunch I was treated to thumbnail sketches of both Mitzi's hopefuls, and Charles's old chums, who came very late, in force, debouching from a vast American car: "muscling in, for all the world like a bunch of GIs set on liberation"; and were last heard planning to carry Kate off to some five-star place in Bucks. That was when Chloë pulled out.

"How many were there?" I asked.

"Oh, three or four, I think. They all look so alike, enormous and blond and tanned, in those sort of 'private eye' macs —Sam Spade, you now—and moaning about the English weather. And demanding dry martinis: they even invaded the pantry, much to Mrs. Furze's consternation—found a cocktail shaker and some olives . . . Rather took over. So I left."

"And Kate?"

"Well, she was amazingly cool and unruffled about all this—rather witty too, I thought, and the Yankees laughed a great deal . . . She's very attractive when she laughs, isn't she?"

"So she was enjoying it all."

"Taking it in her stride, certainly."

"It must have been quite an ordeal after not really entertaining at all for so long: I should have been there to help her . . ."

"Oh, Mitzi Hogan asked about you, of course—and Adrian—*gasping* for gossip; but Kate said you'd gone to London about some job in the Far East. 'Ooh—you would miss the dear creature, wouldn't you? A little bird tells me he's been ever so busy—working in the garden and so forth . . . ?' But she didn't get any joy; Kate has this way of slipping her gears, you know: detaching herself—doesn't she? I remember you called it 'going absent'."

"Yes," I said: "a useful knack. Self-protective opacity."

"Ah!—but now we know where her mind wanders off *to*, don't we?"

"Look here, Chloë: you can't really think that a grown-up woman of her intelligence—"

"All right—all right—forget it! Play it your way, or her way, or what you will: go on! But you still aren't exactly sweeping her off her feet—are you, Laurence—after two months—more!—of being at her beck and call? And I'll bet she doesn't even kiss you on the cheek, does she? She kisses Mr. Hogan . . . That's why you're quitting the field, I suppose? Going off to shoot wild beasts or chase diamond mines or what-ever. Me—I'd be sorely tempted to dress up as the jolly old Noone Walker she's so gone on and make a fairly heavy pass at her. Give her a thrill; bring her to her senses. That's what she needs."

I had thought about it all too often; and even a month ago I might still have considered such a step seriously, if it had served my purpose. But now I wanted to win Kate on my own merits. And the more I studied her, the more it became clear to me that she was putting up a brave front: she was far more delicately balanced between real life and fantasy than Chloë's dismissive "jumpy", or "dodgy", could cover. Her charm, her easy confidences about boring matchmakers, were diversions merely: those "absences" were the nearest one ever got to her true preoccupation. For then she was thinking about the Noone Walker.

Her obsession was eating her away. Only at midday and at midnight did her real life blossom—and then, abortively. For he never came. One morning in the last week of May, I almost believed he had, for she seemed strangely bright-eyed and feverish, and laughed a lot at Henry's terrible jokes. I could do nothing except be there when she wanted me; even—

perhaps—when she might need me. How then should I seriously contemplate that extreme solution? Realise her ghostly lover for her; and, for myself, the scene I had so often enacted in fantasy? "This time I can feel you . . ." But this time more: much more. I would make love to her. Then, in the drowsy convalescence from that fever, persuade her to accept the truth . . . ? It could as easily destroy her reason as open her eyes; such a revelation cannot be fed piecemeal. And, though apparently capable of loving the ghost who had killed her husband, could Kate feel the same about the man?

So May ended, still in macs and wellies, and teas by the fire while the rain slapped at the window panes of Henry's nursery— my nursery: I was reliving my childhood, almost happily, for as long as it was within my grasp. Kate often went out in the evenings now; but never with me. I had suggested it once, and she looked quite scared, and said: "Oh, that's not really us, is it, Laurence?" So I did not press her: flattered, momentarily, that I was different —even special—in her eyes. But I avoided being there when someone was coming to collect her. At least she had the grace never to suggest I baby-sat while she dined *à deux* with "a business chum of Charles's", or "the interesting gallery owner Adrian brought over: just might lead to something—paintingwise . . ."

Now I knew how Jane Eyre must have felt when Rochester went off riding with Blanche Ingram—and I was no penniless governess; no mousy dependant. But, like Jane, I believe I had become familiar; even indispensable.

On the first day of June, the sun came out; and, in the general euphoria, the casting of clouts, and the sudden glory of summer at Noone, Kate Gelhorn proposed to me.

15

"**D**ON'T say anything till you've heard the terms, Laurence: my terms—and, of course, I must hear yours. It's just an idea. Maybe I flatter myself . . . And don't look so incredulous, my dear: I know this is a touch unconventional, but—well, I told you all along you were special. Didn't I?"

She had sent Henry out for a walk with Nanny before I arrived—at twelve-fifteen —to help plant the urns with white nicotiana. Immediately I was surprised, especially when she called me into her upstairs sitting room. This, I remembered, had been arranged as Charles's palatial dressing room; now it was re-papered in the old Chinese pattern chosen by the Noone Walker; and housed her desk, filing cabinet, a low table and a pair of pretty sofas. I thought I must be here for my marching orders—until she sat me down, poured some white wine and said, rather breathlessly: "Cheers, Laurence! I wondered if you'd consider marrying me?"

I don't remember saying much. She spent some time explaining her position; and, to begin with, she looked out of the window, only glancing at me for my reactions.

"It's not exactly simple being a rich (you know I am, don't you?) and youngish widow—so obviously marriage-worthy, I mean. I have tried to be sociable, and to consider, seriously, finding a good stepfather for Henry—"

"But not a husband for you."

"No. I've *been* in love—ages ago, in my twenties—and lived with him for four years. I've got to tell you all this because it's relevant, you see. Anyway, it didn't work out. He left me, in fact, and it—it broke my heart. And I knew I'd never love anyone again . . . Then Charles came along. He could give me everything I wanted: essentially, I suppose, time and space to paint. No strings. All he wanted was an heir: I was his third wife. Oh, we got on very well"—she squinted through her wine-glass at the green garden. "I mean, I quite amused him; and he was

very generous, always. He seemed to—
well, he reckoned I had 'class': good
breeding material, with an 'Hon.' to my
name—somewhat tarnished, perhaps, by
my Bohemian period. Anyway, he spelt it
out, and I knew what I was taking on. I
got pregnant, and we were married. No
complaints."

"Really, Kate?"

"None. Well—I did get a bit upset,
actually—more so than I expected—when
he had other ladies. One quite serious, I
believe, at the time he died: the Principessa, so called. He was . . . Oh, he was
thinking of leaving me: even talked about
it, the evening he was killed. Weird. I was
fearfully mixed up about all that . . . Oh,
I'd have been all right, financially, of
course. But Henry—well, by then, and
being so much more together at Noone,
he'd begun to be very important to me . . .
And, you see, for a moment—when
Charles was going on about it: 'no harm
in Henry's having a brace of Moms' and
so forth—well, I actually wished him dead
. . . God—I can't think why I'm
unloading all this, Laurence. Quite
unnecessary: I'm sorry. I suppose it's all

this raking over the past, trying to tell you everything I think you should know before you consider taking me on."

"Fine. Please continue," I said.

"Dear me, how chilling! You sound like a lawyer, or a headmaster."

"Not at all, Kate: you have set out to be rational about this, and so must I. Sometimes I express myself in a rather old-fashioned manner, perhaps: the rector in me." A startled glance from my interviewer. "I come from a long line, remember, albeit on the distaff side. So: you are not looking for someone to love. And in that case can I assume you are not in love with someone you can't marry?"

She got up and put a piece of ice in her wine. "Oh, yes," she said, her back towards me. "You can assume that with the utmost assurance. I'm not likely to go and desert you for another."

All very close to the chest, these cards. And no Shakespearian riddles, like: I love no living man. She went on smoothly: "I've been subjected to more than my fair share of fortune-hunters recently—and some sexual philanthropists—'The poor sweetie hasn't had it in yonks,' or 'Relax:

let me do you a favour.'" My turn to reach for the ice-bucket; and quickly she said, "I'm embarrassing you now . . . But this isn't some sort of boasting, my dear: I'm determined to make you see my state of affairs—sorry: my situation, warts and all."

"I understand: don't apologise. The point is: I don't threaten you—right? They've been pouncing, and I'm just—"

"One even dropped a condom on the carpet when he pulled out his cigarettes! Oh dear, you gotta laugh . . ." She was; and so did I. Amidst all the past-raking, the pouncers, and the earnest insistence she was not looking for love, I suddenly realised that I was going to marry Kate Gelhorn. That was all I needed. The rest would follow.

She reached over and poured me some more wine; and I could smell her hair, her skin, and the light daytime scent she used. It was like this when we were consulting over plans, or doing a tricky job in the garden together; and I still kept my black costume gloves in a drawer of my desk, wrapped up carefully to hold that perfume. As with magic wishes one dare not spend, I rationed the luxury of unwrapping them and breathing it in. Now I had cornered the source of supply. Kate was mine—and I only saw later that never for one moment did I think twice about my choice. Meanwhile, I had to stay cool, taking my cue from her; and she could talk terms till the cows came home. But for me, there was no choice.

She did not sound cornered.

"Now then, Laurence. Brass-tack time: my terms. (I'm pulling a 'Charles' on you, aren't I? But you can always refuse, of course. I do hope you won't . . .) It's as I've implied, I guess: *chambres séparées*. You go your way and I go mine. I don't like calling it a 'marriage of convenience', as he did: this is so much more. And I don't see myself sleeping around. But you can do as you wish; discreetly, of course. You're young—twenty-eight, right?—and it would be perfectly natural for you to have affairs—"

"But not with the governess, or the upstairs maid. Or the porter, come to that." I was stunned, but still walking.

"Right. Or one's best friends: that's a

bit messy . . . I wondered about Chloë Bender."

It was my turn to laugh first; and she smiled, watching me.

"So—not Chloë."

"Oh, no, Kate: she's just a pal."

"*Touché*." She bowed her head briefly in acknowledgement; and while I could, I struck again, and with a broader blade, at the exposed neck that I loved so much.

"Her younger sisters, maybe. Is that too close to home?"

"You must give me notice of that question," she said. She was looking down at her list—yes, she had a list—and I could not see her eyes; her voice was thin and colourless. A very palpable hit, I thought; but I did not enjoy it much. "Now," she said, "shall I go into wills and so on?"

"Not now."

"Just this, then. Basically, if I die first, you get Noone for life, and half of everything; plus the use, with wise management, of Henry's half until he's eighteen, on condition you bring him up as your own."

"I'm surprised that isn't a precondition for 'my' half too," I said. "That sounds fine: generous. Caring for Hen goes without saying, as far as I'm concerned: indeed, it might be one of my own preconditions—though I'm not yet ready with my list: you have, I confess, taken me somewhat unawares."

"Sorry, Laurence; but, as I said, I don't demand an immediate answer. And we can work out the finer print if and when you say yes . . ."

"I don't believe this. It isn't happening—" I heard myself mumble. Whether it was the wine on an empty stomach (I had driven back from London at first light when I saw the summer had come), or the new-found fortune, or simply Kate's suddenly being mine—on whatever terms—I felt dazed, and covered my eyes. Her voice went on, evenly.

"Laurence: you love Noone and so do I. You get on with Henry; and I believe you're fond of him. He adores you. You are civilised and interesting and gentle and good company; we're used to each other and can be together without talking, without needing to explain. We're both very private, I think, and enjoy being alone. And we like the same things—Noone apart."

I looked up. She was still studying her list. "Kate, are you reading out the 'pros' to me now?"

"Well, yes: I had to work out the pros and cons: it's a big decision. I've had to think about every angle. Do you find that very cold-blooded?"

"No, not at all—given the basic premiss. Actually, Kate, I'm impressed. Do go on."

"Well, that's it really: quite a string of good reasons, I think. And of course the fact that you don't *need* my money . . . But you can surely see why it's you I've chosen—so to speak. Chosen to propose to. Can't you?"

"Do you really think you know me well enough, Kate? Suppose you found I had some terrible secret in my past."

"Well, d'you want to tell me about it? I mean, have you? You see—" she did not pause for an answer: too preoccupied with her own. Another unspoken pact: you keep yours and I'll keep mine. Hardly a fair exchange; I had discovered hers, and it was clear she suspected me not at all.

"You see, I believe we know each othe
better than most people who get married
certainly better than I knew Charles
We've sort of—bumbled along together
making plans and seeing them through
coping with setbacks, talking about the
things we like. Listening; demanding
nothing. Sharing Henry; and you've go
closer to him than his real father ever did
We've spent *ordinary time* together: so
much more like real life than the usua
courting couple; and I think you're my
best friend. Isn't that a hell of a lot?—Bu
I won't go on. I feel a bit silly anyway, in
case I'm flogging a dead horse . .
Speaking of which, I could eat one. But—
do *you* have any questions?"

"Yes. What happens to Henry's inherit
ance—Charles's money—if we have
another? Another child."

"We won't, Laurence; separate rooms
Anything else? No, wait: I can't jus
dismiss that, can I?—Not the money so
much: the question it raises . . ." Now
maybe, to qualify this *chambres séparées*
I thought; but she went on: "You're only
twenty-eight, and I'm imposing childless
ness on you for life; though I guess we

410

can well afford the odd—again discreet—
paternity suit. Not the same as having
your own children, though. It's quite a
price to pay, for a man who likes kids."

"Not 'kids'; Henry. Another Henry."

"Well, that's not on. So; think about it
carefully. Most women couldn't accept
that clause . . . Funny: it's the reverse of
Charles's terms—except for the money.
But the same money: his."

"I'm going to work, you know."

"As you wish. And I shall go on
painting. Yes, it's a good idea, I should
think—though we'd both miss you badly
. . . Oh—but not in the Far East,
Laurence? No, that is not a precondition"
—she laughed and stood up, draining her
glass—"I'm not *that* unreasonable! Just—
well, it would rather defeat the object of
the exercise: to live here, all three of us,
at Noone." All four of us, I thought.
"Lunch," she said. "Unless, of course,
you want to go. To go away and think
about it? Or because you've decided what
you think, and the answer is no?" All at
once she looked young and nervous,
standing there holding the tray.

I took it from her and put it down. "I

have decided what I think," I said. "The answer is yes." I took her hand and bent and kissed it. Then she put her hands on my shoulders, and kissed me on both cheeks.

Celebration. An alfresco banquet by the lake. No mere picnic: this was far too grand, with Abbott and Stevens the chauffeur and Mrs. Furze carrying down the napkin-shrouded hamper, cloths, silver, glasses, a bucket of ice. Kate supervised the packing of the hamper: there were caviare and sour cream on fresh muffins, and poached salmon and asparagus, and imported raspberries with cream, and champagne.

"So you knew I would accept," I said.

"No: I gambled—though it's not like me to tempt providence, actually. I think the weather put me in reckless mood: the sky so clear all night—" (had she waited till her candles went out, and waited on, watching the stars?)—"then the sun this morning—and the radio saying it had set fair. Did you hear it, in London?"

"Yes; and I started down about six; I couldn't wait."

"My poor one—but you must be

ravenous!" And the way she looked right into my eyes and smiled was different now. "As soon as you phoned and said you'd be over, I sent Stevens to collect this lot from Colchester."

"And Pepsi! *And* Jungle-juice iced-lolly!" said Henry. He was helping Mrs. Furze tuck the double-damask corners into the basket.

"Fine," said Kate. "And we'll just carry the cushions."

We ran down the garden with cushions under each free arm, and Henry holding our hands in the middle. Mere symmetry, I told myself; and it will be just as symmetrical with a child on each side and us between them, holding hands: if she has waited this long for me to appear in my eighteenth-century rigout from Nathan & Berman, I can wait too.

My quarry, moreover, was more worth the hunting: very much flesh and blood. Kate's weariness seemed to fall away—like her interview manner and her crumpled list—as soon as I said yes. Hearing Henry come in from his walk, she had run to the top of the stairs to tell him the good news; then Mrs. Furze, and Abbott, and

Stevens. Even the builders working on the dairy, and the contractors digging the swimming pool in the walled garden, seemed to know there was something afoot; and I found later she sent a case of cold beer out to them, "to celebrate Mr. Gill's joining the team". Everyone was smiling on us and winking and raising their thumbs in salute. As we waved back —like minor Royalty—I thought: And the best of British to you too; and wondered what they might say if they knew no broad marriage bed was involved.

But Kate was happy, and looked so lovely, I put away dark thoughts about her "Christmas tree" face in the mirror one cold night in March. I knew very well that face was not for me. Not yet. I was marrying her, but I had yet to win her. And she was so cleverly setting up this arrangement whereby she would be protected from fleshy, pawing suitors, and still be free for her midnight love. I knew that, some time—and it might take time —I would have to lay the Noone Walker once and for all.

That evening I took her out to dinner: our

first date. Afterwards, lingering over our coffee and brandy, under one of the romantic garden alcoves the restaurant used in summer, I watched her gazing silently into the candle-flame, and thought of some of the questions I might have asked. Did you know, Kate, when you decided to propose, that I was hopelessly in love with you? And, if so, do you even begin to see the cruelty of your demands? —Or have you, in your obsession with the pale cleric, quite forgotten the needs of mere mortals? And, setting that on one side (as if one could), is it fair to suggest so unequal a partnership, with all the love on one side? Or do you consider your money weighs so much . . . ? But I had not asked them, because I already knew my answer: You only have to refuse.

Kate was neither cruel nor unreasonable —though she might be a little mad. She did not realise I was so far gone in love, because she was in the self-same state, and she could not see past it. She was obsessed. And I knew all about that: indeed, my obsession with Noone, and the steps I took to repossess it, had given birth to this monstrous triangle. I was in love with a woman who was in love with a ghost. Impasse.

"What are you thinking, Laurence?"

"Are we allowed to ask that?"

"Certainly: neither of us need answer. Demanding nothing—right?"

"Right. I was thinking how little we really know each other. No, not cold feet. Just thinking; and that it will be good finding out more . . . For example, do you always chew your brandy?"

She laughed. "I don't chew it: I 'squelch' it—though I try not to if I'm on my best behaviour. I take a sip, then squeeze it through my teeth and all round —well, my gums, I guess. Charles was shocked: 'Do all Hons behave like that?' But you get twice the flavour: try it. Gets you twice as intoxicated into the bargain, according to my first boyfriend; we were both fairly broke, and decided it was a fine way of having two for the price of one."

"It feels marvellous," I said. "I can see us on either side of the fire in our old age, squelching away—"

"Oh, Laurence . . ." Kate was tender; then suddenly serious, busy moulding the candle-wax. "Laurence, it will work,

416

won't it? Us?—I mean we are 'suited', don't you think? If we're prepared to take time and trouble over it?"

"Well, you convinced *me*." I wasn't going over the top for her—though that might be what she wanted: her with her good reasons, me with my poetry. I trusted I was learning some of her cool. "And you're right: we both need time, for different reasons."

"But I haven't bulldozed you into this? It was a bit odd, the whole business: sitting there with my list . . . Seems so long ago now."

"I don't feel bulldozed, Kate," I said. "I feel somewhat—solemn, I think. And happy."

I knew the best, the only sure, way of convincing her we were "suited", and smoothing out her lovely forehead. But not yet; nowhere near yet, I warned myself . . . Even to stroke her arm (as she had mine once, so passionately; by candlelight, too) would be a threat: "sexual harassment", they call it.

Tantalised, I reached out and touched her hand. "I must get you a ring, Kate, now that we are engaged. Would you like to choose it with me?"

"Have you a family one—your mother's, maybe?"

"Yes. In the bank. A dark sapphire. It would be good with the eyes ... And what sort of wedding ring?"

She was no longer wearing Charles's broad platinum band; she must have removed it before she came out for dinner: I liked that. Now she studied the pale stripe on her brown left hand, as tanned as mine from gardening, and the broader stripe under the slender gold watch she wore for best—then started and reached for her purse.

"God! D'you know the time? I had no idea it was that late."

"Half-past eleven? Afraid of turning into a pumpkin?"

"Come, Laurence—please. Can we go quickly? It's terribly late."

I finished my brandy, and asked for the bill. I could have queried it, or lost my way driving home, or left vital papers at the restaurant and insisted on going back. I could have kept her out until well after midnight. But, because I was in love myself, I knew what she was going through. When I got her back to Noone at ten to twelve, she said: "See you tomorrow—ring me early? Oh—thanks, Laurence!" and pecked me on the cheek.

I could perfectly fairly have said, "I'm coming in for a night-cap, Kate"; like all the pouncers—except that I was within my rights. But, as I learned over the following weeks, night time is uncertain ground. Night time is about "sleeping", and about 'bed". Even quite early, long before the witching hour, Kate used to grow oddly shy and prickly, more like a spinster than a woman who had lived with men for most of her adult life. Soon after dinner she would claim she was tired, it had been a long day, and so on. She looked tired too; and I would leave her, knowing she needed sleep before her vigil. Knowing, moreover, that if I stayed, I would ache even more with the need to hold her, and love her, and keep her from that vigil. At the end of our engagement day, I only drew her back to kiss her cheek in return; then let her go, and headed for home. In a little while, I comforted myself, Noone would be home; then things would change.

Everyone was delighted, and not the least surprised: "We all knew something was going on over there at the Rectory," they said.

Chloë was triumphant; and hid her surprise very well: only she had known the sort of "fine romance" it had been. "Oh, but it's perfect! Absolutely—and I feel especially pleased of course, as I introduced them in the first place. Too satisfactory for words—and *so* right for each other, bless them."

To me, alone, and later—for I had dropped in next morning to tell her, and found her with Percival, children and weekend guests—she said: "So, Laurence. Did you pounce after all?—*She* proposed to *you*? Well! I mean, it's right in the tradition, where so much wealth is involved—but I'm still somewhat startled . . . And so terribly pleased for you, my dear! Well, you've stolen her away from her ghostly parson, haven't you? Maybe a descendant seemed the next best thing— better, on cold winter nights . . ."

We planned a quiet wedding, very soon, at Noone Ampney church. Kate flew her sister and brother-in-law over from Canada; I asked the second cousin I used to lunch with in my City days to be my best man. Neither of us had much family to speak of: a maiden aunt of Kate's, and her Anglesey cousins; my father's brother —my other godfather—whom I had not seen since prep school. These, the Glyn-Joneses, the Benders, Flavia, Mordecai and the Hogan gang, a few friends from London—like Sarah and her man— together with the Noone dependants and certain Noone Ampney worthies, made up the party of thirty or so. They nearly filled the tiny church that my piratical forebear had built soon after the death of his patron, Elizabeth I; any remaining space was crammed, by Jean Glyn-Jones and Mrs. Furze, with June flowers from their own gardens, and from Noone.

Clifford Hogan gave away the bride. She wore a grey-blue satiny dress that flowed and eddied when she moved; and she left her thick hair down, all shiny and swinging, on my demand.

"Is that a precondition?" she asked.

421

I smiled (smiled most of the time that fortnight, as the day came closer and I fell more in love with Kate) and shook my head. "I just want to marry the Kate I know," I said.

I had in fact produced not one precondition.

Edward Glyn-Jones, when I told him of our engagement—and after the celebratory sherry, and congratulations, and tactfully phrased approval that Noone was coming back into the family after all—insisted we should talk seriously about marriage settlements and the rights of future children.

"Though naturally you will have discussed that with Mrs—with your fiancée: but so important, for the heirs' sakes, to make sure such arrangements are cut-and-dried. Likewise your will, Laurence: you will have to redraft it, in consideration of your own children—Oh, certainly before the 'happy expectations', dear boy: a deceased male, after all, may still have offspring nine months later."

All our friends—some sooner than others—seemed to get round to the subject of children: little brothers and sisters for

Henry. Dickie Bone, the retired pop-star, who, for my money, gave the best value in the Hogan gang, said siblings were In this year—"and all the rage among the Chinese backlash, they tell me. One-child families are absolutely passée."

"Shut up, Dickie: Kate will hear you."

He stopped goofing for a moment. "Oh God—doesn't she want one, then?"

"No, she doesn't."

"What? Not even her own little couture sibling, and in time for Henry as a wee Easter surprise? With the new-wave 'Iroquois' markings?" He always said my scar-lines made me look like a Red Indian brave; and referred to me as "Little Chief Sitting Duck" (he was six-foot-four), because, he said, I was "so sickeningly eligible".

"Well, *you* won't be making a speech at the wedding," I said: "that's for sure . . ."

Keeping up the appearance of a normal engaged couple was something we both worked at, without consultation; and I liked being in company with Kate because she would link arms with me, or take my hand when it was time to go. When dancing came up at a party, we danced rather formally, in an old-fashioned way; and she did not nestle, nor kiss me, nor sit with her hand on my knee for form's sake: careful, perhaps, not to put me through more than was necessary. Maybe it was simpler than that: she did not want to. But there was an electric current, a connection: in a look, or such brief physical contact as we had—and especially in public: as though we shared a secret— that made our engagement, too, pleasantly old-fashioned. I, at least, found it deliciously tantalising, keeping the weighty lid of formality on my passions: I was convinced it would not be for long. Just what Kate felt, I could not know—except that she liked being with me. And when I received that electric charge, surely she felt it too? In the miniature world of synapses and nerve-endings, surely it took two to tango?

We did have a secret, of course: our unconventional contract. Not on paper, naturally. Anything binding would have had to be handled by solicitors; and Glyn-Jones, watching over my interests, would point out—after a decent pause for shocked disapproval—that such terms as

Kate demanded immediately rendered any contract of marriage null and void: conjugal rights were recognised by law.

I knew this; but I did not make it one of my questions at our strange "proposal" interview. I knew that I could sue Kate for the denial of such rights, divorce her, and probably be awarded half her wealth. She would keep Noone of course; and she could claim I had agreed to abrogate those rights. But my brief would simply counter, "That is not what my client understood by your term '*chambres séparées*'—though he did agree not to demand children of his own: another matter entirely."

I am sure no such scenes flashed, even subliminally, through my mind when Kate proposed and I accepted. Sometimes at night, in my mill cottage, I had glimpses of them. But I did not really believe in Kate's extraordinary "terms" during those weeks: I was exclusively preoccupied with the prospect of loving her and getting her to love me. My doubts were very few, and based only on the sober realisation— usually in the small dark hours of those nights—that, by her proposal, Kate was making a nutty, desperate bid for security and peace. Like her infatuation with an imaginary lover, it was to escape from reality.

In which case she needed my help far more than she knew.

The wedding was at five. Kate's Anglesey cousins had requested it might be around midday, so that they could get back to their busy farm that evening; but Chloë offered them beds, and I insisted they stay: whenever else, the wedding should not be at noon. I cannot say just what I anticipated; but, knowing what I did, it seemed fairer to Kate.

As it was, no sepulchral voice raised "cause or just impediment". For a moment before her first response, Kate glanced back over her shoulder down the church, and I felt a tingle of alarm. The bishop waited, smiling expectantly; and I leant close to her, catching and holding her eyes, and whispered: "You do, don't you?" And she said clearly, "I do."

During the reception on the terrace and west lawn at Noone, Chloë murmured, "Dodgy little moment, that . . ."

"And I suppose everyone's talking about it."

"Not unkindly at all: she's had a rough time, and they all know it—and she's bloomed so, Laurence, since all this happened. Carry on the good work, my dear!"

"I intend to," I said.

We did not want to go away for a honeymoon: the garden was suddenly repaying all our hard labour, the pool was finished and filled, the weather still lovely. Henry, roaring around in best bib-and-tucker, was excited about going back to Anglesey with his female cousins for a fortnight of cows and sea. We wanted to be at Noone.

Not even Chloë knew; and we went through the whole charade of changing and leaving in Kate's beribboned Mercedes, then returning to the stables by the back way, where my car was hidden, and driving to Orford for dinner.

Noone was quiet and tidy when we returned at eleven.

"I am going to have a night-cap, Mrs. Gill," I said. "What about you?"

She glanced at the hall clock. "Why not?" she said. "Brandy?"

We took it into the library, and I put a match to the neatly laid fire. Mrs. Furze knew, of course; and had set on the hearth the two pairs of patchwork velvet slippers she had been working away at to give us as wedding presents.

"Bless her: so she finished them in time! Well," said Kate collapsing into a chair and kicking off her elegant shoes, "and how does it feel to be at home?"

16

DICKIE BONE would have been able to recommend at least fourteen different ways to spend the nights of a honeymoon, without even starting on the Kama Sutra. I am proud to say I never did the same thing twice. Scrabble, *War and Peace*, astronomy (with my telescope on the roof), Wagner, china-mending, woodcarving, catching up on the geological journals, cooking and eating an elaborate second supper, painting one of the attic rooms, getting drunk slowly in four different ways—brandy, malt whisky, Calvados, claret—and writing away for jobs. Late-night television also became a friend, and especially at weekends when it went on until two.

Sometimes, of course, I did more than one thing. The night I got drunk on Calvados, I delivered Henry's cat, Julie Andrews, of four kittens. The night I listened to *Rhinegold* and *The Valkyries*, I also discovered the joys of *Logic*

Problems—a slim magazine I had picked up months before in Brookall. The night I played Scrabble was after two hours' driving round the countryside, and having a late hamburger in Southend.

That was one of the worst, towards the end of the fortnight, when I was longing to have Henry home as a diversion—not, of course in the small hours, but to tire me. I went up to the nursery about ten, to sort his toys, lay out a new railway track; and on her way to bed Kate found me there.

"Are you all right, Laurence dear?" she said—as she had so many times before.

"No, I'm not, Katy dear" (the first time I had said that). "But don't worry, I'm not going to get drunk again: that was yesterday. You see, I try a different leisure activity each night, to keep my interests broad, open new horizons." I picked up the Scrabble box. "D'you want a game?"

"No, thanks: I'm off to bed . . . You sound very bitter."

"Do I? How odd. I can't think why."

"What did you do at the mill cottage?"

"You asked me that before, and I said I listened to records and thought about you. But you didn't like that. I also saw my friends—Chloë or Adrian or Dickie—or indulged in affairs: they take quite a lot of time."

"Maybe you should get out more—at least after this fortnight's over and we're officially 'back'."

"Maybe I'll go out now: it's a good idea. Don't worry: I won't stop in at the local and give the game away. I'll range far and wide. Broad horizons: that's the ticket."

I drove, rather too fast, halfway to London; then decided I was hungry, and that Southend, as a popular resort, would have junk-food cafés open late. When I got back, the Scrabble was still there on the landing where I had left it; and I took it to my room and played against an egg-timer through the watches of the night.

I resisted sleeping-pills: I could not tell how long a course I might be in for, at the present rate of progress, and did not want to become dependent on them. I am sure we both found it hard; and we made a point of being particularly thoughtful and affectionate—verbally—in the morning and all day. We always did. But, like a child, I began to dread the dark, the need to come in from the garden, to close doors and turn on lights.

Supper was usually left ready, or nearly ready, by Mrs. Furze; Kate was an excellent cook and made one dish most evenings: gazpacho or a soufflé or a syllabub. If we wanted to watch something on television, we had supper on the low table in the library; or we ate at the kitchen table, with candles, and talked.

Kate was quite right: we got on excellently, and there was never a moment of boredom. We talked a great deal about practical things: the games room we planned for Henry and the friends he would bring home from school next year; the fittings for my large attic study: showcases for my mineral samples, broad, shallow drawers for my diagrams and drawings, underlit surfaces for my slides. We even planned a billiards room in the stables: Kate was going to teach me snooker if I taught her the real thing.

(Like a ribald parrot on my shoulder, Dickie Bone haunted me with apt comments. The "real thing" set him off, as did ball games in general; and any talk of digging or sowing, or pollinating the melons, stimulated him—my own Imaginary Friend—to locker-room bawdry. I disowned him; actually caught myself brushing him off my shoulder, the night of the long claret. But I saw by daylight it was just another form of safety valve, this silent ventriloquist act.)

We talked of the garden, and often brought catalogues to the dinner table; but never books. Not yet. Sometimes we listened, through meals and afterwards, to whole operas. Kate was introducing me to *The Cunning Little Vixen*; I played her *Dido and Aeneas*. We both had fair enough voices—hers surprisingly low and sweet: an excellent thing in a woman—to remind each other of leitmotivs or Cole Porter songs. With Henry, we used to sing in the car.

She often hummed while she weeded. Indeed, this brought to a head one of our few confrontations. Working on the other side of the border, I said, "Kate: could you stop humming that particular tune?"

"Sorry. What is it?" And she hummed it again quickly, feeling for the words. "'You can say your lips are not for . . .' Oh, Laurence"—she stood up—"does *every* touch draw blood . . . ? And d'you know how it goes on? 'But you can't hide—'"

"Yes, I know: 'the kiss that's in your eyes'. No, dammit: if all such cheap lyrics touched me, I'd be a very poor man. Those are just the mushy American words. No: it's by Léhar."

"Well—and very nice, too . . . What are the real words, then?"

"Its title is 'Chambres Séparées'."

"Sorry, Laurence." She picked up the watering can and went off towards the walled garden.

After a moment, I followed her. I said: "You must have known: subconsciously, anyway . . . Kate, does that mean you're —that our present arrangement is on your mind? That it bothers you?" She was silent, watering. "Would you like to talk it over?"

"No, thank you. We have."

"Not really. I said yes to you on any terms, because—as you know now, if you didn't know then—I love you."

"I don't think I knew. Or I couldn't have asked you. That would not be quite fair . . . I just thought you were fond of me; that we were in sympathy. I thought that was enough. As I told you, I've managed with less. Maybe you should have said. I mean—I can't change now . . . Is that enough talking? It is for me."

She put down the watering can and went off to her barn. She had said she would have a holiday from painting just for a fortnight: "There's so much to do, and we can get a lot more done, together." But that afternoon she started painting again, and spent part of every day painting from then on.

I looked round for a taxing job: I needed total immersion. We had planned a low wall in the back yard, incorporating a barbecue, a stretch for sitting and watching, and open-topped ends to fill with plants. Now I got busy, carting the old bricks for it up from the stables.

"Why on earth don't you wait till Abbott and his lads are back?" Kate said, passing through the stable yard with hammer and tacks. "Only till Monday. They'll take them up for you."

"I want them now," I said.

On my next journey, I looked into the

barn. "What are you up to?" I asked. "Can I fix something for you?"

She shook her head, her mouth full of tacks.

"I'll hold for you," I said.

She stopped and took out the tacks. "Look, I've always stretched my own canvases—OK? Thanks anyway."

That was the Calvados night. The next night I wrote off about a job in Cambridge, advertised in the Sunday papers; and the next day, Henry, Mrs. Furze, Abbott and co.—normal life—returned.

So did our friends, ringing or dropping in. Once they had got over the admiration of our tans, the hearty jokes—"Laurence is looking very short of sleep"—and all the other formalities, plus the astonishment over our having been at Noone all the time ("Clearly keeping a very low profile, Little Chief: positively horizontal . . ."), it was good to have them there. And marvellous to have Henry, and show him the kittens. He claimed he had improved his diving, and had learned to milk a cow; "And I'll demonstrate, if you like—on that one of Farmer Growl's, over there—shall I?"

"No, darling: I wouldn't. That one's a bull . . ."

Our evenings became social and more relaxed, with dinners and parties, and even trips to London for plays or the opera. Kate never wanted to dine out afterwards, claiming she got too sleepy to enjoy it; but twice we did, at our host's insistence, and returned long after midnight. The first time this happened, I could not stop myself taking a stroll round the garden after she had gone to bed; and I saw, as I had on many such late walks—all ill-advised, and all regretted—the curtains drawn back, the two candles. And I knew that, if I went up as far as the ha-ha, I would be able to see the dark oval of the looking glass, the bright curve of her left shoulder beyond it.

Twice I went over to Cambridge for interviews. This was a job I had heard of by word of mouth, back in the dark days (or so they had seemed then) before we were engaged. The Sumatra-based firm had mentioned it was coming vacant, and would certainly suit "the more academic kind of geologist"; but as I clearly wanted to travel, then their own offer, etc. etc. Once I found Kate and Noone were to be mine—and despite my stated decision to work—I turned down the offers I had, and even put the Cambridge post out of my mind: caring for my new wife and winning her heart would more than occupy my time. Now, casting around, I was sure the job would have gone; till I saw the advertisement.

It was a university post, chiefly funded by a mining conglomerate, but attached to a college. It promised the best of both worlds: research, largely for specific projects, and some overseeing of work at thesis level: "Mineral, with animal attachments," as one of the dons put it.

"Not the least of the latter being the nubile Donna," another chipped in: "you will meet her later: your assistant metallurgist. The original Great Red Rock-Eater."

"Who will take over when you need to travel—though I suppose we should continue to employ the subjunctive outside these four walls. If only for the long ears of other candidates."

The second, the "short-list" interview, was brief; mainly to tell me I could almost certainly have the job if I felt it was right for me; and to introduce me to "my" college. There I came across an old friend and correspondent of Uncle Laurie's: the college chaplain. That clinched it for me; and possibly for them.

The one drawback was that the job did not start till September. After another week on the rack at Noone, I rang them and asked if I could start now, without pay. It offered a respite; a means of spending time away from Kate's impossible proximity, using my brains on more soluble problems than our impasse, and even spending the odd night or two in college. I was glad when the dons agreed.

"Rack" is a touch melodramatic. It was more like being starved out—and, after the first cavalry charge of Henry and our friends, the siege had tightened. I was running short of resources, and morale was low. Being disciplined, British, and Nice, our manners only improved under such stress. We were fond, considerate, harmonious; as Kate said (and only once), we had "so much else to share". There was drawing, music, the house, the garden, reading, playing with Henry—and she was clearly enjoying him more than ever with a resident man to help control him, to smooth their frictions, or jolly them out of their grouches. Henry was happy and looking forward to school in September. Kate was pleasant and charming; friends said she too was so happy. But I knew she was not really there.

She had gone absent again, as in the early days of our acquaintance; and even making allowances for her as a committed artist—"living in a world apart", as Mitzi Hogan had said, a little stung by her coolness—Kate's privacy, behind her bright smile and her dreaming eyes, was almost pathological. It would have worried me even if she had simply been a friend.

She would paint nearly all morning, starting early; sleep heavily for an hour in the afternoon, and paint again until the light was going; then attack the garden. She did not neglect the house; on the contrary, she was hyperactive: "so much to fit in, and the summer flashing by," she would say. I watched her driving herself; working up little routines, and racing herself: this much to be done before the kettle boiled, including putting away the caddy, brushing up the tea she had spilt in her haste, opening the kitchen shutters, laying the tray with a pretty cloth, cups, milk, spoons—and closing the fridge door. Intervals on television were the same: as soon as she could see the flickering square in the corner of the screen that preceded the advertisements, she would get ready.

"Why do you do it?" I asked. "Are you trying to prove something? Or is it just superstitious: such and such will come right if one can beat the kettle—or the ads—or the clock striking?"

"A bit of both, I guess," she said. "Sorry if it bothers you. Please don't watch if you find it irritating . . . But remember you once said I was never on time? . . . All right: that I 'was not precise about time'. Well, maybe I'm just trying to improve . . . And"—brightly—"this way I fit so much more into the day. Anyway, you won't have to watch if you're getting a job—will you, Laurence?"

"Do you mind my starting right away?" I asked.

"Not at all. I'm painting: at least I'm not like Mitzi was, with nothing to fill her days. Poor old Cliff . . ." (Mitzi had walked out on him two weeks before; gone off with a younger man. It had surprised me; but Adrian claimed they'd all seen it coming.) "And you'll have your job in Cambridge. Hen's got Noone, and Nanny, and Abbott—"

"And an imaginary friend or two. But maybe he's growing out of those . . ." I could not resist. A few days before, when I was busy with my wall, I had heard her going by below me, along the rose terrace, with Henry. "But I want to help Laurence," he was saying. "Later, why not? You haven't seen poor Doddy for ages, have you? Let's just go and see if he's there . . ." She had been painting all morning, then come up from the garden. My watch said five minutes to twelve, as they headed for the walled garden.

When I thought back to the very end of winter—living within sight of Noone, and unable to enjoy it; knowing of the snowdrops, the aconites; and fearful of what might be going on inside, where no binoculars could reach—I saw I should have been well prepared for this marriage.

But nothing could prepare me for the process of discovering, day by day, how terribly my love for Kate would grow; and I mean "terribly", not as Chloë Bender would use it. My need for her expanded geometrically, it seemed, doubling with each single, solitary night; and the renascent beauty of my house and garden, all—as I had thought then, before that fatal night in March—that I had ever wanted, only increased the agony, piercing my very heart. (The romantic script-writer was sticking with us, busy with the "Boy Loses Girl" section; and I could not promise him a happy ending: not the way things were heading now.)

There was ample time, those nights, to explore possible courses of action and define alternatives, if only to give myself the task of sane reasoning, and put away insane desire. Two basic facts I always started from: one, Kate was very dodgy and, two, I had killed Charles. I could not sit her down, as any good husband would, to discuss the former, without revealing the latter; couldn't explain away her "madness" and her "ghost" without admitting to murder . . . Sometimes I even wondered if it might be worth the gamble. Half-truths, I knew, would be useless: she was too bright. But total revelation? Dangerous; possibly fatal.

I played it through. "You must know, Kate, that you had a nervous breakdown when Charles died; and, while you were low, you attached yourself to Noone, and to the ghost that was the spirit of the place. They became completely identified, as you busied yourself with old plans, old portraits, and the restoration of beauty and order to the house he had so fiercely defended against Charles's changes: changes you had not liked. You even accepted his having killed your husband: you found this ghost had set you free. You believed he was still there; and you longed for him to come back to you and approve; to reward you for all your good work.

"Then he did, one night in March, and laid his hands on you: you could actually feel him. And it only made you love him more. But, Kate, that ghost was me: it was me, all along. It is me you love. Here are the clothes I used: the gloves still smell of your scent. Don't you see? Don't you believe in me now? I am the Noone Walker."

Lying there in the darkness, I imagined Kate's face as I stripped her bare and unbuilt the world she had escaped into, leaving her nothing to stand on. Even her gentle, civilised husband/brother would crumble, leaving only deceit, shame, loss, panic. Like the last reel of a horror movie, she would find herself alone in the big old house with the best friend suddenly revealed as the villain, the murderer. It would drive her insane.

No: talking would be useless. Even a normal, hearty female on the evenest of keels, who simply didn't fancy sex with her spouse, would be justifiably outraged by such elaborate, such continuous deception; and having him arrested for the murder of her first husband would be only the beginning of her revenge . . . All of which was hardly germane, I decided, since my first proposition was missing. Our impasse sprung, not merely from my guilt, but from her sick infatuation with her imaginary friend, a lover who demanded no service from her except what was already nearest her heart: preserving the splendour that was Noone. With him, or the idea of him—even just the hope— she felt safe. The real men in her life had treated her badly. She had been set up and betrayed by her one great physical passion, then used and abused by Charles Gelhorn as a brood mare. So she fell in love with a man who could not touch her; and, for protection, married one who was not allowed to.

The bitterest realisation was that, with my companionship, Kate would almost certainly have let the Noone Walker fade out of her life, quite naturally, as Henry had. But back in March I spoiled all that. I had blown my hopes, and her sleeping senses, to smithereens—by laying hands on her. I only took a step forward and grasped her neck to frighten her; and she awoke. It did not even take a kiss.

All the passion was there from that moment on, disastrously misdirected. If, as myself, I had patiently wooed and won her, to the point where I could touch her, hold her, I should not be alone now . . . It had been a mistake of mine, in my unhinged state last year, summoning up the Noone Walker to scare the barbarian from Noone; but I had compounded it when I took on his widow, alone before her glass. I was fairly hoist with my own petard.

July; and Cambridge, and the Great Red Rock-Eater helped a little.

Donna comfortably took the place of Flavia, who was back home in Turin by now, in the bosom of her large family. Donna was very different: nothing spiky or eaglish about her—though she was very bright, and almost as ambitious. She was big; all curves, with a bright red mane of hair, elaborately done in the evenings, and not her natural colour, I found. She was tough and funny, with enormous energy. When I showed her, on demand, a snap of Kate, she said: "Laurie baby, that's just the up-market model of me, give or take a few kilos—and the fact that she's a beauty. God! Eyebrows and cheekbones to break your heart, eh? And I'm just plain sexy. Hair's the same—if she just zapped up the rinse a bit . . . Would she mind you cheating on her?"

"Not really."

"Huh! 'Open marriage'?"

"Sort of."

"I had one of those: wide open. He walked out the door with my small dark secretary and hasn't looked at another woman since. Not allowed to, poor bugger . . ."

There was work as well, in quiet libraries and nearly empty labs. A nice balance: in Donna's flat there was usually loud Puccini, a blast of good cooking smells, a bunch of friends. I stayed in college three nights the first week, then two, then one, as the Rock-Eater encroached.

Kate did not know; or knew, and did not care. The drive home was always full of longing and dread; wondering if she had changed, had missed me. And after even three days away, I was still surprised by her beauty. She was looking sensational; I think she had been sleeping more; sunbathing, certainly. I did not think the pale skin that comes with conker hair could turn so deeply gold; and her back, in low-cut summer dresses, was like the finest suede.

We contrived to be very social on the evenings I was home. Clifford (more wifeless than I) needed diverting. Most Fridays we were bidden to dine with him; and, unless he had a house party, he was usually included in our outings and plans. But I spent the daytime almost entirely with Henry, ranging far afield, to steam fairs and aeroplane museums; and stopping at village fêtes when we passed them. He helped me buy two Kelims for the nursery at a carpet sale in Amersham, and we went on and lunched at the Compleat Angler. I missed Kate.

I missed her even when I was in bed with Donna. Walking to the library alone one morning after a hearty breakfast—she was on holiday now, and spent a lot of time cosseting me—I was deep in the pros and cons of an alternative solution. I could file for divorce on "failure to consummate", without apportioning blame: "It didn't work," I would tell Glyn-Jones. I could simply leave her, and divorce would follow automatically after two years or so: the time hardly mattered since I did not anticipate remarriage—certainly not to my Rock-Eater. But that way I should lose Noone.

If I hoped to keep it, I would have to

appeal to Kate; strike some sort of bargain. She was quite sensible enough to know that her terms would not stand up in a court of law, and reasonable enough to appreciate the need for cooperation in avoiding such exposure. She must accept that the gamble on my platonic devotion had failed; that I could not carry on. But I would have to play rough; assert I'd been misled, and spell out, if I must, how the Law would apportion her wealth. Then offer her my half if I could keep Noone: with its grounds, it represented about one fifth of the whole. And she would be wise to accept . . .

But I did not like it. Noone without Kate would certainly bring relief from this insupportable pain; but only loss and emptiness would fill its place. Suppose I told her, straight, the truth about the spectral saboteur—the spanner in the building works, keeping it light but contrite; stopping well short of the visit to her room —might she then dismiss her fantasies? Come round to loving me? And is it true, I wondered, that a wife cannot give evidence against her husband? But then, if the murder were committed before their marriage, surely she could . . .

At which point I found myself standing in one of the narrow city lanes, staring foolishly at a traffic sign, as though it were a divine ultimatum. ONE WAY.

And I turned, and walked to the college car park, and drove back to Noone. For there was only one; and I must take it. I wanted her too much to go on like this— so I must return as the Noone Walker.

That way she would love me in return.

I took the costume from the rucksack in which I had hidden it at the back of my cupboard; hung it up, sponged down the black broadcloth, and pressed it. My spare bands and stock were clean; I brushed off the flat hat, laid them all away, with the gloves, in a drawer of my attic study, and locked it. Then I went to find Kate.

Mrs. Furze told me she was still painting; Henry had gone shopping with Stevens in Colchester. I walked across the west lawn, and through into the walled garden. Two weeks of good rains had given us a huge crop of vegetables, and Mrs. Furze was busy freezing the surplus

451

for winter. I stepped through into the poplar alley—and there was Kate, sun-bathing naked.

She was half on her side, a little turned away from me, with her head in the dappled shade. A dark tartan rug framed the curving golden icon, that rufus hair glinting as the shadows shifted. She lay there, not ten yards away from me, asleep: the pale gold breast in profile rose and fell evenly; ripe for plucking.

I did not want to rape her—and that is what it would have been. I stepped back silently through the door in the wall. I remembered how I used to scare Bill Abbott away from my secret hide-outs: "Beware the Noone Walker! For his haunts are sacrosanct . . ." Kate felt the same way about the poplar walk. However gently I woke her, however subtly took her over in her drowsy, golden state, she would open her eyes—before, during or after—and for her, it would be rape.

She walked into the morning room half an hour later, all showered and crisp and bright.

"How lovely! We did know you were

coming back today. Henry and Stevens will soon be home with the shopping—you won't mind a picnicky sort of lunch, will you?"

"Not at all, Kate: you know me."

She glanced at me, her eyes very blue against the fresh tan. "Fine," she said. "When did you get here?"

"Can I pour you a drink?" I said.

"Lovely. What are you having?"

"Well—brandy, actually; but there's some white wine open."

"Brandy, Laurence . . . ? When *did* you get back?"

"I don't know—an hour ago, maybe more? Rather lose track, working away up in my study." She breathed more freely, as they say; and I could tell by the way her breasts moved that she was wearing nothing under the thin cotton shirt. Maybe nothing under the shorts either . . . Christ, was I turning into a dirty old man? Damn that, I thought: I have been married to this lady for seven weeks and I have just seen her body for the first time. "Ice?" I asked.

"No, thanks." She took the glass,

smiled, and raised it: "Nice to have you back," she said.

I was outside her door just before midnight. It was closed now; but I knew she always opened it as the clock struck: unlocked it, turned the handle and left it —another little routine, and using the chiming to conceal any noise from her unsuspecting spouse, only a dressing room away. I stood behind a pillar on the landing until the last stroke of twelve; then crossed the lobby and pushed the door slowly open.

My mirror-portrait faced me. I did not need a glass to tell me I looked like him. My makeup was immaculate: so much easier now that the scars were smooth, mere lines of paler pigment like boundary marks around the burned area. The hat was fairly low over my eyes: she would see the Noone Walker.

I closed the door silently and went across to her.

The ghost she had waited for so long put his black-gloved hands on her shoulders; and she smiled, and reached up for them.

"I knew you would come back . . ."

He held her eyes in the mirror as he opened the white silk dressing-gown and peeled it slowly downwards. For a moment she closed her eyes, and I saw Kate Gill in a state of pure ecstasy—then I leaned across her and blew the candles out.

17

A N hour later, maybe more, I felt her sleeping, and left her. Back in my own room, I hid the cleric's clothes. It was a reflex action: I could not think of little things like consequences— aware only of peace at last, the ghost laid. And I slept.

Next morning I woke slowly and lay remembering. I wanted to lie there for ever, warm and smoothed out like fresh ironing, to mull it over—though I could recall, consciously, little beyond the extra- ordinary fact, and its consummate perfec- tion. It was my body, my hands and skin that remembered it all, as intricately printed and encoded in our interlocking as DNA. All through that day, even when I was working, or buying a newspaper, or negotiating a roundabout in busy traffic, this physical recall would ambush me— suddenly, and quite perilously: as though with some fierce, internal pain, it closed my eyes for a moment while it passed over.

"Anything wrong, my duck?" said the motherly newsvendor. "Sure . . . ? Wait now—here's your change."

Even on waking, I knew I must get up at my usual hour, and behave completely normally. I dressed, shaved my foolishly smiling face, and straightened it. I heard Kate go downstairs; watched from the landing window, and made myself wait until she had come out through the back door, fed the cats and set off towards the barn. It was early and I felt too vulnerable: I needed breakfast and Henry to cover for me. Knowing, too, that she wanted to be alone, I just watched her.

On warm summer mornings she would often wear her old blue kimono for the pre-breakfast painting session—the builders did not arrive until eight—then come up to change and eat only when Mrs. Furze called her. This morning she was wearing a crumpled white silk dressing-gown, thin as a poppy; and she did not go straight down the hill, but disappeared round the end of the west wing. I went through to one of the guest bedrooms, and saw her again. Emerging from shadow, her

457

back was in the sun. She suddenly stopped and stretched, like a luxurious cat. She kicked off her espadrilles—and then she was running down the lawn towards the end of the walled garden. I felt like some peeping Tom, observing such naked and unconscious grace, as she ran and twirled away from me through the morning sun, all flying white silk and long golden legs, and leaving a tousled track across the silver bloom of a heavy dew.

At breakfast, she was neat and sane, avoiding my eyes; very lenient with Henry when he demanded a miniature packet of Coco-pops, usually kept as a Sunday treat; generous and thoughtful with me. "No, you have all the paper, Laurence: I don't need it . . . Let me know your plans some time. No hurry . . ." I looked over the paper at one point and saw her gazing raptly right through the milk jug. The Soul's Awakening.

"I'll be going back to Cambridge," I said; "I may have to work late, now that I've got the stuff I needed from my files."

"And back tomorrow? Or not till Friday?"

"Oh, I should be back this evening," I

said. "Do you want to go out? Or—what about a day in Cambridge? We could lunch together; maybe do some shopping. And there's that private view you told me about."

"You go," she said: "I must really paint."

When she was speaking, she was restless, snapping a dead-head from among the flowers on the table, brushing up toast crumbs, fetching a damp cloth to wipe the marmalade pot. When she was silent, she was not there: serious, and properly attentive when addressed. But her eyes, even with lowered lids, were glittering away under a bushel of good manners. It was very testing simply to say and do the ordinary, morning things: hard for both of us. At least she had changed out of that white dressing-gown.

She gave me a tight little smile as she passed me to refill her teapot. "Coffee OK? So, we'll see you when we see you."

I wanted to pull her down on to my lap, and cradle all that warmth again; tuck her head into my neck and say: I know, Kate —I was there . . . I said: "I'll telephone if I'm going to be very late." Maybe, I thought, I'll make you wait in vain tonight: all the sharper tomorrow.

"We'll be fine," she said, standing by the window, her face up to the sun. Oh, cool lady, I shall make you burn for your next helping. Stay hungry.

She called goodbye on her way down to the barn. I was talking to the builders. "See you—" I called out back. At least, I thought, until I blow the candles out . . .

I wondered how much she painted. I could not work. I missed lunch trying to make up lost time; then gave in and went shopping. I bought, on impulse, a linen jacket, and a peacock-blue shirt of very fine cotton, for the honeymoon we would have. The possible consequences of my latest deception still seemed oddly distanced, as though lost from view in dead middle-ground. I could see nothing between this evening and escaping to some Greek island together; and I bought her a straight, wine-dark, silk shift with small pearl buttons—a "shirt-dress", they called it—for her to wear nothing under at our late suppers down by the small harbour, as we watched the lights of the fishermen's boats, bringing us our langoustine . . .

The Truth, and the need to reveal it, had become unimportant. The only true revelation was the one that still contained us: the dazzling cloud we shared so separately. Midnight fireworks branded into the sky.

With my parcels under my arm, I walked along the Backs, staring into the black water through a glaze of sun; remembering. Kate's greeting had been the only words spoken throughout our lovemaking. There was a moment when I wondered about ghosts and weightlessness, quickly forgotten in the following storm. I realised I had never made love in total darkness before. Maybe, like being blind, it freed the other senses: certainly it blotted out all individual consciousness, all thought. I retained—but only examined later (a magic memento, clutched tight, still there)—the experience of becoming one creature, with a single purpose. We knew each other so well, and perfectly. Certainly we were suited.

There was a message from Donna when I got back to my office.

"So what happened? You vanished. Last night's supper (v. special!) on ice. If no

461

word, will promote next in line—Love D."

Knowing she would not be there, I escaped to the private view; good early watercolours at a small gallery; and bought a pretty pen-and-wash of a mother and child in a cottage garden.

A colleague came in as I was leaving.

"You look very pleased with yourself, Laurence. Swallowed the canary?"

"Actually, I could do with one. Somehow I missed out on lunch."

"Lightheaded, then: come and take pot-luck."

I thanked him and bowed out. "I'm heading for home," I said: still uncertain whether I was; clear only about the desire to be alone and consider it. There was a wine bar near the library, where they served hot food. I had a glass of some fortifying red and a plate of shepherd's pie; then I was back at work, thinking about Kate.

At nine I rang her and apologised for missing dinner.

"I wasn't expecting you, actually. But you will eat, won't you, my dear."

"Oh, I have. I may go on working a while longer."

"Why not stay there, Laurence? Why drive back after a long day? You've been looking tired: have an early night and finish the work tomorrow, why not?" Transparent Kate.

"Fine—if you don't mind. Be back some time tomorrow, then: maybe for lunch, with luck."

"Don't hurry. Whenever. I'll just be painting. I'll give your love to Henry."

"Goodnight, Kate: sleep well . . ." Burn for me, lady: burn alone.

But by eleven-thirty my total physical recall had abandoned its hit-and-run tactics, its sly ambushes, for fire and the sword on open ground. I was weary, and surrendered; deserted my books and made for the car park. I drove fast but with great care: Kate was waiting for me.

I left the car in the same old lay-by and went along the thick, summer hedgerows and up through the woods—enough of a gibbous moon tonight to manage without the car torch over the open ground—till I reached my lair. Inside the house, and up the back stairs this time. I dare not hurry nor blunder. I must make no sound; and a few minutes more no longer mattered, I decided, waiting in the shadows for the chimes of twelve-thirty to cover the click of my bedroom door: tonight she would certainly wait.

It was a quarter to one by the time I stood, white-faced and black-suited, on her threshold; and outstared my pale rival above the mantelpiece, my wife's face in the oval glass. But this time—as I had so often dreamed—she turned quickly and came to me.

Together, and close, there was no more need for haste. I stayed sensible long enough to blow the candles out; then took her to the window and undressed that dark gold body in the light of the waning moon. No words at all, this time. Our lovemaking was longer, slower and far greater.

Finally—I do not know when—I fell asleep.

Kate Gill woke first.

The moon shone low and yellow through the other window now: low enough to show her their clothes strewn on the floor nearby—the black and the white—and reached to the foot of the bed; but no further. She sat up carefully and turned to her sleeping lover: still there, still close, this time. She knew he would leave before first light. Till then she could hold him and feel him breathing, and watch him sleep: her monochrome idol, her secret god.

Like Psyche before her, she must see him.

Gently she unwound her legs, and eased her way out of the bed; took a candle from the dressing table, found the matches, lit it and carried it back, shading its flame from the draught. She bent over him.

Psyche feared to find some monster, and discovered the sleeping Eros. Kate looked for her household god, her monochrome idol, and found a mere man, frail and faithless, flushed and warm. Most of the white makeup had gone and the scars were quite clear in that raking light. Dazzled, he opened his eyes and had one last brief vision of a golden body bending over him; of dark ruffled wings of hair swinging forwards, and the wild eyes between; the mouth wide in a silent cry. Then the

candle fell, and the cry came. The sheet
caught fire, as Kate ran screaming from
the room.

18

I WOKE up in a narrow, strange bed, and smelt disinfectant, and saw one fat, bandaged wrist close by me on the pillow. Beyond it was my second husband, head in hands; a nurse over by the door. I screamed again but it was only a sort of rasping noise. "Get that man out of here— Get him out—" And I shut my eyes tight, willing myself to die, to disappear. It was no good. I tried to get the dressings off, but my fingers felt blunt and rubbery. They held me still and gave me an injection. It was something at least to disappear again, dissolving into blackness, just the way He does.

Next time I was clearer; enough to realise I had not managed to die. I should have an ordinary razor, with blades, instead of the disposable sort. The nail scissors seemed more like it—but were hopelessly ineffectual; messy. Very painful, now: a lot of surface tissue damage; not deep and clean and quick. I

suppose someone broke the door down
before I'd been bleeding long enough.
Quite a basinful, it looked, with the warm
water to keep them going—but not
enough: ineffectual. You've simply got to
think more clearly and set yourself up so
that, even when you faint, it keeps going.

That wretched man had left. The nurse
was sitting by me; and I told her all the
stuff about warm water to keep the blood
going. Which was stupid. I was getting
clear enough to realise it was, and shut up.

Sometimes they came and tried to make
me talk—about what I'd done, and what
happened just before. Sometimes they
abandoned the stalking-horse and said,
"What made you do it?" I was clear
enough by now not to make more trouble
for myself or the "other parties" (the ones
you don't go to?), and kept mum. I just
longed for them to stop and go away; and
in the end they always did.

Then I was alone again and could think
about the good times. Waiting for Him in
the poplar walk, in the sun; and the first
time I saw Him there, so long ago. The
time I met Him in the corridor, and was
so afraid—but knew suddenly that He was

still at Noone. Then the first time He came to my room. And the next time I could actually feel Him, and knew He was getting closer to me. Then, towards the end of May, when He was so sad, and would not even touch me . . . But most of all, the last time: the time we made love. I knew it would happen: it had to, once He had come so close, and touched me . . . When I woke, I wanted to ask Him so much, in the dark, all close to me: whether He really liked what I had done to Noone; whether He loved me as much as I loved Him. And I wanted to tell Him how He had saved me: yes, even though I knew very well He killed Charles; and that I forgave Him. My avenging angel. How, at first, I thought it was all *my* doing, from wishing my husband dead; that I had some awful destructive power. And I felt so horrified, and riddled with guilt. I suppose that was the nervous breakdown.

But I knew there was something that I had seen, like a secret door, black and white: an escape. I made myself relive that evening, over and over. I counted the statues: made myself count them, again and again. When I was leaving the nursing-home, they told me that the first time I smiled was one day when I suddenly said "—Three—Four!" I wanted to tell Him all that; and how He had set me free.

But when I woke, He was gone. And I waited for Him the next night—waited so long—and then . . . But I could not think of that. Of what happened then. That was what all the doctors kept asking.

Next they started trying to get me to see my second husband, Laurence. They'd say, couldn't I appreciate I was better, so much calmer; and surely I could understand my husband was worried. "You know, it's all of ten days now," they said, "since you Had a Go at yourself . . ." That must have been the hearty, bearded one: just his style. But I did not look up to check; they were all the same really: clones, and not to be trusted. I guess the mistrust was mutual; and I realised I would have more of a chance at home. In which case I must, obviously, see the second husband—desperate measures; but a means to an end. Madly Machiavellian of me; for I was quite determined to die.

How else could I join Him and be with Him always?

I believe I put up a very good front. Not too quick giving way, of course; the gradual defrost: "controlled melt", the ad-men call it. I agreed to parley.

Preparing to see him again, I tried (as an exercise: studying the opposition) to imagine what he felt. I knew, after all, that the wretched man had loved me in his way. Not *our* sort of love, but maybe the best he had. I assumed he felt responsible for my suicide attempt; and he must have been pretty worried, wondering what I had revealed in my drugged state: such a proud, cool, disciplined young man—or so he had seemed. He would abhor scandal.

All my woolly altruism evaporated, however, as soon as he came into my hospital room: the superficial likeness was obscene, violating my memories with the horror of that night—of discovering . . . But I knew even then I must seem calm: the end justifies the means. I behaved well; was reasonable, I think. Simply avoided looking at him. He was reasonable too, and quiet. He always had been, in everyday life. Henry needed me at home, he told me; and that the doctors thought I was better, and Noone would be good for me. He said he would go away from home if I wished; and I could have a day-nurse and a night-nurse to look after me.

"Your presence or absence is immaterial," I said. It sounded quite dignified.

"Good," he said. "Then I shall stay, and keep Henry from tiring you, and work in the garden. It's looking good. You'll be able to sit outside. Would you like to come home tomorrow?"

"Why not?" I said: "Home's the best place." A nice little touch, I thought. "I don't need any more nursing now; just time. *Reculez, pour mieux sauter*—as the chef said to the chips." I was dazzling even myself.

He laughed, and said it was good to see me back on form; but that I might need a night-nurse at first: "Mrs. Furze will be there during the day—and Henry and Abbott and all, fetching and carrying for you: they all look forward so much to your coming home . . . Well, tomorrow then. Stevens will fetch you in time for lunch. With Mrs. Furze." Did they suspect I would leap from the moving car? Credit me with a bit more finesse, I thought; and nodded to indicate the conclusion of the audience. Apart from when he walked in —which was quite upsetting—I did not actually look at him once.

It was oddly moving to come home: so beautiful—in spite of the drizzle. So comfortable; and everything—sheets, bathroom, flowers, food—smelt lovely, and familiar. I had been dreading it, remembering how it was after the nervous breakdown: not just the wasteland of Charles's half-finished works—those brutal steel joists and cantilevers, still unclad, and the plaster-dust, and grubby windows looking out at the sad winter garden—but the weight of it all on me alone: *my* baby now, however battered; and no one to boss me or protect me or pay the bills. Or blame for things. Quite some challenge, as Clifford Hogan said; and told me I could turn to him any time.

I'd always known it was Charles who had made things happen, gathered people around, jollied life along; and that I was freezing off a lot of sympathy with messages through Mrs. Furze saying I could

not be disturbed. So I was grateful to Mr.
Hogan for his interest and advice. But
soon I wanted to manage on my own. By
then I knew more about my money, and
buried myself in the reconstruction of
Noone: clearing the mess, making endless
sketches, starting to follow up the old
plans—and then the old pictures. Getting
that portrait back was a turning point, as
the faded photograph had been in its time.
From then on I had Him to help me. He
had always been there, of course, but so
elusively: the painting made Him real.

It was the other reason that drew me
back to Noone. Simply to see the portrait
again, to lie in bed watching it, made me
very calm and clear. I knew every line so
well, and the landscape behind His head:
green fields with sheep safely grazing, and
comfortable trees, and that all-purpose
sky, sunny one side and stormy on the
other—a crude, village-dramatic-society
backdrop in the manner of Gainsborough.
Certainly it was no masterpiece, and badly
needed cleaning and retouching. But I
could not part with it for so long. The pale
eyes in the shadow of the low, wide hat,
the angular young face (the mouth so

severe) almost as white as the high stock and bands; and I felt His silent approval of my return—and smiled to myself, remembering the heat there was behind that austere façade. That He'd had seven children, the last in His sixty-seventh year.

A long and happy life. Once He had taken on the wealthy Church as a partner, it was He who landscaped the gardens, decorated the ceiling of the great hall, and encouraged His sons to make the Grand Tour and bring treasures from Europe home to Noone. He had known all about the Good Life, both sacred and profane: adored by His parishioners, and living on in village myth as its guardian and protector. The oldest inhabitants still believed it was He who caused the well-timed earth-tremor that clinched the re-routing of a motorway; and I felt sure He enjoyed taking credit for it. But His greatest victory was the saving of Noone Rectory itself. I believe He came back for this; then lingered on to oversee its restoration, and began to love me.

That was one of the things I would have asked Him; and whether He had made some sacrifice—some pact or fearful compromise; with God, or the Devil—in order to take on substance for my sake. Or if it was simply the strength of my love that had brought it about; if, perhaps, it was I that must pay the price . . . But when I woke, He was gone; the bed beside me cool and empty.

And the next night . . . *No!*

No. He would come again, and wipe away the filthy imprint of the impostor. (I wondered if He knew; had watched it all . . . Whether He might not kill the second husband as He had the first: possessive—and He clearly was—about Noone and me.) If He did not come, then I would go to Him. It was so simple. I wasn't afraid, now I was back with my portrait.

The first two days were rainy, and I stayed upstairs. I found I was weaker than I thought, and thinner. My tan had faded out to an unattractive jaundice colour: I wondered if He could still love me. I started exercising seriously, eating more; and Mrs. Furze fixed up a sun-lamp that had been bought for me. I oiled my skin and fed conditioner to my drab hair.

Sometimes I read, mostly books I knew —Trollope, Jane Austen—and listened to records; hi-fi had been installed in my sitting room. Henry came and played on my floor, and his step-father carried up a television for us to watch; "Though we hope you'll be coming down soon, when the weather improves."

It did, that weekend. He took Henry off somewhere in the car all day, and I went down to the terrace, where Mrs. Furze had arranged a long garden chair, new and very comfortable. Later on, about midday, I walked round the garden, to see my precious plants. But I didn't visit the poplar walk: I felt too tired. And I looked such a mess. I spent the afternoon sun-bathing. That evening my nurse, changing the light dressings on my wrists, said I could swim in the pool very soon.

That was also the evening that the impostor tried to lecture me. He had put Henry to bed, and came along to my sitting room; offered to pour me a drink. I had finished the course of rather sinister pills, and accepted a glass of wine. He took one too, and said that some time soon we would have to "talk"; he believed it was "important", and that I was now "up to it". I wanted to watch the television, but I agreed to an appointment the following evening. He said as he was leaving, "Can't you look at me, Kate?" I said I couldn't. "Because I'm too like Him?" he asked; and I turned up the volume—just a bit— breaking the rules of Good Conduct we had lived by. I knew it. But he had broken everything.

They were out again all next day. I did a little gentle gardening, mostly dead-heading my roses. I lay in the sun and listened to Verdi on my transistor: very luxurious and peaceful, with not a cloud in the sky. Mrs. Furze's sister spent the day, though I told them it wasn't necessary. I didn't want her sitting there working away at her pink woollen hearthrug on a perfect August afternoon and saying, "That's a nice melody, isn't it—?" She got too hot, and went indoors; but I saw her keeping an eye on me from the library, where she was watching Esther Williams on Film Matinée.

Only this surveillance, and the evening's appointment hanging over me, marred my day. I felt He was not far away: down in the woods, maybe, or basking in his summerhouse (it had been rebuilt to His design; the old wistaria, and the Kiftsgate rose, trained back over it). If it had not been for the Pink Woollen Rug, and "Going for a little walk, are we? I'll just pop on my other shoes . . .", I would have looked for Him. I knew I was better; that the flesh of my arms and legs was firmer, getting smooth and brown again. I lay with leaves on my eyes, thinking of Him: black gloves on my shoulders, then bare hands on my breasts in the darkness—and the strong young legs of the hunting parson— who (as an odd memorial note in the old parish broadsheet put it) "had ridden hard, prayed hard, drunk deep and fathered seven . . ."

At my husband's request I stayed down that evening: I saw it would be easier to terminate the conversation by leaving the library and going upstairs, than having to ask him to get out of my sitting room. I had found something of Henry's to mend, so there was no need to look up. I knew this would have to happen some time: better to get it over with. As long as they watched me so closely, what hope was there of looking for Him?—and even less of making my ultimate escape. Only calm, reasonable behaviour would lull them; and I could not, reasonably, fob off this "talk" indefinitely.

"Kate," he said.

"Present," I said: "fire away." Keeping it light: no way was he going to put me through it—get me to relive that desperate night. "And just remember, please, that it was you who insisted on this 'talking' thing, not me; and that it is pretty upsetting to face you at all."

"But you don't, Kate. You haven't since I first walked into your room in hospital . . . We are going to have to work out a *modus vivendi*, and that involves speaking the truth, I believe. Our fantasies have got rather out of hand—don't you agree?"

"Speak for yourself: the truth if you like, or as you see it. And I wouldn't know about your fantasies. I mean, you didn't think I was in love with you—secretly or something—did you? If so, you misled yourself." I stitched away all the time, and kept my voice even, reasonable.

"Kate, listen: there is something you must know, and must face up to. Nothing

480

I tell you now can be as bad as what I've put you through so far—and apologies are no use for that . . . Whether you accept it or not, I passionately regret my mistake— my third mistake—and feel entirely responsible for your—drastic reaction. Trying to kill yourself. And, for someone who loves you, that is quite a punishment. But there is something you *must* accept: you know it by now, of course; it just needs facing up to. I played the part of the Noone Walker all along: the vandalism, the hauntings, 'Doddy', the lot. And naturally, if you still doubt it, I can give you chapter and verse . . . And so you see, Kate, it was me you loved."

It was very quiet in the room. I think he may have gone on talking to me; but there was a sort of roaring in my ears, and the sky outside was growing dark. I asked what time it was, it seemed so dark. Then I felt water on my face and a cool breeze. I was on the window seat. I felt cold, and he put a rug round me. The tartan rug I used for sunbathing.

Back on the sofa, I sipped the brandy he gave me. I could hear properly now;

not that he spoke much. He closed the window, lit a fire, switched on the lamp in the corner. Outside, it was a clear, twilight evening, still bright enough to see a yellow branch high in the beech tree; cool enough to feel autumn coming. The summer was going so fast . . . But inside everything seemed curiously slow. I tried hard to think. It was as though all but my brain believed him; and my brain was not working.

He was saying things like ". . . And you can see, if you think back, how I managed to sabotage Charles's building works, now I've told you about the passages—can't you? And my knowing the house and grounds so well . . ." He enumerated his appearances to the workmen; briefly he described his greatest coup, the staircase, the scaffolding and the audio room; and how he had waited behind the yew hedge that day and watched me run past. I did not say, That is correct: old Angus saw you from the attic. The brandy was warming me, getting my blood going again, making me careful. Then he described our encounter in the scrapbook corridor. "No one else knew of that."

"Yes: Henry did . . . Now you said—didn't you?—that you had made three mistakes. That your pretending to be Him—dressing up, and—and going to bed with me, that night, was the third mistake. What did you mean?"

"It was something of a simplification, I suppose. My first was that I ever conjured—that I posed as the ghost to get the intruders (as I saw you) out of Noone; I was still a bit crazed, anyway, at that time. Then coming back, that night in March. If I had simply appeared . . . But I—well, I put my hands round your neck, to frighten you. And the net result—to cut a long story short—was that I fell in love. And didn't exactly frighten you away, either. The reverse. And then the third . . . So. After that there was really no alternative: I simply had to confess to all this and hope you'd—"

"Laurence—" I glanced up at him: an odd sensation. I had been in bed with this man. I could not let myself think about it before; and it was only possible now because all at once I saw the gaps in his "chapter and verse", and knew he was

483

wrong. Not entirely: but enough to make me right.

"Yes, Kate?"

"When did you come back to England?"

"At the beginning of June last year. Why?"

"I thought so," said I. "I mean, the burns you suffered were real enough; and you were on your way back to the auction when you got them."

"So? How is this—?"

"Wait. Now you said you came, one night in March, and put your hands round my neck. Was that the first time?"

"The first time I touched you? Yes."

"The first you came to my room."

"Yes. But I'd met you in the scrapbook—"

"Let me finish—please. There was the night Charles died. Was killed. By an accident."

"But you didn't see him then. Did you?"

"You don't know, do you? *Or* the other times . . . All you need to know, really, is that no less than four times, my dear—*you were not there*."

Now I could look at him; and I saw he was outfaced.

"That's right: go on—" I said smoothly: "pour yourself a good strong drink"—for he had abandoned his careful lager, and picked up the whisky decanter. "That's what one does to cover confusion, or in moments of stress—right? Poor Laurence: you look as if you'd seen a ghost . . . And now you're doing the pacing bit too, I see."

He stopped and looked down at me. The eyes were right, I thought: the family eyes. But I still could not look at the hands that, for an hour of that night, had stroked and held me, or the neck, the V of chest, I had kissed so trustingly. I could not forgive him for that night, when he had made me unfaithful to the Noone Walker.

Now he was saying he couldn't know what I meant if I would not tell him; but that I was quite bright enough to see the soundness of his arguments, and where they led. He had told me everything, he said; he had come clean; and had done so, not just to make himself feel better—that would take time—but to prove to me, his wife, that my infatuation (his word) was with *him*. "I don't think you're really facing the facts, Kate—and they are facts. That we have made love together, not once, but twice."

"Only once," I said. "And then I saw who it was, when I lighted—"

"No, Kate: twice. We've both of us rather—well, skated over that first night together, when—"

"*No!*" I cried. "*No*. You can't—you *can't* take that away too—"

I wept, muffling my face in a cushion, blotting out the world I would soon leave. After a while I felt his hand on my shoulder, felt him smooth back my hair. I jerked away from him and sat up.

He gave me a handkerchief to wipe my face. "It's just the next bit," he said, "where he gives her his handkerchief to mop her face. When he's finished the pacing bit, of course—Oh, come on, Kate! Don't you see the net result of all this? What we've *got*?"

Then I snapped out of it, and stood up, facing him. "That's it? The sum total? Nothing more to confess? Fine: I'll add it up then, shall I? Well—doesn't look as if you've done too well, Laurence, considering it was you—remember?—who wanted this little talk. You've got a lot off your chest; and hope, in time, to feel better. But the bottom line reads: you still don't really *know*; and I do. I was *there*."

"You may be right, my love; I can't prove you wrong—but neither can I bring myself to believe in ghosts—Wait: just give me time, and I may . . . But, Kate, can't you accept the proof of your feelings? Your sensations? Don't you see that we are —suited? Haven't we got *that*?"

I glanced out of the window. Dark blue dusk: it was late, and I felt tired and terribly hungry. "Oh, sure," I said: 'it was good."

"Look at me and say that."

His voice shocked me, and I looked at him. This pretty youth I married had tricked me into infidelity. I hardened my heart: he would get no more satisfaction from me.

"Sure," I said: "I agree. It was good. Now, what about some supper?"

"I don't think I want anything just now," he said, turning at the door. "You go ahead . . . Thank you for hearing me out, Kate. Maybe things will get better, now that you know. Simpler, anyway. Goodnight."

I ate most of the cold meal that Mrs. Furze had left for us in the larder. I ate it standing there on the quarry tiles in bare feet, feeling the cool night breeze on my face through the open window; tearing chunks of chicken from the tidy roast, so beautifully glazed and decorated; licking the mayonnaise off my fingers. I took a drumstick back to the library with me and washed it down with some wine; then felt a sudden desire for a cigarette. I found some in the pocket of Mrs. Furze's overall, and had it with a short, sharp brandy, as a night-cap.

I reckoned I needed it; I deserved it, after going through the mincer and coming out on the other side. How naïve of me to think that he'd destroyed everything that night . . . But now—surely—he had finished; and, through the dust of demolition, I could see that my true lover had never even touched me.

And yet, for the first time since that dreadful moment (only two weeks ago? It seemed endless, like Hell), when I bent over the bed with my candle, and my whole precious, secret world exploded— for the first time since then, I felt powerful and strong. I had not simply hurt Laurence, struck him to the heart: I had mystified him. He could not easily dismiss me as mad; of that I felt sure. And I had planted a seed of doubt that would grow and spread in the dark like a fungus.

As for me—I was traduced; but not entirely deceived. Three times clearly, I had encountered my ghost. Now I was surer than ever He was there, and waiting for me to join Him. That was the only way we could be united completely. I would be able to feel Him, once I was dead too.

I drained my glass, put across the fire-guard, and went slowly upstairs. It was nearly midnight—not that He would come, with my night-nurse snoring softly in the dressing room.

She was leaving at the end of the week.

19

MY beautiful wife lay stretched out in the sun, on the luxurious, long chair I had got, among other things, to welcome her home. Her hair was swept up above her head against the blue cushions; and she wore a pair of pointed green leaves on her eyelids.

I had watched so long from my attic window as she lay there, facing towards me into the strong morning sun, that she floated in my vision like some messenger of the gods: brighter than the sky she plunged through, hair streaming upwards, one knee bent, one foot reaching down to land on our earth; the face so serene and inscrutable, a golden mask with slanting, green, vacant eyes. Even her modest white bathing suit, tied on one shoulder, was not out of keeping.

(A minimal, bright bikini was often drying on the line; but she never wore it if I were around. Twice now I had seen her naked: her back and one breast in sunlight; the full glory by moonlight. My painful confession had got me nowhere, it seemed; I thought of what Chloë would have said about our relationship, and shied away. Pouncing had yielded two hours of ecstasy, a heap of charred bedclothes, and two cut wrists . . .)

Below me on the terrace, the green eyes snapped open like a doll's. She called, "There you are, Laurence. Tell me, which night are we dining with the Benders? I need to get my hair cut."

Life was back to normal, with quotes. To spectators who did not know we had remodelled the boat from the waterline up —still working hard to compensate for the crazy angles of everything that lay below it—we were on an even keel. Back in the social swim: Adrian Pearce and Clifford Hogan had been over for a swim and a drink on Sunday; earlier in the week, Chloë came to tea; and Mordecai was dining tonight. No one talked about Kate's suicide bid; nor was there any question of concealing it. They all knew, and commiserated with me in their different ways: Adrian said something very BBC about "life in its fragile cup", Chloë stroked my arm repeatedly and rather firmly as though I were a nervous steed with a stone in its hoof, and Clifford gripped me by the shoulders, gave me a long look with the bright blue eyes, and told me he was right behind me. Even without gossip, there was no hiding the fact; Kate used makeup, bracelets, and a new, broad watch-strap, but the scars still showed. Going shopping, she wore long sleeves.

Mrs. Furze and Nanny, of course, knew even more. There had been no question of concealing the charred bedding, or washing away every trace of blood from the bathroom. Once I had smothered the flames with a blanket, and failed in my desperate attempt to break down the bath-room door (two-hundred-year-old oak does not easily splinter away from its bolts and hinges, I found), I was forced to fetch tools and unscrew it patiently, while the soft, continuous gurgle of running water drained my heart away. After that it was just a matter of tying up her wrists and driving her to the nearest hospital, in Brookall Newtown; as fast, I thought, as waiting for doctors or ambulances. I rang Nanny early, and Mrs. Furze a little later.

It would seem (I said) that my wife had had a nightmare; certainly she had been sleepwalking, for she fetched a candle from the dressing table; then must have dropped it, and been woken by the blaze. I had yet to discover what terrified her so much that she had attempted to cut her wrists: at least she was out of danger.

"The delicate balance of her mind was disturbed, I expect," said Nanny; and we stuck with that.

When I got home later, Henry was off with Stevens. I told the good ladies the doctors had talked to my wife now; but she could not really help: she remembered nothing, except the fire, and waking up in hospital.

"Poor soul!" said Mrs. Furze. "Ah, but poor you, Mr. Laurence! Why, it's almost like going through your own dreadful experience again—!"

"'History repeats itself'—" said Nanny darkly.

"Anyway—I'm making you some nice hot soup, Mr. Laurence dear; and I've cut these roses for you to take to Madam:

493

they're her favourites, aren't they?—poor lady!"

Both she and Nanny were splendid, diverting Henry, clearing up: everything aired and spotless when I got back. And they were tactful, too. They must have wondered often enough about our love-life, and probably discussed it in euphemisms appropriate to their status—though it was perfectly correct for us to have our own separate bedrooms, bathrooms, dressing rooms; indeed, they would expect it. It was, of course, this convention that had made Kate's "terms" feasible—and her escape into French that enforced the literal interpretation, with that touch of "*pas devants les enfants, ou les bonnes. C'est entendu.*"

However, for newlyweds with the briefest of engagements, we must have seemed remarkably undemonstrative. Kate's "dodginess" ("delicate state", Nanny would say; "nerve trouble", Mrs. Furze) covered all eccentricities, I assumed. This last—so nearly final—crisis was simply a "spot of bother" (Nanny) or "hoo-ha" (Mrs. Furze), to be coped with like the first, "when poor Madam was widowed all so sudden: can't expect her just to mend overnight—even with all what you've done for her, Mr. Laurence dear". And I saw this was the best way to play it. Her friends assumed it was another breakdown: and Kate silently assented when the forthright ones (Chloë, and Dickie Bone, certainly) congratulated her on the speed of her recovery "this time".

But both Kate and I knew it was no breakdown; and the doctors confirmed this: far too careful, too rational, they said, once she was off their sedatives. Far more likely that she had suffered some quite overwhelming shock, some discovery, maybe, and made a serious attempt to escape from it permanently. I listened and nodded, but could throw no light on the nature of her discovery. They questioned me at length, referring frequently to the notes passed on by the nursing-home, as to whether it might be some skeleton from her first marriage—or her more distant past—of which she had told me. They asked me about our relationship, our sex-life (as I knew they must), and concluded by saying: "Well, if all that side of things is in good working order, and you can't think of any reason for her freaking out like that" (this was a bluff, bearded psychiatrist who kept insisting he was "into straight talk") "then I can only give you the name of a good therapist and leave you to it. You, er—Laurence—must try and root out what's nasty in the woodshed —yours or Kate's or whatever: she won't straighten up and fly right until she's said yes to it—slotted it into her own structure —know what I mean?"

I did. In our different ways we were on the same track: and I had medical backup for my talk with Kate. Ironically, it was the glimpse she granted me into her "woodshed" that stayed with me after our twilight exploration that evening: was I forever doomed to make plans, execute them, and back off in confusion? I could not blame the shrinks; should not, I suppose, have forced my confession on her as I did: another shock, too soon. She had seemed so marvellously recovered. But quite unbearably remote: I could not stand that, after all we had been through; both of us, together, however separated by her refusal to see me. Surely I only needed to show her how large a part I played in her precious fantasies; and that only my guise was fantastical: all the rest was true—and even more precious. She only had to listen, understand, accept. Surely?

And so I concluded my destruction, and fired her remaining patch of dreams, the better to plant anew; but, in that brutal denial of our ecstasy, Kate had symbolically sown salt on the cleared ground: nothing could grow there now. Except these doubts. Had she sown dragon's teeth as well? Three armed skeletons had sprung from the bare earth; and these haunted me. Despite my nagging memories of my unseen childhood companion in the woods of Noone, I could not accept the reality of such spectres; but as long as she did (and she was so precise, sighting for sighting: so reasonably, so horribly, sure), I could not advance. Kate was safe behind her golden mask, her green blinkers, encircled by paranormal forces she believed in. Might there really be a ghost at Noone? And was it I who had so irresponsibly summoned Him from the grave . . . ? Now, as in the early days of our marriage, my bride was in better shape than I: and now I was staying awake deliberately, to avoid my dreams.

She was triumphantly restored: lovely, relaxed and fit; "positively blooming", so friends assured me. She had easily convinced the doctors she needed no more nursing, and certainly would not "try anything foolish".

So relaxed that, when the bearded shrink patted her on the head and left— he had wanted to "get a feel of the home situation"—I reopened the subject in an attempt to strike a bargain with her.

"Look here, Kate: if I admit you are psychic, will you meet me halfway?"

"That's what marriage is all about," she said sweetly, stitching nice and easy at the Bargello work: her new hobby, both convenient and therapeutic. Doctor Beard had admired it so.

"Will you promise me you won't try to kill yourself again?"

She looked up and laughed. "What, when you are routed? Be reasonable, Laurence: you are in no position to parley at all . . . ! But of course, my dear, within the conventions of the marriage, I will meet you halfway: of course my answer will be yes. And you know I'm dotty and won't believe me. It's a sort of bargain, if you like."

That is what I was up against; and, within me, the fifth column of my own guilt: I still had not admitted my part in Charles's death. Now it was too late: under the faultless manners, all Kate's fondness had turned to hatred. I dared not cede her so much power.

And now at last I became aware—again, too late—of the steady advance of a totally unexpected new force; indeed, the big battalion itself.

The end of August was still hot, with thunderstorms and sun. I had started working two or three days a week, knowing that Mrs. Furze, with Nanny's help, would watch over Kate: they did not need telling. I would leave very early; and always came home in time for a late tea with Henry—with my wife too, when the light was poor for painting—and a social evening. Or we busied ourselves, separately.

One day Henry met me halfway down

the drive in a state of high excitement. "Guess what, Laurence?" he cried, climbing across me into the passenger seat: "Mr. Hogan's going to take me up in his plane to Scotland! For the day! To a sirliberty football match—all terribly famous people from TV and things—all dressed like clowns, you see—and we've got very special seats—and we'll *meet* them all cos he gave them all this food—pawns and salmons and fancy stuff from his business for this Good Cause and when we've done all that then we'll fly down again, Laurence, in his plane—he flies it, you know—and it's *red*!! *Imagine*! And just Mr. Hogan and *me*!—Just *think* of—"

"But how simply terrific! How absolutely spiffingly fantastic!—But, Henry, are you sure? I mean, he only just gave you that go-kart last week . . ."

And Clifford Hogan had been so good so often, one almost took him for granted: coming to the rescue during those first two days when Kate was in hospital, and I spent most of my time there—whisking Henry and Nanny away on a trip out to the oyster beds, having them to stay for the night and sending them back with a great pail of fresh prawns and a video of the latest kids' blockbuster. And, before that, the toy boat for the lake, radio-controlled: so generous . . .

Before we were through the front door I had run a complete plot through my head—playback and fast-forward—with time to recognise this as a supercharged update of the wooden-horse ploy which carried me into Noone. (But I had been fond of Henry. So? Why shouldn't he be . . . ?) Already I was way out ahead, observing sagely that the snag about a marriage of convenience is your bride's liability to fall in love at any moment: no need to delay till she tires of you . . . And the latest *bombe surprise* I'd served up might well have put her off her phantom, leaving her hungry. Here was a far more nourishing dish: Clifford was a Lovely Man, the original Sugar Daddy; the "sexy teddy-bear figure", as Chloë had put it. So often, since Mitzi's departure, he would drop in on us, or ask us back for the best pot-luck in the county. By spending time with him—as she did—Kate was only repaying his kindness and generosity over her own loss.

That evening I asked her about Clifford Hogan.

"This treat for Henry," I said: "he really is too generous."

"Cliff enjoys him," she said. "Don't worry; he won't get spoilt. School starts in a week: that'll cut him down to size again."

"It's not Henry I was thinking of, actually."

"You mean it would be better for Cliff to pick on someone his own size, when he's at play."

"Well, Chloë seems sure he's the marrying sort; I just wondered if he'd got a lady in his life."

"Oh, lots, I should think. No one he's actually installed."

"He's quite attractive, isn't he?"

"Absolutely. Universally. And very eligible. Incredibly generous—to Henry, anyway; and I imagine—"

"He's lonely, I suppose. Comes round here a lot, doesn't he?"

"And you fear the Greeks especially when bearing gifts, right?"

"No," I said quickly: "that would be uncharitable. Clifford's a good guy."

"*The* Good Guy. No silver spoon maybe, but born with a white hat on. No doubt about it."

Henry's first day at school. Kate was taking him, so I went off early as usual, and arranged to come back in time to collect him. I rang about ten to hear how it went.

"What, dropping him? Oh, he never looked round; not even to wave. No problem."

"Tell me, did he join up with his pals? Or just pitch in—?"

"Oh, Laurence—I'm in a rush, my dear —and you'll hear all this afternoon, when you collect—so, even before I do. I'll be back later: off to London for the day, impulsively—to celebrate, now I feel he's OK. Rushing—No, not a train: I've got a lift with Clifford and he's waiting. Oh, give him my love—"

She got back well after Henry was in bed; but he heard the Bentley—stopping only long enough to drop her off—and came down to tell her his day.

She moved about, assembling supper and listening to him.

"I can do that," I said. "You take him back upstairs and get him settled." I wanted to have her to myself.

She came down again, still gorgeous and alien in London clothes—a purple silk flying-suit affair I had not seen before.

"You wouldn't have. I got it today. Silly, but very comfortable . . . And, no, Clifford Hogan did not give it to me."

"It wouldn't occur to me that he had," I said. "I've eaten already, by the way, with Henry; but I'll share your bottle. And probably have some pudding: it looked good."

"Sorry I'm so late," she said, tucking in. "Oh, thanks. I really shouldn't drink any more: quite pissed enough as it is . . . He was going to bring me back early, you see, but when I met him he said he'd have to go to this party in Chiswick and he could either put me on the train or take me along—wouldn't let me just get on a Tube or—"

"OK, Kate—fine. Relax. So you went to the party."

"Yes. Was Hen fearfully disappointed not to find me here?"

"No, not 'fearfully'—and I warned him

it was late-closing and you might be late
. . . No: much too full of tales and
triumphs; and then the so-called homework—doing a picture of his family.
Rather fun, having homework in the old
house again. I sat him down at the refectory table, just like I used to—"

"Oh, good. Well, it was quite an interesting party, really. No one I knew—but
the purple silk helped; made me bold. And
later, Sam and Zee (have I told you about
them? That's right: the hydraulic billiards
table)—they turned up . . . And *they* liked
it—the new garment."

"It's very dashing," I said. It was, with
long sleeves and romantic cuffs that
covered her wrists. "Kate, what *is* all this
Clifford stuff? I mean, has he rather fallen
for you, d'you think?"

"Yes, a bit. Actually, he told me today
that he was quite upset when you and I
got engaged . . . Well, you know things
had been hopeless with Mitzi for ages. I
mean—Charles used to say they had their
ups and downs—but apparently it never
worked . . . Though she must have known
being married to Cliff would be no—"

"So he had his eye on you? Poor chap."

"Quite. Then Mitzi clearing off—and with one of his young chums: that's what really hurt . . ."

"Are you having an affair with him?" I asked. Blurted.

She gasped, then laughed—over-heartily, I thought. "Dear me, no. No, I'm not—nor likely to. Though I don't see why I should answer such a question. Really, Laurence. Is that what you thought? No . . . Actually, he is one of the deeply conventional ones: wants a good, respectable marriage. Something like Charles—but differently motivated, of course. *Nouveau riche* Brits *are* rather like Americans, I think—don't you? Snobby, conventional; 'hot for certainties'—and instant culture, too: the season party tickets at Glyndebourne and all that. We're asked, by the way. If we're still all present and correct."

I thought for a moment, not wishing to blurt again.

"Is that an oblique reference to your possible suicide, or our—putative—separation?"

"Poor old Laurence: you are mixed up, aren't you?" She was on her feet, clearing the table neatly; she fetched the pudding, talking all the while, in a careful, preoccupied, terribly sane voice: "no way mixed up", it proclaimed. "Look, I've had a lovely day, zooming off, being frivolous. Clifford Hogan gave me a lift. The 'declaration', such as it was, sort of grew out of driving—both looking ahead, you know: so much easier to talk. Not planned, I'm sure. He's pretty miz. I mean, imagine: first getting fond—visiting me through all that ghastly nervous breakdown, and afterwards too: the little widow, needing protection—though I did rather go into my shell . . . And then all that collapsing because you came on the scene. And Mitzi doing a bunk. OK, masses of chums; but no 'set-up'—which is what he needs a wife for. Well, it came out in rather a rush."

"What a bloody nerve!" I was the one standing up now. "Trying to seduce a friend—and the wife of a friend?—For whom he stood, virtually *in loco parentis*, not three months ago, giving you away in marriage? *Christ*—"

"Laurence, he did not try to seduce me. Nor would he want to. I'm not his 'bag', as Charles would have—"

"Not *want* to? Next I suppose you'll tell me he's gay! Pull the other, Katy: it's got bells . . ." She was staring at me, and so I stopped.

She said, "But of course he's gay. D'you mean you didn't *know*? Dammit, man; he fancies *you*! Hadn't you *noticed*?"

"No. It didn't occur to me."

"But, Laurence: at least half of Mitzi's 'eligible men' were patently lovers—his—she was trying to torpedo—No: *not* hers—though she'd have tried it on, I'm sure. And in the end of course succeeded—ran off with one . . . Oh don't look so aghast, Laurence! Most of them are AC/DC like those ads in *Time Out*. As Clifford is. For God's sake! He did father children—a while back, I grant you . . . Oh, here: try some Apple Charlotte. It's good . . . Gosh, I was hungry. Funny old day—But the flying suit is OK, I think."

My mind was not so much racing as skidding through two complete U-turns. First, the relief: sexual jealousy—disallowed anyway, according to her terms—was right off the map. And then—suddenly—I saw that Clifford was just the man she should have married: the kind,

508

powerful, older man who needed neither her money nor her body. No threat at all. He only wanted a "set-up". Just as she did. Her first marriage, but with all the bugs ironed out—and it left the Mark Two standing. She would be perfectly free to pursue her antique vicar while Cliff chased his young men. Custom-built . . .

"Aren't you having any, then? Any Apple Charlotte. Right: I'll put it in the larder. And whipped cream in the fridge, if you change your mind. I'm dead tired —OK, 'tired and emotional': I said it first. I'm off to bed. Goodnight—and stop frowning—do." She gathered up her bright shopping bags, and turned in the doorway. "You haven't been compromised, you know. The family name remains untarnished . . ."

I sat on in the kitchen, staring at the tablecloth. All I could see was that dazzling butterfly in her purple finery—a covering so far removed from the pale, folded chrysalis I had watched over in hospital; so disturbingly like the dark indigo shift I bought her for our Greek isle —and that still lay, dormant, in my desk drawer, with a bunch of fragrant khuskhus in its folds.

I was right: the brown skin, and the bright lipstick she wore to be smart in, stood up well to that intensity of colour. I had seen how her irises picked it up, and how even the under-edge of hair, the bell's rim, reflected it. And I closed my eyes, as I felt all of this—hair, silk, golden arms, and the long, clever hands, wearing my mother's ring—all slipping through my fingers like the finest sand.

20

HENRY'S Scottish jaunt was to be on Saturday—as we were unlikely to forget: he talked of little else; and, in sheer self-defence, a broad spread of pellets became essential ammunition. "Well, Henry, Saturday doesn't look too busy: you'll be able to tidy up your room, won't you? Oh, and the dentist appointment, of course . . ." "Oh, *Mum!*" Or "Hey, Hen, you heard the news? They've banned red aeroplanes in Scotland: debarred from entering their airspace . . ." "Oh, *Laurence!*" He even started a countdown on Friday morning, and got up especially early to catch me before I left and work out a "calendar" of hours and minutes.

"Better allow a bit of room at the end in case Mr. Hogan is late fetching you."

"Oh, no, he's never late. He says that's how he's got where he is. And he's jolly rich, isn't he, Laurence? Must be."

"I should imagine so; but it's not polite,

you know, to speculate on the wealth of one's friends. Now, what about the hours when you're asleep, Henry?"

"Yes, I must have those too, please. D'you think you could cross them off for me?—cos I got to *look* asleep, don't I?"

"Mum will do it for you. She'll have to sleep a bit too, of course; but it'll be rather fun crossing off those ones early on Saturday morning, won't it? Ask her to save some for you; and you can do them in this lovely dark blue inky pen, to show that they're night time. No, I can't— because I'll be away, you see." (Now I wanted to stay. But was it just to see him cross out the last ones and print, in red, "We have lift-off!" on the dotted line provided? No: jealously clinging on, as well . . . Now the punctual Mr. Hogan would be there to guide his hand. Maybe I'd have breakfast in bed with the Rock-Eater instead . . .)

"Will you? Oh, well . . . Hey, that looks *great*! Laurence, will you miss me on Saturday?"

"I will, actually. But I'm probably going to stay up in Cambridge to finish some work—so I won't actually eat my heart out. I'll have a hamburger instead and think of you noshing away at your salmons and pawns . . ."

He did a lap of the kitchen squealing softly, as I had told him to be quiet; his mum was still asleep.

"Come on," I said: "I've ruled it up. You can do the numbers." I wanted to say, Will *you* miss *me*? D'you like Mr. Hogan and his red plane better than me?

He was concentrating over his figures, frowning, and breathing hard.

"That two's back to front, Henry."

"What? I thought it looked rather sumpshus."

"Super curves, yes; but according to the rules—remember?—you can't have—"

"Baby swans facing downstream, can you?—cos the stream goes like you read: thataway—and they'll get swept out to sea . . . Oh *dear*. Is Tippex cheating?"

I produced some from my briefcase, repaired the damage, and left it there, indulgently. "And don't you let that make you sloppy," I growled. I scribbled a note to Kate saying I'd be back on Saturday evening, and left. It was opting out; but I could not face being at Noone alone with her—and, for Saturday at least, Clifford Hogan would not take my place. As for Donna, I even knew before I turned out of the gates that two short hours of Kate Gill had spoiled my sport. I would be staying in college tonight.

I worked, not well but long, dined in hall, and drank late with the chaplain before retiring to my narrow bed. We talked of my uncle, and God, and Life, and the Bishop of Durham.

"Simply not a *Practitioner!*" he said. "Intellectuals make bad doctors and worse priests. They should be walled up alive in old universities: pure research is their true *métier*—His theories are not unsound: simply too rarefied—no *nourishment* in them. 'The hungry sheep look up and are not fed' . . ."

It was refreshing; and, for a while, I thought of Uncle Laurie and forgot Kate. That night I dreamed of Noone as it used to be, with its fragile old curtains and shrouded chandeliers. But then the tune went false. I saw a scrawny black bat-creature creeping across the plaster ceiling of the hall, like Spiderman; and watched

Him, complete with shovel hat, as he gnawed and crunched his way through the taut chain of the chandelier. I knew that my wife was sitting at the refectory table with Henry and my uncle, discussing her Will, and I shouted Get out! Get out . . . ! It fell very slowly, tinkling as it went. I ran through thick wet sand to save them; but I saw that the front door had been "gelhornised" into an up-and-over affair, like a suburban garage, and a large car was backing in—all grilles and lights and exhaust fumes—and Kate and Henry and Uncle Laurie piled in with picnic baskets and Mr. Hogan drove them off, honking his horn.

The paper shade swinging in a gust from my open window; a cross motorist blocked by a delivery van in the narrow street below—it was all very simply explained. "And the consequence was . . ." that we were left alone at Noone: me and my shadow—Tonto and the Noone Walker. "That's a very wise old young man: he won't lead Tonto into any trouble—"

I got up quickly, rather hung over; wondering if I needed a therapist more than Kate did—and deciding, with case-book dreams like mine, who needs to pay out good money?

I worked all day; and now it was my turn to get home long after Henry was in bed. The outing had apparently been an unqualified success. And I had timed my return well. "No Mr. Hogan?" I asked.

"He stayed for a drink—hoping to see you. It's quite late."

"Sorry. I just wanted to get this work finished."

"Have you a mistress in Cambridge?" Kate said, in a light, conversational tone.

"Naturally," I said. "But I didn't see her this time. Instead I got a hangover drinking with the college chaplain, and woke up indecently late."

"Oh, Laurence—and you talk about the other one having bells on! Spare me the—"

"All true," I said. "We talked about the Bishop of Durham, and he quoted *Lycidas*. Not that it matters much. Lies, white lies, and strategics—and always with the best of intentions . . ." I raised my glass in a toast.

"Are you all right, Laurence?"

"Yes, thank you. Tired, and a bit the worse for wear. As you've eaten, I'll just grab a butty and a glass of milk, and go to bed." I had the feeling she wanted to talk; and I was afraid, from the awful, sanitised brightness with which she had inquired about mistresses, that this might prefigure: Then why didn't we stop messing about, and separate?—since neither of us was happy—surely just a question of admitting it hadn't worked out . . . And so on. I could hear it all: so reasonable.

But I did not want a justified failure. And I could not face any more "good reasons" for anything: I wanted to lose myself in a warm, dark world of senses only . . . The world I must never share with my glorious wife, according to our pact. The world that I had tricked her into; and discovered—of course—she was as much at home in as I.

I lay in a hot bath drinking my ice-cold milk, and saw how naïve I had been, how childish, to make a promise with my fingers crossed; and yet how readily, under stress, I was right in there, pact-making again. For, while I was driving her to the hospital, praying she would not die, I promised whatever gods were listening that I would be content with just that—even a tricky wife who "saw things", even a potential suicide, always at risk—and never lay a finger on her, if only she would not die. I remembered how, later, sitting in her room, knowing she was out of danger, I watched the slow plasma-drip to keep my eyes away from her face, and repented that desperate deal: I could not live with her for ever and not make love to her . . . It must have been then that I decided to tell her everything just as soon as she could take it—everything except about Charles—and start wooing her all over again.

It seemed (as the saying goes) a good idea at the time: such a pity that whole new cans of worms are not more clearly labelled. Well, now there was no time to re-establish my mild, dependable, platonic image: The Man She Married; and even less to woo and win her to my way of loving. Now I had another rival, and a very serious one.

In bed, I tried to read and forget him . . . I liked Clifford Hogan; always had.

He was big and bluff and good-looking; turned fifty, and still immensely strong: rough trade, I suppose, evolved into smooth business. Not an exciting man; in fact he was rather a bore. A good friend. Kate could do worse. She had.

But I was certain he would never, deliberately, take her from me: he was too white. I wondered if he guessed how fragile our marriage was—for I was equally certain Kate would not talk of it: she had far too much to conceal ever to betray me. No: between Clifford and Kate there would be no call for steamy confidences. He might not know it, or allow himself to consider it, but once he had so ruefully recounted his sad tale of devotion, he only had to wait. In time Kate would abandon her second "marriage of convenience" ("It just didn't work"), and —after a decent interval—would propose a third. She would soon be a dab hand at proposals (a Roneo'd list, in time?). This way, moreover, she would not need to try such desperate means to find her fine and private meeting place: this good guy in the white hat would fly Henry in his plane, give her the moon, protect her from harm, and never once invade that privacy; leaving her free to devote life, and painting, to her mystical passion. She could see visions, and dream dreams . . .

I woke with her shaking me. I was sitting up in bed, terrified; I was still crying out when I woke.

"Laurence! Laurence—? You've been having a nightmare—"

"Yes," I said. "Yes, so it was. Thank God . . . It was just a nightmare. Are you all right . . .? Oh, Kate! I dreamt you were drowning in fine sand—and you *were* sand and you slipped—just slipped away —all so fine—through my . . . Oh, no—"

"Hush, Laurence. It's over now. Don't think about it. Shall I make you a mug of tea? I wouldn't mind one . . ."

She was so warm and close and gentle, and smelt of herself, and of muffins, fresh from the oven—"Oh, Kate—I do love you so."

She got up from the edge of my bed, but let me hold her hand. "My dear—don't. Please. I'm going to make some tea. And I'll get one of my sleeping powders to make sure you—"

"No, Kate: I don't want to dream again."

"You wouldn't; they're marvellous: something they gave me when I left the hospital, for when I felt I couldn't face— oh, being inside my head. They put you to sleep fast, and very deep—well below dreaming level. Just for a few hours; no bad after-effects."

"Thanks; but not for me. I haven't resorted to drugs so far, and I'm not starting now."

"Still, we'll have a cup of tea."

Soon she was back, wearing her old kimono over the cotton nightdress, and carrying two mugs. "There, get that down you."

"Stay a little while—and talk."

"No. Talking isn't the solution: sleep is. Drink up and settle down. I'll leave the dressing-room light on, OK?" She bent over swiftly and kissed my forehead—my hands, full of the hot mug, were tied— and she was gone.

I woke up with the sun already high, and Henry standing by with another cup of tea. He sat up on the end of the bed while I drank it, and told me about his great

day, leaping down to act out the clowns
and the stuntmen and the giant, blow-up
frog that had invaded the pitch in the
grand finale.

"And the announcer said 'He just needs
kissing—he's really a prince—really—!'
And all these sort of dancing girls—ever
so pretty with feathers and white boots and
things—made a circle and kissed it—and
lots of silly little girls out of the audience
rushed on too to have a go—but they got
shooed off—But it was *huge*, Laurence!
I mean, they could only reach his toes
and bum and then *wham*! It exploded
into little shreds and there was—*Barry
Manilow*!!! Wearing a crown! *And* singing
. . . And I *met* him afterwards with Mr.
Hogan—look! I've got a *photo*—'To
Henry'—See? And Mr. Hogan wants to fly
us to France for a day trip—wouldn't that
be neat?"

"Is it a big plane then? And where did
you sit?"

We got on with his go-kart circuit in
the field all morning; but at lunch he was
yawning, and Kate insisted he should have
a sleep. I decided to go out, ostensibly to
observe the collection of autumn-flowering

clematis at a small country house in Norfolk that was open for the day. Kate stayed to sunbathe—"It may be the last of it, you see"—and be there when Henry woke, despite Nanny's offer to forgo her Sunday constitutional.

This would be Kate's first time virtually alone at Noone since her return. I knew she would do nothing "foolish" with Henry asleep upstairs, but I felt all the old fears surfacing. On my way to tell her I was off, I stopped in the library and watched her. She lay stretched out flat on her face, wearing a thin shirt over the minimal bikini. The shirt would come off, no doubt, when she heard my car leave. The pruning knife lay beside her on the ground; she had asked for it at lunch: "So much that's finished flowering needs cutting back now."

I wondered what was going on in her head; and how much this Clifford business —of which she had said no more—was just a diversion. She was behaving so normally. Was she just lulling my suspicions? "You know I'm dotty and won't believe me . . ." She was quite clever enough. Or was it much simpler than that? Did she just lie there and dream of that weightless body covering hers? Could she, perhaps, actually feel him, I wondered—or partly feel him? A subtle and ingenious lover perceived only by the erogenous zones . . . ?

I drove faster and farther than I need, stopped on open moors and climbed up to a small cairn; chiefly to clear myself of the persistent, dull headache I had woken with. I had been thirsty, too; but it could not still be my hangover. Then I realised that Kate had drugged me. I had no memory of wakefulness nor anxiety: a black space—then morning sun, and blessed Henry with tea. Looking back, I could see the mug had been removed from my bedside table.

When I got home, Clifford Hogan's runabout was parked on the gravel. I heard voices in the garden. I went quickly through to the kitchen and looked in the bin. I had to search, but I found a small, white envelope, and read, through the coffee grounds, "One to be taken at night when necessary, well stirred into a hot beverage."

When I had changed into my gardening

things, I went up to my study; delaying. The terrace below was empty, except for the remains of tea; Henry came round the corner on his bike, with White Fang in hot pursuit, and disappeared behind the dairy. I must go down and be friendly and hostly to Clifford Hogan; even if they hadn't heard the car, Henry would have seen it and told them I was back.

From the lawn, before I had called out, I saw them. They were walking slowly by the great border along the lower terrace, a little below me, arm in arm. She wore shorts, and the shirt—open—over her bikini top. They looked like father and daughter, with him beaming down at her indulgently from his great height, the king-sized teddy-bear (what else do you give the young widow who has everything?); and Kate so relaxed, letting go of him to crouch down and tug out a weed. Then she stood up, slipped her hand through his seersucker elbow, and they paced on. She was chattering away, pointing things out. And I knew that look: absent, at ease. He was silent; watching, smiling, nodding.

I called out, "I'm back . . . Hullo,

Clifford. Is she giving you the low-down on succulents?" It was not meant to sound so racy, and I blundered on, "Or is it the lesser potentilla . . . ?"

Kate said, "You've missed tea: I'll make a fresh pot, and we'll all have some. Hen saved some cake, I think . . ." She was doing up the buttons of her shirt, now. For my eyes only . . .

Something inside my head seemed to snap. Details became exquisitely clear as they stood there below me, by my border: the ironed crease on her "good" shorts; his thick, manicured fingers adjusting his buttonhole; and that buttonhole, the first of my autumn crocuses, that I had planted in April.

"Thank you, Cliff, for Henry's superb outing. Yes, Kate, I should love a fresh pot of tea. And, while you're doing that, would you excuse me? I just have to make a couple of phone calls. I shan't be long."

I went up to my study. Three telephone calls: one to Heathrow, one to Edward Glyn-Jones, and one to Chloë. Then I went down for my tea.

Next morning, Monday, I was up early;

but I did not go to Cambridge. As soon as I knew Kate was down in her barn, I went into her dressing room and packed a zipper-bag of thin, holiday clothes: some festive, like the flying suit; some casual; a few of the old, scruffy favourites—her faded shorts, and the collarless shirt of her father's, fine and much-mended, still bearing its "Utility Mark" from the war years: an odd garment for so rich a lady. A skirt and a long-sleeved shirt were on the chair in the bathroom, obviously clean and laid out for taking Henry to school. I left those, but took the bikini from the towel rail, gambling on her being in too much of a hurry to notice its absence, along with all the other things I had removed.

It was still well before Mrs. Furze was due; but Nanny and Henry were moving about. I took the bag down to my car and locked it in the boot along with my own, ready packed from the night before. Then I went back upstairs, and into her sitting room: I needed her passport, fast; at any moment she might tire of painting and come up to get ready for the school run. Not in one of the locked drawers, please,

God . . . No: in an open pigeonhole. I put it in my pocket and went down to make breakfast.

She came up in a rush, flying into the kitchen through the back door and glancing wild-eyed at the clock before she looked at us, with our cornflakes and our school bags.

"That can't be the time! Oh, Laurence, haven't you gone? Did you oversleep? I'm madly late. Henry, are you nearly ready? I will be—only got to get some clothes on . . ."

"Mum . . . ! Laurence is taking us both! You're *both* taking me!"

"Oh, fine! but . . ." She looked at me.

"But why? Because it would be fun: family outing, eh, Hen? since Mum and I missed the one on Saturday—then I'll drop you back here and go on to Cambridge, OK? Get on with it then: get dressed and I'll butter some toast for you . . ."

While she was upstairs I poured her a cup of tea and stirred in the contents of one of the small white envelopes I found in her medicine cupboard. For a brief moment, in all the excitement of taking action at last, it felt like another mistake; and my reasonable, careful soul cried out to me: If it is, matey, it'll be your last . . . "Ah, Kate: I poured you some tea to cool it."

"Thanks. Great—" Already she was gulping it thirstily. "I'll just grab some toast—"

"I've done some," I said: "sit down and eat it and drink up and get into the car —my car—OK? Anything you need from upstairs? I'm going to my study for some papers I've forgotten, so—"

"My bag—but I won't need that if I'm coming straight back."

I took my briefcase and the large carrier from the hall and went straight to her room, where I gathered up her handbag, her makeup, brushes, and the clearly favoured face-cream, pills and two paperbacks from her bedside table. There were the sandals I dared not take before (she had come down in some bright, flat, balletic things—useful, I thought, for sightseeing; if we had time for that), and her espadrilles, still warm. I did not pack a nightdress; but, as an afterthought, I added the white dressing-gown: it took up so little room in the carrier bag—and was just as much mine as His.

At the head of the stairs, I masked the bag with my briefcase and called, "All in the car? Get a move on, or I'll beat you to it—"

Henry raced out and across the hall, just ahead; Kate ran after him, laughing, toast in hand, and I let them rush past, then followed them. "We're off, Nanny! Goodbye, Mrs. Furze!" we called. I unlocked the boot, threw in the briefcase and the bag. And we left.

It was about fifteen minutes to the nursery school, and I drove fast. Henry talked all the way about who we might see if we were lucky and what he might do today; like, tell everyone about his jaunt. Apart from warning him not to boast or bore the socks off his chums, there was hardly any need to say a word. Kate was certainly very quiet in the back. We saw Henry in through the gates; and two small, rough characters charged up to him and hailed him with much thumping and cackling. He turned and waved; then ran back to us.

"Hey, that's Bleep—the little one—and

hat's Basher, like I told you of: my special friends! See ya . . ."

He disappeared into the hurly-burly. Kate was smiling, the proud mother.

"He's awfully nice and normal, isn't he?" she said, walking back to the car slowly.

"He'll survive," I said. "Kate, are you feeling OK?"

"Short of sleep, I guess—I shouldn't be . . ."

"Get in the back again and you can have a snooze on the way home. I'll drive gently . . . No, I'm not in a rush today."

I drove like a saboteur with a load of nitro-glycerine on board. I could see in my rear-view mirror that she was fast asleep when we passed the gates of Noone, and headed for the motorway. There was lots of time: our plane was not until after midday.

21

"**B**UT you can't kidnap your *wife*, Laurence! Do stop being ridiculous and let's go home."

"I'm deadly serious, Kate. And I don't believe it's against the law to take your wife on a surprise holiday, is it? Unless you make a scene at the airport—which you won't, will you? You don't like scenes. I was relying on that."

"No question of scenes: I just won't be there. You can do what you like: I'm going home."

"And suppose I don't let you?"

"And how could you stop me?"

"Well, the child-locks are on all the doors and I'm here in the driving seat, the only exit: how do you propose to get out? We can sit here till Doomsday; there are lots of planes—and empty seats, out of season—and a whole fortnight to play with. You might as well co-operate: the weather's nicer in Greece. But there's no hurry: this is quite a pleasant spot. Take your time to accept the situation, Kate: you haven't got much of an alternative . . . And don't try fighting me, will you?"

"Suppose I did?"

"I would not hesitate to knock you out —Oh, nothing so crude as a rabbit-chop: there are subtler means in the mysterious East; and most companies insist on valuable employees learning the basic skills, if only to protect their investment. Then it would simply be a matter of ordering a wheelchair at Heathrow."

"You take my breath away . . ."

"That was the general idea. So you can either sleep sweetly all the way, or behave yourself. And it's worth remembering that my word carries somewhat more conviction than yours, in view of your recent medical history: I have only to explain, and they can check with Dr. Pond and the shrinks . . . Kate? I'm not bluffing, you know: if the worst came to the worst and you persisted in behaving—uncooperatively, then I'd have no choice. I would understand you were refusing me the chance I've asked for."

"And then?"

"Then Plan B comes into effect. I'd take

you home and get you certified. Plenty of
witnesses—airport officials and doctors
and porters. At that point I would not
hesitate; I'd hit you with everything, Kate:
your crazy 'terms', your obsession with a
dead vicar—the lot . . . You've been very
protected so far, because I've loved you so.
Even now, dammit: I only want you to
come on a holiday, away from Noone.
When I give up, you'll find real life
flooding in—and not even your wealth will
save you."

"Clifford Hogan will."

"Not when he hears what he's up
against: respectability matters far too
much to him . . . Think of the *News of
the World*—"

"You couldn't."

"You'd be surprised what—"

"You couldn't—because I would
explain how you had sabotaged Charles's
building works. You'd go to prison."

"So? What proof have you?"

"There must be proof. The police would
find it. You can't have covered your tracks
perfectly: there must be footprints, clues
—threads—hairs—in the passages. In the
cellars—"

"Certainly; why not, in my own house? I've been around Noone—officially—for the last six months. Why shouldn't I explore the cellars of my own—?"

"The clothes, then. Your costume."

"That went into the boiler weeks ago, when you were in hospital."

"Some record—kept by the firm you got it from."

"Yes, indeed: good thinking, Robin. But under an alias of course. No connection."

"They'd recognise you—the scars."

"You underestimate me: I ordered it by phone; sent a taxi—with cash—to collect it. No connection. And, no, they are not going to remember a taxi driver eighteen months ago. Come on, Kate, you're getting a bit desperate, aren't you?"

"So would you—shut up with a madman in a layby somewhere in the Chilterns . . . If I'm meant to be delicately balanced, aren't you pushing it a bit?"

"Would you like to get out and walk around? It's a concession you can bargain for."

"Another bargain? Could you trust me?

You know how easy they are to break . . .
OK, what?"

"Just that you won't be silly and try to
run away. I will have to hold your arm, of
course."

She was silent; and I gazed out across
the brown-and-blue distances of Bucks and
Oxon, and listened to her quick, anxious
breathing. She was still in the back seat,
of course; and better that way. I did not
want to crowd her.

"OK," she said. "I just can't stand
being shut up any more."

I got out and unlocked her door for her.
In the open, she stretched, and breathed
deeply. Then, still not looking at me, she
held out her arm.

I put it through mine, companionably.
"Look—no handcuffs," I said, and we
walked through the gate and out on to the
sloping field. The sky was overcast now,
and there was a chill breeze, up here on
our eminence. I let her go, took off my
jacket and put it round her. She took my
arm, and we paced on.

She seemed to have run out of steam;
temporarily, at least.

I said, "I'm not mad, you know . . .

Put yourself in my position, Kate, and just imagine what has pushed me to such lengths. My marriage is threatened by two rivals—and rivals I can't really compete with: a homosexual, and a ghost. It sounds like the beginning of a bad joke: 'Heard the one about the gay, the spook and the virtuous—?'"

"Stop it, Laurence. I do think you've gone mad. And dammit—what marriage is there to save?"

"Christ, Kate! And you've called *me* cynical . . . Remember swearing something rather quaint and old-fashioned about loving and cherishing, till death us do part?"

"But you broke our agreement; you renegued on the terms—"

I turned her to me, took both her hands and held them firmly.

"Kate, you, of all people, must understand what it is to believe in something you know simply can't be so: *can't*—according to all the rules; according to reason. No, listen: you waited and hoped and kept on believing, night after night. Are *you* going to tell *me* that putting one's shirt on the Impossible cannot pay? I'd

have accepted any terms; and waited . . .
But I discovered I wasn't as strong as you:
that I could not wait for ever. So. Harder
for me, maybe—having you there. Very
much there."

She glanced up at me; and I felt her
hands tense, like a cat about to leap from
a too-warm lap. I let her go, and walked
beside her. Near, but not touching. She
said nothing; when we stopped at a natural
look-out point, clear of the trees, she very
deliberately stepped sideways, putting
space between us.

From her safe distance she said
defiantly, "Is this—this comparative
freedom—another concession? Some
bargain I've made without knowing
it . . . ? What small print didn't I read,
then . . . ?" Leaning forward to see my
face. Whistling in the dark.

I looked away and said, "No bargain
this time, Kate. Nor do I entirely trust
you. But you have actually been listening
to me. Didn't you notice?"

She laughed. (She had before:
nervously, angrily; and, when she first
woke up, and I explained where we were,
outlined the situation, she had laughed in

sheer disbelief—which turned a little hollow when she saw my face; that I meant it. She was suddenly very wide awake; furious, incredulous again, then coldly arguing. Next came her "humouring the psychopath" stage: quickly over, possibly because it angered me. "Don't dare soft-soap me, Kate! *Don't* say you know how I feel and let's go home and have a nice day together—*Christ*, woman—you're not stupid! Credit me with just a little insight —I mean, you have been my Special Subject, so to speak, over the last six months; and, before that, I used to listen to you humouring Charles when he went over the top—as he seemed to do fairly regularly . . .")

I think I must have talked myself down, and reassured her a little. I had to remind myself I was still the dangerous saboteur of last summer; and that, by my own confession, I had been "still a bit crazed" by my experiences. "Once more the dangerous saboteur" might be nearer the mark: ever since that moment last evening on the lawn at Noone, when I stood looking down across the border at Kate and Clifford, and felt something snap in my head, I had—as I could see now—reverted to that role. The swift decisions, the crisp phone calls, the planning and packing and attention to detail; and, all the while, that heightened capability, that (deceptively?) clear vision, and the blessed adrenalin rushing, almost audibly, through the system. Heady stuff, action. However —said my careful soul, as I stood there with Kate, looking out from our high place over one of the loveliest kingdoms of the earth—however: not necessarily the right action, not even morally justifiable in terms of emotional need—

"Shut up . . . ," I said out loud.

"But I didn't say anything, Laurence."

"No. Just me, being bloody reasonable again. Inside my head. 'Just the natives: pay no attention . . .'"

"Is being reasonable so bad? After all—"

"Hush, Kate." I turned and put my finger on her mouth, very lightly; then turned back to the view. "It can paralyse everything. Look at poor bloody Hamlet. Lovely little mover when he got going; totally tied up most of the time, seeing the other side of the question . . . You must be thirsty, Kate. And hungry, too: didn't have your usual egg-and-bacon fix this morning, did you?"

"I am, actually: mostly thirsty. That foul drug does dry one out."

"So I found." (We'd been through that bit: the first "angry" phase; mercifully short. I didn't give her time to lie; just produced Exhibit A—the small, coffee-stained envelope—from my pocket and rested my case. But I couldn't resist asking if she'd locked her door as well; and she moved on into the silent, sulking stage.)

"Please, Laurence," she was saying, "can't we go home and talk this over? I've got a bit of a headache, too—partly being shut up, I guess—and I really am pining for a cup of something—even water. Couldn't we?"

"No need to go home: there's a Thermos of tea and some Marmite sandwiches in the boot, along with all our holiday gear."

"I see. You've thought of just about flaming everything, haven't you . . . ? Right: so what's the deal this time?"

"Just that you come to the airport and get on the plane with me."

"For a mug of tea and a Marmite—? You must be joking!"

"Why? Folks have been known to sell their souls for far less; with the Marmite thrown in I'm counting on your body as well . . . 'Ooh, Miss Berry—you're ever so lovely when you're angry!' And now you should turn and pummel me with your little fists—"

She made a sort of choking noise; and laughed, then stopped herself short and cried out *"Christ!"* at the grey sky. She turned and started walking back to the car.

Now we were both glad of the shelter. We drank our tea in silence; and she started on the pile of sandwiches I had made that morning. Halfway through, she said, rather muffled—perhaps intentionally—by the sandwich she was holding: "What did you mean about 'co-operating' or whatever—?"

"Just that: coming peaceably on holiday with me. Not a lot to ask: a last chance."

"And that's all? All the 'co-operation' required of me?"

"Yes, Kate. 'Holiday' as in 'holiday brochure'. And not even in the finest print

—the bit about 'possible surcharges'—will you find the word 'rape'."

She ate another sandwich in silence; then, "So you told Nanny you might persuade me to come to Cambridge for the day. When do they start worrying about us? What about breaking it to Henry?"

"I told you: Chloë will take over. If I don't ring her by teatime, she swings into action; tells everyone we're off on an impulsive holiday . . . Yes, and Adrian this evening, and the gala ballet do on Thursday: everything. All arranged. She may have Henry to stay a night or two—and you know how often he's wanted to; it was only your still being a bit suspicious of Chloë that—"

"Me? Not for a moment—"

"OK, just plain jealous, right? Ssh—Listen: it's all fixed; notes left for the builders—they're starting on the front parapets, and the pointing, this week: very straightforward to be getting on with. Philip knows about the swimming pool, and finishing the paving—and Nanny and Mrs. Furze will cope. They've got Chloë at the end of a phone if they can't; even

Edward Glyn-Jones is on red alert for crises and major decisions—"

"Oh God—do they *all* know you've kidnapped me—? I'll never be able to face—!"

"Think, dammit, Kate: am I likely to admit I need to kidnap my own wife? Come on. All is well, believe me. Don't you see that, if you run a household as well as you do, you create a machine that can at least tick over without you?"

I took her silence as assent, and started the engine.

"Wait, Laurence. Now I want to have a pee."

I caught her eye in the rear-view mirror and she looked shiftily away. She said, "But I suppose you've thought of that too . . ." Suddenly she hit the back of my seat with some force. "And I am *not* going to have you standing over me while I do."

I switched off the engine and waited.

"So—what?" she said grudgingly. "Have you brought a very long coil of rope to let me out on?"

"You'd make a great accomplice, you know," I said. "Powerful string, actually, from the kitchen drawer; in haste."

"I don't *believe* it!" She laughed harshly; and I feared we might be back at square one.

"But," I went on, turning round and looking at her, "since you've already made a bargain over your tea and sandwiches to come with me on to the plane, I don't need it, do I? You won't go breaking your word."

"You did."

"But 'Hons' don't, do they?"

She grimaced; and I turned back again and did up my seat belt.

"I must go, Laurence," she said. "Please: I'm desperate."

I got out and opened the door for her. "Shall I count?" I asked. "Like playing lurky? Up to a hundred—then I come looking for you?"

"You won't need to," she snapped.

It was a very long couple of minutes after she had disappeared into the trees; long enough to wonder if I'd blown it. She could get almost up to the motorway, two miles off, under cover, and hitch a ride. No bag, no coat, thin shoes; but it could be done. Kate could do it. She had—so

some would say—married me ruthlessly;
could she not leave me so?

Then she appeared through the spinney
and walked slowly to the car. "OK then,"
she said haughtily: "let's get this famous
holiday over and done with. Dammit,
Laurence: I'm not even properly dressed
for it . . ."

I squealed softly, like Henry, under
cover of the engine noise: I was on my way
—no more than that. It was a start.

The Greek island was planned as the *coup
de grâce* in our long duel; the blows and
the mercy to be equally divided, and no
taking of prisoners.

However, by the time we had flown to
Athens, caught a taxi to the central depot,
endured a three-hour bus ride and a boat
trip in the dark to the island of my choice,
then walked to the nearest of the two
tavernas in the small port, it was very late,
and the fight had gone out of us. I booked
us into single rooms. Kate was too
exhausted, she said, in body and spirit, for
food, and went straight up to bed. I had
a beer and a fresh roll in a café by the
water's edge. I was the last, apart from

owner and his friends drinking at the bar. I felt the balmy night and watched the stars; the soft slap of the waves, and the Greek voices, flowed over me, marvellously unintelligible, demanding nothing.

It had been an odd journey, with little talk and less complaining. Apart from visiting Paris, and Amsterdam with her father long ago, Kate had only been to Rome and North America, both with Charles. Greece was new to her. On the plane, she studied the phrase-book I had brought, until she fell asleep; slipping down with her pillow against the window, not against me.

Physical contact, however, is inevitable in travel; and especially in a Greek bus. When the sun had gone and there was no more to see outside, Kate slept once more, heavily; falling against my shoulder, starting awake, nodding off again. Then I eased her down on to my lap and watched her as she slept. When I looked up and saw the indulgent, well-worn faces looking down at us, I did not feel foolish. "English?" asked the conductor, stopping to look. "Is new marry?" I nodded. "Very tired," I whispered. The conductor and the indulgent watchers smiled broadly. "Is correct for new marry, is very tire, heh?" Then he said it in Greek and hushed the laughter. "Slip good!" he said, and moved on.

We did, that night in our separate rooms; and woke to cloudless blue. We breakfasted on fierce Greek coffee and pastries filled with fetta cheese at the same small café by the water.

"Do you feel up to walking?" I asked. "It's going to be quite hot; but I want to explore along the coast for this little taverna on the peninsula I remember. I don't know how far. I don't even know the name."

"I don't mind heat." She was very still and easy, her dark glasses pushed back, her eyes wide to the dazzle of sun and water, almost as though she were drinking the light. "It's incredible here," she said: "I didn't know sea could be such a colour."

"Even better if you look down into it from a height."

"From your peninsula."

"If they haven't built a hotel complex on it by this time."

"Seven years . . . ," said Kate: "a smooth-faced little sprig from Cambridge. I can't imagine you without the scars." She studied me for a moment and then looked out to sea again. "I'm not sure I'd like it."

"I didn't think you—"

She leaned over and put her hand firmly across my mouth, silencing me; then pushed away her coffee cup and got to her feet. "When do we start?" she asked.

I was sitting gazing at the water; stunned. "We have," I said.

By noon we were climbing down the rough path from my taverna to bathe in a peacock-green bay. We had a late lunch, of tomatoes, onions, bread and oil, on the deserted terrace, and swam again, and slept; and walked back to the port three miles along the shore, to collect our bags and find a taxi. By then the sun was going down in splendour, and had to be watched. We settled, with a bottle of wine, at our bar, to see the hot penny drop into those fabled mountains of the mainland: Parnassus was there—Olympus, too, we were told, on a good day.

"Too much . . . ," said Kate, shaking her head.

"It is rather. With luck there'll be an army exercise, or a shoal of jellyfish in our bay, to make it all a bit more real . . ."

We watched the hypnotic scarlet disc until it had gone. Then Kate said, "Did you come here with a girl?"

"I thought you'd never ask . . . No, as a matter of fact: just two rather hearty friends from Cambridge, whose sailing holiday had fallen through. I was afraid they'd get bored, but even they were caught by it; bought lilos and drifted about all day quite happily rudderless, it seemed. A bit of the Greek dancing in the evenings, I remember. But that's not compulsory."

We sat hand in hand, knee to knee, "squelching" our Demestica and watching the silken sea turn purple.

"I prefer the idea of the phosphorus. Bathing at night," said Kate. "Look, since we're going to be living and eating at your dream taverna after this, why not have supper here and then get the taxi back?"

"Fine. I wouldn't mind changing, though; and washing off some of the salt.

I'm sure they'd let us at last night's place; and the bags are there."

One of the rooms was still free, they told us: we were welcome. I suggested I find a restaurant while Kate showered and dressed. I still did not want to crowd her. When I saw her again, she was wearing the flying suit: I watched her coming along the front past the string of small cafés, heads turning in her wake.

"It's not too over the top, is it?" she asked.

"No. It's fine," I said. "You're quite gorgeous."

"Good. Thanks for packing it, Laurence."

She had started on the small eats, the *mezze*, when I rejoined her.

"New? The shirt?" she said. "And the jacket!"

"Not precisely; but new on. I got them in July. In Cambridge."

"The same time as that lovely dress I found in my bag? You know what I like, don't you? It's for tomorrow. So . . . you've been planning all this quite a while."

"On and off."

"'You're a deep one and no mistake', as my old Nanny used to . . . Oh God—I sound like Lady Chloë . . ."

"Never."

"*Did* you and Chloë—?"

"No, Kate. I do speak the truth most of the time, you know."

"Just omit parts of it, I suppose."

"Well, I will—eventually—drop you back at Noone, Kate."

"And you would, eventually, have told me you were the fourth statue, I'm sure."

I was completely thrown. At last I said, "How long have you known?"

"Since you told me about being responsible for all the vandalism, I guess . . . No: not right away; I was in too much of a state. I took longer to work it out. You see, the night when Charles died, and I looked up—it was all so shadowy, and quick. And fraught. I couldn't be sure. I still wondered."

"You didn't say anything. You wanted to keep me guessing—give me hell."

"'Not precisely'—she assumed my donnish tone. "I saw you couldn't possibly have admitted to that 'visitation'—not as things were . . . So I—yes, I suppose I used it against you. Handy: I was very short of weapons by then, if you remember."

"Yet when you really had your back against the wall—"

"Hijacked and re-routed—" She was enjoying my discomfiture.

"—you still didn't use it."

"I nearly did. I wasn't sure—oh, what you'd do, I guess."

"You weren't sure if I was a murderer."

"Just so. Not the moment to choose, really."

"Oh, Kate."

"Well, I still don't know. Only that it was you above me on the porch. You've confirmed that."

"Do you still think I could have murdered Charles?"

"Even more—now I've seen you in action—'lovely little mover' and all that. I realise you're perfectly capable of it . . . What seemed to me out of keeping, when I thought about it, was the—the *unplanned* aspect: that if someone saw you, or you were caught by the police, then or later, you couldn't possibly prove it was an accident—could you? I mean, there'd been plenty of chances to kill Charles—easier, and neater. No: thinking it over, I reckoned it was an accident. It didn't fit. I even wondered all over again if it could have been Him . . . Until yesterday, when I nearly said it—and I caught a glimpse of your face in the car mirror. Then I *knew* you were the fourth statue; and I shut up. Suddenly I was scared. I'm not now—though I'm still not sure, really . . . And you're not saying anything. You mean—I suppose—that I've got to make up my own mind."

"After so many truths and half-truths, Kate, it's probably the only way for you to be sure . . . And, speaking of half-truths," I said, as lightly as I could, "what about the other—'sightings'?" Very busy; taking more bread, not looking at her. Not wanting to hear.

"Those were true." Then she put her hand over mine, and said, "It's my favourite place, Noone; but it's good to get away from it."

We both ate langoustine, just as I so often dreamed we would. And the colour left the water and the sky, stars came out, and bobbing lights across the bay. It was suddenly cooler; still balmy.

"Why don't we get the taxi now," said Kate, "and have our coffee and brandy and things back at the taverna?"

We did; but, as I had so often dreamed, we did not get round to the coffee and the brandy.

22

THE birds of the peninsula woke us before first light, and we made love again. There was even less need to hurry this time, with our whole lives ahead of us. Then we lay close, talking. Kate got up and opened the windows wide so she could hear the sea better; and came back, cool and smooth, into the warm bed. And it's all true, I told myself.

"It's all true, isn't it?" I said.

"I think so," said Kate. "It's certainly not a Scotch mist."

Later, when it was light, she told me I'd had another nightmare: "Only for a moment. You started to cry out—but it was easy to calm you down."

"I wonder why I did that."

"Never mind. I like calming you down."

At breakfast on the terrace, she looked like a beautiful, sleek, auburn cat, full of cream.

"What are you thinking about?" I said.

"Nothing much. 'Chapter and verse' . . . Proof it was you, visiting me. Both times, I mean. No need to take your word for it."

We were very idle over the next three days; slow meals and long siestas; bathing, lying in the sun, lying in the shade reading the paperbacks we had picked up at the airport. I started on the Edith Wharton I'd found on her bedside table.

"I didn't know she wrote ghost stories," I said. "Or, come to think of it, that you'd feel like reading them, my darling: maybe it helps give them distance—puts them in their place. Ghosts, I mean . . . But I suppose you still believe in them."

"For people who can see them, yes. So do you, actually—though you won't accept it. And that, my love, is what your night-mares are all about."

"Am I still having them?"

"Can't you remember, then? I don't go on about them—stirring them up—because *you* haven't . . . Last night—don't you *really* remember?—you were fussing about Henry and Him—the Noone Walker. Doddy. Frantically telling Henry to hide quickly: *He* was coming. Through the wood."

That night, while Kate slept spread-eagled across me, breathing warm along my collarbone, I stayed awake. I could not stop thinking of her words: "Those were true." No glimmer of doubt.

After a while she stirred and woke, sensing my sleeplessness.

"Kate," I said: "tell me more about Him. Are you sure it couldn't have been me? The other sightings?"

She told me about the first, her encounter in the poplar alley on the day of the auction. "April, you see—when you must have been in Sri Lanka; half-dead . . . That alley is His favourite spot, it seems: several sightings there—though not by me . . . I remember Henry saying—it was one of those hot days just after we got engaged—that Doddy was there, pacing up and down—and 'ever so gloomby'— You know how he picks up these expressions from Mrs—"

"*Henry* saw Him? I mean *really* saw Him—not me?"

"Oh, yes: often—*far* more often than I

did. He's the 'psychic' one. Children often are . . . But didn't you know?"

"I thought he'd grown out of all that—once I'd stopped playing the part."

"He has, I think. He's a bit embarrassed by it now—as one is about old toys, old games—even old friends, I guess. That's probably why he hasn't told you . . . No, darling: not so much 'secretive'—just wanting your admiration. Your approval."

"And I was pretty cutting about Doddy once, I remember . . ."

"Well—even now, I gather—Doddy still keeps turning up. Just hanging about, not talking. Out of sorts. Rather babyish, really, as Henry remarked: 'jealous of us playing with Laurence'."

"How extraordinary, Kate. I didn't know any of this."

"Don't worry. Really. Even earlier on, it was only when Henry was fed up with everyone else for some reason; or lonely. Which he seldom is now he's got you, darling. Look, so stop fussing, and—"

"No, wait. Tell me more. About His coming to your room."

"Oh—just twice, I guess, when it was *Him*. Well—I know, now . . . But quite scary, that first time—in there. And midnight . . . I was brushing my hair, I think. Yes; and He came slowly forward till He was very close behind me, and I could actually see His hands on my neck —but couldn't feel a thing—except, after being so frightened, suddenly very peaceful. It was strange: I could see—and *feel*—that He loved me, Laurence . . . He stood there—maybe a minute, maybe more—sort of stroking my neck and my hair; then He stepped back, out of the light, and I turned round and He'd gone . . . Way back in February, that must have been."

"And later? I mean, apart from me— complicating your life—Was the next time near the end of May? A few days before your proposal?"

"How did you . . . ? Oh, from the way I behaved, I guess. Well, that time he didn't come near me; stood over by the fireplace. I tried to talk to him, but he just gazed sadly at me. Then he moved over to the end of the bed. I went across to—to lie down. And I felt this extraordinary peace-fulness again—and terribly sleepy—must have closed my eyes. And then he wasn't there . . . Look, is there any point in all this?" She sat up and dragged the counterpane round her. "*Why* do you want to know . . . ? Laurence? What's up? You can't be jealous of him. Or simply prying . . . Tell me this—at least: do you believe in Him now? I mean, d'you admit that you do?"

"Yes," I said, and my voice sounded oddly shaky. I sat up too, and reached for a jersey. "Kate. He'd pretty well lost Henry, you said; and now He's lost you. But old Hen's still there, and we've gone off."

"What do you mean?" Her voice was frightened. She was out of bed now, standing up; a pale shape in her winding sheet. "You don't think that He could harm Henry? That He'd *want* to?"

"Kate," I said carefully: "if these—these restless spirits have feelings, and characters, well—I just wonder what they're like. I would have expected them merely to repeat—to relive—the events and emotions of their lives, wouldn't you? But it sounds otherwise. OK, so the Noone Walker came back to his rectory the very day it was sold. You were sympathetic—clearly: but He did not approve of Charles's work."

"*You* didn't, Laurence. D'you mean . . . ? He sort of drove you?"

"No. I'm a sceptic, Kate. But I did feel —yes: a bit 'driven'. At times, certainly. Inspired. And, as I said, a bit crazed . . . Either way, it was as He intended—and you carried on from there, restoring His precious Noone. Maybe He inspired *you*: you say you sensed His approval. But, even though His mission was accomplished—so to speak—He stayed on: He enjoyed Henry's company; and He'd fallen in love with you, it seems. Now, this is also a jealous spirit, remember; about people as well as places. Vetting the new owners on the day of the auction, going into a decline when you decide to get married, hanging around Henry—all of which sounds quite funny. I just wonder about, well—funny-peculiar. I wonder if He'd actually do anything."

"Could spirits hurt people, Laurence? Poltergeists, maybe: they could knock you out with a flying saucepan. Maybe a ghost could scare you into danger—you run, you fall down the lift-shaft . . . But

Hen wouldn't be scared of dear old Doddy . . ." She was standing over by the window looking out. "On the other hand, a 'friendly' ghost could simply lead you into danger, like a will o' the wisp in a swamp . . . And there are dangerous places around Noone. But He wouldn't want to harm Henry."

"Not 'harm' him; no. But—well, Henry trusts Him, you say." I started again. "It's a very odd situation (something of an understatement, what?), in which you three have become extraordinarily close; too close. And for some time He had you, both of you, all to Himself. Not so long ago, Kate, He nearly landed you for keeps . . . Well, it would only take an accident in the home, a common enough occurrence, after all, and He'd—He'd have old Hen."

I had phoned Noone on our first morning: all was well, Henry at the Grange for two nights, and the good ladies quite delighted we were "taking a proper break" (Nanny); "a late honeymoon, if I may be so bold, Mr. Laurence dear . . ." (Mrs. Furze).

Now it was Saturday. Henry would be home again.

"It's four-thirty," said Kate: "how soon can we phone?"

"Seven? It'll be only six in England. We could use the time to walk into town and phone from there."

"And for seats on the plane—if that's what we really want."

"Is it? Do you want to go anyway, Kate?" I said.

"Yes. I'm worried. It may seem silly—and I don't want this holiday to end—but."

"But we'd both be worrying . . . OK. No phoning, no messing about. We leave our luggage and a note, reserving the room, saying we'll be back on Monday; take an overnight bag, walk along to the port, get a taxi to Athens—down the island and across the bridge: quicker than waiting for boats and buses—and catch the first plane. OK? No more decisions, then. Let's go."

It may have sounded decisive; and Kate was patently relieved to stop thinking in circles and act. But at least a dozen times during that long morning I felt it was sheer madness: a pair of dotty ladybirds, flying away home.

If we could simply have asked the right questions on the phone, we might not have been so precipitate; but how could we? "Ah—Nanny? Everything fine? Good. By the way, you haven't noticed a small black-and-white vicar—Nanny? Can you hear me? Bad line, I'm afraid . . . A black-and-white minister—have you? Hanging around Henry? No, not 'minstrel', Nanny: 'minister'—priest—parson; a dead one, actually—yes, a ghost . . . Well I wonder if you'd just pop out, would you—and have a look . . . ?"

Things moved quickly, once we had taken the first step—though it felt desperately slow, like being back in the old nightmare, running through wet sand. There was light enough to walk fast along the rough road to the port; and we did not try to talk of other things, still busy reassuring ourselves and each other.

"We're not panicking really, are we?" Kate said more than once. "Not being utterly ridiculous?"

"No: we're just breaking our holiday and checking up and coming back."

"Yes. Rather extravagant and fun. A surprise visitation. Sorry, darling! Not too happily expressed."

"Don't worry, Kate: lean on the clichés —'no news is good news', 'better safe than . . .' Look, everything's fine—or we'd have heard."

"Absolutely . . . Oh, Laurence—"

"It'll be all right, my love—and we'll feel so foolish when we find it is—and we'll all have a spiffing weekend in the old home."

"That's just what we'll do . . . Laurence, d'you think there'll be a taxi this early?"

"I think everything starts early: fishing ports do. There'll be a taxi—or some car we can hire—or somebody who knows of one: it'll be all right. And we're not panicking."

But I kept thinking of the dangers that lay about or within Noone; the accident blackspots. Our man-made hillside with its decorative cliffs and grottoes; the passages, some rendered impassable by old rock-falls; the lake, and my Riding Tree that leaned out over the water. But Henry could swim . . . Not if he were caught in the water-lilies we had planted and allowed to run riot over the summer.

"He's too sensible . . . ," I said out loud.

Kate said, "But he's only five."

There was a taxi in the square; we found its driver having breakfast at the bus depot bar, and drank down a short, sharp coffee ourselves while he finished.

The one road took us the length of our island and over the long bridge that linked it to the mainland; and we comforted ourselves with another cliché: the longest way round *was* the shortest way home. We were at the airport before nine. A matter of urgency, we said; and they rushed us through to a boarding plane that still had a few empty places.

We could not sit together. It was like being cut in half. Kate was back in the smoking section: "I'd like it, actually," she said; and accepted all the cigarettes she was offered by her neighbours. I would certainly have done the same. She stayed behind her dark glasses, but adequately sociable: inspecting someone's holiday snaps when I took along her book. She said, "Our watches are an hour ahead of England, aren't they?" I reassured her, and so did the beefcake with the snaps. When I next looked round, he was altering her watch for her. I wanted to hit him and take his place; but we were both of us, without admitting it, superstitiously queasy about midday (does the Walker observe British Summer Time, I wondered?): it was probably more sensible to accept diversions than pool our fears. Still, I went up and got two hundred duty-free cigarettes—"for Mrs. Furze," I said—so that she would not have to accept any more of his; and found even such petty jealousy a welcome pastime.

Heathrow. Ten-fifteen. No baggage, no pack-drill. The first out.

"How long will it take to get the car?" said Kate.

"I'm going to rent one while you phone," I said.

I told them I would take the fastest one they had if it was ready now. It was waiting outside, just back, tank full; it only needed "valeting". I said I'd take it as it stood, and signed. It turned out to be a red Porsche—"I thought he said 'posh'!" Kate whispered—and then we were out in the mild English sunshine, heading north-east, moving fast; thankful to be under our own—considerable—steam, and together.

Everything was fine at home, she said—"as we knew it would be," she added. "I didn't speak to Our Hen—he was outside playing; Nanny surprised, delighted, thrown into a tiz: would soup and cheese be adequate? You can imagine . . ."

She sat close to me, her hand on my thigh. It was only five days since we had passed this way as separate and silent antagonists.

I said, "This would be far worse if you were in the back, grinding your teeth at me."

Kate smoothed out her brow and smiled. "It does help . . . That seems a long while ago. So much has happened."

"Making up for lost time. We've fitted a lot in."

"Boasting again . . . Oh God, darling—and it would all be spoiled if something bad happened. Because of us. Not being there when—"

"The nearer we get, the surer I feel that this is all a lovely, self-indulgent, wild-goose chase," I said. "Perfect day, and you, and going home to see the lad—"

"And we needn't feel foolish—though Nanny and Co. will be frightfully shocked by such extravagance. Just have us our family weekend and fly off again, like very exotic commuters."

"The sort of work that gives Monday a good name"—and we sang "Monday, Monday, so good to me . . ." But I was thinking: Why do I feel so scared? It was a senseless, childish dread, like the smell of hospitals; and I kept seeing the flames and the faces at the window and the railway crossing ahead . . .

Kate was saying that we'd be able to check up on the work that had been going on: the paving round the pool; the builders —"Not that they'll be there of course; but we'll see how they're getting on with the pointing, and mending the parapet, and if—"

I swerved violently as we turned to each other.

"The scaffolding," said Kate quietly.

"He wouldn't," I said firmly.

"He's far too sensible."

"Of course he is," I said. And I thought: But he trusts old Doddy. And he's only five . . . Nanny would be busy getting the lunch together, prinking the flowers, opening the windows; preoccupied.

I swung off the motorway and raced along the narrow lanes.

"Nanny wouldn't let him," I said out loud.

Kate was looking at her watch. I could not ask her how late it was, nor peer too obviously at my own watch. I wondered if the car clock was right: eleven forty-five.

"That's slow," said Kate looking straight ahead.

All slow: underwater ballet. But the end, when it came, came quickly.

We turned in at the gates and ran the long, chill gauntlet of the lime-trees' shade; then we could see the flash of the fountain ahead, and were parking in the sunny gravel circle. We got out and looked up. I think we had both seen them for a moment as we emerged from the avenue; but, blinded by the light, I was not certain that I had.

A tower of scaffolding ran up the famous protected front of Noone, to the left of the porch, with a ladder to the first platform. From where I stood I could just see the tracery of balustrade like old, worn lace against the sky; but not beyond it. Kate was already on the far side of the circle looking up, shading her eyes.

"Oh, Christ . . . ," she said. "Oh, no."

I ran back. She was calling up: "Stay there, darling . . . ," and her voice was very calm. "Stay there: I'm coming . . ." To me she said: "Take too long, getting the keys to those windows . . ." And now, dazzled by sun, I could see something too.

High above us, beyond the balustrade, and dark against the noon-day sky, there seemed to be two figures, pared away to thin ciphers by the glare: one small, one taller; standing quite still. I squeezed my eyes shut for a moment, and looked again. They appeared to merge, as though the taller one had taken the little one's hand and they were moving along the ledge.

I ran to the ladder and started up it after Kate.

Climbing close under the building as we were, unable to see even the parapet—that was the worst. Kate, a little way above me, stopped and craned out as far as she could, and called: "Stay there, Hen! We're just . . ." But her voice cracked.

"We're coming, Henry!" I called, and climbed up the scaffolding past her. I saw her face.

"Go on," she said: "I'm OK." She called up again, clearly and calmly: "Stay there, darling. Don't move—OK?"

No answer. Grimly I hauled myself up to the next stage.

There was a high, bloodcurdling yell and we both stared upwards, sick with fear, through the crossbars, to the distant coping and bare blue sky beyond, dreading we might see something. Nothing could lean out that far: anything visible would be falling. Then the yell modulated into a yodel—Henry's Indian war-cry—and clearly behind us, though still reflected by the cliff in front. I turned and saw him rushing out from the shrubbery in his chieftain's feathers.

"You're *back*!" he squealed. "And it's

stripey ice-cream for lunch! And—Hey. Now I can climb up too!"

Kate, crouched against a steel upright, was laughing and sobbing.

"Hi, Hen!" I called in tremolo. "How's tricks?" And started climbing down.

"Hey-hey-hey!" He was dancing around at the bottom. "Can I come up too? Nanny said I mustn't—but Doddy and Fish are up there—did you see them?"

I helped Kate down; and we were on the ground, hugging him and laughing.

"Oh, Mum—you're all wet! I say—you *have* been missing me, haven't you . . . ? You silly old mother-bear . . ."

"So . . . ," I said. "And just who is this 'Fish' character, may I ask?"

"Oh yes . . . ! And I can go up too, Laurence? And guess what? He's another 'Laurence', like you . . . ! But everybody calls him by his nickname: 'Fishface'—so you won't get muddled up, will you?"

I felt very cold in the noon-day heat; I thought of my "little death".

"You see," Henry was saying, "Fishface (well, he says I can call him 'Fish' cos it's shorter)—he says he's come home. He's travelled a terrible long way, you see—and he told me all about a horrid fire and all these men with long sticks and things— And *do* come and see the stripey ice-cream: it's *three colours*! And . . . Hey, Mum—don't worry about *him*: Doddy's up there too. And he'll be OK, Fishface will. He knows his way around."

THE END

GUIDE
TO THE COLOUR CODING
OF
ULVERSCROFT BOOKS

Many of our readers have written to us expressing their appreciation for the way in which our colour coding has assisted them in selecting the Ulverscroft books of their choice.

To remind everyone of our colour coding— this is as follows:

BLACK COVERS
Mysteries

★

BLUE COVERS
Romances

★

RED COVERS
Adventure Suspense and General Fiction

★

ORANGE COVERS
Westerns

★

GREEN COVERS
Non-Fiction

ROMANCE TITLES
in the
Ulverscroft Large Print Series

The Smile of the Stranger	*Joan Aiken*
Busman's Holiday	*Lucilla Andrews*
Flowers From the Doctor	*Lucilla Andrews*
Nurse Errant	*Lucilla Andrews*
Silent Song	*Lucilla Andrews*
Merlin's Keep	*Madeleine Brent*
Tregaron's Daughter	*Madeleine Brent*
The Bend in the River	*Iris Bromige*
A Haunted Landscape	*Iris Bromige*
Laurian Vale	*Iris Bromige*
A Magic Place	*Iris Bromige*
The Quiet Hills	*Iris Bromige*
Rosevean	*Iris Bromige*
The Young Romantic	*Iris Bromige*
Lament for a Lost Lover	*Philippa Carr*
The Lion Triumphant	*Philippa Carr*
The Miracle at St. Bruno's	*Philippa Carr*
The Witch From the Sea	*Philippa Carr*
Isle of Pomegranates	*Iris Danbury*
For I Have Lived Today	*Alice Dwyer-Joyce*
The Gingerbread House	*Alice Dwyer-Joyce*
The Strolling Players	*Alice Dwyer-Joyce*
Afternoon for Lizards	*Dorothy Eden*
The Marriage Chest	*Dorothy Eden*

FICTION TITLES
in the
Ulverscroft Large Print Series